Michael didn't stir, but he watched Caroline...

He was perfectly aware that there was more going on than the obvious, and equally certain she was determinedly ignoring at least one thread in their interaction.

Finally, relaxed once more on the chaise, she spread her hands and asked directly, "Well, will you help?"

He met her gaze. "On two conditions."

A sudden wariness slid behind her lovely eyes; she blinked and it was replaced by an expecting-to-be-amused smile. "Conditions. Good heavens! What?"

"One—it's too lovely a day to spend sitting inside. Let's take this discussion on a stroll through the gardens. Two"—he held her gaze—"that you'll stay for lunch."

She blinked slowly; he was very sure she was wary of him physically. Of getting physically close.

"Very well—if you insist," she said.

He fought to keep his smile from deepening. "Oh, I do."

By Stephanie Laurens

THE IDEAL BRIDE
A GENTLEMAN'S HONOR
THE LADY CHOSEN
THE PERFECT LOVER
ON A WICKED DAWN
ON A WILD NIGHT
THE PROMISE IN A KISS
ALL ABOUT PASSION
ALL ABOUT LOVE
A SECRET LOVE
A ROGUE'S PROPOSAL
SCANDAL'S BRIDE
A RAKE'S VOW
DEVIL'S BRIDE
CAPTAIN JACK'S WOMAN

And in Hardcover

THE TRUTH ABOUT LOVE

STEPHANIE LAURENS

The Ideal Bride

A CYNSTER NOVEL

AVON BOOKS

An Imprint of HarperCollinsPublishers

This is a work of fiction. Names, characters, places, and incidents are products of the author's imagination or are used fictitiously and are not to be construed as real. Any resemblance to actual events, locales, organizations, or persons, living or dead, is entirely coincidental.

AVON BOOKS
An Imprint of HarperCollins*Publishers*
10 East 53rd Street
New York, New York 10022-5299

Copyright © 2004 by Savdek Management Proprietory Ltd.
Excerpt from *The Truth About Love* copyright © 2005 by Savdek Management Proprietory Ltd.
ISBN: 0-06-050574-5
www.avonromance.com

First Avon Books paperback printing: March 2005
First William Morrow hardcover printing: March 2004

Avon Trademark Reg. U.S. Pat. Off. and in Other Countries, Marca Registrada, Hecho en U.S.A.
HarperCollins® is a registered trademark of HarperCollins Publishers Inc.

Printed in the U.S.A.

10 9 8 7 6 5 4 3 2 1

To my four fellow "Rogue Authors"—
Victoria Alexander, Susan Andersen,
Patti Berg, and Linda Needham—
I wouldn't stay sane without you.
With much love,
SL

The Ideal Bride

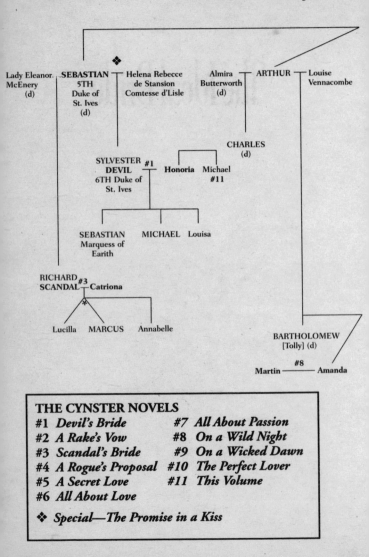

The Bar Cynster

Lady Eleanor McEnery (d) — **SEBASTIAN** 5TH Duke of St. Ives (d) — Helena Rebecce de Stansion Comtesse d'Lisle

Almira Butterworth (d) — ARTHUR — Louise Vennacombe

CHARLES (d)

SYLVESTER DEVIL 6TH Duke of St. Ives — **#1** — **Honoria** Michael **#11**

SEBASTIAN Marquess of Earith   MICHAEL   Louisa

RICHARD SCANDAL **#3** — Catriona

Lucilla   MARCUS   Annabelle

BARTHOLOMEW [Tolly] (d)

Martin — **#8** — Amanda

THE CYNSTER NOVELS

Family Tree

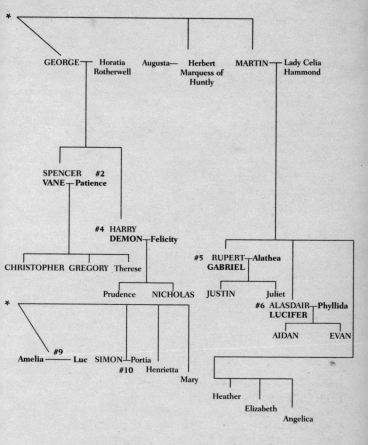

GEORGE—Horatia Rotherwell   Augusta—Herbert Marquess of Huntly   MARTIN—Lady Celia Hammond

SPENCER   #2
VANE—Patience

#4 HARRY
DEMON—Felicity

CHRISTOPHER   GREGORY   Therese

#5 RUPERT—Alathea
GABRIEL

JUSTIN   Juliet

Prudence   NICHOLAS

#6 ALASDAIR—Phyllida
LUCIFER

AIDAN   EVAN

Amelia   #9
———Luc   SIMON—Portia
#10   Henrietta

Mary

Heather
Elizabeth
Angelica

MALE CYNSTERS in capitals
* denotes twins
Children born after 1825 not shown

The Ideal Bride

CHAPTER

1

Late June, 1825
Eyeworth Manor, near Fritham in the New Forest, Hampshire

Wife, wife, wife, wife.

Michael Anstruther-Wetherby swore beneath his breath. That refrain had plagued him for the last twenty-four hours. When he'd driven away from Amelia Cynster's wedding breakfast, it had run to the rhythm of his curricle's wheels; now it was playing to the steady clop of his bay gelding's hooves.

Lips setting, he wheeled Atlas out of the stableyard and set out along the drive circling his home.

If he hadn't gone to Cambridgeshire to attend Amelia's wedding, he'd already be one step closer to being an affianced man. But the wedding had been one event he hadn't even thought of missing; aside from the fact that his sister Honoria, Duchess of St. Ives, had been the hostess, the wedding had been a family gathering and he valued family ties.

Familial links had helped him immeasurably in recent years, first in gaining his position as Member of Parliament for this district, and subsequently in forging his path upward through the ranks, yet that wasn't the wellspring of his appreciation; family had always meant a great deal to him.

Rounding his house, a sturdy, three-storied manor house built of gray stone, his gaze went —as it always did when he passed this way—to the monument that stood on the verge halfway between the house and the gates. Set against the dark-leaved shrubs filling the gaps beneath the tall trees, the simple stone had stood for fourteen years; it marked the spot where his family—his parents and younger brother and sister racing home in a curricle in the teeth of a storm—had been killed by a falling tree. He and Honoria had witnessed the accident from the schoolroom windows high above.

Perhaps it was simply human nature to value highly something one had lost.

Left shocked, grieving, and adrift, he and Honoria had still had each other, but with him barely nineteen and her sixteen, they'd had to part. They'd never lost touch—they were, even now, close—but Honoria had since met Devil Cynster; she now had a family of her own.

Slowing Atlas as he approached the stone, Michael was acutely aware that he did not. His life was full to bursting, his schedule perennially crammed; it was only in moments like this that the lack shone so clearly, and loneliness jabbed.

He paused, studying the stone, then, jaw setting, faced forward and flicked the reins. Atlas picked up his pace; passing through the gates, Michael held him to a steady canter along the narrow lane.

The nightmarish sound of horses screaming slowly faded.

Today he was determined to take the first step toward establishing a family of his own.

Wife, wife, wife, wife.

The countryside closed around him, embraced him in its lush green arms, welcomed him into the woods and forests that to him were the essence of home. Sunlight flickered, glimmered through shifting leaves. Birds called and twittered; beyond the rustle of the canopies, there was no other sound to punctuate the clop of Atlas's hooves. Narrow and winding, the lane led nowhere but to the Manor, joining a wider road that led south to Lyndhurst. Not far from that junction, another lane wended east to the village of Bramshaw, and Bramshaw House, his destination.

He'd decided on his course some months ago, but once again government concerns had demanded his attention and he'd let matters slide . . . when he'd realized, he'd pulled himself up short, sat down, and laid out a schedule. Despite the distraction of Amelia's wedding, he'd stuck rigidly to his self-imposed timetable and left the wedding breakfast in good time to drive down here. To his necessary destiny.

Leaving Somersham in midafternoon, he'd stopped with a friend at Basingstoke overnight. He hadn't mentioned his reason for heading home, yet it had weighed—preyed—on his mind. He'd set out early and arrived home midmorning; it was now two o'clock, and he was determined to delay no longer. The die would be cast, the matter, if not finished with, then at least begun—halfway arranged.

A constituency matter?

You might say that.

Amelia's question, his answer, perfectly true in its way. To a sitting Member, one who'd reached the age of thirty-three unwed and been informed he was being considered for advancement into the ministry, marriage was definitely a "constituency matter."

He accepted he had to marry—indeed, he'd always assumed he would someday. How else was he to establish the family he craved? Yet the years had rolled by and he'd become caught up in his developing career through that and his close links with the Cynsters and the haut ton, increasingly cognizant of the breadth of experience the state of marriage encompassed, he'd become less and less inclined to pursue it.

Now, however, his time had come. When Parliament had risen for the summer, he'd been left in no doubt that the Prime Minister expected him to return in autumn with a wife on his arm, thereby enabling him to be considered in the cabinet reshuffle widely tipped to occur at that time. Since April, he'd been actively seeking his ideal bride.

The peace of the countryside wrapped him about; the *wife, wife, wife* refrain remained, but its tone grew less compulsive the closer he got to his goal.

It had been easy to define the qualities and attributes he required in his bride—passable beauty, loyalty, supportive abilities such as hostessly talents, and some degree of intelligence lightened with a touch of humor. Finding such a paragon proved another matter; after spending hours in the ballrooms, he'd concluded he'd be wiser to seek a bride with some understanding of a politician's life—even better, a *successful* politician's life.

Then he'd met Elizabeth Mollison, or rather remet her, for strictly speaking he'd known her all her life. Her father, Geoffrey Mollison, owned Bramshaw House and had been the previous Member for the district. Brought low by his wife's unexpected death, Geoffrey had resigned the seat just as Michael had approached the party with his grandfather Magnus Anstruther-Wetherby's and the Cynsters' backing. It had seemed a stroke of fate. Geoffrey, a conscientious man, had been relieved to be able to hand the reins to someone he knew. Even though he and Geoffrey were from different generations and markedly different in character—namely in ambition—he'd always found Geoffrey encouraging, always ready to help.

He hoped he'd help now, and support his notion of marrying Elizabeth.

She was, in his estimation, remarkably close to his ideal. True, she was young—nineteen—but she was also well bred, well groomed, and unquestionably well brought up and, so he judged, capable of learning all she needed to know. She was a very English beauty, with pale blond hair and blue eyes, a fine complexion, and a slender figure well suited to the current fashions; most important, however, she had grown up in a political house. Even after her mother had died and Geoffrey had retired from the fray, Elizabeth had been placed in the care of her aunt Augusta, Lady Cunningham, who was married to a senior diplomat.

What's more, her younger aunt, Caroline, had been married to the British ambassador to Portugal; Elizabeth had spent time at the embassy in Lisbon under her aunt Caro's wing.

Elizabeth had lived all her life in political and diplomatic households. Michael was perfectly certain she'd know how to manage his. And, of course, marrying her would strengthen his admittedly already strong position locally;

that wasn't something to sneeze at, given that by all accounts in future he'd be spending much of his time on international affairs. A wife who could be relied on to keep the home fires stoked would be a godsend.

Mentally, he rehearsed what he would say to Geoffrey. He did not yet wish to make a formal offer for Elizabeth's hand—he needed to get to know her better and allow her to get to know him—but given the connection between himself and the Mollisons, he deemed it wise to sound Geoffrey out; no sense in proceeding if he was set against it.

Michael doubted that would be the case, but it wouldn't hurt to ask, to keep Geoffrey firmly in his camp. If over two or three meetings Elizabeth proved as pleasant and amenable as she'd appeared in town, they could progress to an offer, and thence to the altar, all in good time for autumn.

Cold-blooded perhaps, yet in his opinion a marriage based on mutual affection rather than passion would suit him best.

Despite his links with the Cynsters, he did not consider himself as one with them when it came to marriage; he was a different sort of man. They were passionate, determined, high-handedly arrogant; he would admit to being determined, but he'd long ago learned to disguise his arrogance, and he was a politician, ergo not a man given to the wilder passions.

Not a man to allow his heart to rule his head.

A straightforward marriage to a lady close to his ideal—that was what he needed. He'd discussed the prospect and specifically Elizabeth Mollison with his grandfather, and also with his aunt, Mrs. Harriet Jennet, a political hostess of note; both had supported his stance, in both cases with typical Anstruther-Wetherby ascerbity.

Harriet had snorted. "Glad to see Honoria and that lot haven't turned your head. The position of your wife is too important to be decided by the color of a lady's eyes."

He doubted that the color of a lady's eyes had ever featured highly in any male Cynster's mind as a deciding factor in marriage—other physical attributes perhaps . . . of course, he'd held his tongue.

Magnus had made various stringent comments about the unwisdom of allowing passion to rule one's life. Strangely, however, although almost daily prodding him to get on with the business of securing Elizabeth's hand, at Amelia's wedding at Somersham, Magnus had ignored the perfect opportunity to press . . . then again, history had it that all weddings celebrated at Somersham Place were love matches. Perhaps it was that—that the marriage he was set on, indeed, needed to be set on, would not be one such—that had persuaded his grandfather to cling to wisdom and in that company hold his tongue.

The lane wended on; a strange impatience rose within him but he held Atlas to his steady pace. Ahead, the trees thinned; beyond, glimpsed through their trunks and the thick undergrowth, he could see the rippling fields lining the Lyndhurst lane.

A feeling of certainty gripped him; it was the right time for him to go forward and marry, to build another family here, the next generation, to put down deeper roots and grow into the next phase of his life.

The lane was a succession of curves, the trees and undergrowth thick enough to screen sounds at any distance; by the time the rattle of the fast-approaching carriage, the thud of flying hooves, reached him, the carriage was almost upon him.

He just had time to draw Atlas to the side of the lane before a gig, out of control and careening wildly, exploded around the bend.

It flashed past, heading toward the Manor. Grim-faced, pale as death, a slim woman wrestled with the reins, desperately trying to control the horse.

Michael cursed and wheeled Atlas. He was thundering in the gig's wake before he'd even thought. Then he did, and cursed again. Carriage accidents were his worst nightmare; the threat of witnessing another sank like a spur into his side. He urged Atlas on.

The gig was rocketing, almost flying; the horse would soon tire, but the lane led only to the Manor—and that would be reached too soon.

He'd been born at the Manor, had lived his first nineteen years there; he knew every foot of the lane. Atlas was fresh; dropping the reins, Michael rode with hands and knees.

They were gaining, but not enough.

Soon the lane would become the drive, which ended in a sharp turn into the forecourt before the Manor steps. The horse would take the curve; the gig wouldn't. It would overturn, the lady would be thrown . . . onto the rocks edging the front beds.

Inwardly cursing, he pushed Atlas on. The big gelding responded, stretching out, legs flashing as they gained inch by inch on the wildly rocking gig. They were almost alongside. . . .

The gates flashed up, then were behind.

No more time.

Gathering himself, Michael sprang from the saddle to the gig. He caught the seat, dragged himself half over it. Lunging across the lady, he grabbed the reins and yanked hard.

The lady screamed.

So did the horse.

Michael hung on with all his strength and hauled back. There was no time—no drive left—to worry about anything but halting the horse.

Hooves skidded; the horse screamed again, swung sideways—and halted. Michael grabbed the brake—too late. Momentum whipped the gig around; pure luck kept it upright.

The lady was flung out of the gig onto the grassy verge.

He was thrown after her.

She landed facedown; he sprawled half atop her.

For an instant, he couldn't move—couldn't draw breath, couldn't think. Reactions—dozens—poured through him. The slender, fragile body trapped beneath his, delicate yet elementally womanly, sent protectiveness flaring—only to trigger horror and nascent fury over what had so nearly transpired. Over what had been risked.

Then fear welled, black, roiling, irrational and old, dark and deep. It swelled, gripped hard, strangled all else.

Hooves shifted on the gravel—he looked around. The

horse, blowing hard, tried to walk, but the gig dragged; the horse stopped. Atlas had halted on the other side of the lawn and stood watching, ears pricked.

"*Ooof!*"

Beneath him, the lady struggled. His shoulder lay across her back, his hips anchoring her thighs; she couldn't move until he did.

He rolled back, sat up. His gaze fell on the stone monument, two yards away.

The terror of screaming horses filled his mind.

Jaw setting, he drew in a tight breath and got to his feet. Watched, grim-faced, as the lady pushed back, then swung around to sit.

He reached down, grabbed her hands, hauled her unceremoniously to her feet. "Of all the stupid, *witless*—" He broke off, fought to shackle his temper, soaring on the wings of that roiling, irrational fear. Lost the battle. Hands rising to his hips, he glared at its cause. "If you can't handle the reins, you shouldn't be driving." He snapped the words out, didn't care if they cut. "You came within yards of serious injury if not *death*!"

For an instant, he wondered if she was deaf; she gave no indication she'd heard him.

Caroline Sutcliffe dusted her gloved hands, and thanked her stars she'd worn gloves. Ignoring the solid lump of male reverberating with aggravation before her—she had no idea who he was; she hadn't yet seen his face—she shook out her skirts, inwardly grimaced at the grass stains, then straightened the bodice, the sleeves, her gauzy scarf. And finally consented to look up.

And up—he was taller than she'd thought. Wider of shoulder, too . . . the physical shock when he'd appeared beside her in the gig, compounded when he'd landed atop her on the grass, flashed back into her mind; she thrust it out again. "Thank you, sir, whoever you are, for your rescue, however ungracious." Her tone would have done a duchess credit—cool, confident, assured and haughty. Precisely the right tone to use on a presumptuous male. "However—"

Her rising gaze reached his face. She blinked. The sun

was behind him; she stood in full light, but his face was shadowed.

Lifting her hand, she shaded her eyes and unabashedly peered. At a strong-featured face with a square jaw and the harsh, angular planes of her own class. A patrician face with a wide brow delimited by straight dark brows over eyes memory painted a soft blue. His hair was thick, dark brown; the silver tracery at his temples only made him more distinguished.

It was a face that held a great deal of character.

It was the face she'd come there to find.

She tilted her head. "Michael? It is Michael Anstruther-Wetherby, isn't it?"

Michael stared—at a heart-shaped face surrounded by a nimbus of fine, sheening brown hair so light it was flyaway, puffed soft as a dandelion crown about her head, at eyes, silver-blue, slightly tip-tilted . . . "Caro." The name came to his lips without real thought.

She smiled up at him, clearly delighted; for one instant, he—all of him—stilled.

The screaming horses abruptly fell silent.

"Yes. It's been years since we've spoken. . . ." Her gaze grew vague as she cast her mind back.

"At Camden's funeral," he reminded her. Her late husband, Camden Sutcliffe, a legend in diplomatic circles, had been His Majesty's Ambassador to Portugal; Caro had been Sutcliffe's third wife.

She refocused on his face. "You're right—two years ago."

"I haven't seen you about town." He had, however, heard of her; the diplomatic corps had dubbed her the Merry Widow. "How are you faring?"

"Very well, thank you. Camden was a good man and I miss him, but . . ." She shrugged lightly. "There were more than forty years between us, so it was always going to be this way."

The horse shifted, ineffectually dragging the braked gig. Recalled to the present, they both went forward; Caro held the horse's head while Michael untangled the reins, then checked the harness. He frowned. "What happened?"

"I have no idea." Frowning, too, Caro stroked the horse's nose. "I was coming from a Ladies' Association meeting at Fordingham."

The crisp clop of hooves had them both glancing toward the gates. A gig came trotting smartly through; the large lady driving saw them, waved, then briskly steered the gig toward them.

"Muriel insisted I attend the meeting—you know how she is." Caro spoke quickly, beneath the rattle of the gig's approach. "She offered to drive me, but I decided if I was traveling all that way, I would use the trip to call on Lady Kirkwright. So I drove over early, then attended the meeting, and Muriel and I drove back in tandem."

Michael understood all she was telling him. Muriel was Camden's niece, Caro's niece-by-marriage, although Muriel was seven years the elder. She, too, had grown up in Bramshaw; unlike the pair of them, Muriel had never left. Born and raised at Sutcliffe Hall at the far end of the village, she now lived in the village center in Hedderwick House, her husband's residence, a stone's throw from the drive of Bramshaw House, Caro's family home.

More to the point, Muriel had elected herself the organizer of the parish, a role she'd filled for years. Although her manner was often overbearing, everyone, themselves included, bore with her managing disposition for the simple reason that she did a necessary job well.

With a stylish flourish, Muriel brought her gig to a halt in the forecourt. She was handsome in a mannish way, undeniably striking with her upright carriage and dark hair.

She stared at Caro. "Great heavens, Caro!—were you thrown? You've grass stains on your gown. Are you all right?" Her tone was faint, as if she couldn't quite credit her eyes. "The way you took off, I never would have believed you'd succeed in reining Henry in."

"I didn't." Caro waved at Michael. "Luckily Michael was riding out—he bravely leapt into the gig and performed the necessary feat."

Michael met her eyes, saw the lurking, gracefully grateful smile. Managed not to smile in return.

"Thank goodness for that." Muriel turned to him, nodding in greeting. "Michael—I didn't know you'd returned."

"I arrived this morning. Have you any idea why Henry bolted? I've checked reins and harness—there doesn't seem to be any obvious cause."

Muriel frowned at Henry. "No. Caro and I were driving home together, then Caro turned into your lane and waved. She was just a little way along when Henry started, then"— Muriel gestured—"off he went." She looked at Caro.

Who nodded. "Yes, it happened just like that." She stroked Henry's nose. "Which is strange—he's normally a placid beast. I drive him whenever I'm home."

"Well, next time we meet at Fordingham, I'll take you up with me, you may be sure." Muriel widened her eyes. "I nearly had palpitations—I expected to come upon you bloody and broken."

Caro made no direct answer; frowning, she studied Henry. "Something must have startled him."

"Possibly a stag." Muriel gathered her reins. "The bushes are so thick along that stretch, it's impossible to see what may be lurking."

"True." Caro nodded. "But Henry would have known."

"Indeed. But now you're safe, I must get on." Muriel glanced at Michael. "We were discussing arrangements for the church fete, and I must make a start. I assume you'll be attending?"

He smiled easily. "Of course." He made a mental note to learn when the fete was. "My regards to Hedderwick, and George if you see him."

Muriel inclined her head. "I'll pass your wishes on." She exchanged a gracious nod with Caro, then eyed Caro's gig, presently blocking the exit from the forecourt.

Michael glanced at Caro. "Let's take Henry to the stables. I'll have Hardacre examine him, see if he can suggest anything to account for his start."

"An excellent notion." Caro waited while he reached over and released the gig's brake, then she waved to Muriel and led Henry forward.

Michael checked that the gig was undamaged and the

wheels rolling freely. Once it cleared the forecourt, he saluted Muriel. With a regal nod, she trotted her horse past and around toward the gates. He turned to follow Caro.

Atlas was still standing patiently; Michael clicked his fingers and the bay ambled up. Catching the reins, he wound them about one hand, then lengthened his stride. Coming up on Henry's other side, he looked across at Caro—at the section of her face he could see over the horse's head. Her hair glimmered and shimmered in the sunshine, totally unfashionable yet it appeared so soft, it simply begged to be touched. "Are you fixed at Bramshaw House for the summer?"

She glanced at him. "For the moment." She patted Henry. "I move around between Geoffrey here, Augusta in Derby, and Angela in Berkshire. I have the house in London, but I haven't yet reopened it."

He nodded. Geoffrey was her brother, Augusta and Angela her sisters; Caro was the baby, the youngest by many years. He glanced at her again; she was murmuring soothingly to Henry.

A peculiar disorientation still gripped him, as if he were slightly off-balance. And it had to do with her. When they'd briefly met two years ago, she'd been recently bereaved, draped in widow's weeds and heavily veiled; they'd exchanged a few murmured words, but he hadn't truly seen or spoken with her. Prior to that, she'd spent the previous decade or so in Lisbon; he'd occasionally glimpsed her across ballrooms or crossed her path when she and Camden were in London, but had never shared more than the usual social pleasantries.

There were only five years between them, yet although they'd known each other since childhood and had spent their formative years growing up in this restricted area of the New Forest, he didn't truly know her at all.

He certainly didn't know the elegant and assured lady she'd become.

She looked at him—caught him looking at her—and smiled easily, as if acknowledging a mutual curiosity.

The temptation to assuage it grew.

She looked forward; he followed her gaze. Summoned by the crunch of the gig's wheels, Hardacre, his stableman, had come out of the stable. Michael beckoned; Hardacre came over, bobbing a deferential greeting to Caro, who returned it with his name and one of her serene smiles. While they walked the gig into the stableyard, Michael and she explained what had happened.

Frowning, Hardacre ran knowledgeable eyes over both horse and gig, then scratched his balding pate. "Best leave him with me for an hour or so—I'll unharness and check him over. See if there's some problem."

Michael looked at Caro. "Are you in a hurry? I could lend you a gig and horse if you are."

"No, no." She waved aside the offer with a smile. "An hour of peace would be welcome."

He recalled, reached solicitously for her arm. "Would you care for tea?"

"That would be delightful." Caro smiled more definitely as he settled her hand on his sleeve. With a nod for Hardacre, she let Michael steer her toward the house. Her nerves were still flickering, twitching, hardly surprising, yet the panic of being in a runaway gig was already fading—who could have predicted that near-disaster would turn out so well? "Is Mrs. Entwhistle still your housekeeper?"

"Yes. None of the staff have changed, not for years."

She looked ahead at the solid stone house with its gabled roof and dormer windows. They were walking through an orchard, the dappled shade sweet with the scent of swelling fruit. Between that and the back door lay a rambling herb garden bisected by a flagged path; to the left beyond a low wall lay the kitchen garden. "But that's what draws us back, isn't it?" She glanced at him, caught his eye. "That things stay comfortingly the same."

He held her gaze for a moment. "I hadn't really thought . . . but you're right." He stopped to let her precede him up the narrow path. "Will you be remaining at Bramshaw for long?"

She grinned, knowing he, now behind her, couldn't see. "I've only just arrived." In response to a panicked summons from Elizabeth, her niece. She glanced back at him. "I expect to be here for some weeks."

They reached the back door; Michael leaned past her to open it, conscious as he did of her—just her. As he followed her into the dim corridor, directing her to the drawing room, he registered how not simply feminine, but female she was. How much as a woman she impinged on his senses, with her slender yet curvaceous figure gowned in filmy muslin.

There was nothing the least unusual about the gown; it was Caro herself who was unusual, and that in more ways than one.

Following her into the drawing room, he tugged the bellpull. When Gladys, the maid, appeared, he ordered tea.

Caro had strolled to the long windows at the end of the room; she smiled at Gladys, who bobbed and left, then she looked at him. "It's such a lovely afternoon—shall we sit out on the terrace and enjoy the sunshine?"

"Why not?" Joining her, he set the French doors wide. He followed her onto the flagged terrace to where a wrought-iron table and two chairs stood perfectly placed to capture the sunshine and the vista over the front lawns.

He held one chair for her, then, circling the table, took the other. There was a frown in her eyes when she lifted them to his.

"I can't remember—have you a butler?"

"No. We did years ago, but the house was closed up for some time, and he moved on." He grimaced. "I suppose I should look around for one."

Her brows rose. "Indeed." Her expression stated that a local Member should certainly have a butler. "But if you're quick, you won't need to look far."

He looked his question; she smiled. "Remember Jeb Carter? He left Fritham village to train as a butler under his uncle in London. He apparently did well, but was seeking to return to the district so he could better watch over his mother. Muriel was searching for a butler—again—and she hired him. Unfortunately Carter, as so many before him, failed to meet Muriel's exacting standards, so she let him go.

That was only yesterday—he's currently staying at his mother's cottage."

"I see." He studied her eyes, hoping he was reading the messages in the silvery blue accurately. "So you think I should hire him?"

She smiled one of her quick, approving, warming smiles. "I think you should see if he would suit. You know him and his family—he's honest as the day is long, and the Carters were always good workers."

He nodded. "I'll send a message."

"No." The reproof was gentle, but definite. "Go and see him. Drop by while passing."

He met her eyes, then inclined his head. There were few he would take direct guidance from, but Caro's edicts in such matters he judged to be beyond question. She was, indeed, the perfect person—the unquestionably best-qualified person—to sound out regarding his direction with Elizabeth, her niece.

The tea arrived, brought by Mrs. Entwhistle, who had clearly come to see Caro. She took her celebrity in stride; he watched as she said all the right things, asking after Mrs. Entwhistle's son, complimenting her on the delicate cream puffs arranged in a dish. Mrs. Entwhistle glowed and retreated, thoroughly pleased.

While Caro poured, Michael wondered if she even registered her performance, if it was calculated or simply came naturally. Then she handed him his cup and smiled, and he decided that while her responses might once have been learned, they were now ingrained. Essentially spontaneous.

Simply the way she was.

While they sipped and consumed—she nibbled, he ate—they exchanged news of mutual acquaintances. They moved in the same circles, were both extremely well connected on both diplomatic and political fronts; it was supremely easy to fill the time.

The knack of making polite conversation came readily, fluidly, to them both, a skill attesting to their experience. In substance, however, he would bow to her; her comments displayed an insight into people and their reactions that surpassed his own, that struck deeper and truer, illuminating motives.

It was pleasant in the sunshine. He studied her while they traded information; to his eyes she glowed with confidence, not the sort that sparkled and gleamed, but a quiet, steady assurance that shone through, that seemed bone-deep, infinitely sure, almost serene.

She'd grown to be a remarkably calm woman, one who effortlessly cast an aura of peace.

It occurred to him that time was passing—oh so easily. He set down his cup. "So, what are your plans?"

She met his gaze, then opened her eyes wide. "To be honest, I'm not sure." There was a hint of self-deprecatory humor in her tone. "I traveled for some months while in mourning, so I've satisfied that urge. I did the Season this year—it was lovely to meet friends again, pick up the threads, but . . ." She grimaced lightly. "That's not enough to fill a life. I stayed with Angela this time—I'm not sure yet what I want to do with the house, if I want to open it again and live there, hold court like some literary hostess, or perhaps immerse myself in good works. . . ." Her lips lifted, her eyes teased. "Can you see me doing any of those things?"

The silver blue of her gaze seemed layered—open, honest, yet with intriguing depths. "No." He considered her, sitting so relaxed on his terrace; he couldn't see her as anything other than she'd been—an ambassador's lady. "I think you should leave the good works to Muriel, and a court would be too restricted a stage."

She laughed, a golden sound that merged with the gilded afternoon. "You have a politician's tongue." She said it approvingly. "But enough of me—what of you? Were you in London this Season?"

It was the opening he'd been angling for; he let his lips twist wryly. "I was, but various committees and bills proved more distracting than anticipated." He elaborated, content to let her draw him out, to form for herself a picture of his life—and his need of a wife. She was too knowledgeable for him to need to spell it out; she would see—and be there to explain and assure Elizabeth when the time came.

There was a subtle attraction in speaking with someone who knew his world and understood its nuances. Watching Caro's face was a pleasure—seeing the expressions flit over her features, watching her gestures, so elegant and graceful, glimpsing the intelligence and humor in her eyes.

Caro, too, was content, yet as he watched her, so she, too, from behind her polished facade, watched him, and waited.

Eventually, he met her gaze and simply asked, "Why were you heading this way?"

The lane led here and only here; they both knew it.

She let her eyes light, beamed a brilliant smile his way. "Thank you for reminding me. What with all this catching up, I'd quite forgotten, yet it's all very apt."

Leaning her forearms on the table, she fixed him with her most beguiling look. "As I said, I'm staying with Geoffrey, but old habits die hard. I know quite a few people from the ministries and embassies who are spending their summer in the neighborhood—I've organized a dinner for tonight, but . . ." She let her smile turn rueful. "I'm one gentleman short. I came to prevail on you to help me balance my table—you, at least, will appreciate how necessary to my peace of mind that is."

He was charmed and had to laugh.

"Now," she continued, ruthlessly gilding the lily, "we have a small party from the Portuguese embassy, and three from the Austrian, and—" She proceeded to outline her guest list; no politician worth his salt would refuse the opportunity to bump such elbows.

He made no pretense of doing so, but smiled easily. "I'll be delighted to oblige."

"Thank you." She gave him her very best smile; she might be a trifle out of practice, but it still seemed to work.

A rattle and clop on the graveled drive reached them; they both looked, then rose as Hardacre walked Henry, once more harnessed to her gig, around.

Hardacre saw them and ducked his head. "Seems right as rain now—you shouldn't have any trouble with him."

Caro gathered her reticule and rounded the table. Michael took her elbow and steadied her down the terrace steps. She thanked Hardacre, then allowed Michael to help her up to the gig's seat. Taking the reins, she smiled at him. "At eight o'clock then—I promise you won't be bored."

"I'm sure I won't be." Michael saluted her and stepped back.

She flicked the reins and Henry obliged; in perfect style, she trotted out along the drive.

Michael watched her go—and wondered how she'd known he'd be here to ask. It was the first day in months he'd been home, yet . . . just luck? Or, given it was Caro, was it good management?

Beside him, Hardacre cleared his throat. "Didn't want to say anything to Mrs. Sutcliffe—no point. But that horse . . ."

Michael looked at him. "What about him?"

"I reckon the reason he bolted was because he'd been stung with pellets—found three tender spots on his left hindquarter, like marks left by stones from a slingshot."

He frowned. "Boys—for a lark?"

"Dangerous lark if that be so, and I have to say I can't think of any lad hereabouts silly enough to do such a thing."

Hardacre was right; all the locals lived on horses—they'd know the likely outcome of such foolishness. "Perhaps there are visitors from London in the vicinity. Lads who wouldn't know."

"Aye, that's possible," Hardacre admitted. "Anyways, can't see any likelihood of it happening again, least not to Mrs. Sutcliffe."

"No, indeed. That would be like lightning striking twice."

Hardacre headed back to the stable. Michael stood for a full minute staring down the drive, then he turned and climbed the terrace steps.

It was too late now to call on Geoffrey Mollison, especially not if his household was at sixes and sevens preparing for Caro's dinner party. Indeed, there was now no need as he himself would be attending and thus would meet Geoffrey later.

Yet his impatience had eased; he was inclined to view

Caro's dinner as an opportunity rather than a distraction. Such an event would be the perfect setting in which to refresh his memory and further his acquaintance with Elizabeth, his ideal bride.

Feeling indebted to Caro, he strolled inside—he needed to unpack his evening gear.

"The enemy is engaged! Our campaign is under way." A triumphant smile wreathing her face, Caro dropped into a chintz-covered armchair in the family parlor at Bramshaw House.

"Yes, but will it work?" Perched on the chaise, picture pretty in a ruffled gown of sprigged muslin with her long fair hair coiled at her nape, Elizabeth eyed her, hope and trepidation in her big blue eyes.

"Of course it will work!" Caro turned her triumph on the only other occupant of the parlor, her secretary, Edward Campbell, who was seated beside Elizabeth on the chaise. A sober, earnest, and reliable gentleman of twenty-three summers, Edward did not look at all the sort of gentleman to have swept Elizabeth off her feet. Appearances, as Caro well knew, could be deceptive.

Letting her smile fade, she met Edward's eyes. "I assure you that when a gentleman like Michael Anstruther-Wetherby makes up his mind you are the ideal candidate for the position of his wife, the only way to avoid having to say the word 'no' and cling limpetlike to it in the teeth of the considerable pressure that will—make no doubt—be brought to bear, is to convince him *before* he makes his offer that he's made a mistake."

Although her words were for Elizabeth, she continued to watch Edward. If the pair were less than rock solid in their resolve, she wanted to see it, know it, now.

Until five days ago, she'd been happily ensconced in Derbyshire with Augusta and had expected to spend the summer months there. Two urgent summonses from Elizabeth, one to her, one to Edward, had brought them hotfoot to Hampshire via London.

Elizabeth had written, panicked at the prospect of finding

herself facing an offer from Michael Anstruther-Wetherby. Caro had thought it a sham—she knew Michael's age and his circle—but Elizabeth had related a conversation with her father in which Geoffrey, having ascertained that Elizabeth had formed no *tendre* for any gentleman she'd met while in town during the Season, had proceeded to sing Michael's praises.

That, Caro had had to admit, sounded suspicious. Not because Michael wasn't perfectly praiseworthy, but because Geoffrey had sought to point that out.

Edward, too, had had doubts over Elizabeth's conjecture, but stopping in London on their way down, he'd dropped in on certain friends, like him aides and secretaries to the politically powerful. What he'd learned had brought him home pale and tense. The whispers had it that Michael Anstruther-Wetherby had been put on notice for a cabinet position; part of that notice concerned his marital status and the suggestion he alter it by autumn.

Caro had delayed another day in town, long enough to pay a morning call on Michael's formidable aunt, Harriet Jennet. They'd spoken political hostess to diplomatic hostess; Caro hadn't even had to broach the subject—Harriet had seized the opportunity to drop a word in her ear regarding Michael's interest in Elizabeth.

That had been more than confirmation enough. Matters were, indeed, as serious as Elizabeth had supposed.

Caro shifted her gaze to her niece. She herself had been a diplomatic bride, a young and innocent seventeen-year-old swept off her feet by the supremely polished attentions of an older—in her case much older—man. She, admittedly, had had no other love in her life, but not for the world would she wish such a marriage on any other young girl.

Although she'd never known love herself, she had every sympathy for Elizabeth and Edward. It was in her household in Lisbon they'd first met; she'd never encouraged them, but to her mind that also meant not opposing them. If love was to be, it would be, and in their case, it had indeed grown. They'd remained steadfast for more than three years, and neither showed any sign of wavering in their affection.

She'd already been thinking of what she might do to further Edward's career, at least to the point that he could offer for Elizabeth's hand. That, however, was not a matter for today. Michael's prospective offer had to be dealt with first. Now—immediately.

"You have to understand," she explained, "that once Michael makes an offer, it will be much harder to get him to withdraw it, and harder still for you, placed as you are, your father's daughter, to refuse it. Our wisest course therefore is to ensure the offer is never made, and that means changing Michael's mind."

His brown eyes serious, Edward looked at Elizabeth. "I agree. It's by far the best way—the tack most likely to succeed with least damage to all."

Elizabeth met his gaze, then glanced at Caro. Then sighed. "Very well. I concede you're right. So what must I do?"

Caro smiled encouragingly. "For tonight, we must concentrate on raising the question of your suitability in his mind. We don't need to repulse him all at once, but simply make him pause and consider. However, whatever we do can be neither overt nor obvious."

Imagining the possibilities, she narrowed her eyes. "The key to manipulating the opinions of a gentleman like Michael Anstruther-Wetherby is always to be subtle and circumspect."

CHAPTER
2

Michael climbed the steps of Bramshaw House at ten minutes past eight that evening. Catten, the butler, knew him well; he conducted him to the formal drawing room and announced him, then deferentially stepped back. Michael walked into the long room, into a fractional pause in the buzz of conversation, smiling easily as eyes, then smiles came his way.

Engaged with a group about the fireplace, Caro saw him. Pausing a few paces inside the room, he waited while she disengaged and came to greet him, the skirts of her oyster silk gown softly shushing.

"My savior!" Smiling, she gave him her hand; when he released it, she confidently tucked it in his arm, swirling to stand beside him as she surveyed the guests. "I suspect you know most, but I doubt you'll have met the Portuguese contingent." She slanted him a glance. "Shall we?"

"By all means." He allowed her to steer him toward the group she'd recently left.

She leaned close, murmured, "The ambassador and his wife are dancing attendance at Brighton, but both couples here are, if anything, even more influential."

She smiled as they joined the group. "The Duke and Duchess of Oporto." With a gesture she indicated a dark gentleman with a cadaverous face and a tall, equally dark and haughty matron. "The Count and Countess of Albufeira."

Another dark-haired gentleman, but quite different from the first—a portly soul with twinkling eyes and the high color of one who was fond of his wine—and a brown-haired, handsome but severe lady. "And this is Ferdinand Leponte, the count's nephew. Allow me to present Mr. Michael Anstruther-Wetherby. Michael is our local Member of Parliament."

Everyone exchanged bows, murmured polite greetings. Relinquishing Michael's arm, Caro placed a hand on the duke's sleeve. "I think it would be wise for you to get to know each other." Eyes gleaming, she glanced at Michael. "I've heard a whisper that in future Mr. Anstruther-Wetherby will be spending more time in our diplomatic circles as distinct from the purely political."

He met her gaze, arched a brow, not entirely surprised she'd heard the rumors. She hadn't, however, revealed such knowledge earlier in the day.

Interpreting their interplay as confirmation, the count quickly engaged him; within minutes, the duke had joined in. Their wives were equally interested, with a few well-directed questions quickly establishing his background and connections.

He was content to encourage them, to listen to their views on what they saw as the most important aspects in the relationship between their two countries. They were keen to sow the right seeds, to influence his opinions before he'd truly formed them—or more particularly before he heard the views of the Foreign Office mandarins.

Caro gently touched his arm and excused herself. Although he continued to give his attention to the duke and count, he was aware that Ferdinand Leponte followed her, claiming the position by her side.

Other than exchanging greetings, Ferdinand, unlike his countrymen, had evinced not the smallest interest in him. Ferdinand looked to be around thirty years old; he was black-haired, olive-skinned, and outrageously handsome, with a brilliant smile and large dark eyes.

A womanizer almost certainly—there was something about him that left little room for doubt. He was typical of many foreign embassy "aides"; relatives of those such as the count, their positions were little more than passports into diplomatic circles. Ferdinand was definitely a hanger-on, but it wasn't the count on whom he was intent on hanging.

When Caro returned ten minutes later, swooping in to artfully extract him and lead Michael to meet her other guests, Ferdinand was still trailing at her heels.

Excusing himself to the other Portuguese, Michael met Ferdinand's eyes. He bowed as if in farewell. Ferdinand smiled ingenuously. As Caro took his arm and led him to the next group, Ferdinand fell in on her other side.

"You are *not* to twit the general," Caro hissed.

He glanced at her, and realized she was speaking to Ferdinand.

Ferdinand grinned, all Latin charm. "But it is so difficult to resist."

Caro threw him a repressive glance, then they reached the group before the long windows, and she launched into introductions.

Michael shook hands with General Kleber, a Prussian, then the Hapsburg ambassador and his wife, both of whom he knew.

The general was an older gentleman, bluff and severe. "It is good that we now have peace, but there is much to be done. My country is very interested in the building of ships—do you know much of the shipyards?"

Denying any knowledge of the industry, Michael moved to draw the ambassador into the conversation. The general pointed out that Austria had no seaport and thus no navy. Michael swung the conversation to agriculture, unsurprised when Caro seized the moment to steer Ferdinand away.

She returned minutes later alone. Rescuing Michael, she introduced him to the other guests—three English diplomats and their wives; a Scots parliamentarian, Mr. Driscoll; his wife and two daughters; and a notoriously attractive Irish peer, Lord Sommerby, whom Mrs. Driscoll was eyeing askance.

Finally, with a softening smile, Caro turned to the last group in the room. She waved at her brother in affectionate dismissal; exchanging grins, Michael shook hands with Geoffrey. He was a large man, heavyset, with sloping shoulders that accentuated a care-worn air; for all he'd been the local Member for years, a gathering of this caliber was in some ways beyond him.

"I understand you and Elizabeth met in town." With a fond smile, Caro indicated the slim young woman standing beside Geoffrey.

At last. "Indeed." Michael took the slender hand Elizabeth extended. "Miss Mollison." He'd seen her when he'd entered, but had been careful not to show any particular interest. He now tried to catch her eye, tried to gauge her reaction to him, but although she smiled sunnily up at him and their gazes met, he could detect no real attentiveness behind her blue eyes.

They deflected almost instantly as Caro introduced the younger man standing somewhat diffidently beside Elizabeth. "My secretary, Edward Campbell. He was Camden's aide, but I grew so used to relying on him that I decided he was simply too valuable to let go."

Campbell threw her a look as if to remind her he *was* only her secretary. He offered his hand; Michael shook it, visited by an urge to recommend Campbell keep his eye on Ferdinand. Suppressing it, he turned instead to the most urgent matter on his plate: Elizabeth Mollison.

"I hear you're in line for advancement," Geoffrey said.

He smiled easily. "That's for the Prime Minister to say, and he won't, not until autumn."

"He always did play his cards close to his chest. So, what's the state of the Irish these days? Think you'll head that way?"

Exchanging political news with Geoffrey was the perfect cover for looking over his daughter. Elizabeth stood beside her father and idly surveyed the room; she affected no interest in their conversation—indeed, seemed oblivious of it. Caro claimed Campbell's arm and went to circulate. Michael shifted so he could better observe Elizabeth.

There was something not quite right . . .

He glanced at Caro, then back at Elizabeth, then surreptitiously noted the gowns the other two young ladies, Driscoll's daughters, were wearing. One was soft pink, the other pale primrose.

Elizabeth had chosen to wear white.

Many unmarried young ladies did, especially during their first Season. Elizabeth had just completed hers, yet . . . white didn't suit her. She was already so fair, and with her pale blond hair the result was poor. Especially as she'd chosen to complement the gauzy gown with diamonds.

Considering the outcome, Michael inwardly frowned. He would never presume to instruct a lady in what to wear, yet he was aware of the difference between a well-dressed lady and a poorly dressed one. In political circles, one rarely saw the latter.

Seeing Elizabeth as she was was something of a jolt. Quite aside from the white making her appear washed out, the combination of the virginal gown with the blatant fire of the diamonds struck a definitely wrong note.

He glanced again at Caro. Oyster silk, draped to perfection, outlined the seductive curves of her body; the color subtly complemented her fair but warm skin, while her gloriously untameable mass of fine hair shimmered under the candlelight in a medley of browns and golds. She wore silver and pearls, echoing her eyes and their curious silver-blue hue.

Looking at Elizabeth, he couldn't imagine that Caro hadn't advised against her present attire. He concluded that behind Elizabeth's innocent air lay a will of some strength—one at least stubborn enough to ignore Caro's injunctions.

His inward frown deepened. A stubborn and headstrong will—was that good? Or not so good? An inability to take advice from those patently well qualified to supply it . . . ?

A number of guests had arrived late; Caro brought them around, performing the introductions. While two newcomers were chatting with Geoffrey, Michael turned to Elizabeth. "As I recall, we met at Lady Hannaford's ball in May—did you enjoy the rest of your first Season?"

"Oh, yes!" Elizabeth's eyes lit; she turned a glowing face to him. "The balls were such fun—I do so adore dancing.

And all the other entertainments, too—well, except for the dinners. They were often boring. But I made a large number of friends." She smiled ingenuously up at him. "Do you know the Hartfords? Melissa Hartford and her brother, Derek?"

She paused, waited, clearly expecting an answer. He shifted. "Ah . . . no." He had a suspicion Derek Hartford would prove to be twenty, and Melissa even younger.

"Oh. Well, they've become my best friends. We go all over town together, exploring and gallivanting. And Jennifer Rickards joins us, too, and her cousins Eustace and Brian Hollings." Elizabeth paused in .her bright prattle, then frowned across the room. "Those two girls look rather lost, don't you think? I'd better go and speak with them."

With that, she flashed him a brilliant smile and swanned off—without properly excusing herself.

Michael watched her go, feeling rather . . . disoriented. She'd been treating him like a family friend, one with whom she didn't need to stand on ceremony, yet . . .

Silk sussurated beside him; the scent of honeysuckle, faint and elusive, teased his senses.

He looked down as Caro slid her hand onto his arm. She'd followed his gaze to Elizabeth; she glanced up and pulled a face at him. "I know, but you needn't think it was my idea."

He smiled down at her. "I didn't."

Looking again at Elizabeth, she sighed. "Unfortunately, she was adamant over the white and simultaneously desperate to wear the diamonds—for courage. They were Alice's, you see."

Alice was—had been—Elizabeth's mother, Geoffrey's wife. Michael blinked. "Courage?"

"She's not used to evenings of this ilk, so I suppose she felt in need of bolstering." Caro looked up at him, her expressive face and brilliant eyes both teasing and somehow communicating. "It's just a passing phase—a part of learning to deal with this sort of gathering. She'll soon find her feet."

She looked away. He stared at her profile. Had she guessed his thoughts vis-à-vis Elizabeth?

Should he speak, enlist her aid—

She came up on her toes, stretching to see over the crowd. "Is that . . . ?"

He followed her gaze and saw Catten standing in the doorway.

"At last!" Caro flashed him a brilliant smile, sliding her arm from his. "Do excuse me while I organize."

He watched her glide away, smoothly performing the hostessly ritual of pairing her guests according to the recognized order of precedence. With the company boasting English, Irish, and foreign dignitaries, that was no mean feat, yet she organized them all without a hitch.

As he strolled to offer his arm to Mrs. Driscoll, he wondered how Elizabeth would have managed it.

"Well, we'll hope to see you in Edinburgh sometime in the next year." Mrs. Driscoll helped herself to green beans from the dish Michael held, then relieved him of the dish and passed it on.

"I'd enjoy visiting again, but I fear the Prime Minister may have other plans." Picking up his knife and fork, he applied himself to the fifth-course meats. "When duty calls . . ."

"Aye, well, all of us here understand that."

Mrs. Driscoll's gaze briefly circled the table. Inclining his head in acknowledgment, he, too, glanced around. For all that she saw him as a potential opportunity for one of her daughters, Mrs. Driscoll had not been overly pushy; their conversation had not become awkward.

Her comment, indeed, was apt. All those about the table knew how things were done, how to behave in this select and somewhat esoteric circle so heavily influenced by the vicissitudes of politics, both local and international. He felt more at home, certainly more engaged than he did at similar purely tonnish gatherings.

Between Mrs. Driscoll on his right and the countess on his left, he didn't lack for conversation. The whole table was engulfed in a pleasant hum. Glancing along the board covered with white damask, silver, and crystal, he noted the younger ladies, Elizabeth and the two Driscoll girls, together with two younger gentlemen and flanked by Edward Campbell, sitting in a group midway along.

Seated on the opposite side of the table, Elizabeth was engrossed in some discussion, animatedly describing something, hands flying.

Michael turned to reply to a question from the countess.

He was turning back to Mrs. Driscoll when a sudden peal of laughter drew all eyes—to Elizabeth.

The sound was abruptly cut off; fingers pressed to her lips, Elizabeth's gaze darted up and down the table. A blush suffused her pale cheeks.

One of the Driscoll girls leaned forward and made some comment; Edward Campbell answered and the awkward moment passed. The other diners turned back to their conversations. One of the last to do so, Michael saw Elizabeth, head now bowed, reach for her wineglass.

She took a sip, choked—tried to replace the goblet and nearly tipped it over. The clatter and her coughing again drew all eyes. Goblet finally safe on the table, she grabbed her napkin from her lap and ducked her head.

Beside her, Campbell patted her on the back; her coughing eased. He asked her something—presumably if she was all right. Her fair head bobbed. Then she straightened, lifted her head, and drew in a deep breath. Smiling weakly around, she breathlessly said, "I'm so sorry—do excuse me. The wine went down the wrong way."

Everyone smiled easily and returned to their discussions.

Talking to the countess, Michael found his mind wandering. The incident was a small thing, yet . . .

His gaze drifted up the table to Caro at its end, engaged in what appeared to be a scintillating discussion with the duke and the general. If she had choked . . . a big "if" admittedly, but if she had, he was certain she'd have passed the moment off in a much more charming way.

Still, as Caro had said, Elizabeth was young.

He smiled at the countess. "I hope to visit your country again in the not-too-distant future."

* * *

When the company reassembled in the drawing room, Michael continued to observe Elizabeth, but from a distance. She remained surrounded by the younger crew, leaving all hostly duties to her aunt and father, giving him no chance to evaluate her abilities in that sphere.

He felt oddly frustrated. Joining that younger group . . . he simply wasn't one of them. It had been a very long time since events such as curricle races had dominated his mind. Yet he was determined to learn more about Elizabeth. He was standing by the side of the room, momentarily alone, wondering how best to further his aim, when Caro materialized at his side.

He knew she was near an instant before she stopped beside him and claimed his arm. She did it so naturally, as if they were old friends with no social barriers between them, he found himself responding to her in the same vein.

"Hmm." Her gaze was fixed on Elizabeth. "I could use some fresh air and I daresay Elizabeth could, too." Looking up, she smiled warmly, but there was a determined glint in her eye. "Besides, I want to separate her from that crowd. She really should do the rounds and widen her acquaintance." Her hold on his arm firming, she arched a brow at him. "Would you care for a stroll on the terrace?"

He smiled, careful to hide the depth of his approval. "Lead on."

She did, steering him across the room, with a few glib words extracting Elizabeth from her circle. Still on his arm, she swept them through the open French doors out onto the moon-drenched terrace.

"Now!" Walking briskly, whisking Elizabeth down the terrace, Caro studied her. "Are you all right—is your throat sore?"

"No. It's truly quite—"

"Caro?"

The soft call had them all turning. Edward Campbell looked out from the French doors. "I think you'd better . . ." He gestured back into the drawing room.

"Peste!" Caro looked at Edward for a moment, then glanced at Michael, then Elizabeth. Releasing Michael's

arm, she caught Elizabeth's hand and placed it on his sleeve. "Walk. To the end of the terrace at least. And then you can return and practice by charming the general for me."

Elizabeth blinked. "Oh, but—"

"No buts." Caro was already stalking back to the drawing room. She flicked a hand back at them, rings flashing. "Go—walk."

She reached Edward; taking his arm, head rising, she swept back into the drawing room.

Leaving Michael alone with Elizabeth; suppressing a grin—Caro was quite amazing—he looked down at her. "I suspect we'd better do as instructed." Turning her, he started slowly strolling. "Are you enjoying your summer thus far?"

Elizabeth threw him a resigned smile. "It's not as exciting as London, but now Aunt Caro is here, there'll be lots more happening. More people to meet, more entertainments to attend."

"So you enjoy meeting new people?" A healthy attitude for a politician's wife.

"Oh, yes—well, as long as they're *young* people, of course." Elizabeth pulled a face. "I do find 'making conversation' with old fogeys or those one has nothing in common with a trial, but Caro assures me I'll learn." She paused, then added, "Although I have to say I'd much rather not have to learn at all."

She flashed him a brilliant smile. "I'd much rather just *enjoy* the parties, the balls, the routs and not worry over *having* to talk to this one or that. I want to enjoy being young, enjoy dancing and riding and driving, and all the rest."

He blinked.

Leaning on his arm, she gestured widely. "You must remember what it was like—all the fun to be had in the capital."

She looked up at him, clearly expecting him to smile and nod. After leaving Oxford, he'd spent most of his time as a secretary to important men; he had been in the capital, yet he suspected he'd inhabited a parallel universe to the one she was describing. "Ah . . . yes, of course."

He bit back an admission that it had been a long time ago.

She laughed as if he'd been twitting her. Reaching the end of the terrace, they turned and ambled back. She continued telling him of her wonderful months in London, of events and people he didn't know and had little interest in.

As they neared the doors to the drawing room, he realized she'd shown no interest in him—in his likes, acquaintances, his life.

Inwardly frowning, he glanced at her. She was treating him not just as a family friend, but worse, as an uncle. It hadn't occurred to her—

"Finally!" Caro emerged through the doors, saw them, and smiled. She glided toward them. "It's so balmy out here—perfect for a pleasant interlude."

"Ah, my dear Caro, you read my mind—"

Caro swung back. Ferdinand had followed her onto the terrace; he broke off as he realized there were others present.

She reversed direction, intercepting him. "Mr. Anstruther-Wetherby and Elizabeth have been enjoying a stroll—we were just returning to the drawing room."

Ferdinand flashed his white smile. "*Excelente!* They may go in and we can stroll."

She'd intended to turn him back into the drawing room. Instead, deftly, he turned her. Half turned her—she caught his arm and was about to correct him when she sensed Michael move close.

"Actually, Leponte, I believe that's not what Mrs. Sutcliffe meant."

The delivery was urbane, his tone impossible to take exception to, yet steel rang beneath the words.

Mentally rolling her eyes, resisting an urge to pat Michael's arm and assure him she was perfectly capable of dealing with would-be gigolos like Ferdinand, she shook Ferdinand's arm, dragging his gaze, belligerently locked with Michael's, back to her. "Mr. Anstruther-Wetherby is right—there's no time for a stroll for me. I must get back to my guests."

Ferdinand's lips set, but he was forced to accede.

Knowing he would sulk, suddenly perceiving an unexpected opportunity, she swung to Elizabeth; her face momentarily screened from both men, she signaled with her eyes, directing Elizabeth to Ferdinand. "You're looking refreshed, my dear—perhaps you could help?"

Elizabeth blinked, then summoned an ingenuous smile. "Yes, of course." Drawing her hand from Michael's sleeve, she turned her smile on Ferdinand. "Perhaps you could take me to your aunt, sir? I've had very little chance to speak with her."

Ferdinand was too experienced to let his chagrin show; after only the most fleeting hesitation, he smiled his charming smile and with a courtly half-bow, murmured his delight.

Ferdinand reached for Elizabeth's hand; behind Caro, Michael shifted. It was a tiny movement, but both she and Ferdinand noted it. Ferdinand's smile took on an edge. Grasping Elizabeth's hand, he drew her nearer, settling her hand on his sleeve. "I will do more than that, my pretty one. I will stand by your side and . . ."

Whatever else he planned, Caro didn't hear as he bent closer to Elizabeth and lowered his voice.

Caro knew Elizabeth—and Edward—far too well to imagine Ferdinand would get any joy there, but Elizabeth had the sense to laugh delightedly as she and Ferdinand reentered the drawing room.

Feeling quite pleased with Elizabeth's performance, Caro turned to Michael, ignoring the irritation behind his polite mask. He was reasonably adept at hiding his emotions, but she was a diplomatic hostess of long standing, ergo an expert in divining people's true reactions.

He was—as she'd hoped—not just frustrated, but puzzled, and starting to be wary. She—they—needed him to reassess; she almost crossed her fingers as she reclaimed his arm. "The duke mentioned he'd like to speak with you again."

Recalled to duty, he accompanied her back into the drawing room.

She ensured he was kept busy, away from Elizabeth. Whether he noticed Ferdinand flirting with Elizabeth, who wisely played the innocent, thus encouraging Ferdinand to even greater efforts, Caro couldn't be sure; the duke truly had wanted to speak with him. Michael had already made the right impression there; they remained locked in serious discussion for some time. While continuing to patrol her guests—there was never any time during diplomatic entertainments when a hostess could relax—she tried to keep an eye on him, yet toward the end of the evening, she suddenly discovered him gone.

One quick survey of the room informed her Geoffrey was also absent.

"Damn!" Plastering on a smile, she swept up to Edward. "You're on duty for the next while." She lowered her voice. "I have to go and haul your irons out of the fire."

Edward blinked, but he'd stood as her deputy through far worse crises; he nodded and she moved on.

Casting a last glance about the room, reassured there were no other impending disasters threatening, she slipped into the front hall. Catten stood guard there; he told her Geoffrey had taken Michael to his study.

Her heart sank. Surely after all he'd seen of Elizabeth that evening, all the serious questions Elizabeth's performance *ought* to have raised in his mind, Michael wasn't so bone-headed as to persist with an offer?

She couldn't believe he was that stupid.

Almost running, she hurried to the study. With barely a tap, she opened the door and swept in. "Geoffrey, what . . ."

With one glance she took in the scene—both men leaning over the desk, poring over some maps spread on its surface. Relief swept her; she hid it behind a disapproving frown. "I know you're unused to these affairs, but really, this is not the time for"—she gestured at the maps—"constituency matters."

Geoffrey grinned apologetically. "Not even politics, I'm afraid. There's a blockage on a tributary to the river. It's in Eyeworth Wood—I was just showing Michael."

With a fine show of sisterly exasperation, she linked her arm in Geoffrey's. "What am I to do with you?" She bent a mock frown on Michael. "You, at least, should have known better."

He smiled and followed as she led Geoffrey from the room. "But the woods are mine, after all."

Her heart no longer beating in her throat, she ushered them back into the drawing room. Elizabeth glanced over and saw them enter; her eyes flared—Caro smiled serenely back. And made sure Michael had no further opportunity to speak with Geoffrey by retaining her hold on her brother's arm and taking him to talk with General Kleber.

The end of the evening drew near. Gradually, the guests took their leave. The diplomatic contingent, more accustomed to late nights, were the last remaining. They'd gathered in a group in the middle of the room when Ferdinand spoke.

"I would like to invite all those who would enjoy it to join me for a day's cruise on my yacht." He looked around the circle; his gaze came to rest on Caro's face. "It is moored in Southampton Water close by. We could sail for a few hours, then find a pretty spot to anchor for lunch."

The offer was generous. Everyone present was tempted. With a few questions, Caro ascertained that the yacht was sizeable, large enough to accommodate them all easily. Ferdinand assured her his crew would arrange a luncheon; it was too good a prospect to dismiss—on more than one count.

She smiled. "When should we go?"

They all agreed that the day after next would be perfect. The weather was currently fine and not expected to change; having a day to recover before they came together to enjoy each other's company again would work nicely.

"An excellent notion," the countess declared. She turned to Caro. "Aside from all else, it will put that boat to better use than I suspect it has been put to date."

Caro hid a smile. The arrangements were quickly made. Michael accepted; she'd been sure he would.

As everyone turned to leave, Elizabeth tugged her sleeve. She stepped to the side, lowered her voice. "What is it?"

Elizabeth glanced past her to Michael. "Have we done enough, do you think?"

"For tonight, we've done all we reasonably can. Indeed, we've done brilliantly." She glanced at the group filing through the doorway. "As for the cruise, I couldn't have planned that better myself. It'll be the perfect venue to develop our theme."

"But . . ." Still looking at Michael, who was talking to General Kleber, Elizabeth bit her lip. "Do you think it's working?"

"He hasn't offered for you yet, and that's the most important thing." Caro paused, reassessing, then patted Elizabeth's arm. "Nevertheless, tomorrow's another day—we should make sure he's occupied."

With a swish of her skirts, she returned to the group. A quick word in the countess's ear, a quiet moment with the duchess and the ambassador's wife, and all was arranged. Or almost all.

As he followed the bulk of the guests out of the front door, Michael found Caro beside him.

She slipped her hand in his arm. Leaning closer, she murmured, "I wondered if you'd like to join us—me, Elizabeth, Edward, and a few others—on a trip to Southampton tomorrow. I thought we might meet in town late morning, have a look around, then lunch at the Dolphin before a quick visit to the walls, and a gentle journey home."

Looking up, she arched a brow at him. "Can we count on your escort?"

Another—and quieter—opportunity through which to evaluate Elizabeth. Michael smiled into Caro's silvery eyes. "I'll be delighted to join you."

He hadn't realized Caro had intended a shopping expedition. Nor that Ferdinand Leponte would be one of the party. Arriving at Bramshaw House at eleven, he'd been bidden to join Caro, Elizabeth, and Campbell in the barouche; the day was fine, the breeze light, the sunshine warm—all had seemed in place for a pleasant outing.

The others joined them at Totton on the road to Southampton. The duchess, the countess, the ambassador's wife, and Ferdinand Leponte. Ferdinand predictably tried to engineer a reallocation of seats, suggesting Michael join the older ladies in the duchess's landau, but Caro waved the suggestion aside.

"It's barely a few miles, Ferdinand—too close to bother rearranging things." With the tip of her furled parasol, she tapped her coachman's shoulder; he started the barouche rolling. "Just have your man follow and we'll be there in no time, then we can all walk together."

She sat back, then glanced at Michael, sitting beside her. He smiled, let his gratitude show. Her lips twitched; she looked ahead.

They spent the half-hour journey discussing local events. Caro, he, and Edward were less well informed about local affairs than Elizabeth; encouraged, she filled them in with the latest news.

He was pleased to discover she kept abreast of local matters.

"The church fete is the next big event." Elizabeth grimaced. "I suppose we'll have to attend, or Muriel will be after us."

"It's always an entertaining day," Caro pointed out.

"True, but I do so hate the feeling of being *obliged* to be there."

Caro shrugged and looked away. Inwardly frowning yet again, Michael followed her gaze out over the expanse of Southampton Water.

They left the carriages at the Dolphin and wandered along High Street, then the ladies determinedly turned to the shops along French Street and Castle Way.

The gentlemen—all three of them—started to drag their heels. Started to realize they'd been inveigled into being packhorses under false pretenses, to wit, by having elusive carrots dangled before their noses.

Edward, doubtless more accustomed to such trials, merely sighed and accepted the parcels Caro and the ambassador's wife dropped in his arms. Michael found himself landed with a bandbox tied with wide pink ribbon, bestowed on him by Elizabeth with a sweet smile.

Chattering together, the ladies entered the next shop. Michael glanced at Ferdinand. Holding two gaudily wrapped packages, the Portuguese looked as discomposed and disgusted as he himself felt. Looking at Edward, at the relatively innocuous brown packages Caro had handed him, Michael raised his brows. He met Edward's eyes. "Want to swap?"

Edward shook his head. "The etiquette pertaining here is that you have to hold on to whatever they hand you, or else they'll get confused."

Michael held his gaze. "You're making that up."

Edward grinned.

By the time the ladies finally consented to return to the Dolphin, where luncheon awaited them in a private parlor, Michael was burdened with the bandbox and three other parcels, two tied with ribbon. The only aspect of the situation that lightened his mood was that Ferdinand was all but invisible behind the ten parcels his aunt and the duchess had stacked in his arms.

Michael felt something perilously close to fellow feeling when, together with Ferdinand, he tumbled the packages onto a settle in the inn parlor. They exchanged glances, then looked at Edward, who had escaped relatively lightly. Reading their expressions, Edward nodded. "I'll arrange to leave these here."

"Good." Michael made it clear by his tone that any other outcome would precipitate mutiny.

Ferdinand just glowered.

The luncheon started well enough. Michael sat on one bench beside Elizabeth, with Caro on his other side and Ferdinand beyond her. The other four sat on the bench opposite. He wanted to question Elizabeth as to her aspirations, angling to learn what she looked for from marriage, but the two leading comments he introduced both somehow ended back with the balls, parties, and entertainments of London.

On top of that, the countess and the duchess, speaking across the table, distracted him. Their comments and queries were too needle-sharp, too acute to be lightly turned aside. They may not be their husbands, yet they were assuredly sounding him out; he had to pay them due attention.

Edward came to his aid once or twice; Michael met his gaze and nodded almost imperceptibly in appreciation. Elizabeth, however, seemed sunk in her own thoughts and contributed nothing.

Then the desserts arrived and the older ladies shifted their attention to the crème anglaise and poached pears. Seizing the moment, he turned to Elizabeth, only to feel a sudden warmth against his other side.

Turning that way, he realized Caro had shifted along the bench, realized with an eruption of hot anger that she'd shifted because Ferdinand had shifted into her.

He had to fight down a surprisingly powerful urge to reach behind Caro and clip Ferdinand over the ear. It was what he deserved for behaving like such a boor, yet . . . diplomatic incidents had arisen from less.

He fixed his eyes on Ferdinand's face; the Portuguese was currently intent on Caro, looking down, trying to read her face. "So, Leponte, what sort of horses do you keep in town? Any Arabs?"

Ferdinand glanced up at him, momentarily at sea. Then he colored faintly and responded.

Michael kept asking questions, about carriages, even the yacht, focusing everyone's attention on Ferdinand until the meal ended and they stood to leave.

As she followed him out from the bench, Caro squeezed his arm lightly. It was the only acknowledgment she made that she appreciated his support, yet he felt an unexpected, somewhat righteous glow.

They'd planned to take a postprandial stroll along the old walls. The view afforded over Southampton Water and south to the Isle of Wight, taking in all the commerical and private shipping that dotted the blue expanse in between, was superb.

The wind whipped the ladies' skirts and tugged at their bonnets; conversation was difficult. The ambassador's wife linked her arm with Elizabeth's; heads together, they discussed some feminine thing. The duchess and countess walked alongside, captured by the view. Behind the four ladies, Caro followed, Ferdinand close beside her. Michael got the distinct impression Ferdinand was groveling, trying to get back into Caro's good graces, knowing he'd stepped over that invisible line.

The Portuguese was exceedingly charming; he'd probably succeed.

Bringing up the rear with Edward, watching Ferdinand's artful performance, Michael couldn't help but wonder if the Portuguese had misinterpreted, or rather missed altogether, the irony in Caro's nickname, and thought the "Merry" in the "Merry Widow" meant something it did not.

CHAPTER
3

$\mathcal{T}$he next day dawned bright and clear. At Caro's suggestion, Michael joined them at Bramshaw House. She, Elizabeth, and Geoffrey climbed into the barouche; Michael and Edward kept pace on their horses during the short journey to the landing stage just south of Totton.

Smiling across at Michael as the carriage rolled along, Caro reviewed her plans for the day—her order of battle. Ferdinand, anxious to please after his faux pas of the day before, had agreed to bring his yacht into the northernmost reaches of Southampton Water, thus shortening the time they, and all the others, too, needed to travel before embarking on their cruise.

Reducing time spent in the carriage had seemed wise. If Elizabeth spent too much time in Michael's sight while in ordinary situations, she might inadvertently start to correct the image they were working to project.

They had to walk a fine line. While alone with Michael or with only herself or Edward present, Elizabeth could behave in ways she couldn't if others were about to witness her performance; the only restriction was what Michael would believe. In public, however, if she was ultimately to marry Edward and support him in *his* career, she couldn't paint herself as a silly flibbertigibbet; those in diplomatic circles had long memories. When among others, all she could do was stumble in minor ways—like her white gown and diamonds or her choking at table—that would be forgiven her youth or excused as inexperience.

Thus far they'd managed exceedingly well. Caro was pleased, but knew better than to rest on her laurels. Not yet.

They rattled through Totton, then turned off the main road and headed down the incline to the water's edge. The twin masts of Ferdinand's yacht came into sight, then they rounded the last hill and there it lay, bobbing gently at the jetty.

Most of the others were already there; the ambassador and his wife were boarding as the Bramshaw House party drew up beside the landing stage. A wooden platform built out from the bank, being on the western shore of the estuary, well away from the bustling port on the opposite shore, the jetty was used almost exclusively by pleasure boats.

Michael dismounted, gave his horse into the care of the ostler hired from the tavern in Totton for the day, then came to open the carriage door. Smiling with very real anticipation, Caro gave him her hand; momentarily aware of the strength of his grasp, she allowed him to help her down.

He met her gaze, then glanced at the yacht.

"It's quite something, isn't it?" she said.

He looked back at her, paused, then admitted, "I wasn't expecting anything quite so large. Most 'yachts' aren't that big."

She settled her shawl about her shoulders. "I understand Ferdinand uses it up and down the Portuguese coast, so it would have to withstand the Atlantic breakers. They're even more ferocious than the Channel in a storm."

The carriage shifting behind them recalled Michael to his duty. He turned and helped Elizabeth down.

Caro walked to the narrow gangplank leading onto the yacht. While she waited for Edward and Geoffrey to join her, she scanned those already on board. She was delighted to note Mrs. Driscoll and her daughters. She'd suggested Ferdinand invite them, too; clearly he'd complied.

She couldn't yet see if the Driscolls had lived up to her expectations. Glancing back, she took in the delightful picture Elizabeth made in her summery gown of sprig muslin, ruffled at the neckline, sleeves, and hem. She carried a matching ruffled parasol; the outfit was perfect for a garden party, or to impress impressionable males at any outdoor event.

Of course, no woman with the slightest modicum of common sense would wear such a gown aboard an oceangoing yacht.

Noting Michael's silent but patent approval of Elizabeth's appearance, Caro inwardly grinned; he wouldn't be so approving by the time they headed home. She summoned Edward with a look; leaving Elizabeth to Michael, he came to give her his arm and aid her in picking her way up the gangplank.

"I sincerely hope you know what you're doing," he murmured, steadying her as she swayed.

Tightening her grip on his arm, she laughed. "Oh, ye of little faith. Have I failed you yet?"

"No, but it's not you directly I doubt."

"Oh?" She glanced at him, then back at Elizabeth, tripping prettily toward the gangplank on Michael's arm.

"No, not Elizabeth either. I just wonder if you're reading *him* aright."

Caro drew back to look at Edward's face. "Michael?"

Looking ahead, Edward's face hardened. "And not just Anstruther-Wetherby."

Facing forward, Caro saw Ferdinand, the smiling convivial host, waiting at the gangplank's head. He looked like a handsome wolf—too many teeth were on show. Smiling in return, she covered the last yards and gave him her hand; he bowed her aboard with courtly grace.

Straightening, he raised her hand to his lips. "You are the last, as befits the most important, dear Caro. Now, we may set sail."

With a twist of her wrist, she slid her fingers from his grasp. "Do wait until my brother and niece and Mr. Anstruther-Wetherby come aboard."

With an amused glance, she directed Ferdiand's attention to where Elizabeth was unsteadily negotiating the narrow gangplank. "It's the first time Elizabeth's been aboard a yacht. I'm sure she'll find the experience rewarding." She patted Ferdinand's arm. "I'll leave you to greet them."

She was aware of the irritated look he cast her as she swept forward. Edward strolled in her wake; they were both excellent sailors, quite at home on the lightly rolling deck.

"Countess. Duchess." They exchanged bows, then Caro greeted the gentlemen before turning to Mrs. Driscoll. "I'm so glad you and your daughters could join us."

As she'd predicted—it was so nice to be proved right— both the Driscoll girls were sensibly attired in twill walking dresses, plain and unadorned. Her own gown of bronze silk twill was made high to the throat, with long fitted sleeves and only slightly flared skirts. Her shawl was a plain one without any fringe. Other than a strip of flat lace around the collar and the placket of her bodice—safe enough—there were no frills or furbelows to catch on anything.

Unlike the fine ruffles of Elizabeth's gown.

"Oh!"

As if on cue, the feminine cry had everyone turning. Elizabeth's hem had snagged in the gap between the gangplank and the deck. Ferdinand had his hands full holding her upright, while Michael crouched precariously on the gangplank, struggling to unhook the fine material.

Reining in her smile to the merely happy, Caro turned back to the others. With a wide gesture, she directed all attention to the brilliant blue swath of water before them, the surface ruffled by a gentle breeze. "It's going to be a glorious day!"

It certainly started out that way. Once Elizabeth, Michael, and Geoffrey were safe aboard, the gangplank was drawn in and the ropes untied; a trio of swarthy sailors swarmed up the rigging, then the sails were unfurled and the yacht leapt before the wind.

With "oohs" and "aahs" and shining eyes, all the guests clung to the bow rails and watched the waves rush to meet them. Fine spray kicked up as the yacht gained speed, sending the ladies back from the rails to the chairs grouped behind the forecastle. Leaving Elizabeth to her own devices—she had strict instructions on what line to take—

Caro linked her arm in Geoffrey's and set out to stroll, determined to stay clear of Michael and Ferdinand both.

It was easy to pass among the ladies, to share the enjoyment as the yacht sped smoothly down the western shore of the estuary. Other than when they crossed the wake thrown up by a larger commercial ship, the journey was relatively calm.

While passing the spot along the port bow where Michael, Elizabeth, and the Driscoll girls stood chatting, Caro listened in.

Elizabeth, eyes shining, was holding forth. "The suppers are really nothing at all to comment on, but the dancing, especially close by the rotunda, is quite thrilling—one can never be sure *whom* one is rubbing shoulders with!"

Vauxhall. Caro smiled. The pleasure gardens did not rate highly among the political and diplomatic set. As she and Geoffrey moved on, she saw Elizabeth lean against a rope to steady herself; when she tried to straighten, the ruffle at her shoulder caught on the rough hemp. One of the Driscoll girls came to her rescue.

Elizabeth had already tried to open her parasol. Michael had had to grab it, wrestle it closed, then explain to her why she couldn't use it.

Caro risked a quick peek at his face; he was looking a trifle harassed, even a touch grim. Subduing her smile, she glided on.

As Ferdinand had to play the host, it would be some time before he would be free to chase her. She was aware of his intent, but confident of her ability to fend him off. As Camden Sutcliffe's much younger wife, she'd been the target of far more experienced seducers—rakes, roués, and licentious noblemen—for more than a decade; Ferdinand stood no chance with her. Indeed, no man stood any chance with her; she had absolutely no interest in what they were so eager to offer. In fact, they wouldn't be so eager to offer if they knew . . .

Beside her, Geoffrey cleared his throat. "You know, m'dear, I've been meaning to ask." From beneath his heavy brows, he studied her face. "Are you happy, Caro?"

She blinked.   •

"I mean," Geoffrey rushed on, "you're not that old and you haven't opened up the London house and, well . . ." He shrugged. "I just wondered."

So did she. Smiling lightly, she patted his arm. "I haven't opened the house because I'm not sure what I want to do with it—whether I really want to live there at all." That much she could explain. Indeed, voicing her feelings solidified the strange equivocation she felt about the house in Half Moon Street. She and Camden had used it as their London residence; located in the best part of town, it was neither too big nor too small, had a pleasant rear garden, and was filled with exquisite antiques, yet . . . "I'm honestly not sure."

She liked the house, but now when she went there . . . something simply wasn't right.

"I, ah, wondered whether you were thinking of marrying again."

She met Geoffrey's gaze. "No, I'm not. I have no intention of remarrying."

He colored slightly, patted her hand as he looked forward. "It's just that—well, if you do, I hope you'll stay closer this time." His voice turned gruff. "You've family here . . ."

His words trailed away; his gaze remained fixed ahead. Caro followed it, to Ferdinand, standing beside the wheel giving his captain orders.

Geoffrey snorted. "I just don't want you marrying some foreign bounder."

She laughed, hugged his arm reassuringly. "Truly, you can set your mind at rest. Ferdinand is playing some game, but it's not one in which I have any interest." She met Geoffrey's gaze. "I won't be throwing my cap into his ring."

He read her eyes, then humphed. "Good!"

Half an hour later, she thanked the gods that Geoffrey had spoken of his concerns sooner rather than later, and so given her the opportunity to allay them before Ferdinand made his move. As soon as he'd finished with his captain, he fixed his sights on her. With considerable flair, he displaced Geoffrey at her side, then cut her out from the crowd congregated behind the forecastle. She permitted him to take her strolling about the deck—for the simple reason that it was an open deck; there was a limit to what he might even think to accomplish within plain sight of all the others.

Including his aunt, who, somewhat to Caro's surprise, seemed to be keeping a sharp eye on her nephew, although whether that eye was severely disapproving or simply severe, she couldn't say.

"Perhaps, my dear Caro, as you are so enjoying the trip, you could return tomorrow and we could go out again. A private cruise just for two."

She assumed a considering expression, sensed him holding his breath, then resolutely shook her head. "The church fete is quite soon. If I don't make an effort, Muriel Hedderwick will be unbearable."

Ferdinand frowned. "Who is this Muriel Hedderwick?"

Caro smiled. "She's actually my niece-by-marriage, but that doesn't adequately describe our relationship."

Ferdinand continued to frown, then ventured, "Niece-by-marriage—this means she is Sutcliffe's—your late husband's—niece?"

She nodded. "That's right. She married a gentleman named Hedderwick and lives . . ." She continued, putting Muriel and her history to good use, totally distracting Ferdinand, who wanted to know only so he could counter Muriel's supposed influence and inveigle Caro away on his yacht.

Poor Ferdinand was destined for disappointment, on that and all other scores. By the time he realized he'd been diverted, they were nearing the bow once more.

Looking ahead to where Michael and the girls had been standing, Caro saw the group clustering by the rail. She could see Michael's back, and the Driscoll girls' gowns, and Edward, all pressing close.

Edward glanced around and saw her. He beckoned urgently.

Both she and Ferdinand hurried across.

"There, there." One of the Driscoll girls murmured. "Here, take my handkerchief."

"You poor thing—how dreadful." Seeing Caro approaching, the other sister stepped back.

Edward looked grim as he quickly stepped in, taking the arm of the wilting figure slumped over the rail.

"*Oohhhh*," Elizabeth moaned, a sound of abject misery. Michael, on her other side, was supporting most of her weight.

Edward cast a speaking glance at Caro; she stared back at him. They hadn't thought . . .

She blinked. Turned to Ferdinand. "Do you have a cabin—some place she can lie down?"

"Of course." Ferdinand squeezed her shoulder. "I will have it prepared."

"Wait!" Michael turned his head and spoke to Ferdinand. "Tell your captain to turn around. We're now in the Solent— he needs to get back into calmer waters, and closer to shore."

Caro realized the ride had become considerably more choppy; used to tipping decks—this was mild compared to the Atlantic—she hadn't truly noticed when they'd emerged from the relatively protected reaches of Southampton Water and heeled southwest into the Solent.

Glancing at the limp figure Michael was holding upright, Ferdinand nodded curtly and left. On the way to the wheel, he called orders to one of his crew; the sailor scurried to open the doors to the companionway leading to the lower deck. Looking Caro's way, he beckoned, called "Come, come" in Portuguese, then disappeared down the steep stairs.

Caro exchanged glances with Michael and Edward, then moved to the rail, taking Edward's place; stroking Elizabeth's back, she tried to look into her face. "Don't worry, darling. We'll get you downstairs. Once you're lying down, you won't feel so poorly."

Elizabeth gulped in air, tried to speak, then weakly shook her head and moaned again.

She slumped even lower. Michael tightened his hold. "She's close to fainting. Here—stand back."

He stooped, then lifted Elizabeth into his arms. He settled her, then nodded at Caro. "Lead the way. You're right—she needs to be horizontal."

Getting Elizabeth—who truly was as good as unconscious—

down the narrow stairs was no easy feat. With help from Caro and Edward, Michael managed it; once he gained the lower deck, Caro looked past him and called to Edward, who'd been helping from behind. "Cold water, a bowl, and some cloths."

Grim-faced, Edward nodded. "I'll get them."

Caro turned and hurried ahead to hold the door to the stern cabin open. Michael angled his awkward burden through, then walked to the bunk bed the sailor had hurriedly made up, and laid Elizabeth down.

She moaned again. She was whiter than the proverbial sheet—her fine skin looked almost green.

"She lost her breakfast over the rail." Michael stepped back, met Caro's worried eyes. "Is there anything else you need?"

She bit her lip, then shook her head. "Not at present—just that water."

He nodded and turned for the door. "Call me when she wants to come up again—she won't be able to manage the stairs without help."

Distractedly, Caro murmured her thanks. Leaning over Elizabeth, she brushed tendrils of damp hair off her forehead. She heard the door softly close; glancing around, she confirmed the sailor had left, too. Gently, she folded Elizabeth's forearm over her chest.

Elizabeth moaned again.

"It's all right, sweetheart—I'm going to loosen your laces."

Edward brought the water in an ewer with a basin; Caro met him at the door and took them. "Is she all right?" he asked.

"She will be." Caro grimaced. "It never occurred to me she might be seasick."

With a worried glance, Edward left. Caro bathed Elizabeth's face and hands, then eased her up so she could sip from a glass. She was still very pale, but her skin no longer felt quite so clammy.

She sank back on the pillows with a sigh and a little shiver.

"Just sleep." Unwinding her shawl, Caro draped it over Elizabeth's shoulders and chest, then brushed the pale curls from her forehead. "I'll be here."

She didn't need to look out of the portholes set across the stern to know the yacht had heeled and turned. The chop and slap of the Solent's waters had faded; the hull was once more riding smoothly, slowly gliding back up the estuary.

Elizabeth dozed. Caro sat in the cabin's only chair. After a time, she rose and stretched, then crossed to the row of portholes. She studied the catches, then opened one, pushing it wide. A faint breeze drifted in, stirring the stale air in the cabin. She opened two more of the five round windows, then heard a rattle and a great splash.

Glancing at the narrow bunk, she saw Elizabeth hadn't stirred. Peering out, she glimpsed the shore. The captain had dropped anchor. Presumably lunch would be served soon.

She debated, but decided against leaving Elizabeth. With a sigh, she sank back onto the chair.

Sometime later, a soft tap sounded on the door. Elizabeth slept on; crossing the cabin, Caro opened the door. Michael stood in the corridor holding a tray.

"Campbell picked out what he thought you and Elizabeth would like. How is she?"

"Still sleeping." Caro reached to take the tray.

Michael gestured her back. "It's heavy."

With her shawl covering her, Elizabeth was decent enough; Caro stepped back. Michael carried the tray to the table; she followed, studying the plates as he set the tray down.

"Once she wakes, you should try to get her to eat something."

She glanced at him, then grimaced. "I've never been seasick—have you?"

Michael shook his head. "But I've seen plenty of others who were. She'll feel weak and woozy when she awakes. Now that we're back in calmer waters, eating something will help."

Caro nodded, looked back at Elizabeth.

He hesitated, then said, "Geoffrey's a trifle queasy, too."

Caro turned back to him, eyes widening in concern.

"That's why he hasn't been down to ask about Elizabeth. He's not as badly affected as she—he'll be better off in the open air."

A frown creased her brow; he suppressed an urge to run his thumb over her forehead and ease it away—squeezed her shoulder lightly instead. "Don't worry about Geoffrey— Edward and I will keep an eye on him." With a nod, he indicated Elizabeth. "You've enough on your hands."

Caro followed his nod, remained looking at Elizabeth. He hesitated, then turned away. As he opened the door, he heard Caro's soft "Thank you." Saluting her, he stepped out and softly closed the door.

Back on the main deck, he joined the other guests around the tables Ferdinand's crew had set up to display the delicacies of an alfresco meal. He chatted with General Kleber, who'd spent the previous day touring Bucklers Hard, the center of the local shipbuilding industry, then moved on to speak with the duke and the count, furthering his understanding of their country's views on a number of pertinent trade issues.

Once the meal was over and the tables cleared away, the ladies gathered behind the forecastle to gossip. Most of the men drifted to the rails, finding spots to lounge and enjoy the sunshine. The breeze, previously brisk, had faded to a gentle zephyr; the soft slap of rippling waves was punctuated by the raucous cries of gulls.

A postprandial peace settled over the yacht.

Michael found himself at the stern, for the moment alone. Ferdinand, deprived of Caro's company, had initially sulked. Now he'd cornered Edward Campbell; the pair were lounging against a capstan. Michael would have wagered a considerable sum that Ferdinand was trying to learn more about Caro via her secretary. In that, he wished him luck; despite his relative youth, Campbell seemed well up to snuff, experienced enough and sufficiently devoted to Caro to ensure he revealed nothing useful.

Drawing in a breath, filling his lungs with the tangy air, Michael turned his back on the rest of the yacht and leaned on the stern rail. The junction of Southampton Water and the Solent lay some distance away; beyond, the Isle of Wight rose, a silhouette across the horizon.

"Here—try some of this. It's quite bland."

Caro's voice. He glanced down, and noticed the open portholes. Elizabeth must be awake.

"I'm not sure . . ."

"Try it—don't argue. Michael said you should eat, and I'm sure he's right. You don't want to swoon again."

"Oh, heavens! How on earth am I to face him—or any of them? How *mortifying*."

"Nonsense!" Caro spoke bracingly, but it sounded as if she, too, were eating. "When things like this happen, the correct way to handle it is to create no further fuss. It was unforeseen, nothing could be done to avoid it, it happened, and now it's over. One deals with it in the most straightforward manner and gives oneself no airs, nor must you appear to be making yourself interesting because of your illness."

Silence, punctuated by the clink of cutlery.

"So . . ." Elizabeth's voice seemed to have gained some strength; it sounded almost normal. "I should simply smile and thank people, and . . ."

"And put it behind you. Yes, that's right."

"Oh."

Another pause; this time, Caro broke it. "You know, being subject to seasickness is not a great recommendation for a diplomat's wife."

Her tone was musing, considering.

Michael raised his brows. Recalled his earlier suspicion that Caro knew of his interest in Elizabeth.

"Well, we'll just have to make sure Edward fixes his sights somewhere other than the Foreign Office."

Michael blinked. *Edward?*

"Perhaps the Home Office. Or maybe under the Chancellor."

He heard Caro shift.

"We really must give the point some serious thought."

Her voice faded as she moved further from the portholes; she and Elizabeth continued to discuss this and that, but he

heard nothing more about diplomats' wives and the requirements and criteria for same.

Straightening, he strolled to the starboard corner, propped
a hip against the side, fixed his gaze on the shore, and tried
to fathom just what was going on. He'd thought Caro knew
of his tack regarding Elizabeth and had been aiding him. Yet
clearly she recognized and actively supported a connection
between Elizabeth and Campbell.

He stopped his thoughts—focused on what he felt about
Elizabeth being Campbell's wife instead of his. All he could
summon was a mild observation that Elizabeth and Edward
might indeed suit.

Grimacing, he folded his arms and leaned one shoulder
against a nearby rope. That, assuredly, was not what he
would feel had he been seriously set on winning Elizabeth to
wife, if he'd felt convinced she was the wife he needed. He
might not be a Cynster, yet if he'd been truly engaged by the
desire to secure Elizabeth as his wife, his reaction would be
considerably more profound.

As things stood, he felt far more exercised about Ferdinand's pursuit of Caro than about Campbell's apparent success with her niece. That, however, wasn't what was
pricking him.

Looking back on the last three days, ever since he'd
returned home and set out to evaluate Elizabeth—or more
specifically from the moment Caro had so dramatically
reentered his life—matters had progressed smoothly with no
real effort from him; the situations and opportunities he'd
needed and wanted had simply appeared.

Looking back . . . he felt increasingly certain Caro had
been playing fairy godmother, waving her wand and managing the scene, yet her touch was so light, so masterly, it
was impossible to be absolutely sure. He had no doubt she
was an accomplished player of diplomatic and political
games.

The question was: What sort of game had she been playing with him?

He might not be a Cynster, but he was an Anstruther-
Wetherby. Being manipulated had never sat well with him.

* * *

Once the anchor was hauled in and the yacht was once more slowly tacking up the western shore, at Elizabeth's insistence Caro left her resting and climbed the narrow companionway back up to the main deck.

Stepping into the open air, she lifted her head and filled her lungs; lips curving, lids at half-mast against the sinking sun, she turned—and walked into a hard male body.

One she'd connected with before; even as the certainty over who it was registered, she fleetingly wondered why, with him, her senses simply seemed to know. More, why they leapt, hungry to experience the solid, powerful strength of him, greedy for his nearness. She'd been sliding her hand onto his arm and stepping close for days—she'd told herself she needed the nearness to capture his attention and direct it, but had that been her only reason?

She'd certainly never craved close contact with any man before.

Looking up, she smiled in easy apology. She would have stepped back, but his arm suddenly tightened about her waist, supporting her, gathering her close as if she'd been in danger of falling.

She gripped his arms. Her heart lurched; her pulse accelerated.

Eyes widening, she looked into the blue of his—and for one minute couldn't think, wasn't truly sure what was going on. . . .

They were intent, those sky blue eyes of his; they searched hers—she returned the favor. To her surprise, she couldn't fathom what was passing through his mind.

Then his lips curved easily; his hold on her slackened and he set her on her feet. "Are you all right?"

"Yes, of course." She could barely breathe, but smiled her thanks. "I didn't see you there—the sun was in my eyes."

"I was just coming to ask how Elizabeth was." He waved toward the bow. "Geoffrey's growing anxious."

"In that case I'd better go and set his mind at rest." Resisting the urge to claim Michael's arm, she turned.

Only to have him offer his arm. Inwardly shrugging, she

took it in her usual trusting, close, and confiding way, the way she'd been dealing with him for the past days. Regardless of her susceptibilities, until he definitely lost interest in Elizabeth it would be wise to maintain that level of interaction—the better to steer his perceptions.

"Has she recovered?"

They strolled down the deck. "She's considerably better, but I suspect it'll be best if she remains in the cabin until we reach the landing stage." She met his gaze, could read no overt concern there, nothing more than polite inquiry. "If you could lend her your arm then, I know she'll be grateful."

He inclined his head. "Of course."

Michael steered her to where the others sat grouped in the lee of the forecastle. For most, the day had gone well—even Geoffrey had enjoyed the outing, his only anxiety being Elizabeth's well-being. Caro assured everyone Elizabeth was largely recovered, with her usual tact smoothed over the incident, then refocused the conversation away from Elizabeth's indisposition.

Leaning against the yacht's side, he watched her. Wondered. She refused Ferdinand's offer to stroll about the deck, settling instead between his aunt and the duchess to exchange reminiscences of the Portuguese court.

An hour later, the yacht was tied up at the landing stage. The company disembarked; with expressions of goodwill and thanks all around, they piled into the waiting carriages.

Elizabeth and Caro were the last of the ladies to attempt the gangplank. Together with Caro and Edward, he went down and helped Elizabeth, still weak but determined to maintain some dignity, up the stairs to the main deck.

At the head of the gangplank, Elizabeth paused and very prettily thanked Ferdinand, apologizing for the inconvenience she'd caused. Caro stood beside her; waiting behind Caro, Michael noted that the appropriate words came readily to Elizabeth's tongue. Caro was not tense or expectant; she wasn't anticipating any need to have to step in and assist.

Ferdinand bowed and made the best of it, smiling and gallantly waving aside Elizabeth's apologies, his dark gaze shifting to Caro's face as he did.

Then Edward took Elizabeth's hand and stepped onto the gangplank; Elizabeth followed unsteadily. Caro stepped aside and let Michael move past her; he followed Elizabeth closely, one hand hovering at her waist, steadying her, ready to catch her if she overbalanced. The tide was in; the rise and fall of the waves at the jetty was greater than it had been that morning.

Slowly progressing at Elizabeth's heels, over her shoulder Michael saw Edward's face every time he glanced at Elizabeth. His concern was open, and clearly personal. Although he couldn't see Elizabeth's expression, Michael sensed she clung to Edward's support far more than his own.

Any thought that he'd misinterpreted and there wasn't some definite understanding between the two vanished.

And if he could see it, Caro certainly had.

The necessity of his assisting with Elizabeth had left Caro to Ferdinand's care. When Edward, Elizabeth, then he stepped off the gangplank and onto the jetty, he left Edward to see Elizabeth to the carriage; Geoffrey was already in it. Turning back, he waited at the gangplank's end, and offered his hand to Caro when she reached him.

She gripped firmly, using his support as she stepped down to his side; he didn't wait for her to take his arm but placed her hand on his sleeve and covered it with his as she turned to say her good-byes to Ferdinand.

Who was clearly irritated at being denied his moment alone with her.

His eyes met Michael's, his gaze hard, challenging. But he had to maintain a mask of civility—more, he was given no option but to accept Caro's definition of him as an amusing acquaintance, nothing more.

Exactly how she accomplished it, Michael couldn't have said, yet her decree was there in the tone of her voice, in the light smile she bestowed along with her gracious nod of farewell. Both he and Ferdinand had no difficulty interpreting her message. Ferdinand had to pretend to accept it; he didn't, however, like it.

Michael, on the other hand, wholeheartedly approved.

As he walked with Caro along the landing stage to where

their carriage, the last remaining, stood waiting, he wondered if, perhaps, a word in the handsome Portuguese's ear—a simple gentleman-to-gentleman explanation of the truth behind Caro's nickname—might not be wise.

Despite Caro's consummate performance, Ferdinand hadn't given up.

CHAPTER
4

*T*he next morning at eleven, Michael set out to ride to Bramshaw House. Atlas, eager over once again being ridden every day, was frisky; Michael let the powerful gelding shake off his fidgets in a light canter along the lane.

He hadn't made any arrangements to call on the Bramshaw House household. The drive back from Totton yesterday had been subdued; Elizabeth, unnaturally pale, had remained quiet and withdrawn. He and Edward had dropped back, letting the carriage roll ahead, leaving Elizabeth in relative privacy.

They'd parted at the top of Bramshaw lane, yet he'd continued to brood on Caro's performance. The suspicion that she'd manipulated him, subtly steered him in the direction she'd wished while he'd imagined his direction and hers were the same, had grown, had pricked, prodded, and nagged at him. He'd spent the evening thinking of her, reliving their exchanges.

Normally, in any political or diplomatic sphere he'd have had his guard up, but with Caro it simply hadn't occurred to him that he might need to guard against her.

Betrayal was too strong a word for what he felt. Irritation, yes, lent an edge by the definite prick to his pride she'd delivered. Given he was now sure quite aside from any manipulation that he definitely did not need or want Elizabeth as his wife, such a response was perhaps a touch irrational, yet it was, quite certainly, how he felt.

Of course, he didn't know *absolutely* that Caro had exercised her manipulative wiles on him.

There was, however, one way to find out.

He found Caro, Elizabeth, and Edward in the family parlor. Caro looked up, her surprise at seeing him immediately overlayed by transparent delight. Beaming at him, she rose.

He grasped the hand she offered. "I rode over to tell Geoffrey we've unblocked the stream through the wood."

"Oh, dear—he's out."

"So Catten told me—I've left a message." He turned to greet Elizabeth and Edward, then met Caro's eyes. "I—"

"It's *such* a glorious day." She gestured to the wide windows, to the brilliant sunshine bathing the lawns. She smiled at him, stunningly assured. "You're right—it's a perfect morning for a ride. We could visit the Rufus Stone—it's been years since I last saw it, and Edward never has."

There was a fractional pause, then Elizabeth suggested, "We could take a picnic."

Caro nodded eagerly. "Indeed, why not?" Swinging on her heel, she headed for the bellpull.

"I'll organize the horses while you're changing your gowns," Edward offered.

"Thank you." Caro beamed at him, then looked at Michael. Her expression sobered as if she'd been struck by a sudden thought. "That is, if you're willing to spend your day gallivanting about the countryside?"

He met her wide earnest eyes, noted again how artlessly open her silvery blue gaze seemed—and how, if one looked deeper, there were layers, refracting, diffracting, in those fascinating eyes. Anyone who took Caro at face value—as a passably pretty woman of no particular power—would be committing a grave error.

He hadn't intended going for a ride, certainly hadn't suggested it, yet . . . he smiled, as charmingly beguiling as she. "Nothing would please me more." Let her continue to think she was in the saddle, with the reins firmly in her hands.

"Excellent!" She turned as Catten appeared at the door.

She quickly gave orders for a picnic lunch to be packed. Elizabeth slipped upstairs to change her gown; when Caro turned to him, he smiled easily. "Go and change—I'll help Campbell get the horses. We'll meet you on the front steps."

He watched her go, confident and assured, then followed Edward from the parlor.

Upstairs, Caro scrambled into her riding habit, then sighed with relief when Elizabeth, already correctly attired, slipped into her room. "Good—I was about to send Fenella to waylay you. Now remember, it's important you don't overplay your hand—don't try to appear too awkward or obtuse. In fact . . ."

Frowning, she tugged the tightly fitted bodice of her maroon habit straight. "I really think we'd be better served by you being yourself as far as possible today. Riding and a picnic without any others present is such an easy, informal affair. If you're truly silly, it'll appear too strange—there won't be any camouflage."

Elizabeth looked confused. "I thought you suggested a ride so I'd have another opportunity to demonstrate my unsuitability? He hasn't yet changed his mind, has he?"

"I don't think so." Caro picked up her gloves and quirt. "I suggested a ride because I didn't want him asking to take you for a walk in the gardens."

"Oh." Elizabeth followed her into the corridor; she lowered her voice. "Is that what he was going to ask?"

"That, or something like it. Why else is he here?" Caro tugged on her gloves. "I'd wager my pearls he was going to ask to speak with either you or me alone, and in neither case would that be a good idea. The last thing we need is to let him engage us in any private discussion."

She led the way down the stairs.

Michael and Edward were waiting before the front steps, each holding his horse and one other. Josh, the stable lad, was tying the bags in which their picnic had been packed to the saddles. To Caro's surprise, Michael held the reins of her gray mare, Calista, not those of Elizabeth's Orion.

The sight made her even more wary; if Michael was intent

on speaking with her, rather than seeking further time with Elizabeth . . . the only points he was likely to discuss with her were Elizabeth's diplomatic experience, and how she thought Elizabeth would respond to an offer from him.

Hiding her speculation, determined to divert him from progressing along such lines, she went down the steps, an easy smile on her lips.

Michael watched her approach. Leaving Atlas's reins dangling, he draped those of the gray mare over the pommel as he moved to the mare's side. He waited, reached for Caro as she neared. Closing his hands about her waist, he gripped, drew her a fraction closer, preparing to lift her to her saddle; her gloved hand came to rest on his arm. She looked up.

Suddenly—unmistakably—desire flared, like heated silk caressing bare skin. Simultaneously, he felt the quiver that rippled through her, that made her breath catch, made her silver eyes, for just one heartbeat, glaze.

She blinked, refocused on his face—let her lips curve as if nothing had happened.

But she still wasn't breathing.

Eyes locked with hers, he tightened his grip—again felt her control quake.

He lifted her to her saddle, held her stirrup; after an instant's hesitation—disorientation, he knew—she slid her boot into place. Without looking up, without meeting her eyes, he crossed to Atlas, caught his reins, and swung up to the saddle.

Only then did he manage to fill his lungs.

Elizabeth and Edward were already mounted; chaos momentarily reigned as they all turned their horses toward the gate. He was about to turn to Caro—to meet her gaze, to see—

"Come on! Let's be off!" With a laugh and a wave, she rode past him.

Laughing in return, Elizabeth and Edward set off in her wake.

For an instant, he hesitated, suppressing an urge to glance back at the steps . . . but he knew he hadn't imagined it.

Eyes narrowing, he tapped his heels to Atlas's flanks, and followed.

Caro. He no longer had the slightest interest in Elizabeth. However, when reaching the main road, Caro slowed and they caught up and proceeded in a group; it was abundantly clear she intended to ignore that unexpected moment.

And his reaction to her.

And even more hers to him.

Caro laughed, smiled, and gave the performance of her life, gaily enjoying the summer day, delighting in the cloudless sky, in the larks that swooped high above, in the tang of cut grass rising from nearby fields basking in the sunshine. Never before had she been so glad of the discipline the years had taught her; she felt rocked to her soul, as if an earthquake had struck—she had to shield herself quickly and absolutely.

As they cantered down the road to Cadnam, then turned south onto the leafy lane that led to the site where William II had been struck down by an arrow while hunting in the forest, her heart gradually slowed to its normal rhythm, the vise about her lungs gradually eased.

She was aware of Michael's gaze touching her face, not once but many times. Aware that behind his easygoing, amenable, ready-to-enjoy-the-beauties-of-the-day expression, he was puzzled. And not entirely pleased.

That last was good. She wasn't *aux anges* over that unlooked-for development either. She wasn't at all sure what had caused such a potent and unsettling reaction, but instinct warned her that it, and therefore he, was an experience she'd be wise to avoid.

Given that he was interested in Elizabeth, the latter shouldn't prove at all difficult.

Edward was on her left, Elizabeth on her right; just ahead, the lane narrowed. "Edward." Checking Calista, she caught Edward's eye and dropped back. "Did you get a chance to ask the countess about Señor Rodrigues?"

She'd chosen a topic that Michael would have no interest in, yet before Edward could react and drop back to join her, Michael had.

"I take it the countess is an acquaintance of old?"

She glanced at him, then nodded. "I've known her for years. She's a member of the inner court—very influential."

"You were in Lisbon for what? Ten years?"

"More or less." Determined to steer matters back on track, she looked ahead and smiled at Elizabeth. "Elizabeth visited us on several occasions."

Michael's gaze went to Edward. "Over the last few years?"

"Yes." Caro saw the direction of his glance; before she could decide if he actually meant anything by his comment—had deduced anything she'd rather he didn't—he looked at her and captured her gaze.

"I imagine the life of an ambassador's wife would have been one of constant and giddy dissipation. You must feel quite adrift."

She bridled, felt her eyes flash. "I assure you the life of an ambassador's wife is hardly a succession of relaxing entertainments." She lifted her chin, felt her color, along with her temper, rise. "A constant succession of *events*, yes, but—" She broke off, then glanced at him.

Why on earth was she reacting to such an unsubtle jibe? Why had he, of all men, made it? She continued rather more circumspectly. "As you must be aware, the organization of an ambassador's social schedule falls largely to his wife. During the years of our marriage, that was my role."

"I would have thought Campbell would have handled much of it."

She felt Edward's glance, his offer to intervene; she ignored it. "No—Edward was Camden's aide. He assisted with legal, governmental, and diplomatic details. However, the arena in which most important decisions are actually made, the venues at which such matters are most directly influenced is, as it always has been, in embassy drawing rooms, ballrooms, and salons. In other words, while the ambassador and his aides may execute the battle plan, it's the ambassador's wife who secures for them the field on which they may maneuver."

Looking ahead, she drew a calming breath, reached for

her customarily unshakable social poise, surprised that it had temporarily deserted her. There was, after all, an obvious reason for Michael's probing. "If rumor speaks true and you're shortly to find yourself at the Foreign Office, you'll need to remember that without the right wife, an ambassador, no matter how able, will be hamstrung."

Coolly, she turned her head and met his blue eyes.

His lips curved, but his self-deprecating smile didn't reach his eyes. "I've been told the same holds true for government ministers."

She blinked.

Michael looked forward, the curve of his lips deepening as he saw Elizabeth and Edward had pulled ahead; the lane had narrowed, allowing only two horses abreast. "Everyone knows," he murmured, voice low so only Caro would hear, "that Camden Sutcliffe was a master ambassador."

He brought his gaze back to her face. "Doubtless he understood—" He broke off, startled to see some hurt, some fleeting expression so painful it stopped his breath, flash through her silver eyes. What he'd been about to say vanished from his head; he'd been baiting her, wanting to provoke some reaction and learn more . . .

"Caro?" He reached for her hand. "Are you all right?"

She refocused, abruptly shifted her mount away, avoiding his hand, and looked ahead. "Yes. Perfectly."

Her voice was cool, distant; he didn't—couldn't bring himself to—test her again. Although her tone was even, he sensed it had cost her an effort to achieve it. He felt he should apologize, but wasn't sure for what. Before he could think of any way to put right whatever had gone wrong, Edward and Elizabeth kicked up their mounts and drew ahead as the lane opened into a wide clearing.

Tapping her heels to her mare's flanks, Caro went forward to join them; increasingly frustrated, he sent Atlas after her.

The clearing was as wide as a field, dotted here and there with oaks. Close to the middle stood the Rufus Stone, a monument erected by Earl De La Warr some eighty years before to mark the spot where William II, due to his red hair known as Rufus, had fallen on August 2, 1100. Although commemorating a pivotal moment in history, the stone, inscribed with the bare facts, stood relatively unadorned or in any way celebrated, surrounded by the deep stillness of the forest.

Edward and Elizabeth had reined in under the spreading branches of an ancient oak. Edward dismounted and tied his reins to a branch. He turned, but before he could go to where Elizabeth waited to be helped from her saddle, Caro rode up; with an imperious gesture—for her, out of character—she summoned Edward to her side.

Without hesitation, Edward went.

Reining Atlas in, Michael dismounted, watched Edward lift Caro to the ground. Securing Atlas's reins, he went to Elizabeth and lifted her down.

Smiling brightly, Caro pointed to the stone and made some comment to Edward; they set out across the sward toward it. With an easy smile for Elizabeth, Michael fell in beside her as they followed the other two to view the monument.

That moment set the pattern for the following hour. Caro seemed bent on enjoyment; she smiled, laughed, and encouraged them all to do the same. So subtle was her performance—never overdone, totally believable with not so much as a word to jar anyone's suspicions—Michael had to admit it was instinct alone that insisted it was a performance, all for show.

After admiring the monument and revisiting the tale of how William had been slain by an arrow fired by Walter Tyrrell, one of William's hunting party, and how that had led to the younger Henry's seizing the throne over his older brother, Robert, and after exclaiming over how the loosing of a single arrow had resounded through the centuries, they retired to spread a rug and investigate the morsels packed in the saddlebags.

Caro directed them as was her wont. He behaved as she wished, more to placate her, to calm her, than for any other reason. Deploying his own mask, he smiled and charmed Elizabeth, sat by her side—opposite Caro—and talked to her of whatever she wished. Today, Elizabeth didn't try to convince him she was a featherbrain interested only in balls and dancing, yet although he sensed she was being her genuine self, and was far more attractive without her assumed traits, he was acutely aware she did not possess sufficient depth or complexity in her character to fix his interest, not on any level.

Throughout the interlude, from behind his mask, his attention remained riveted on Caro.

Across the rug, separated from him and Elizabeth by the assembled feast, she and Edward talked easily, exchanging comments with the rapport of old friends. He judged Edward to be about four years Caro's junior; although he watched closely, he detected not the smallest hint of any loverlike connection. Campbell clearly admired and respected Caro's abilities; more than any other person, he would have seen the evidence on which to base such an assessment. In Michael's experience, political and diplomatic aides were the shrewdest and most accurate judges of their masters' talents.

Edward's attitude to Caro, and the impression Michael received that he viewed her as a mentor and was happy with, indeed felt grateful for, the opportunity to learn from her, dovetailed with the picture Michael himself was forming of Caro.

That, however, was not what he was waiting to learn, not why he remained so intensely focused on her.

Something he'd said had hurt her, and she'd retreated behind the highly polished persona she showed to the world.

It was, he reminded himself as he searched for cracks and found none, a persona she'd perfected over a decade under the most exacting circumstances. Like a highly polished metal mask, that facade was impenetrable; it gave nothing away.

By the time they packed up the remnants of their feast and shook out the rug, he'd accepted that the only way he would learn more about Caro was if she consented to tell him. Or consented to let him see her as she truly was.

He mentally paused, wondering why learning more about

her, the real Caro who hid behind the mask, was suddenly so vitally important. No answer came, yet . . .

They reached the horses and milled about, retying the saddlebags. Caro was having difficulties; he circled behind her intending to help—her mare shifted, bumping Caro back—into him.

Her back met his chest, her bottom his thighs.

His hands went to her waist, instinctively gripping and steadying her against him. She stiffened; her breath had caught. He released her and stepped back, acutely aware of his own reaction.

"Whoops! Sorry." She smiled up at him ingenuously but didn't meet his eyes as, moving to her side, he reached up to take the laces she was struggling to tie.

She drew her hands away too swiftly, but he caught the laces before they unraveled.

"Thank you."

He kept his gaze on the laces as he tied them. "That should hold it."

His expression easy, he stepped back. And turned to help Elizabeth into her saddle, leaving Edward to lift Caro to hers.

Walking to where Atlas stood waiting, he glanced back at the others. "There's still hours of sunshine left." He smiled at Elizabeth. "Why don't we ride through the forest, skirt around Fritham, and stop by the Manor for afternoon tea?"

They exchanged glances, brows rising.

"Yes, let's." Elizabeth faced him, simple pleasure in her smile. "That will be a lovely ending to a pleasant day."

Michael looked at Caro. One of her charming smiles curving her lips, she nodded. "An excellent suggestion."

He swung up to Atlas's saddle and they turned into the forest. He, Caro, and Elizabeth knew the way. They rode through the glades, sometimes galloping, then slowing to amble along the path to the next open ride. Whoever was in the lead steered them. The sun filtered down through the thick canopies, dappling the track; the rich forest scents rose around them, the quiet punctuated by birdcalls and the occasional rustle of larger beasts.

No one attempted to converse; Michael was content to let the companionable silence lengthen and take hold. Only among friends would Caro not feel it necessary to chat; that she didn't make the effort was encouraging.

They approached the Manor from the south, emerging from the outliers of Eyeworth Wood to clatter into the stableyard. Hardacre took charge of their mounts; they walked up through the old orchard to the house.

Leading the way along the corridor to the front hall, Caro glanced back at him. "The terrace? It'll be lovely out there."

He nodded. "Go ahead. I'll speak with Mrs. Entwhistle about tea."

Mrs. Entwhistle had heard them come in; the prospect of providing tea and sustenance for their small party quite delighted her, reminding Michael of how little the housekeeper generally had to do.

He found the others seated about the wrought-iron table. The sun, still above the treetops to the west, bathed the area in golden light. His gaze on Caro's face, he drew out the last chair and sat, once again opposite her; she seemed to have relaxed, yet he couldn't be sure.

Elizabeth turned to him. "Caro was just telling me she'd heard a rumor that Lord Jeffries was to resign. Is it true?"

Lionel, Lord Jeffries had been appointed to the Board of Trade only the year before, but his tenure had been marked by diplomatic incident after incident. "Yes." Across the table, he met Caro's gaze. "Inevitable after his latest gaffe."

"So it's true he called the Belgian ambassador an extortionist to his face?" Caro's eyes twinkled.

He nodded. "Burnt his last bridge in the process, but I can imagine it was almost worth it to see Rochefoucauld's face."

Her eyes opened wide. "Did you? See his face?"

He grinned. "Yes—I was there."

"Jupiter!" Edward whistled through his teeth. "I heard Jeffries' aides were beside themselves—it must have been an impossible situation."

"The instant Jeffries set eyes on Rochefoucauld, the die was cast. Nothing—not even the Prime Minister—could have stopped him."

They were still discussing the latest diplomatic scandal when Jeb Carter carried out the tea tray.

Immediately, Caro looked at Michael; he was waiting to catch that look—to see her understanding in her quicksilver eyes, to bask in her approval.

Little by little, step by step; he was determined to draw closer to her, and would exploit any tool that came to hand.

"Will you pour?" he asked.

She reached for the pot, flashing a delighted smile Carter's way, inquiring after his mother before letting him, blushing at being remembered, escape.

Elizabeth took her cup, sipped, a frown in her eyes—then her face cleared. "Of course—he's Muriel's last butler, the one she recently turned off." Her puzzlement returned. "How did you know him?"

Caro smiled and explained; Jeb had been away training in London for so long Elizabeth hadn't remembered him.

Of course, Caro had been away for even longer. Sipping his tea, watching as she reminded Elizabeth of various others in the district, workers and their families and where they were now, who had married whom, who had died or moved away, Michael wondered if she ever forgot anyone. Such a memory for people and personal details was a godsend in political circles.

The minutes passed easily; the afternoon waned. The pot had gone cold and Mrs. Entwhistle's cakes had disappeared when, at Caro's request, he asked for their horses to be brought around. They'd risen and were walking down the terrace steps to wait in the forecourt when the rattle and clop of an approaching gig reached them.

Caro halted on the steps; raising a hand to shade her eyes, she looked to see who it was. The aftereffects of her momentary weakness as they'd approached the Rufus Stone had gradually faded; her nerves had settled—she felt reasonably calm once more. Later, she'd castigate herself for reacting as she had—when she was safely in her room and a long way from Michael.

Otherwise, the day had gone more or less as she'd wished; she doubted they'd advanced their cause, yet neither had they harmed it—and Michael had had no chance to make an offer, or even to discuss such matters with her.

It had been a positive day by default; she was content with that.

The gig came into sight, the horse trotting smartly up the drive with Muriel on the seat. She was an excellent whip; she halted the gig before the steps in some style. "Caro. Michael."

Muriel exchanged nods with them and with Edward and Elizabeth, then looked at Michael. "I'm giving one of my suppers for the Ladies' Association tomorrow evening. As you're home, I came to invite you to attend—I know all the ladies would appreciate the opportunity to speak with you."

Michael stepped down to stand beside Caro; she felt his gaze touch her face. Guessing what was behind his hesitation, she glanced at him, smiled. "Do come. You'll know most of us there."

Despite their earlier contretemps—and she had to forgive him, he couldn't know—she was in reasonable charity with him. Since that painful moment, he'd behaved with exemplary tact.

He read her eyes, then glanced at Muriel, his politician's facade sliding seamlessly into place. "I'd be delighted to take supper with the ladies. You must have some new members since last I was down."

"Indeed." Muriel smiled graciously; the Ladies' Association was her pride and joy. "We've done well this past year, but you'll hear of our successes tomorrow."

Her gaze shifted, going past them as Hardacre came up, leading the three horses. Muriel looked at Caro. "If you're heading home, Caro, perhaps you could ride beside the gig and we could go over the plans for the fete?"

She nodded. "Why not?" Sensing Michael's hand rising to touch her back, she quickly looked down and descended the steps. She started toward Calista, then realized that Muriel was watching everyone like a hawk; the last thing they needed was any question being raised in anyone's mind about Michael and Elizabeth.

Dragging in a breath, she swung around—to see Michael

shaking hands with Edward and nodding politely to Elizabeth in farewell. Releasing Edward's hand, Michael waved her on. "Come—I'll lift you up."

Her smile felt weak, but she could hardly wait for Edward to lift Elizabeth up and then help her, too, not with Michael standing there offering. Steeling every nerve, outwardly calm, she walked to Calista's side. Dragging in another breath, she held it, and turned.

And found he was less than a foot away.

He reached for her—and it was worse than she'd anticipated. Her nerves literally quaked. He was so much taller than she, her eyes were level with his collarbone; his shoulders were so wide, he blocked her off from the world.

He gripped her waist and she felt weak, light-headed, as if his strength somehow drained hers.

He hesitated, holding her between his hands. She felt oddly small, fragile, vulnerable. Captured. Her whole world condensed, drew in. She could feel her heart thudding in her throat.

Then he lifted her, easily, and sat her in her saddle. His grip loosened; his hands slid slowly from about her waist. Reaching for the stirrup, he held it.

She managed to thank him; her words sounded distant to her ears. She settled her boot in the stirrup, then fussed with her skirts. Finally managed to breathe, to swallow. Gathering her reins, she looked up. Smiled at Muriel. "Let's be off, then."

Michael stepped back.

Caro waved in his direction, then wheeled Calista to come up beside Muriel's gig. Edward and Elizabeth waved, too, then sent their mounts to fall in behind the gig.

Michael watched the little cavalcade until it passed out of sight. He remained for some minutes, staring at the gates, then turned on his heel and went inside.

CHAPTER
5

At least he now knew why he needed to know more—a lot more—about Caro.

Relaxed in his chair at the breakfast table the next morning, he wondered why he'd been so slow to correctly interpret the signs. Perhaps because it was Caro and he'd known her forever. Regardless, he was now fully cognizant of at least one of the emotions keeping him so intently focused on her.

It had been a long time since he had, entirely of his own volition, without the slightest encouragement, lusted after a woman. Actively wanted her even though she was intent on running the other way.

Or so he read Caro's reaction. She'd felt the attraction, that spark that required no thought and asked no permissions; her response had been to avoid giving it a chance to strike, and if that wasn't possible, then to pretend it hadn't.

From experience, he knew her tack wouldn't work. As long as they remained in sufficient proximity to ensure they would meet and inevitably touch, the need would grow only more potent, the spark commensurately more powerful, until they let it burn.

The only problem he could see in that was that the woman involved was Caro.

Her reaction wasn't a surprise. Unlike Ferdinand, he

knew the correct interpretation of her nickname. The "Merry Widow" was, as such English nicknames sometimes were, a perverse expression. In Caro's case, she was an outwardly merry widow in that she was a hostess of some note, but the real meaning was that she'd been chased by the best of them, yet had refused to be caught. Just as red-haired men were often called Bluey, she was, in reality, a severely chaste widow who never encouraged anyone to imagine otherwise.

She was the opposite of what the term "Merry Widow" led the naive to suppose.

Which meant he was in for a difficult and uncomfortable time of it, at least until he convinced her that her only option was one that would suit her as well as it would suit him.

Savoring the last of his coffee, he considered how long convincing her might take. Considered the hurdles before him. To be the gentleman who tempted the Merry Widow enough to get into her bed, and her . . .

A challenge indeed.

It would be a diplomatic triumph of an unusual order, even if no one ever knew of his success. But they would, of course; that was part of his plan.

He could pull it off; he was a politician born and bred, and such innate qualities were precisely those required. He just had to finesse his way past Caro's defenses.

And along the way, when he had her defenseless in his arms, he'd learn what it was that had so upset her, and if he could, put it right.

Deeming it wise to let the day go by, to let her normal, natural confidence reassert itself and assure her she was safe, that he posed no threat to her and so didn't need to be kept at a distance, he schooled himself to sit in his study and deal with the months' worth of accounts and minor details his agent had dutifully left piled on his desk.

Two hours later, he was steadily plodding through the pile when Carter tapped on the door and entered.

"Mrs. Sutcliffe has called, sir."

He checked his memory. "Which Mrs. Sutcliffe?" Caro? Or one of Camden's nieces-by-marriage?

"Mrs. Caroline, sir. She's in the drawing room."

"Thank you, Carter." He rose, wondering, then inwardly shrugged. He'd learn soon enough.

When he entered the drawing room, Caro was standing before the windows looking out over the front lawn. Sunbeams lanced through her cloud of frizzy hair, striking copper and red glints from the golden brown. Her gown was a pale blue a few shades darker than her eyes; fine and summer light, it clung to her figure.

She heard him and turned, smiled.

And he instantly knew she was a long way from believing him unthreatening. As usual, however, it was only instinct that told him so; Caro herself gave nothing away.

"I hope you don't mind—I've come to sound you out and pick your brains."

He returned her smile, waved her to the chaise. "How can I help?"

Caro grasped the moment of crossing to the chaise, gathering her skirts and sinking gracefully down, then waiting for him to lounge, relaxed but attentive in the armchair facing her, to marshal her thoughts and dragoon her wits out of the morass of irrational panic they'd developed a habit of sinking into every time the possibility of Michael's coming close to her loomed.

She didn't understand her sudden sensitivity; she could barely believe that after all her years of extensive worldly experience, she was now—here in deepest Hampshire—falling victim to such an affliction. Determined to conquer it, or at the very least ignore it, she clung to her pose of assured serenity. "I've decided to give a ball on the evening preceding the church fete. It occurred to me that with so many from London in the neighborhood, if we hold a ball, invite them all, and arrange to house them locally overnight, then they could spend the next day at the fete before heading off in the afternoon."

She paused, then added, "I suppose what I'm proposing is a condensed house party with the ball as its highlight and the fete as its extension."

Michael's gaze remained on her face; she couldn't tell

what he was thinking. After a moment, he asked, "So your underlying purpose is to use the ball to bolster attendance at the fete, especially with those down from London, which in turn will greatly increase local interest, thus ensuring the fete is a resounding success?"

She smiled. "Precisely." It was a delight to deal with someone who saw not just actions, but implications and outcomes. Of course, ensuring the fete's success was not the ultimate purpose driving her latest project. After yesterday, both Elizabeth and Edward were adamant over bringing the situation with Michael to a head; they wanted to create some situation that would definitely demonstrate Elizabeth's incapacity to adequately fill the role of Michael's wife.

Thus a major social event to be attended by numerous diplomatic and political personages, tied to a major local event. The organization required would be horrendous, and Elizabeth was, indeed, a mere apprentice in that regard.

Caro, of course, could handle such a challenge without a qualm, and would; they were hoping the demonstration of her talents would focus Michael's attention on Elizabeth's lack of such highly evolved social skills.

He was regarding her with what seemed to be faintly amused interest. "I'm sure you're already halfway organized. How can I help?"

"I was wondering if you would agree to put up some of the guests from farther afield for the night of the ball." She didn't wait for a reply, but artfully continued, "And I also wanted to ask your opinion on the guest list—do you think that little difficulty between the Russians and the Prussians has blown over? And, of course . . ."

The conversational reins firmly in her grasp, she set out to create her field of battle.

Michael let her rattle on as she would, increasingly certain her peripatetic discourse wasn't as lacking in direction as it seemed. Regardless of her ultimate goal, her observations were accurate, often cannily acute; when she directed a specific question his way, and actually paused to give him a chance to answer, it was on a subject that was a diplomatic minefield. Their ensuing comments evolved into a discussion of some depth.

After a while, she rose; still talking, she paced, circling the chaise, then sank down onto it once more. He didn't stir, but watched her, conscious of the intellectual challenge of dealing with her on more than one level simultaneously. Indeed, on more than two. He was perfectly aware there was more going on than the obvious, and equally certain she was determinedly ignoring at least one thread in their interaction.

Finally, relaxed once more on the chaise, she spread her hands and asked directly, "Well, will you help?"

He met her gaze. "On two conditions."

A sudden wariness slid behind her lovely eyes; she blinked and it was replaced by an expecting-to-be-amused smile. "Conditions? Good heavens! What?"

He smiled, striving to make the expression as unthreatening as he could, not entirely sure he'd succeeded. "One—it's too lovely a day to spend sitting inside. Let's take this discussion on a stroll through the gardens. Two"—he held her gaze—"that you'll stay for lunch."

She blinked, slowly; he was very sure she was, most definitely, wary of him physically. Of getting physically close. He knew of only one way to address such a problem, and she'd handed him the solution on a platter.

Having set the stage herself, she couldn't now not play; her smile deepening, she refocused on his face. "Very well—if you insist."

He fought to stop his smile from deepening. "Oh, I do."

She rose; so did he, but he turned aside to the bellpull to summon Carter and instruct him about luncheon, giving her the chance to escape onto the terrace.

When he followed her out, she was standing at the top of the steps facing the front lawn. Her hands were clasped before her; her shoulders rose as she drew in a deep breath.

He moved to stand beside her and she very nearly jumped. He met her eyes, offered his arm. "Let's go across the lawn and through the shrubbery, and you can tell me how many guests, and whom, you think would best be quartered here."

Inclining her head, she tucked her hand in the crook of his arm; he resisted the urge to draw it further and cover it with his, to draw her closer. They descended the steps and started strolling.

Lifting her head, Caro focused on the trees lining the drive and forced her mind to the myriad details of organizing the ball—away from the hideously distracting presence beside her. Her lungs had seized again; it was a wonder she could speak. "The Swedes definitely." She threw him a glance. "I won't wish General Kleber on you—we'll keep the Prussians at Bramshaw. The grand duchess will almost certainly attend, and she'll expect to stay with me."

She continued working through the guest list; grappling with logistics did, indeed, make it easier to cope with Michael's nearness. He gave her no cause to panic further, but asked intelligent questions, ones she could answer. He had met, or knew of, most of those she intended to invite; he was aware of the undercurrents between the various groups.

They strolled down a path between the trees, then circled through the extensive shrubbery, eventually reemerging onto the drive not far from the terrace from which they'd set out.

"I've a confession to make," Michael said as they climbed the terrace steps.

She glanced at him. "Oh?"

He met her gaze, and she was struck by a dreadful suspicion that he could see through her social shield. Her lungs locked; her nerves tensed. His gaze traveled her face, but then he smiled, an easy, comfortable, and to her comforting, gesture.

"Despite making me promise to open the fete, Muriel neglected to mention when the event is." His eyes returned to hers, full of self-deprecatory laughter. "Rescue me—when is it?"

She laughed, felt the tension that had gripped her dissolve. Found she could meet his eyes with genuine ease. "A week from tomorrow."

"So"—gaining the terrace, he waved her to the wrought-iron table now set with luncheon dishes—"your ball would be a week from tonight."

"Yes." She sat in the chair he held for her, then waited until he took the one opposite before launching into details of the ball itself; she'd saved that subject so she'd have something to keep him occupied. "I'm not yet sure of my theme."

Michael hesitated, then suggested, "Keep it simple."

When she opened her eyes at him, he elaborated, "More informal than a London ball. Everyone will have had a surfeit through the Season, but in the country in summer there's no reason you need adhere to full ceremony."

If she did, he'd have the devil of a time securing some of her attention on the night.

"Hmm . . . even though we're talking of the diplomatic corps?" Her brows rose higher. "Perhaps you're right."

She paused to consume a forkful of Mrs. Entwhistle's pastry, then, gaze distant, waved the fork. "What about calling it a Midsummer Revels, rather than a ball?"

He knew a rhetorical question when he heard one; he made no reply.

"There's a wonderful group of musicians in Lyndhurst who would be perfect. They're very good with lighter, summery airs and country dances." Her eyes had lit; she was clearly envisioning the event. "It would certainly be something different . . ."

He sipped his wine, then raised the glass to her. "A summer wine to tempt the jaded palate."

She met his eyes, grinned. "Precisely. Yes—that's what we'll do."

The next half hour went in a discussion of potential problems and how best to deal with them. Knowing the importance of foreseeing such hitches and having plans to deal with them before they arose, Caro had composed her guest list with an eye to highlighting Michael's need for a hostess who understood matters such as the esoteric wranglings currently exercising the Russians and their Prussian neighbors.

"So," she concluded, "can I rely on you to keep an eye on the Prussians and the Russians and make sure they don't come to blows? I want Edward to keep a more general eye on things, and I'll be everywhere, of course."

Michael nodded. "The Polish chargé d'affaires will be of some help, I daresay."

"Really?" She raised her brows. "He's always struck me as such a mild sort, rather ineffectual."

Michael's lips curved; he met her eyes. "Appearances can be deceptive."

Inwardly, she stilled; outwardly, she opened her eyes wider, then shrugged. "If you're sure." Pushing back her chair, she laid aside her napkin. "Now I really must go and make a start on the invitations."

Michael rose and came to draw back her chair. "I'll walk you to the stable."

She picked up the gauzy scarf she'd draped over the chair back; she caught it between her hands, intending to flip it over her hair, but stopped. Instead, as they went down the steps and set off around the house, she kept the scarf in her hands, idly playing with the long band, thus obviating him offering her his arm.

Not that he made any move to do so. Instead, he walked beside her, his strides long and easy . . . almost lazy.

They walked through the sun-dappled orchard, and she felt her nerves easing once more. Despite that odd panic that while he was close never seemed to be far away, her latest ploy had played out very well. She'd managed, and survived the whole quite creditably. Surely he could see that an innocent, relatively inexperienced young lady like Elizabeth could never cope with the demands of social events the like of which his wife would need to organize.

As Camden's bride, Caro had been plunged into the higher diplomatic circles with even less preparation than Elizabeth had now; she could still remember the paralyzing panic, the stomach-churning fear—she wouldn't wish that on any young lady, much less her own niece.

Surely, with all the details of the ball and its associated organization laid before him, he'd realize . . .

She drew in a breath, lifted her chin. "Elizabeth's out picnicking with the Driscolls and Lord Sommerby." She flashed a smile Michael's way. "She hates doing invitations—inscribing the same phrases time after time—but . . ."

Michael caught the tension in her voice as she continued, searching for ways to draw attention to Elizabeth's youth and lack of experience without being obvious. That that had been the principal purpose behind her visit, perhaps even behind the ball itself, he didn't doubt; that she was acting to deflect him from offering for Elizabeth's hand he no longer questioned. Yet her manipulation itself no longer concerned him—what had moved her to it, her attitudes, her silences, most of all the vulnerability and occasional, fleeting panics he detected behind her glamour of supreme confidence and capability, did.

Elizabeth's face, and Edward's, too, flashed across his mind, yet it was the need to spare Caro that had him reaching for her hand.

She was gesturing as she spoke; he trapped her fingers in midair, unsurprised when her words abruptly died.

Halting, she faced him, eyes wide, pupils dilating, breath caught. He met her gaze, trapped her silvery eyes; he was acutely conscious that they were out of sight of the house, screened by the orchard's trees, all in full leaf. "You don't need to be so busy on Elizabeth's behalf."

Shifting his hold on her hand, enclosing her fingers in his, he stepped closer, realized from the way she blinked, then, a frown forming in her eyes, searched his, that she wasn't sure of his meaning.

"You don't need to instruct me about Elizabeth anymore." His lips lifted wryly. "You've convinced me."

Caro stared into his blue eyes. She'd never been knocked so far off-balance in her life. He was too close—she was so aware . . .

How long had he known?

The thought jerked her free of the mesmerizing effect he had on her. She narrowed her eyes, concentrated. Did he mean what she thought he did? "You've changed your mind? You won't be offering for Elizabeth's hand?"

He smiled. "I've changed my mind. I won't be offering for Elizabeth's hand." He paused, then raised her fingers to his lips, lightly brushed a kiss across her knuckles. "Elizabeth is not my ideal bride."

The touch of his lips sent a tingling sensation skittering down her arm, but that was overwhelmed, then submerged, by the incredible relief that rose up and poured through her.

Only then did she realize she hadn't been certain of her ability to save Elizabeth, hadn't until then appreciated how important to her saving Elizabeth from an unhappy political marriage had become.

She smiled freely, totally without restraint, making no attempt to mask her joy. "I'm so glad." Her smile only grew. "It wouldn't have worked, you know."

"I realized that."

"Good." She couldn't stop beaming; if she'd been younger, she would have danced. "I'd better go." And tell Elizabeth the good news.

He held her gaze for a moment longer, then inclined his head and released her hand. He waved her on to the stables.

Michael walked beside her, waited with her while Hardacre brought out her gig. Her smile . . . it was radiant. He felt smugly content that he'd spoken the right words to put it on her face. It was a joy to behold; it warmed him from the inside out. He stood basking in the glow, his hands clasped tightly behind his back to make sure he didn't reach for her and spoil the moment.

The gig arrived; he helped her to the seat. She'd continued to fill his ears with plans for the ball, yet her words were now transparently free of any overarching intent; they were straightforward expressions of her thoughts—he heard the ring of clarity, and realized he'd taken a significant step closer to Caro herself, a significant step deeper into her confidence.

He waved her off with considerable satisfaction.

Once the gig and she had disappeared around the drive, he set off, still smiling, to walk back to the house.

His words had lifted a burden from Caro's shoulders; even if he had the moment again, he wouldn't have scripted it otherwise. Her joy had been fascinating, a true delight, even if it had prevented her from realizing that in shifting his attention from Elizabeth, he'd fixed it on someone else.

Someone a great deal more experienced than Elizabeth.

Smile deepening, he looked up at the house and walked steadily on.

He was actually looking forward to Muriel's supper tonight.

"Ah, there you are, Michael!"

Severely handsome in plum silk, Muriel swept forward as he walked into her drawing room.

He shook the hand she offered, then glanced around the room. It was decently filled, largely with ladies although there were some other gentlemen scattered among the skirts.

"Let me introduce you to our new members." Muriel steered him to a group stationed before the French doors presently open to the rear garden. "Allow me to introduce Mrs. Carlisle. She and her husband have recently come to live in Minstead."

His politician's smile to the fore, he shook Mrs. Carlisle's hand and learned she and her husband had moved to the district from Bradford. He progressed around the group, meeting two others new to the area and renewing his acquaintance with the three other ladies who had known him for years.

Although they did not vote, here as in any district it was the ladies who were most active at all levels of community service, organizing gatherings like the church fete and supporting institutions such as the orphanges and workers' refuges. Michael viewed their goodwill and support as a key factor in shoring up his personal standing as local Member; only with that secure could he safely devote his mind to the wider challenges the Prime Minister was intent on handing him. Consequently, he did not begrudge the time he spent at evenings like this; indeed, he was happy to grasp the opportunity Muriel had handed him and make the most of it.

He was engaged in doing precisely that when Caro entered the room. Facing the hearth, he was chatting to two gentlemen before the fireplace when instinct prompted him to glance up into the mirror above the mantelpiece.

Caro stood framed in the doorway, looking around. Dressed in a delicate, simply styled gown of printed silk, she drew the eye, yet seemed to fit perfectly into the setting. Pearls draped her throat and glowed on one wrist, from which a matching reticule hung; beyond that, she wore no other ornamentation, and needed none.

She located Muriel; smiling, she moved to greet her.

Covering his lapse, he continued discussing the corn price, then glibly excused himself and strolled on. To intercept Caro.

She started slightly when he appeared beside her; no one else would have noticed—no one else was watching her so intently. Capturing her hand, he managed to stop himself from raising it to his lips, contented himself with placing it on his sleeve. "I wondered when you'd arrive."

She returned his smile with one that still held a large measure of her earlier joy. "It's such a lovely evening, I decided to walk." She glanced around. "Have you met everyone?"

With his head, he indicated a group by the side of the room. "I haven't spoken with Mrs. Kendall yet." He caught Caro's gaze, let his smile deepen. "She'll want to tell me about the boys' home. Come and support me."

He intended to behave as he meant to go on; he wondered how long it would take her to recognize his new direction.

She steeled herself, faint tension infusing her spine as if to guard against the effect he had on her, but, still smiling, still glowing with that inner happiness, she inclined her head. "If you wish, but I can't think what support you might need from me."

Glancing at Michael's face, Caro saw his smile flash— was it her imagination that, just for that instant, painted it predatory?—but his expression was easy as he met her gaze and murmured, "You're the only one in the room of similar background—you're the only one who truly understands my jokes."

She laughed; as before, the touch of humor soothed her taut nerves. She was content to accompany him while he spoke with Mrs. Kendall, who did indeed want to discuss the boys' home, then they moved on to speak with others, some intent on claiming her attention, some his.

That afternoon, on returning from the Manor floating on a

cloud of unfettered relief, she'd gone straight to the parlor and reported their success to Elizabeth and Edward. They'd celebrated over tea, congratulating themselves and admitting, now they could, that playing such tricks on Michael, mild though they had been and definitely for his own good, had not sat altogether well with them.

But he'd seen, and agreed, and by that agreement absolved them; she felt so thoroughly happy and vindicated, subduing her silly reaction enough to remain by his side for a while seemed a very small price to pay.

An hour passed surprisingly easily, then Muriel announced that supper was laid out in the dining room. Finding herself by Michael's side at the long buffet, with him helping her to herb patties and shrimp in aspic, surrounded by numerous others yet still somehow with him alone, she paused, then slanted him a glance.

He felt it, looked at her. He searched her eyes, then raised a brow, his lips lightly curving. "What is it?"

She glanced down at a platter of cucumber florets. "You should circulate, not stick by my side."

He waited until she looked up again to ask, "Why?"

She narrowed her eyes at him. "As you're perfectly aware, this is one of those occasions when a Member needs to work the room."

His smile was genuine. "Yes, I know."

She decided against the cucumber, stepped away from the table.

Plate in one hand, he took her elbow and steered her toward the bank of windows open to the rear garden. "I just can't see why we can't circulate together."

Because every time he touched her, her nerves seized and she forgot how to breathe.

She kept her tongue between her teeth, kept a serene, relaxed expression on her face, and fought to ignore the way her senses fixed on him, how they reached for and craved the solid strength of him as he walked, languidly assured, by her side. She knew perfectly well how solid his body was; she'd collided with it twice now. For some illogical, irrational, totally witless reason, her senses were luridly, slaveringly fixated on what the third time would be like.

Halting before the windows, he released her; facing him, she drew in a breath. Before she could utter the protest she was certain she should, he said, "Think of it as me claiming your protection."

"Protection?" She sent him a look that stated very clearly she wasn't about to accept any such spurious reasoning—or any appeal to her feminine emotions, either. "You, of all people, in this crowd, need no protection beyond your own gilded tongue."

He laughed, and she felt more comfortable, a touch more in control.

Suddenly realized that with him—and in truth, with him alone, at least within the confines of her private life—she did not, as she did with everyone else, exercise her usual level of mastery. Or rather, she might exercise it, yet it might very well not work. Her ability to manage him was not assured, not something she could take for granted.

They'd been eating, nibbling; she glanced up at him. He trapped her gaze; he'd been watching her face. He studied her eyes, then raised a brow in mute question.

She let her chin set. "Why are you clinging to my side?"

His brows rose; his eyes laughed at her. "I would have thought that's obvious—you're a much more entertaining companion than anyone else here, especially our often over-helpful hostess."

She had to grant him that last. Muriel's attempts at assistance could sometimes be disastrous. Yet she wagged a finger at him. "You know perfectly well you're pleased she's organized this evening—you've been able to do your local rounds without lifting a finger."

"I never said I wasn't grateful—it's merely that my gratitude extends only so far."

"*Humph!* If she hadn't organized this, what would you have done?"

His smile was devastating. "Asked you to do it, of course."

Ignoring the effect of that smile, she humphed again.

His expression turned mock-hurt. "Wouldn't you have helped me?"

She glanced at him, tried to make her look severe. "Possibly. If I was bored. Only I'm not that bored at present, so you should be especially grateful to Muriel."

Before she'd finished speaking, his gaze had turned considering, as if contemplating some different prospect.

"Actually, I should probably do something about the area south of Lyndhurst—"

"No." Realizing what tack he was following, her response was instantaneous.

He refocused on her face, then tilted his head, a slight frown in his eyes; he seemed more intrigued than rejected. Then his expression eased; straightening, he took her empty plate from her. "We can talk about it later."

"No, we can't." She was not going to act as a political or diplomatic hostess for him or any man ever again. In her own right, she might enjoy exercising her true talents, but she would not play that role for any man again.

He'd turned away to set their plates on a side table; when he turned back, she was surprised to discover his expression serious, his blue eyes unusually hard, yet his tone when he spoke was calming. "We can, and will, but not here, not now."

For an instant, he held her gaze; she was looking at the real man, not the politician. Then he smiled, and his social mask overlaid that too-determined look; raising his head, he took her arm. "Come and help me with Mrs. Harris. How many children does she have these days?"

Reminding herself that despite his occasional lapses into what she classified as "presumptuous male" behavior, she was in good humor with him, she consented to accompany him and speak with Mrs. Harris.

And subsequently with a succession of others.

When, courtesy of a speculative glance from old Mrs. Tricket, she realized that his liking for her company was raising hares, rather than argue—in her experience a pointless exercise with a presumptuous male—she seized the opportunity of Muriel's being in the group with whom they were engaged to move to her side and murmur, "Thank you for a very pleasant evening."

Muriel, taking in Michael at her side, currently speaking with Mrs. Ellingham, looked at her in surprise. "You're leaving?"

She smiled. "Indeed. I wanted to mention . . . I've decided to hold a ball on the evening before the fete. There are a number of the diplomatic set presently in the area—I thought if they stay overnight, they can attend the fete the next day, boosting our attendance."

"Ah." Muriel blinked. "I see."

She didn't appear enamored of the notion, but that was almost certainly because she hadn't thought of it first. Patting her arm, Caro went on, "I left Edward and Elizabeth struggling with the invitations—I must go and do my part. Again, thank you—I'll send your invitation around tomorrow."

"Thank you." Muriel nodded, her gaze going past Caro. "If you'll excuse me, there's something I must to see to."

They parted. Caro turned to Michael, who had finished with Mrs. Ellingham. She let her smile deepen. "I'm heading home."

She went to draw her hand from his arm and step away, but he moved with her. She paused when they were clear of the group, but he steered her on. Toward the front hall.

When she looked at him and let her puzzlement show, he gifted her with a smile she knew wasn't genuine. "I'll drive you home."

A statement, not an offer; his tone—determined—was more real than his smile.

Her heels struck the hall tiles as she imagined it—driving home on the seat of his curricle, the night dark and balmy about them, his hard, solid body so close to hers . . . "No, thank you. I prefer to walk."

He halted; they were out of sight of the company in the drawing room. "In case it's escaped your notice, it's now full dark outside."

She shrugged. "It's not as if I don't know the way."

"It's what—a hundred yards or so to your gate, and then four hundred or more to the front steps?"

"This is Hampshire, not London. There isn't any danger."

Michael glanced at Muriel's footman, standing waiting by the door. "Have my carriage brought around."

"Yes, sir."

The footman hurried off to comply. When Michael looked again at Caro, he found she'd narrowed her eyes.

"I am not—"

"Why are you arguing?"

She opened her lips, paused, then lifted her chin. "You haven't taken your leave of Muriel. I'll be halfway home by the time you do."

He frowned, recalling. "She went into the dining room."

Caro smiled. "You'll need to go and find her."

A sound behind them made him glance around. Hedderwick, Muriel's spouse, had just come out of the library. No doubt he'd been imbibing something stronger than sherry, but was now returning to his wife's party.

"Perfect," Michael said beneath his breath. He raised his voice. "Hedderwick! Just the man. I need to be on my way, but Muriel's disappeared. Please convey my thanks for an excellent evening and my apologies for having to leave without thanking her in person."

Hedderwick, a large, rotund man with a round bald head, raised his hand in farewell. "I'll make your excuses. Good to see you again." He nodded to Caro, and continued toward the drawing room.

Michael faced Caro. Raised a brow. "Any further social hurdles you can see?"

Eyes like silver shards, she opened her lips—

"Oh, there you are, Hedderwick—please tell Muriel I enjoyed myself thoroughly, but I have to get back to Reginald. He'll worry if I don't return soon."

Hedderwick murmured soothingly, standing back as Miss Trice emerged from the drawing room and came bustling toward Michael and Caro. A gaunt but thoroughly good-natured lady, sister of the local vicar, she'd kept house for him for many years and was an active member of the Ladies' Association.

Her eyes twinkled as she neared. "*Thank* you, Caro, for making the first move. It's really very *good* of Muriel to give these little suppers, but some of us do have other calls on our time."

Caro smiled. Miss Trice beamed at Michael and bade them both farewell, barely breaking her stride in her march to the door.

The footman swung it open; as Miss Trice went out, the clop of hooves and the crunch of wheels on gravel reached them.

"Good." Michael grasped Caro's arm. "You can stop arguing. It's dark. I'm leaving, too. I may as well drive you home—Geoffrey would expect me to."

She looked at him. Despite her calm expression, he could see the exasperation in her eyes. Then she shook her head, gestured as she turned to the door. "Very well!"

Feeling entirely justified, he escorted her onto the porch. His curricle stood waiting. As they went down the steps, she muttered something; he thought the words were "Damn presumptuous male!"

Having gained what he wished, he ignored them. Taking her hand, he assisted her into the curricle, then gathered the reins and followed. She scooted along the seat, drawing her skirts in so he could sit beside her. He did, then set his matched grays trotting down the short drive.

Nose in the air, Caro said, "What about Miss Trice? She's walking home in the dark, too."

"And the vicarage is what? Fifty yards down the road, with its door at most ten paces from the gate."

He heard a sound suspiciously like a sniff.

Decided to poke back. "Could you please explain why you're being so difficult over me driving you home?"

Caro clung to the front of the curricle as he turned his horses into the street. It was a moonless night, black and balmy; he couldn't see that her knuckles were white. As she'd anticipated, through the turn his weight shifted; his hard thigh pressed against hers—heat flared and sank into her flesh, into her. The curricle straightened; the pressure eased. Yet she remained intensely aware of him, of the hard, masculine heat of him a mere inch away.

Predictably, her nerves were in knots, her lungs tight. She'd never been so afflicted in her life.

How could she explain what she didn't understand?

She sucked in a breath, and prepared to lie. "It's just—"

She blinked, peered ahead.

Shadowy figures were dancing in the darkness along the side of the road. She peered harder.

"Good God!" She grabbed Michael's arm, felt it turn to steel under her fingers. "Look!" She pointed ahead. "Miss Trice!"

Two burly figures were struggling with the thin woman; a half-smothered scream reached them.

Michael saw. With a cry, he flicked the reins and his horses shot forward.

Caro clung to the side of the curricle, eyes locked on the scene ahead. The sudden thunder of hooves erupting out of the black night made the two men look up. She caught a fleeting glimpse of pale faces, then one yelled; they let Miss Trice go and plunged down a narrow path between the vicarage and the next cottage.

The path led directly into the forest.

Michael hauled on the reins; the curricle stopped, rocking wildly on its springs alongside the crumpled figure of Miss Trice.

Caro jumped down without waiting for the curricle to settle. She heard Michael swear as she raced across in front of his horses. As she reached Miss Trice, she was aware of him hauling on the brake, swiftly tying off the reins.

Crouching, she put her arm about Miss Trice, who was struggling to sit up. "Are you all right? Did they hurt you?"

"No. I—oh!" Miss Trice was still struggling to catch her breath. She leaned against Caro's arm; Caro didn't have the strength to lift her.

Then Michael was there; he put one arm about Miss Trice, took her hand, and drew her into a sitting position. "It's all right. They've gone."

They all knew there was no point giving chase; at night it would be easy to hide a regiment in the forest.

Miss Trice nodded. "I'll be recovered in a moment. I just need to catch my breath."

They didn't rush her; eventually, she nodded again. "Right. I can stand now."

Caro stood back and let Michael help Miss Trice to her feet. She swayed, but then caught her balance.

"We'll walk you to the door." Michael kept his arm around Miss Trice; Caro noted the older woman seemed to find his support comforting.

The attack had taken place just yards from the vicarage gate. Once they were through it and walking up the paved path, Michael asked, "I don't suppose you have any idea who those men were?"

Miss Trice shook her head. "They're not local men, that I'd swear. I think they were sailors—they smelt fishy, they had the arms for it, and their voices were terribly rough."

They were within easy riding distance of Southampton. Although it was unusual for sailors to penetrate far into the bucolic countryside, tonight two had, intent on attacking some woman.

Michael glanced at Caro as they reached the vicarage steps; her attention was all for Miss Trice. He wondered whether it would occur to her that if he hadn't insisted on driving her home, and persisted until she succumbed, *she* would have been the first woman to walk this way down the village street.

In the dark, alone.

Without anyone close behind to rescue her.

CHAPTER
6

*A*t least Caro had let him drive her home without further argument. With the morning bright about him, Michael swung Atlas down the Bramshaw lane and let his mind revisit the final scenes of the previous night.

They'd seen Miss Trice into the vicarage, into Reverend Trice's shocked and solicitous care. Between them they'd explained; once assured Miss Trice was indeed unharmed and did not wish the doctor fetched, they'd left.

Almost absentmindedly, Caro had allowed him to hand her into the curricle; she'd made no comment when a few minutes later, he'd turned in between the Bramshaw House gates. The winding drive was lined with old trees; in this season it was heavily shadowed along most of its length. Pulling up before the front steps, he'd walked around, handed Caro down, then escorted her to the door.

Drawing in a deep breath, she'd turned to him; with her face lit by the porch lamp, he'd realized she wasn't, as he'd supposed, affected by shock. Instead, she was puzzled, as puzzled as he. "What a very odd affair."

"Indeed." They'd both turned as Catten opened the door.

She'd held out her hand. "Thank you for seeing me home. As it transpired, it was a stroke of good fortune, especially for Miss Trice."

Frustration had bloomed. He was glad they'd been in time to save Miss Trice, but . . . he'd held on to Caro's hand until her fingers had fluttered and he'd once again had her complete attention. Still he'd waited, until she'd looked up and met his eyes. "Tell Geoffrey."

Her eyes had narrowed at his tone, but she'd nodded— somewhat regally. "Of course."

"Promise."

At that, her eyes had flashed. "Naturally I'll tell him— immediately, in fact. Good gracious! Those men might be hiding on our land. With Elizabeth at home, I'm sure Geoffrey will ensure our gardeners, workers, and woodsmen are alerted."

Geoffrey on guard was what he'd wanted; biting his tongue, he'd accepted her assurance and released her. "Good night."

She'd left him with a distinctly haughty nod. He'd headed home, aware as he'd tooled through the night that no matter what else she'd realized, she hadn't yet divined his true direction.

If she had, she wouldn't have jibbed at his protecting her. To his mind, protecting her now figured more as exercising a right he'd claimed rather than as some polite offer it fell to her whim to accept or decline.

In that respect, there was no longer any choice, any decision for her to make.

A lark's call drew him back to the present. The outlying cottages of the village appeared; he slowed Atlas to a trot.

He'd intended to let matters fall out as they would, to allow Caro to realize his interest in her in her own time—he had the whole summer to secure her as his bride; there hadn't seemed any reason to rush her—yet by the time he'd risen from the breakfast table that morning, he'd accepted that that approach would no longer do.

Aside from all else, he'd discovered he had far more in common with his brother-in-law than he'd supposed.

That Devil would shield Honoria from any and all danger regardless of whether she wished to be shielded was beyond question. Knowing how much that irked his sister, yet equally aware of how ruthless Devil could be, and indeed had been on that point, he'd often wondered at the compulsion that drove his brother-in-law, or rather the source of it. On most other matters, Devil was a willing slave to Honoria's wishes.

Now *he* had caught the same disease. Certainly, he was now victim to the same compulsion he'd long recognized in Devil.

He'd spent a restless night; by the time he'd finished breakfast this morning, he'd accepted that the hollowness centered somewhere below his breastbone wasn't due to hunger.

Luckily, Caro had already been married once; she would doubtless take his reaction—his susceptibility—in her stride.

That, however, presupposed she'd recognized and accepted the true nature of his interest in her.

He was on his way to speak with her, to ensure that whatever else occurred between them, she was completely clear and unequivocally convinced on that point.

On the fact that he wanted her as his wife.

Leaving Atlas in the care of Geoffrey's stableman, he walked up to the house through the gardens. As he started across the last stretch of lawn leading to the terrace, a distinct but distant snip, followed by a rustle, had him glancing to the left.

Fifty yards away, Caro stood in the center of the sunken rose garden clipping deadheads from the burgeoning bushes.

Garden shears tightly gripped, Caro snipped with abandon, plucking the sheared hips from the heavily laden bushes and dropping or tossing them to the flagstone path. Hendricks, Geoffrey's gardener, would tidy up later and be grateful for her industry; meanwhile, attacking the bushes and cutting away the faded blooms, encouraging the rampant canes to flower even more profusely, was distinctly satisfying. Oddly calming, in some strange way soothing the panicky irritation she felt whenever she thought of Michael.

Which was far too often for her liking.

She had no idea what the feeling presaged, no prior experience to call on, but instinct warned she stood on tricky ground where he was concerned, and she'd long ago learned to trust her instincts.

The discovery that she couldn't be sure of managing him, indeed was no longer sure she'd successfully managed him at any point, had undermined her usual confidence. Her exasperated capitulation the previous evening, wise though hindsight had proved it to be, was another cause for worry—since when had she become so susceptible to the pressuring persuasions of a presumptuous male?

True, he'd been absolutely determined, but why had she succumbed? Given in? Surrendered?

Frowning direfully, she viciously decapitated another shriveled set of blooms.

She paused, frown fading . . . and felt a tingle of warmth, felt a lick of rising excitement frizzle along her nerves.

Lungs tightening, she looked up—and saw her nemesis, large as life, lounging against the stone arch, watching her. Inwardly she swore in Portuguese; the effect he had on her—whatever it was—was only getting *worse*. Now she could feel his gaze across a distance of ten paces!

A smile curved his lips. He pushed away from the arch and walked toward her.

Ruthlessly suppressing her wayward senses, she responded with a perfectly gauged smile, one that was welcoming, suitable for an old friend, yet clearly stated that that was the limit of their association. "Good morning—are you looking for Geoffrey? I believe he's gone to look over the south fields."

His smile deepened; his eyes remained fixed on hers. "No. I'm not after Geoffrey."

His long, easy strides carried him to within a foot of her skirts before he halted. She let her eyes widen, outwardly laughingly surprised—inwardly starting to panic. He surprised her even more—panicked her even more—by reaching out, plucking the shears from her right hand while with his other hand he captured her fingers.

Her gloved fingers, she reminded herself, struggling to subdue her escalating tension.

He smiled into her eyes. "It's you I came to see."

He raised her hand; thanking heaven for her gardening gloves, she allowed one brow to rise, waiting for him to realize he couldn't kiss her fingers. Amusement gleamed in the sky blue of his eyes, then he turned her hand, long fingers flicking the wrist-slit of the glove wide, bent his head, and placed a kiss—a disturbingly firm, distractingly hot, far-too-knowing kiss—directly over the spot beneath which her pulse raced.

For one instant, giddiness threatened, then she snapped her gaze to his face, watched him reading her reaction, saw the satisfaction in his eyes.

"Indeed?" Preserving her expression of polite friendliness required considerable effort. She retrieved her hand; she didn't need to tug—he released it readily.

"Indeed. Are you busy?"

He didn't glance around at the severely denuded bushes, for which she grudgingly accorded him several points. A lady of her standing visiting her brother's house . . . if she was filling her hours deadheading roses, there was obviously nothing urgent on her plate.

"No." Determined to meet his challenge, whatever it might be, she smiled. "Did you think of some suggestion for the ball?"

His eyes met hers; she tried but couldn't read them. His expression remained relaxed, unthreatening. "In a manner of speaking. But come, let's walk. There are a number of matters I'd like to discuss with you."

He tossed the shears into the trug by her feet, and offered his arm. She had to take it and stroll beside him, and fight to appear unaffected. Her nerves were screamingly aware of his physical presence, of his strength, and that disturbing, distracting masculine aura that seemed, at least to her fevered imagination, to shimmer about her—reaching for her, enfolding her, as if it would surround and trap her.

She gave herself a mental shake, looked up as he said, "About Elizabeth."

The words focused her wits wonderfully. "What about Elizabeth?"

He glanced at her. "I realize you—you, she, and Campbell—knew my intentions, or rather the possibility of my having intentions in that direction. I wondered how you knew."

It was a reasonable question, albeit one he couldn't have asked of anyone but a trusted friend. She looked down as they walked, rapidly considering how much she should reveal, deciding that in this case, the truth would be wisest. She met his gaze. "Amazingly enough, it was Geoffrey who first alerted us."

"Geoffrey?" His incredulity was unfeigned. "How could he have heard anything?"

She smiled, genuinely this time. "I know it's hard to imagine, but I don't think he knew anything of *your* intentions. As I understand it—and no, in the circumstances, I haven't broached the subject with him—it was *his* intentions he was pursuing. When Elizabeth returned from London and admitted she hadn't developed a *tendre* for any gentleman of the ton, Geoffrey turned his mind to what I believe he thought would be an advantageous match. He tried to sound out Elizabeth, but . . ."

She caught his eye. "Geoffrey singing any gentleman's praises was bound to put the wind up Elizabeth."

He raised his brows. "Especially given her attachment to Campbell."

She smiled, commending his intelligence. "Precisely."

As she watched, his eyes widened, his gaze momentarily distant, then he glanced at her. "Just as well *I* didn't sound out *Geoffrey* over the possibility I came here to assess."

"Indeed not—he would have taken the bit between his teeth and run."

"Which would have been deuced awkward." He caught her gaze. "It appears I have to thank you for stopping me from speaking with him—that was why you came to see me that first day, wasn't it?"

A betraying warmth crept into her cheeks. "Yes." She looked away, shrugged. "Of course, I didn't intend to make quite such a dramatic entrance."

The comment reminded Michael of that earlier incident; a

shaft of pure fear lanced through him. He damped it down, pointing out to his newfound vulnerability that she was here, walking, warm and feminine, by his side.

They strolled for a few paces, then he murmured, "But you—you knew more definitely about my direction. How did you learn of it?" He'd decided the simplest way to make her see and appreciate the rightness of his *new* direction was to lead her mind along the same track his had taken.

"Elizabeth sent frantic summonses to me and Edward—I was staying with Augusta in Derbyshire. We both thought Elizabeth had misinterpreted, so we stopped in London on the way down. There, however, Edward learned about your pending promotion and the Prime Minister's directive. So I visited your aunt Harriet and she told me of your intentions regarding Elizabeth."

"I see." He made a mental note to have a word to his aunt, but reading between the lines, it seemed Caro already knew all she needed to know about his present state and the reason behind his sincere need of a suitable wife.

Indeed, he couldn't see any benefit in explaining further. At least not in words.

He glanced at her. The summerhouse built out over the ornamental lake—his chosen destination—was still some way ahead.

She looked up, caught his eye, and smiled—perfectly genuinely. "I'm so glad you understood about Elizabeth, that you and she really wouldn't suit." Her smile deepened. "I'm relieved and very grateful."

He returned her smile with one he hoped wasn't wolfish. He wasn't above exploiting her gratitude—in her own best interests, of course.

And his.

He searched for topics to keep her distracted until they gained the summerhouse's relative privacy. "I presume you have hopes for Campbell. He'll need to advance further before he and Elizabeth can hope to secure Geoffrey's blessing."

"Indeed." She looked down, then said, "I was thinking of

speaking to a few people when Parliament reconvenes. If there's to be a reshuffle, that might well be a propitious time."

He nodded. Saw no reason not to add, "If you like, I could sound out Hemmings at the Home Office, and there's Curlew at Customs and Revenue."

She looked up, her radiant smile dawning. "Would you?"

Taking her elbow, he guided her up the summerhouse's steps. "Campbell's experience is sound; I'll watch him while I'm here and make my own assessment, but with both Camden's and your imprimatur, it shouldn't take much effort to set his feet on the next rung."

Caro laughed, softly cynical. "True, but it does take connections." Walking across the summerhouse to where open arches with low railings looked out over the lake, she halted, turned, and smiled. "Thank you."

He hesitated, his blue gaze on her, then walked slowly toward her.

Her lungs locked; with every step he took, the vise clamped about her chest tightened, until she felt lightheaded. In the most severely lecturing tones she could muster, she told herself not to be stupid, to simply keep breathing, to hide her silly sensitivity at all costs—how mortifying if he should realize . . .

This was Michael—he posed no threat to her.

Her senses refused to listen.

To her mounting surprise, the closer he got, the more clearly she could read the intentness in his gaze. Realized with a jolt that he'd dropped his politician's mask, that he was looking at her as if . . .

He didn't stop his prowling advance.

Full realization struck. She felt her eyes widen. Abruptly, she swung around. Gestured to the lake. "It's a . . . very pleasant view."

She'd barely managed to squeeze the words out. She waited, tense, almost quivering.

"Indeed." The deep murmur stirred the fine hairs at her nape.

Her senses flared; he was like a caressing flame burning at her back. So near. About to reach around and engulf her. Trap her.

Panic struck, full blown.

"Ah"—she stepped quickly to her right, walked to the far side of the next arch—"if you stand over here, you can see down the lake to where the rhododenrons are in bloom."

She didn't dare look his way. "And look!" She pointed. "There's a family of ducks. There's"—she paused to count—"twelve ducklings."

Senses at full stretch, she waited, mentally scanning for movement from her left.

Suddenly realized he'd circled to her right!

"Caro."

She swallowed a shriek; she was so tense she felt dizzy. He was beside and just behind her; stepping left, she whirled. Her back to the other side of the arch, she stared at him. "What—just *what* do you think you're about?"

Given her panic, her wide eyes, manufacturing a scowl was beyond her. Besides, this was Michael. . . .

Beyond her control, puzzlement and a certain hurt filled her eyes.

He'd halted; he stood perfectly still, his blue gaze on her face, searching, studying . . . the impression she received through the jibbering of her senses was that he was as puzzled as she.

He tilted his head; eyes narrowing, he shifted to face her.

She managed to drag in a breath. "What do you think you're doing?"

Her tone carried her real question; why was he panicking her, frightening her—destroying the easy if distant, comfortable friendship they had in the past, more or less until now, shared?

His lashes flickered, then he sighed and refocused on her face.

Abruptly, she realized he was as tense as she.

"I was, as it happens, trying to get you to stand still long enough to get my hands on you."

The answer sent her panic soaring, yet even so she could

barely believe her ears. She blinked, managed to summon the icily haughty cloak she desperately needed. "Haven't you heard? I'm the Merry Widow. I do not, ever, play games of that sort." Hearing the words, and her firm tone, bolstered her courage; she lifted her chin. "Not with you—not with any man."

He didn't move, but continued to regard her with a frown in his eyes. A long moment passed, then he asked, "What made you think I was interested in any game?"

A disorienting suspicion that they were talking at cross-purposes assailed her—yet she was sure they were not. There was a light in his eyes, an intent she recognized . . .

Michael took advantage of her confusion, taking two steps to stand directly before her. She tensed; before she could bolt, he closed his hands about her waist.

Anchoring her before him with the frame of the arch at her back, he locked eyes with her. "I have no interest whatever in *playing* at anything."

Between his hands, she quivered, but her physical panic, although very much present, was having to fight a strong vein of astonishment. She'd lifted her hands, presumably to hold him off; they fluttered to rest, passive, on his chest.

He ignored the oddly evocative touch, waited, gave her time to calm enough to remember to breathe, to study his face, accept that he had her caught, but that he wasn't to be classed with any of the others who'd pursued her. He was operating on a different plane with a different goal in mind. He watched her thoughts shimmer through her eyes, all but saw her gather her wits.

She moistened her lips, glanced fleetingly at his. "What, then?"

He smiled, slowly, and watched her attention fix on his lips. He bent closer, lowered his head—distracted, she didn't immediately notice.

Then she did. She sucked in a breath and looked up— from a distance of mere inches met his eyes.

He caught her gaze. "I'm in deadly earnest."

Her eyes flared, then her lids fell as he lowered his head the last inch, and kissed her.

Pressed his lips to hers, fully expecting some degree of chilly resistance, fully prepared to overcome it, overwhelm it. Instead . . . while she certainly froze, and didn't respond, there was no resistance in her either.

Nothing to overcome, to overwhelm, to sweep away.

No attempt to hold aloof, much less break away.

No icy, haughty chill. Nothing. Simply nothing.

Caution whispered through his mind, laid a restraining hand on his intentions. Puzzled, he moved his lips gently, teasingly, over hers, trying through that simple touch to gauge, to sense her feelings. Instinct directed him to keep his hands locked at her waist, at least until he understood her, and her unexpected, elusive response.

It came eventually, so hesitant and uncertain he nearly drew back—just to check that this was Caro. Caro—the confidently assured ambassador's wife of more than a decade's standing.

The woman in his arms . . . if he didn't know better, he'd have sworn she'd never been kissed. He kept the caress light, lips skating, brushing, beckoning . . . it was like breathing life into a statue.

She was cool, but not cold, as if waiting for warmth to find her and bring her to life. The fact focused him as nothing else could have—certainly as no other woman ever had; what he was discovering through the kiss, through the slow gradual warming of her lips, all he learned from exploring their rosebud softness, all he suddenly realized from the tentative pressure she eventually returned, was so utterly out of kilter with what he'd expected—with what any man might have expected—she seized and fixed his attention completely.

After that first, brief, uncertain response, she stopped—waited. He realized she was waiting for him to break the kiss, raise his head, and let her go. He debated for a heartbeat, then, moving slowly, angled his head and increased the pressure of his lips on hers. If he let her go too soon . . . he was politician enough to see the danger.

So he teased and cajoled, used every wile he possessed to draw a response again from her. Her hands shifted, restless, on his chest, then she gripped his lapels and abruptly kissed him back, more firmly, more definitely. A real kiss.

Got you.

He swooped and returned the caress, quickly engaged her in a real exchange—kiss for kiss, sliding, tempting pressure for pressure. While she was distracted, he eased his fingers, and slowly slid his hands around, loosely— carefully—taking her in his arms. He wanted her there, secure, before he let her escape from the kiss.

Caro's head was starting to swim. Quite how she'd got trapped into this strange kissing game she didn't know. She couldn't kiss—she was perfectly aware of that—yet here she was, leaning against his chest, her lips beneath his . . . kissing him.

She should stop. Some panicky little voice kept telling her she should, that she'd regret it if she didn't, yet she'd never been kissed like this before—so gently, so . . . temptingly, as if her response was something he actually wanted.

It was strange. Of the others who'd pursued her, few had ever got close enough to steal a kiss. The handful that had had wanted to devour her; her revulsion had been immediate and ingrained—she'd never questioned it, never felt the need to.

Yet now, here, in the safety of her childhood home with Michael . . . was it simply that combination of the familiar that had failed to trigger her usual reaction, that instead had left her open to . . .

This strange and intoxicating exchange.

This tempting and beguiling exchange.

Just how tempting, how intoxicating, how thoroughly beguiling she learned a moment later, when fraction by fraction he slowly drew back, until their lips parted and he lifted his head. Not far, just an inch or so; enough for her to raise her lids and look into the bright blue of his eyes half hidden behind the tracery of his lashes. Just enough for her to draw in a quick breath, and realize his arms were around her—not crushing her or mauling her, yet trapping her all the same.

Enough for her to experience a rush of pure impulse— crazy and thrilling and wholly wanton—that had her pressing closer, stretching up, and touching her lips once again to his.

In the instant she did, she sensed his pleasure. A definite masculine gloat that he'd tempted her so far.

What was she doing?

Before she could pull back, he tightened his arms about her, held her close as he took over, and kissed her again.

Slow, easy, a warm and confident caress. His tongue touched her lips, traced, tantalized . . . she parted them, tentatively, curious . . . not even truly sure it was by her own will and not his.

His tongue traced the soft inner faces of her lips, not so much bold as assured, certain. Then he probed further, found her tongue and stroked, caressed . . .

Warmth seeped through her, unraveling her tensed nerves, soothing and smoothing away her hesitations, her uncertainties, her fears . . .

Michael felt her relax, felt the last of her coldness melt away. Grappled with his desire to take more, to press further, to claim, caged it so artfully she wouldn't know it was there. Regardless of how experienced his rational mind told him she had to be, his instincts knew better than to scare her—to at this stage give her any excuse to flee.

It was he who called an end to the engagement; he was gratified that that was so—she was so caught, now so involved in the pleasurable exchange that returning to the real world—the world in which she was the virtuous Merry Widow—had temporarily lost all appeal.

Drawing back, feeling their lips part, hearing the soft exhalation she gave as they did, he had to fight to hide his triumph.

He let her ease back, steadied her within his arms until she was firm on her feet. She blinked and her eyes met his. A frown came to life, slowly grew until it shadowed the silvery depths of her gaze.

Then she blushed, glanced away and stepped back—remembered she couldn't and stepped to the side. He let his arms fall, turned with her, trying to read her face, wanting to know . . .

Caro sensed his gaze, forced herself to halt, draw in a huge breath, and meet it. She frowned, warningly, at him. "So now you know."

He blinked. A second passed. "Know what?"

Looking ahead, nose in the air, she headed for the summerhouse's door. "That I can't kiss." It was imperative she bring this interlude to a rapid end.

Naturally, he kept pace, falling in, strolling easily beside her. "So what was it we were doing just now?"

He sounded faintly puzzled, also faintly amused.

"By your standards, not a lot, I imagine. I don't know how to kiss." She waved a hand dismissively. "I'm no good at it."

They descended the steps and set off across the lawn. Head up, she walked as fast as she reasonably could. "I daresay Geoffrey will be back by now—"

"Caro."

The single word held a wealth of, not just feeling, but beguiling promise.

Her heart leapt to her throat; determinedly, she swallowed it. The man was a consummate politician—she shouldn't forget that. "Please—spare me your sympathy."

"No."

She halted, turned to stare at him. "What?"

He met her eyes. "No, I won't spare you—I fully intend to teach you." His lips curved; his gaze dropped to hers. "You're perfectly teachable, you know."

"No, I'm not, and anyway . . ."

"Anyway what?

"Never mind."

He laughed. "But I do mind. And I am going to teach you. To kiss, and more."

She humphed, shot him another, more dire, warning glance, and walked on even faster. Muttered beneath her breath. "Damn presumptuous male."

"What was that?" He strolled patiently beside her.

"I told you—never mind."

On reaching the house, she discovered Geoffrey had just returned; with immense relief, she all but bundled Michael into his presence and escaped.

To her room. To sink down on her bed and try to work out

what had happened. That Michael had kissed her—that he'd wanted to and managed to—was strange enough, but why had she kissed him back?

Mortification washed over her; rising, she went to the washstand, poured cold water from the ewer into the basin, and washed her warm face. Patting her cheeks dry, she remembered, heard again his gently amused tone. He'd said he'd teach her, but he wouldn't of course. He'd only said that to gloss over the awkward moment.

She returned to the bed, sinking down on the edge. Her pulse was still galloping, her nerves in a tangle, yet the knot was not one she recognized.

The shadows progressed across the floor while she tried to make sense of what had occurred, and even more what she'd felt.

When the gong for luncheon rang through the house, she blinked and looked up—in the mirror of her dressing table across the room, she saw her face, her expression soft, her fingers lightly tracing her lips.

With a muttered curse, she lowered her hand, stood, shook out her skirts, and headed for the door.

CHAPTER
7

$\int$he would avoid him henceforth; it was the only viable solution. She certainly was not going to spend her time imagining what learning to kiss under his tutelage would be like.

She had a ball to organize and lots of guests to house—more than enough to keep her busy.

And that evening she had a dinner to attend at Leadbetter Hall, where the Portuguese delegation was spending the summer.

Leadbetter Hall was near Lyndhurst. The invitation had not included Edward; in the circumstances, that wasn't surprising. She'd ordered the carriage for seven-thirty; a few minutes past the appointed time, she left her room suitably gowned and coiffed, her rose magenta silk gown draped to perfection, cut to make the most of her less-than-impressive bosom. A long strand of pearls interspersed with amethysts circled her throat once before hanging to her waist. Pearl and amethyst drops dangled from her ears; the same jewels adorned the gold filigree comb that anchored the mass of her unruly hair.

That hair, thick, springy, and all but impossible to tame—to make conform to any fashionable style—had been the bane of her existence until a supremely haughty but well-disposed archduchess had advised her to stop trying to fight a battle destined to be lost, and instead embrace the inevitable as a mark of individuality.

The ascerbic recommendation had not immediately changed her view, but gradually she'd realized that the person most bothered by her hair was herself, and if she stopped agonizing over it and instead took its oddity in her stride—even embraced it as the archduchess had suggested—then others were, indeed, inclined to see it simply as a part of her uniqueness.

Now, if truth be told, the relative uniqueness of her appearance buoyed her; the individuality was something she clung to. Gliding to the stairs, hearing her skirts sussurating about her, reassured that she looked well, she put a gloved hand to the balustrade and started down.

Her gaze lowered to the front hall, to where Catten stood waiting to open the front door. Serenely, she glided down the last flight—a well-shaped head of dark brown locks atop a pair of broad shoulders, elegantly clad, came into view in the corridor running alongside the stairs. Then Michael turned, looked up, and saw her.

She slowed; taking in his attire, she inwardly cursed. But there was nothing she could do; returning his smile, she continued her descent. He strolled to the bottom of the stairs to meet her, offered his hand as she neared.

"Good evening." She kept her smile plastered in place as she surrendered her fingers to his strong clasp. "I take it you, too, have been invited to dine at Leadbetter Hall?"

His eyes held hers. "Indeed. I thought, in the circumstances, I might share your carriage."

Geoffrey had followed Michael from the study. "An excellent idea, especially with those scoundrels who attacked Miss Trice still at large."

She raised her brows. "I hardly think they'd attack a carriage."

"Who's to say?" Geoffrey exchanged a distinctly masculine glance with Michael. "Regardless, it's only sensible that Michael escort you."

That, unfortunately, was impossible to argue. Resigning herself to the inevitable—and really, despite the silly expectation tightening her nerves, what had she to fear?—she smiled diplomatically and inclined her head. "Indeed." She lifted a brow at Michael. "Are you ready?"

He met her gaze, smiled. "Yes." Drawing her to his side, he laid her hand on his sleeve. "Come—let's away."

Lifting her head, drawing in a deep breath, ignoring the tension that had escalated dramatically now he'd moved so close, she regally nodded to Geoffrey and consented to be led to the waiting carriage.

Michael handed her up, then followed. He sat on the seat opposite her, watching while she fussed with her skirts, then straightened her silver-spangled shawl. The footman shut the door; the carriage lurched, then rolled off. He caught Caro's eye. "Have you any idea who else will be present tonight?"

Her brows rose. "Yes, and no."

He listened while she listed those she knew would be present, digressing to give him a potted history of the sort of information most useful for him to know, then elaborating on those she suspected might also have been summoned to sup with the Portuguese.

Sitting back in the shadows of the carriage, lips curving, he wondered if she was even conscious of her performance—the exact response he would have wished for from his wife. Her knowledge was wide, her grasp of what he most needed to know superior; while the carriage rumbled along the leafy lanes, he continued to question, to encourage her to interact with him both as he wished, and also in the manner with which she was most comfortable.

That last was his real goal. While her information would certainly be of help, his primary aim was to put her at her ease. To encourage her to focus on the diplomatic milieu to which she was so accustomed, and in which she was a consummate participant.

Time enough to engage with her more personally later, on their way home.

Aware that on the return journey she'd be in a much more approachable mood, one more amenable to his intentions, if she'd passed a pleasant evening to that point, he set out to, as far as he was able, ensure her enjoyment of the night.

They reached Leadbetter Hall in good time, alighting before the steps leading up to imposing doors. He escorted her through the doors to where the duchess and countess stood waiting just inside the high-ceilinged front hall.

The ladies exchanged greetings, complimenting each other on their toilettes, then the duchess turned to him. "We are delighted to receive you, Mr. Anstruther-Wetherby. It is our hope that we will do so many more times in the coming years."

Straightening from his bow, he replied with easy assurance, sensing Caro's gaze on his face; turning from greeting the countess, he caught her approving glance.

Almost as if she were starting to view him as a protégé . . . he hid the true tenor of his smile. With his customary elegant confidence, he took her arm and steered her into the drawing room.

They paused on the threshold, glancing swiftly around, getting their bearings. There was a brief hiatus in the hum of conversations as those already there turned to look, then people smiled and returned to their discussions.

He glanced at Caro; arrow-straight beside him, she all but vibrated with pleasurable expectation. Confidence, assurance, and serenity, all were there in her face, in her expression, in her stance. His gaze drifted over her, surreptitiously drank her in; he again felt a surge of primitive emotion, a simple possessiveness.

She was the wife he needed, and intended to have.

Recalling his plan, he turned her toward the fireplace. "The duke and count first, I think?"

She nodded. "Indubitably."

It was simple enough to remain by her side as they circled the drawing room, stopping by each knot of guests, exchanging introductions and greetings. His memory was almost as good as Caro's; she'd been right in predicting the presence of most of those there. Those she hadn't foreseen included two gentlemen from the Foreign Office and one from the Board of Trade, along with their wives. All three men instantly recognized him; each found a moment to stop by his side and explain his connection with the duke and the count, and the still-absent ambassador.

Turning back to the group with whom he and Caro were engaged, Michael discovered that Ferdinand Leponte had insinuated himself into the circle on Caro's other side.

"Leponte." He and the Portuguese exchanged nods—polite but, on Leponte's part, suspicious and assessing. Having already taken Ferdinand's measure, he resigned himself to, at least outwardly, ignoring the Portuguese's attempts to—why mince words?—seduce his intended bride.

Creating a diplomatic incident would not endear him to the Prime Minister. Besides, Caro's formidable reputation—the one Ferdinand had yet to properly comprehend—was clear proof that she was unlikely to need any help in seeing the Portuguese off. Better men had tried and fallen at her gates.

While chatting with the Polish chargé d'affaires, from the corner of his eye Michael watched Ferdinand deploy what he had to admit was considerable charm attempting to draw Caro away from him; her hand still rested on his arm. He was acutely aware of the weight of her fingers; they didn't shift, flicker, or grip, just remained steadfastly where they were. From what he caught of their exchanges, the Portuguese was making little headway.

Ferdinand: "Your eyes, dear Caro, are silver moons in the heaven of your face."

Caro, brows rising: "Really? Two moons. How strange."

There was just the right ripple of amusement in her tone to totally depress any loverlike pretensions Ferdinand was nursing. Glancing his way, Michael saw irritation flash fleetingly through Ferdinand's dark eyes, a fractional downward tightening of his mobile mouth before his charming mask re-formed, and he rattled in once more, tilting at Caro's walls.

Michael could have informed him that such an approach was pointless. It was necessary to take Caro by surprise and so get *inside* her defenses; once up, in place, guarding her virtue—why, in her circumstances, her virtue required such vigilant preservation he hadn't yet divined—those defenses were virtually impossible to shake. Certainly not in any social setting. They'd been forged, tested, and perfected in what must have been a highly exacting arena.

Returning to his conversation with the chargé d'affaires, he confirmed that Mr. Kosminsky would, indeed, be attending Caro's ball and was willing to assist in ensuring said ball was not marred by any unhappy occurrence.

The diminuitive Pole puffed out his chest. "It will be an honor to serve in protecting Mrs. Sutcliffe's peace of mind."

Hearing her name, Caro grasped the opportunity to turn to Kosminsky. She smiled, and the little man glowed. "Thank you. I know it's an imposition of sorts, yet—"

She glibly bound Kosminsky to be her willing slave, at least as far as keeping her ball trouble-free.

Standing between them, Michael silently appreciated her performance, then he glanced at Ferdinand and once again caught a glimpse of chagrin. He realized that Leponte, viewing him as a rival for Caro's favors, wasn't bothering to hide his aggravation at her dismissiveness from him.

Leponte was, however, being careful to hide his reaction from Caro.

The realization sharpened Michael's attention. From the corner of his eye, he watched Ferdinand consider Caro measuringly. There was an intensity in that assessment that did not fit the mold of a holidaying foreign diplomat looking for a little diversion in the bucolic bliss of the English countryside.

Caro threw a comment his way; smiling easily, with practiced facility he resumed his part in the discussion.

Yet some part of him remained alert, focused on Ferdinand.

Dinner was announced. The guests paired up and strolled into the large dining room. Michael found himself seated near the duke and count; Portugal had for centuries been one of England's closest allies—those gentlemen's interest in learning his stance on various issues and educating him as to theirs was entirely understandable.

Less understandable was Caro's placement—at the far end of the table, separated from the duchess by Ferdinand, with an ancient Portuguese admiral on her other side and the countess opposite. Although at least a third of those present were English, there were no compatriots near her.

Not, of course, that such a situation would bother her.

It did bother him.

Caro was aware of the peculiarity of her placement. If Camden had been alive and she'd been attending with him, then the position was correct, seating her with the other senior diplomats' wives. However . . .

She wondered, fleetingly, whether her appearing on Michael's arm and remaining by his side in the drawing room had given rise to an inaccurate assumption; considering the duchess's and countess's experience, she jettisoned that explanation. If they'd suspected any pending connection between her and Michael, one or the other would have quietly inquired. Neither had, which meant she was seated where she was for some other purpose; while she smiled and chatted and the courses came and went, she wondered what that might be.

On her right, Ferdinand was charmingly attentive. On her left, old Admiral Pilocet snoozed, waking only to peer at the dishes as each course was set out before succumbing to slumber once more.

"My dear Caro, you must try some of these mussels."

Returning her attention to Ferdinand, she consented to be served with a concoction of mussels and shallots in herb broth.

"They are English mussels, of course," Ferdinand gestured with his fork, "but the dish is from Albufeira—my home."

Increasingly intrigued by his persistence, she decided to let herself be drawn. "Indeed?" Skewering a mussel on the tines of her fork, she considered it, then glanced at Ferdinand. "Do I take it you live near your uncle and aunt?" She popped the morsel into her mouth and watched his gaze lock on her lips.

He blinked. "Ah . . ." His eyes returned to hers. "Yes." He nodded and looked down at his plate. "We all—my parents and cousins and my other uncles and aunts—live at the *castelo* there." He turned his brilliantly charming smile on her. "It is built on the cliffs overlooking the sea." He looked soulfully into her eyes. "You should visit with us there— Portugal has been too long without your fair presence."

She laughed. "I greatly fear Portugal will have to grin and bear my absence. I have no plans to leave England's shores in the foreseeable future."

"Ah, no!" Ferdinand's features reflected dramatic pain. "It is a loss, at least in our little corner of the world."

She smiled and finished the last of her mussels.

Their plates were cleared. Ferdinand leaned closer, lowering his voice. "We all understand, of course, that you were devoted to Ambassador Sutcliffe, and even now revere his memory."

He paused, watching closely. Her smile in place, she reached for her wineglass, raised it to her lips; as she sipped, she met his dark eyes. "Indeed."

She wasn't foolish enough to dismiss Ferdinand and his by-English-standards histrionic behavior. He was probing, searching—for what she had no clue. But while he was good, she was better. She gave him no inkling of her true feelings and waited to see where he would go.

He cast his eyes down, feigning . . . shyness? "I have long harbored a regard bordering on fascination for Sutcliffe—he was the consummate diplomat. There is so much that can be learned from a study of his life—his successes, his strategies."

"Really?" She looked mildly bemused, although he wasn't the first to take that tack.

"But yes! Just think of his first actions on taking up his post in Lisbon, when he—"

The next course was set before them. Ferdinand continued to expound on the highlights of Camden's career. Content to have him thus occupied, she encouraged him; he was extremely well informed of the catalog of her late husband's actions.

By judiciously adding her own observations, she extended the discussion over the rest of the courses; Ferdinand looked up, slightly surprised when the duchess rose to lead the ladies from the room.

In the drawing room, the duchess and countess claimed her attention.

"Is it always this warm during your summer?" The duchess languidly waved her fan.

Caro smiled. "Actually, it's quite mild this year. Is this your first visit to England?"

The slow beat of the fan faltered, then resumed. "Yes, it is." The duchess met her eyes and smiled. "We have spent much of the last years with the embassies in Scandanavia."

"Ah—no wonder the weather here seems warm to you, then."

"Indeed." The countess stepped in to ask, "Is this area usually so favored by the diplomatic set during summer?"

Caro nodded. "There's always a goodly number of the embassy set about—it's pleasant countryside close to London, and close to the sailing about the Isle of Wight."

"Ah, yes." The countess met her gaze. "That, of course, is why Ferdinand would have us here."

Caro smiled—and wondered. After an instant's pause, she turned the conversation into other channels. The duchess and countess followed her lead, but seemed disinclined to let her move on to chat with other ladies.

Or so she felt; the gentlemen returned to the drawing room before she had a chance to test them.

Ferdinand was among the first to stroll in. He saw her instantly; smiling, he came to join her.

Michael walked in some way behind Ferdinand; he paused just inside the door, scanning the room—he saw her by the windows, flanked by the duchess and countess.

For one instant, Caro felt a strange dislocation. Across the room, she faced two men. Between her and Michael, Ferdinand, smiling wolfishly, the epitome of Latin handsomeness and overwhelming charm, approached, his gaze locked on her. Then Michael stepped forward. His attractiveness was more subtle, his strength less so. He walked more slowly, more gracefully, yet with his long-legged stride he was soon only paces behind Ferdinand.

She had no doubt of Ferdinand's intention, but it wasn't the wolf who commanded her senses. Even as she forced her gaze to Ferdinand's face, with her usual easy assurance returned his smile, she was infinitely more aware of Michael slowly, purposefully, advancing.

Almost as if the movement had been choreographed, the duchess and countess murmured their excuses, one on either side lightly touched her hands in farewell, then they swept forward. Flowing around Ferdinand with barely a nod, they closed with Michael.

He had to stop and talk with them.

"My dear Caro, you will forgive me, I know, but you are here." Ferdinand gestured theatrically. "What would you?"

"Indeed, I've no idea," she replied. "What would I?"

Ferdinand took her arm. "My obsession with Camden Sutcliffe—your presence is an opportunity I cannot resist." He turned her; under his direction, they strolled down the long room. With Ferdinand's head bent to hers, it would appear they were deep in some discussion; given the present company, it was unlikely any would interrupt.

His expression one of scholarly interest, Ferdinand continued, "I would, if I may, ask more about an aspect that has always intrigued me. Sutcliffe's house was here—it must have played a considerable part in his life. Must have"—frowning, he searched for phrases—"been the place he retreated to, where he found greatest comfort."

She raised her brows. "I'm not sure, in Camden's case, that his country home—his ancestral home—played as large and important a role as one might suppose."

Why Ferdinand was pursuing such a tack—surely a strange approach to seducing her—escaped her, yet it was a useful topic with which to pass the time. Especially if it served to keep Ferdinand safely distracted from more direct ventures. "Camden didn't spend much time here—at Sutcliffe Hall—during his lifetime. Or at least, during his years of diplomatic service."

"But he grew up here, yes? And this Sutcliffe Hall was his—not just his ancestral home, but it belonged to him, true?"

She nodded. "Yes."

They strolled on, Ferdinand frowning. "So you are saying

he only occasionally visited this Hall during his ambassadorship."

"That's right. Usually his visits were fleeting—no more than a day or two, rarely as long as a week, but after the deaths of each of his first two wives he returned to the Hall for some months, so I suppose it's true to say that the Hall was his ultimate retreat." She glanced at Ferdinand. "By his wish, he's buried there, in the old chapel in the grounds."

"Ah!" Ferdinand nodded as if that last revelation meant much to him.

A disruption within the company had them both looking up; the first of the guests were departing.

Engaged in nodding a distant farewell to the gentleman from the Board of Trade and his wife, Caro didn't register Ferdinand's abrupt change of tack until he shifted between her and the rest of the room and, leaning close, murmured, "Dear Caro, it is such a lovely summer night—come walk with me on the terrace."

Instinctively, she looked toward the terrace, revealed through a pair of open doors that just happened to lie a few paces from them.

To her surprise, she found herself being expertly herded toward the doors.

Instincts briefly warred; it was her practice not to give ground literally or figuratively in such matters, more to spare her would-be seducers than through any concern for her safety—she'd always emerged triumphant from such encounters and had no doubt she always would—yet in this case, her curiosity was aroused.

She acquiesced with a regal inclination of her head and allowed Ferdinand to guide her through the doors and out onto the moonlit flags.

From across the room, Michael watched her slender figure disappear from sight, and inwardly cursed. He didn't waste time considering what Leponte might be up to; deftly—with the skill that had brought him to the Prime Minister's notice—he disengaged from the duke and his aide, ostensibly intending to have a word with the gentlemen from the Foreign Office before they departed.

He'd nominated them because they were standing in a group conveniently close to the terrace doors. Cutting smoothly through the other guests, he was aware that the countess and duchess were watching him with increasing agitation. By the time they realized he wasn't stopping to chat with the last group before the doors . . .

Ignoring the distant rustle of silks as they moved—too late—to intercept him, he strolled with his usual languid air out onto the terrace.

He barely paused to locate Caro and Leponte, then continued toward them. They stood by the balustrade some little way along, wreathed in shadow yet quite visible; the moon was nearly full. Approaching with lazy, unthreatening strides, he took in the prevailing tensions; Leponte stood close to Caro as she apparently admired the play of moonlight and shadow across the manicured lawns. He was not touching her, although one hand hovered, as if he'd intended to, but had been distracted.

Caro was, if not relaxed, then certainly assured—her usual calm and collected self. The tension that had gripped him faded; she clearly didn't need him to rescue her.

If anyone needed rescuing, it was Leponte.

That seemed plain as, hearing him, the Portuguese glanced his way. Befuddlement, utter and complete, etched his face.

Drawing near enough to hear their conversation—or rather, Caro's dissertation on the principles of landscape gardening as propounded by Capability Brown and his followers—Michael understood. He could almost find it in him to feel sorry for Ferdinand.

Caro sensed his approach, glanced his way, and smiled. "I was just explaining to Mr. Leponte that this garden was originally laid out by Capability Brown, and then improved more recently by Humphrey Repton. It's an amazing example of their combined talents, don't you think?"

Michael met her gaze, smiled lightly. "Indubitably."

She rattled on. The duchess and countess had paused in the drawing room doorway; Caro saw them and beckoned. For their part in Ferdinand's scheme to get her alone, she subjected them to a lecture on gardening that would have made an enthusiast wilt. The countess, looking highly conscious, tried to slip away; Caro linked her arm in hers and extolled the theories of coppicing in unrelenting detail.

Michael stood back and let her have her revenge; although she never stepped over any social line, he was quite certain it was that, and so were her victims. Ferdinand looked sheepish, but also thankful to have her attention deflected from him; Michael wondered just how ruthless she'd been in dismissing Ferdinand's advances.

Finally, the duchess, edging away, murmured that she had to return to her departing guests. Still enthusing, Caro consented to follow her back into the drawing room.

Ten minutes later, with the company thinning, he interrupted her eloquence. "We have a long drive ahead of us— we should join the exodus."

She glanced at him, met his gaze. Her eyes were beaten silver, quite impenetrable. Then she blinked, nodded. "Yes—I daresay you're right."

Five minutes more saw them taking leave of their hosts; Ferdinand walked with them to the carriage. When Caro paused before the open carriage door and gave him her hand, he bowed over it with courtly flair.

"My dear Mrs. Sutcliffe, I greatly look forward to being present at your ball." He straightened, met her eyes. "I will look forward to seeing the gardens of Sutcliffe Hall, and to your explanation of their wonders."

Michael gave the man credit for gumption—few others would have dared. Yet if he'd expected to discompose Caro, he'd misjudged.

She smiled, sweetly, and informed him, "I'm afraid you've misread the invitation. The ball is to be held at Bramshaw House, not Sutcliffe Hall."

Noting Ferdinand's surprise and the frown that followed it, the frown he quickly hid, Caro inclined her head, all graciousness. "I will look forward to seeing you and your party then."

Turning to the carriage, she accepted Michael's hand and climbed up. She sat on the seat facing forward. An instant later, he filled the doorway. He looked at her; in the dimness she couldn't see his face.

"Shift along."

She frowned, but he was already looming over her, waiting for her to move so he could sit beside her. An argument with Ferdinand still close enough to hear would be undignified.

Hiding a grimace, she did as he asked. He sat, far too close for her liking, and the footman shut the door. An instant later, the carriage rocked, and they were on their way.

They'd barely started along the drive when Michael asked, "Why was Leponte so put out that your ball will not be at Sutcliffe Hall?"

"I don't really know. He seems to have developed a fascination for Camden—studying what influences made him what he was."

"Leponte?"

Michael fell silent. She was acutely aware of the warmth of his large body on the seat beside her. Even though his thigh was not touching hers, she could sense its heat. As usual, his nearness made her feel peculiarly fragile. Delicate.

Finally, he said, "I find that hard to believe."

So did she. She lightly shrugged, and looked out at the shifting shadows of the forest. "Camden was, after all, extremely successful. Regardless of his present employ, I assume Ferdinand will ultimately step into his uncle's shoes. Perhaps that's why he's here—learning more."

Michael humphed and looked ahead. He didn't trust Leponte, not when it came to Caro, not in any respect; he'd assumed his distrust arose from the obvious source—from those primitive possessive instincts she aroused in him. Now, however, in light of the countess's and duchess's behavior, in view of that final moment beside the carriage, he was no longer so certain at least part of his distrust didn't spring from a more professional reaction.

He'd been prepared to accept and manage, even suppress, a distrust that arose from personal emotions; he was a consummate politician after all. Distrust that arose from prickling professional instincts was something else entirely—that could well be too dangerous to ignore, even for a short time.

Recognizing a landmark outside, gauging how much time they still had alone in the darkness of the carriage, he glanced at Caro. "What did you and Leponte talk about at table?"

She leaned against the plush cushions, through the dimness regarded him. "Initially it was the usual small talk, then he started on his tack as a Camden Sutcliffe accolyte with a detailed overview of Camden's career."

"Accurate, would you say?"

"In all respects he touched on, certainly."

He could tell by her tone, by the way she paused, that she was puzzled, too. Before he could prompt, she continued, "Then in the drawing room he asked about Sutcliffe Hall, theorizing that the place must have been significant to Camden."

Through the gloom, he studied her. "Was it?"

She shook her head. "I don't think so—I don't believe Camden thought so. I never detected any great attachment on his part."

"Hmm." He settled back, reached out and took her hand. Her fingers fluttered, then quieted; he curled his more firmly around them. "I think"—slowly he lifted her trapped hand to his lips—"that I'll be keeping an eye on Leponte at the ball, and wherever else we meet him."

She was watching; he could sense the tension spreading through her. Turning his head, through the gloom he caught her gaze. "For a number of excellent reasons."

He placed a chaste kiss on her knuckles.

She watched, then, gaze locked on her hand, drew in a tight breath. An instant passed, then, frowning, she lifted her eyes to his. "What—?"

He raised her hand again, lightly brushed his lips over her knuckles, then, eyes on hers, slowly, with the tip of his tongue, he traced them.

Her response was immediate and strong. A shudder racked her; she briefly closed her eyes.

Before she opened them, he shifted and pulled her to him,

his other hand rising to cup and frame her jaw, to angle her face so his lips could cover hers.

He was kissing her—and she was kissing him back—before she had a chance to retreat.

Releasing her hand, he reached for her, drew her more definitely to him. As before, her hands rose to his chest, tensed as if she would resist; he deepened the kiss, and her resistance never came.

Instead . . . gradually, step by subtle step, he coaxed not just acceptance but willing participation from her. Initially, she seemed to believe that after the first exchange he'd stop—she seemed to be waiting for him to do so. When he didn't, indeed made it perfectly clear he had no intention of not further indulging, tentatively, hesitantly, she joined him.

Her lips were soft, sweet, her mouth pure temptation; when she offered it, he rejoiced, and took, conscious that some part of her mind was watching, puzzled, almost surprised . . . why he couldn't imagine.

She was a delight, one he savored, stretching out the simple moments as he never had before.

He caressed, claimed, then teased, ultimately taunted and got the response—a more fiery, definite, passionate response—that he'd wanted, that he knew she had it in her to give. He wanted that and more—all she had to give—but was tactician enough to realize that with her, each step and stage had to be battled for and won.

The Merry Widow was not going to yield so much as one inch without a fight.

That, very likely, was why so many had failed with her. They'd assumed they could leap ahead, overlook the preliminaries, and instead had stumbled at the very first hurdle.

Kissing her.

If, as it seemed, for some mystical reason she'd got it into her head that she was hopeless at kissing . . . it was difficult to seduce a woman who wasn't willing to be kissed.

Secure in his victory, he drew her closer yet, angled his lips over hers. Her breasts brushed his chest; her arms started to slide over his shoulders, then stopped, tensed.

The carriage slowed, then turned into Bramshaw Lane.

With a gasp, she pulled back—enough to hiss his name in warning.

"*Sssh.*" Inexorably he drew her even deeper into his embrace. "You don't want to shock your coachman."

Her eyes flew wide. "Wh—"

He cut off her shocked question in the most efficient way. They had at least seven more minutes before they reached Bramshaw House; he intended to enjoy every one.

CHAPTER

8

Caro woke the next morning determined to regain control of her life. And her senses. Michael seemed intent on seizing both—to what end she didn't know—however, whatever, she was *not* going to be a party to it.

As she had been for the last half of their journey home from Leadbetter Hall.

Smothering a curse at her newfound susceptibility, at the tangle of curiosity, fascination, and schoolgirlish need that had allowed him to take such liberties and seduced her into participating as she had, she closed her room door, flicked her skirts straight, and headed for the stairs.

Breakfast and the fresh slate of a new day would give her all she needed to get her life back on track.

Gliding down the stairs, she inwardly grimaced. She was probably overreacting. It had only been a kiss—well, numerous rather warming kisses, but still, that was hardly cause for panic. For all she knew, he might have had enough, and she wouldn't even need to be on guard.

"Ah, there you are, m'dear." Sitting at the head of the dining table, Geoffrey looked up. He nodded to Elizabeth and Edward, both seated at the table, heads together, poring over a single sheet. "An invitation from the Prussians. They've asked me, too, but I'd rather not—other things to do. I'll leave the giddy dissipation to you."

That last was said with a fond smile that included both her

and Elizabeth; while Geoffrey delighted in his family's social prominence, since Alice's death he no longer himself cared for any but the most simple entertainments.

Catten held Caro's chair at the other end of the table; she sat, reached for the teapot with one hand, and imperiously held out the other for the invitation.

Edward handed it to her. "An impromptu alfresco luncheon—by which I assume they mean a picnic."

She glanced at the single sheet. "Hmm. Lady Kleber is first cousin to the Grand Duchess, and is something of a figure in her own right." Lady Kleber had written personally, inviting them to join what she described as "a select company."

There was, of course, no chance of refusing. Quite aside from the discourtesy involved, the general's wife was only returning Caro's hospitality; it had been she who had started this round of entertainments with her dinner to rescue Elizabeth.

Sipping her tea, she suppressed her frown. There was no point trying to escape the outcome of her own scheming. All she could do was hope, almost certainly in vain, that Michael wasn't one of Lady Kleber's selections.

"Can we go?" Elizabeth asked, eyes shining, eagerness transparent. "It's a perfect day."

"Of course we'll go." Caro glanced again at the invitation. "Crabtree House." To Edward, she explained, "That's the other side of Eyeworth Wood. It'll take half an hour by carriage. We should leave at noon."

Edward nodded. "I'll order the barouche."

Caro nibbled her toast, then finished her tea. They all rose from the table together; once in the hall, they went their separate ways—Geoffrey to his study, Edward to speak with the coachman. Elizabeth went to practice her piano pieces—more, Caro suspected, so Edward would know where to find her and have an excuse to linger than from any desire to improve her playing.

The cynical assessment had floated into her mind without conscious thought; it was almost certainly accurate, yet . . . she shook her head. She was becoming too jaded, too scheming—far too much like Camden in her dealings with the world.

Regretfully she dismissed the desperate notion that had blossomed in her mind. There was no situation she could conjure to ensure that Michael would be otherwise engaged for the afternoon.

Reblocking the stream was out of the question.

They turned into the drive of Crabtree House just after half past twelve. Another carriage was ahead of them; they waited while Ferdinand descended and handed the countess down. Then the carriage rumbled on and theirs took its place before the front steps.

Handed down by Edward, Caro went forward, smiling, to greet their hostess. She shook hands with Lady Kleber, answered her polite queries and made Geoffrey's excuses, then greeted the countess while Elizabeth curtsied and Edward made his bow.

"Come, come." Lady Kleber waved them along the front of the house. "We will go onto the terrace and be comfortable while we await the others."

Caro strolled beside the countess, engaging in the usual pleasantries. Elizabeth walked with Lady Kleber; Edward and Ferdinand brought up the rear. Glancing back as she gained the terrace, Caro saw Edward explaining something to Ferdinand. She'd been surprised Ferdinand hadn't sought her attention—clearly he'd remembered Edward had been Camden's aide.

Cynically amused, she followed the countess. Tables and chairs had been set to allow the guests to enjoy the pleasant vista of the semiformal rear garden ringed by the deeper green of Eyeworth Wood.

She sat with the countess; Elizabeth and Lady Kleber joined them. The general emerged from the house; after genially greeting all the ladies, he joined Edward and Ferdinand at another table.

The conversation was brisk; Lady Kleber, the countess, and Caro discussed impressions gained during the recent Season. Their subjects ranged from diplomatic suspicions to the latest fashions. Exchanging observations, Caro wondered, as she had increasingly over the past hours, if Michael had been invited.

She'd half expected him to appear at Bramshaw House and claim a place in the carriage, but such an action would have surprised even Geoffrey—Eyeworth Manor was closer to Crabtree House than Bramshaw was. To join them, he'd have ridden in quite the wrong direction; clearly he'd decided against that tack.

Assuming he'd been invited.

She glanced across as footsteps heralded further arrivals—but it was the Polish chargé d'affaires with his wife, son, and daughter. Caro appreciated Lady Kleber's forethought in inviting the younger pair—they made a natural foursome with Elizabeth and Edward, much to Ferdinand's transparent disgust; he had to swallow it, bow to the ladies, and let Edward escape.

She continued to chat and watch as others arrived. No Russians, of course, but the Swedish ambassador, Verolstadt, his wife, and their two daughters joined them, followed by two of the general's aides-de-camp and their wives.

Caro inwardly frowned. Lady Kleber was an experienced diplomatic hostess, unfailingly correct; she possessed none of her more famous relative's eccentricities. So she *should* have invited Michael. Not only was he the local Member, but she must have heard the rumors. . . .

The minutes ticked by; surrounded by glib conversation, Caro grew increasingly concerned. If Michael was to move to the Foreign Office, he needed to be present at affairs such as this—the more informal, relaxed, private entertainments at which personal links were forged. He needed to be here— he ought to have been invited . . . she tried to think of some excuse to inquire. . . .

"Ah—and here is Mr. Anstruther-Wetherby!" Lady Kleber rose, a patently delighted smile wreathing her face.

Swinging around, Caro saw Michael walking up from the stables. She hadn't heard the crunch of hooves on the drive—he'd ridden over through the forest. She watched him greet Lady Kleber, and felt distinctly irritated over her earlier worry; he clearly needed no champion in the diplomatic sphere. When he wished, he could be disgustingly charming; she watched him smile at the countess and bow over her hand, and inwardly humphed.

Quietly handsome, assured, subtly dominant, his brand of charm was far more effective than Ferdinand's.

Her gaze flicked to Ferdinand; he was edging her way, positioning himself so he'd be able to claim her side when the party descended to the lawn. Glancing around, she looked for escape . . . and realized there wasn't any—other than . . .

She looked at Michael; had he lost interest in pursuing her?

Him or Ferdinand—which would be wiser? Lady Kleber had told them the picnic was to be held in a clearing a little way into the forest; Caro knew the way there—a gentle stroll, and they would hardly be alone. . . .

The decision was taken out of her hands. Via a maneuver she had to admit was masterful, she was the last person Michael greeted.

"Good, good! Now we are all here, we may go and enjoy our picnic, *ja?*" Beaming, Lady Kleber waved to the lawn, then circled, determinedly shooing them off the terrace.

Having just shaken Caro's hand, Michael retained it. Looking into her eyes, he smiled. "Shall we?" Smoothly, he drew her to her feet.

Her senses flickered, and it wasn't, this time, simply due to his nearness. There'd been a glint of steel behind the blue of his eyes, and his grip on her hand, the restrained power behind his claiming of her company . . . he definitely hadn't given up the chase.

He anchored her hand on his sleeve, then looked at Ferdinand. "Ah, Leponte—do join us."

Ferdinand did, very readily, yet it was Michael who had her arm. As they descended to the lawn, then set out in train with the others to stroll to the clearing, she wondered what he was up to—what new tack he was taking with Ferdinand.

They entered the trees following a well-beaten path. She caught the movement as Michael glanced over her head at Ferdinand.

"I understand you're something of a disciple of Camden Sutcliffe?"

Direct attack—more usually a political than a diplomatic gambit, perhaps in this instance to be expected. She glanced at Ferdinand, saw color tinge his olive skin.

He nodded, a touch curtly. "As you say. Sutcliffe's career is a pattern card for those of us who seek to make our way in the diplomatic arena." Ferdinand met Michael's steady regard. "Surely you would agree? Sutcliffe was, after all, your countryman."

"True." Michael let his lips curve. "But I'm more politically inclined than diplomatically so."

That, he felt, was fair warning; there was a great deal of ruthless cut-and-thrust in politics, while diplomacy was by definition more a matter of negotiation. Looking ahead, he nodded toward the Polish chargé d'affaires. "If you truly want to learn about Sutcliffe and what shaped him, you're in luck—Sutcliffe's first appointment was to Poland. Kosminsky was a junior aide in the Polish Foreign Ministry at the time; his professional acquaintance with Sutcliffe dates from '86. I understand they remained in touch."

Ferdinand's gaze had locked on the dapper little Pole chatting with General Kleber. There was a fractional hesitation while he manufactured a suitably delighted mien. "Really?"

His features lit, his eyes didn't. They were curiously flat when he met Michael's gaze.

Michael smiled, and didn't bother to make the gesture charming—or even all that pleasant. "Really."

Caro understood his meaning; she surreptitiously pinched his arm. He glanced down at her, a silent *What?* in his eyes.

Hers flared warningly, then, apparently distracted, she looked into the trees. She pointed. "Look! A jay!"

Everyone stopped, looked, peered, but of course no one else except Edward saw the elusive bird. Which only confirmed that Edward was both loyal and exceedingly quick-witted.

On the other hand, he'd had five years to grow used to his employer's little tricks.

She had more than her fair share of them, Michael had to grant her that. By the time she'd explained to Ferdinand what jays were, and why spotting one was so exciting—something he himself hadn't fully appreciated—they'd reached the picnic site.

It was instantly apparent that the English vision of a picnic—hampers of food spread on cloths with rugs strewn about on which to sit—had not translated directly into Prussian. Various chairs had been grouped about the clearing; along one side, a trestle table groaned beneath numerous silver dishes and a complement of plates, cutlery, glassware, wines, and cordials that would have done a formal luncheon proud. There was even a silver epergne set in the center of the display. A butler and three footmen hovered, ready to serve.

Despite the relative formality, the party achieved a pleasantly relaxed ambience, due largely to Lady Kleber's efforts, ably assisted by Caro, Mrs. Kosminsky and, surprisingly, the countess.

That last put him on guard; there was something going on, some ongoing connection between the Portuguese and Camden Sutcliffe, although of what nature he couldn't yet guess. The countess's uncharacteristically cheery behavior made him even more determined to keep his eye on Ferdinand—her nephew.

He pretended not to see the countess's first two attempts to attract his notice. Sticking to Caro's side—something she seemed to be growing more accustomed to—plate in hand, he moved with her as she circulated, group to group, while they all savored the meats, fruits, and delicacies Lady Kleber had provided.

Caro's agenda quickly became clear; personally, she didn't have one—her application was entirely on his behalf. She was patently intent on using her considerable contacts and even more formidable talents to smooth his way, to give him a step up into what had been her world, a world in which she still, if not reigned, then at least wielded a certain power. Her unsolicited support warmed him; he tucked the feeling away to savor later and focused his attention—more than he most likely would have if left to his own devices—on making the most of the opportunities she created for him to make those personal connections that were, at bedrock, what international diplomacy most surely relied on.

The company had disposed of the last strawberry and the footmen were packing away the plates when he felt a gentle touch on his arm. Turning, he looked into the countess's dark eyes.

"My dear Mr. Anstruther-Wetherby, dare I claim a few minutes of your time?"

Her smile was assured; he couldn't very well deny her. With an easy gesture, he replied, "You perceive me all ears, Countess."

"Such a strange English saying." Claiming his arm, she waved to two chairs set at one side of the clearing. "But come—I have messages from my husband and the duke, and must discharge my duty."

He had his doubts about the importance of her messages, yet her citing of duty struck an oddly true note. What was going on?

Regardless of his curiosity, he was acutely conscious of being led away from Caro. He would have made some effort to include her, even in the teeth of the countess's clear wish for a private discussion, but when he glanced around, he saw Ferdinand deep in conversation with Kosminsky.

The little Pole was in full flight; Ferdinand was presently engaged.

Relieved on that score, he went without argument, waiting while the countess settled in one chair, then sitting in the other.

She fixed her dark eyes on his. "Now . . ."

Caro glanced at Michael, leaning forward, relaxed yet focused on whatever the countess was telling him.

"Sure you won't come?"

She looked back at Edward. He met her eyes, flicked his gaze to Ferdinand and back, then raised his brows.

"Ah—no." Caro looked past him at the youthful group heading down the path that led to a pretty dell.

The afternoon had grown warm; the air beneath the trees was heavy, redolent with the scents of the forest. Most of the older guests were showing definite signs of settling for a postprandial nap, all except Mr. Kosminsky and Ferdinand, and Michael and the countess, who were absorbed with their discussions.

"I'll . . . sit with Lady Kleber."

Edward looked unimpressed by her strategy. "If you're sure?"

"Yes, yes." She flicked her hands, shooing him toward where Elizabeth and Miss Kosminsky dallied, waiting for him. "Go and enjoy your ramble. I'm perfectly capable of dealing with Ferdinand."

Edward's last look plainly said, *In this setting?* but he knew better than to argue. Turning, he joined the girls; within minutes, the group had disappeared along the path through the trees.

Caro rejoined Lady Kleber, Mrs. Kosminsky, and Mrs. Verolstadt. Their talk, however, quickly became desultory, then faded altogether. A few minutes later, a gentle snore stirred the air.

All three older ladies had their eyes closed, their heads back. Caro glanced swiftly around the clearing; most others, too, had succumbed—only Kosminsky and Ferdinand and Michael and the countess were still awake.

She had a choice—pretend to fall asleep, too, and fall victim to whichever of the two men pursuing her first came, like Sleeping Beauty's prince, to wake her—as she would wager her best pearls they would—or . . .

Quietly rising, she drifted around the chairs—and kept drifting, silent, wraithlike, until the trees closed around her, and she was out of sight.

Quite what she'd hoped to achieve—by the time she reached the stream, sanity had returned.

Sinking onto a flat rock nicely warmed by the sunshine, she frowned at the rippling stream and decided it had been her vision of Sleeping Beauty, trapped, forced to wait and accept the attentions of whichever handsome prince turned up to press a kiss to her lips . . . it really had been too reminiscent of her own situation, so she'd done what any sane woman would have—even Sleeping Beauty if she'd had the chance. She'd upped stakes and run.

The problem was that she couldn't run far, and was therefore in danger of being run to earth by one or the other of her princes—pursuers. On top of that, one knew this piece of forest even better than she.

Worse still, if she was destined to be caught by one, and had to choose, she wasn't sure which of them she should opt for. In this setting, Ferdinand would be difficult to manage; Edward had been right there. However, regardless, Ferdinand had little chance of sweeping her off her feet and into any illicit embrace. Michael, on the other hand . . .

She knew which of the two was more truly dangerous to her. Unfortunately, he was the one with whom she felt immeasurably safer.

A conundrum—one for which her considerable experience had not prepared her.

The distant snap of a twig alerted her; concentrating, she heard a definite footfall. Someone was approaching along the path she'd taken from the clearing. Quickly, she scanned her surroundings; a thicket of elder growing before an ancient birch offered the best hope of safe concealment.

Rising, she hurriedly climbed the bank. Circling the thicket, she discovered the densely growing elder did not extend to the trunk of the massive birch, but instead formed a palisade screening anyone standing under the birch from the stream. Beyond the birch the ground rose steadily; she might be visible from higher on the bank, yet if she stood in front of the birch . . .

Slipping into the screened space, she took up a position before the huge birch trunk and peered toward the stream. Almost immediately, a man came striding along the bank; all she glimpsed through the elder leaves was a shoulder, the flash of a hand—not enough to be certain who he was.

He halted; she sensed he was looking around.

Stretching this way and that, she tried to get a better sight of him—then he moved and she realized he was scanning the bank, the area where she stood, simultaneously realized the coat she'd glimpsed was dark blue. Ferdinand; Michael was wearing brown.

She held her breath, still, eyes locked on where Ferdinand stood . . . childhood games of hide-and-seek had never felt so intense.

For long moments, all was silent, unmoving, the heavy heat beneath the trees a muffling blanket. She became aware of her breathing, of the beat of her heart . . . and, suddenly, a disconcerting ruffling of her senses.

Those senses abruptly flared; she knew he was there before she actually felt him, moving silently toward her from around the tree. Knew who he was before his large hand slid around her waist; he didn't urge her back against him—her feet didn't move—yet suddenly he was there, all heat and strength at her back, his hard body, his solid masculine frame all but surrounding her.

She hadn't been breathing before; she couldn't now. A rush of warmth flooded her. Giddiness threatened.

Raising a hand, she closed it over his at her waist. Felt his grip firm in response. He bent his head; his lips traced the sensitive skin below her ear. Suppressing a reactive shiver, she heard his whisper, low, deep, yet faintly amused, "Stay still. He hasn't seen us."

She turned her head, leaned back into him, intending to tartly tell him "I know"—instead, her gaze collided with his. Then lowered to his lips, mere inches from hers . . .

They were already so close their breaths mingled; it seemed strangely sensible—meant to be—that they shifted, adjusted, closed the distance, that he kissed her and she kissed him even though they were both highly conscious that mere yards away Ferdinand Leponte searched for her.

That fact kept the kiss light, lips brushing, caressing, firming even while they both continued to listen.

Eventually came the sounds they were waiting for, a faint curse in Portuguese followed by the sound of Ferdinand's footsteps retreating.

Relief swept Caro, softening her spine; she relaxed. Before she could collect her wits and retreat, Michael seized the moment, juggled and turned her fully into his arms, closed them about her, parted her lips and slid into the honeyed cavern of her mouth.

And took, tasted, tantalized . . . and she was with him, following his script, content, it seemed, both to allow and appreciate the slowly escalating intimacy that each successive encounter brought. Wrought. A reflection of the steadily escalating desire building within him and, he was sure, in her.

He felt confident of that last even though she was extremely difficult to read, and apparently set on denying it.

Recalling that, recalling his real purpose in coming after her, and accepting that greater privacy would be wise, he reluctantly eased back from the kiss.

Lifting his head, he looked into her face, watched the shadows of emotions swim through her eyes as she blinked and reassembled her wits.

Then she glared, stiffened, and pushed back from his embrace.

Managing to keep his lips straight, he let her go, but caught her hand, stopping her from stalking off.

She frowned at his hand, locked about hers, then lifted a chilly gaze to his face. "I should return to the clearing."

He raised his brows. "Leponte is lurking somewhere between the clearing and here—are you sure you want to risk running into him . . . alone, under the trees . . ."

Any lingering doubts over how she saw Leponte—any inclination to view the man as a rival—were banished, reduced to ashes by the aggravation in her eyes, by the nature of her hesitation. Her gaze remained locked with his; her expression eased from haughty dismissal to exasperation.

Before she could formulate some other plan, he said, "I was on my way to check the pond, to make sure the stream is still running freely. You may as well come with me."

She hesitated, making no secret that she was weighing the risks of accompanying him against those of inadvertently running into Leponte. Unwilling to utter any promise or assurance he had no intention of keeping, he kept silent and waited.

Eventually, she grimaced. "All right."

Nodding, he turned away so she wouldn't see his smile. Hand in hand, they left the protection of the elders and headed further along the stream.

She threw him a suspicious glance. "I thought you said the stream was unblocked?"

"It was, but as I'm here"—he glanced at her—"with nothing better to do, I thought I'd make sure we've got the problem permanently fixed."

He walked on, leading her deeper into the forest.

The pond was well known to locals, but as it was buried deep in Eyeworth Wood, a segment of the forest and part of his lands, few others knew or even suspected its existence. It was located in a narrow valley, and the surrounding vegetation was dense, less easy to penetrate than the tracts of open forest.

Ten minutes of tramping along forest paths brought them to the pond's edge. Fed by the stream, it was deep enough for the surface to appear glassy and still. At dawn and dusk, the pond drew forest animals large and small; in midafternoon, the heat—not as heavy here, yet still considerable—wrapped the scene in somnolence. They were the only creatures awake, the only ones moving.

They glanced around, drinking in the quiet beauty, then, still holding Caro's hand, Michael led the way around the bank to where the stream exited the pond.

It was gurgling merrily, the sound a delicate tinkling melody falling into the forest silence.

Halting at the stream's head, he pointed to a spot ten yards along. "A tree had lodged there—presumably it came down in winter. There was debris built up around it, almost a dam. We hauled out the tree and the worst of it, and hoped the stream would clear the rest itself."

She studied the free-flowing water. "It seems to have done so."

He nodded, gripped her hand and stepped back. Drew her back with him—without warning released her hand, locked his about her waist, lifted and whirled her; setting her down at the base of a huge oak, her back to the bole, he bent his head and kissed her.

Thoroughly this time.

He sensed her gasp—knew she tried to summon and cling to outrage—felt a spurt of very masculine delight when she failed utterly. When despite her clear intent to resist she instead met his thrusting tongue, when within seconds her lips firmed and, for her almost boldly, with that lick of elusive passion, not only met his demands, but seemed intent on gaining more.

The result was a kiss, a succession of increasingly heated exchanges that, to his considerable surprise, evolved into a sensual game of a type he'd never played before. It took him some moments—it took effort to tear even a part of his mind free enough to think—before he realized what was different.

She might not have had much experience kissing, believing, wrongly, that she didn't know how; he'd expected her, once he'd seduced her thus far, to be eager to learn—as indeed she was. What he hadn't expected was her attitude, her approach to that learning, yet now he was dealing with it, lips to lips, mouth to mouth, tongue to tongue, it was, indeed, pure Caro.

He was starting to realize she did not possess an acquiescent bone in her body. If she agreed, she went forward, determined and resolute; if she disagreed, she would resist equally trenchantly.

But being acquiescent, going along with something without any real commitment, was simply not Caro.

Now he'd forced her to face the question, she'd obviously decided to take him up on his offer to teach her to kiss. Indeed, she seemed intent on getting him to teach her more—her lips, her responses, were increasingly demanding. Commanding. Matching him, step by step, meeting him toe to toe.

If the complete capture of his senses, the total immersion of his attention in the exchange, the increasingly definite reaction of his body were anything to go by, she didn't need any more teaching.

Abruptly, he pulled back, broke the kiss, aware of just how dangerously insistent his own desire was growing. Aware of the rising beat in his blood. He lifted his head only inches, waited until her lids fluttered, then rose—searched her silver eyes.

He needed to know if she was where he thought she was, if he was reading her responses accurately. What he saw . . . was at first surprising, then intensely gratifying. A degree of amazement—almost wonder—lit her lovely eyes. Her lips were full, a lusher pink, slightly swollen; her expression turned considering, assessing, yet he sensed beneath it all that she was pleased.

She cleared her throat; her gaze dropped to his lips before she quickly raised it and attempted to frown at him. She tried to ease back, but the bole was behind her. "I—"

He swooped, cut her off, shut her up. Shifted closer and slowly, deliberately, pinned her against the tree.

Felt her fingers tense on his shoulders, then ease.

She'd been about to protest, to insist they stop and rejoin the others—it was what she'd feel she had to say. Not necessarily what she wanted.

Most of her would-be suitors, he would wager, had failed to grasp that point. Caro played by the social rules; while she was an expert at bending them to her cause, she also felt bound by them. She'd been married for nine years; she would have got into the habit of refusing all invitations to dalliance. Her reaction was doubtless now ingrained; as he'd just proved, the only way to get inside her defenses was to ignore them, and the rules, entirely.

Simply act—and give her the opportunity to react. If she'd truly wished to stop, she would have struggled, resisted; instead, as he deepened the kiss and, leaning one shoulder against the tree, eased her body against his, she slid her arms up and twined them about his neck.

Caro clung to him, drank in his kiss, brazenly kissed him back—and ignored the tiny, dwindling voice of reason that kept insisting this was wrong. Not only wrong, but seriously, dangerously stupid. Right now, she didn't care, swept away on a tide of exultation she'd never before experienced—never expected to experience.

Michael truly *wanted* to kiss her. Not once, not twice, but many times. More, he seemed . . . she didn't know what the burgeoning compulsion she sensed in him truly was, but the word that came to mind was "hungry."

Hungry for her, for her lips, for her mouth, to take and savor as much as she would allow. As he could seduce her to allow, yet in terms of seduction, to her his very wanting was the ultimate temptation. Just as well he didn't know, and she was far too wise to tell him.

His lips, hard and commanding, on hers, the way his tongue filled her mouth, savoring and caressing, then retreated, luring her to reciprocate, was no longer an education but a fascination. A sensual delight she, now reassured, could indulge in and enjoy.

The notion of kissing—at least kissing Michael—no longer filled her with dread. Instead . . .

Shifting her hands, she spread her fingers, speared them through his thick locks, and gripped, holding his head steady so she could more forcefully press a deep, soul-satisfying kiss on him. A curious heat was building within her; she let it rise and suffuse her, pour through her—and into him.

His reaction was immediate, a surge of ravenous hunger that was acutely satisfying. She met it, urged him on—felt her whole body tighten deliciously when he sank deep into her mouth and plundered.

Indeed, her body seemed to heat even more; the warmth spread in greedy licks beneath her skin. Her breasts felt tight . . . the weight of his chest against them was curiously soothing, yet not enough.

He suddenly increased the intensity of their exchange with a flagrantly incendiary kiss—one that curled her toes and left parts of her she'd never imagined could be affected throbbing.

Her breasts ached—then he eased back. She gathered her wits to protest—

His hand at her waist released, glided up and settled, hard and definite, his palm spread over her breast.

Her protest died, frozen in her mind. Panic awoke with a jerk—

His hand closed, firm, commanding; her senses splintered. The odd ache eased, then swelled anew.

Eased again as he caressed, kneaded.

For one instant she teetered, uncertain . . . then heat rose in a wave, rushed through her—and he kissed her more deeply, she kissed him back, openly sharing, and his fingers firmed again.

Panic was smothered beneath a welling tide of sensation; deep and very real curiosity held it down. He'd succeeded in teaching her how to kiss. Perhaps he would, perhaps he could, teach her more. . . .

Michael knew the instant she decided to allow him to caress her; he felt no inward smirk, only heartfelt gratitude. He needed the contact as much as she; she might have starved for years, yet his desire was, at least at this point, the more urgent.

That, he promised himself, would change—he had a very definite vision of what he wanted from her—but that time was not yet. For now . . .

He kept his lips on hers, artfully distracting her every time he edged their intimacy deeper. Instincts prodded him to open her bodice, to savor her exquisitely fine skin, yet they were standing in the middle of the woods and too soon would need to return to the picnic clearing.

That last prompted him to gradually lighten the kiss, until, without jarring her, he could lift his head and study her face while he continued to caress her. He needed to know her thoughts, her reactions, so he would know how and where to recommence when next they met.

When next he managed to whisk her away and trap her in his arms.

Her lashes fluttered; her lids opened a fraction. Her eyes, bright silver, met his. Neither of them was breathing all that evenly. The first step toward intimacy—the inital commitment to explore what might be—had definitely been taken; their gazes touched, acknowledged.

Caro drew in a tight breath, eased her hands from his

neck, his shoulders, and looked down—at his hand, large, strong, long fingers skillfully caressing her breast, circling her now tightly furled nipple, sending sensation streaking through her, leaving her nerves tight, tense, skittering. Her fine voile dress was no real barrier; taking her pebbled nipple between his fingertips, he gently squeezed.

She sucked in a breath. Closed her eyes, let her head fall back—then forced her lids open again and fixed her gaze on his face. His lean, austerely handsome face. If she could have frowned, she would have; she had to content herself with a studiously blank expression. "I didn't say you could . . . do this."

His hand closed again. "You didn't say I couldn't, either."

A faint frown finally came; she narrowed her eyes on his. "Are you saying I can't trust you anymore?"

His face hardened, so did his eyes, but his hand never faltered in its languid caressing. He studied her for a moment, then said, "You can trust me—always. That I promise. But I'll also promise more." His hand firmed about her breast; his eyes held hers. "I won't promise to behave as you expect." His gaze lowered to her lips; he leaned closer. "Only as you want. Only as you deserve."

She would have frowned harder and argued, but he kissed her. Not with ravenous heat, but in a straightforward, deeply satisfying exchange. One that left her social conscience feeling somehow appeased, as if there was no reason she couldn't simply accept all that had happened between them, adult to adult, and leave it at that.

Despite his high-handed, domineering behavior, she didn't feel overwhelmed. She knew, absolutely, that he would never hurt or harm her, that if she struggled, he would release her . . . both actions and words suggested he simply wasn't going to let her deny him, or herself, purely on the grounds of social strictures.

If she wanted to deny him, she'd need to convince him she really didn't want to fall in with his plans. Simple enough—except . . .

Her head was pleasurably swimming, her mind detached, her body warm and heated under his hand.

Suddenly, he broke the kiss. Lifting his head, he looked past her, past the tree. She turned her head, but couldn't see past the bole.

He'd frozen—all except his fondling fingers. She drew in a tight breath, about to ask what was there—his gaze flicked back to her face, his eyes widening in warning.

Then, swift and silent, he moved, stepping to her side, turning and drawing her with him around the tree; he ended with his back to the bole, more or less to the pond itself, while she stood trapped against him, her back to his chest, facing away from the pond, shielded from whatever danger threatened.

Glancing over her shoulder, she saw him looking over his, peering around the tree toward the pond. Then he looked back, met her gaze. Lowering his head, he nudged hers until he could whisper in her ear, "Ferdinand. Keep quiet. He doesn't know we're here."

She blinked. He straightened again; she sensed he was keeping watch, yet . . . while his attention had diverted and his fingers had slowed, they hadn't stopped. Her skin still felt hot, her breasts tight, her nerves jangling.

Worse, his other hand had risen to minister in apparently absentminded concert.

It was, she discovered, extremely difficult to think.

Regardless, she couldn't protest.

Minutes of nerve-tingling tension passed, then the alertness gripping him eased. He turned back to her, leaned close, and whispered, "He's heading away from us."

Valiantly ignoring the preoccupation of his hands, she turned and peered past him, and glimpsed Ferdinand striding into the forest, following a path leading away from the pond's opposite side.

Michael had seen, too. He caught her eye, closed his hands firmly, then eased his hold, trailing his palms down her body as he released her.

She dragged in a fractionally deeper breath.

He studied her eyes, then bent his head and kissed her— one last time. An ending, and a promise—until next time.

Lifting his head, he met her gaze. "We'd better get back."

She nodded. "Indeed."

They set out around the pond; when they reached the opening of the path that led back toward the clearing, she paused, looking further around the pond to the path Ferdinand had taken. "He's going the wrong way."

Michael met her gaze; his jaw hardened. "He's a grown man."

"Yes, *but*—" She looked down the other path. "You know how easy it is to get lost in here. And if he does wander off and lose his way, the whole company will get caught up trying to find him."

She was right. He sighed, and waved toward the other path. "Come on—he can't be far ahead."

With a quick smile in acknowledgment of his capitulation, she led the way. Fifty yards on, the path hit a downward slope badly crisscrossed with roots; he stepped past her and went ahead, giving her his hand to ensure she didn't slip.

They were concentrating on their descent, not speaking but watching their feet, when low voices reached them. They paused, looked ahead; both knew another small clearing opened to the side of the path a little way along.

He glanced back, put his finger to his lips. Frowning, Caro nodded. This was his land, but it wasn't fenced; he'd never prevented locals from using it. But they'd both caught the furtive note of the murmured conversation; it seemed wise not to walk into a situation where they might not be welcome. Especially not with Caro by his side; there were at least two men, possibly more.

Luckily, it was easy to step off the narrow path, then continue between the trees. The undergrowth was sufficient to screen them. Eventually they reached a spot where they could look through a large bush into the clearing.

In it, Ferdinand stood talking to two men. They were slight, rather weaselly, dressed in threadbare frieze. They were definitely not Ferdinand's friends; from their interaction, however, it seemed likely they were his employees.

Michael and Caro had arrived too late to hear any of the discussion, just assurances from the weaselly two that they would perform whatever job Ferdinand had hired them for, and Ferdinand's curt, aristocratic dismissal. That delivered, he turned on his heel and walked back out of the clearing.

They held still and watched him stride away, back toward the pond.

Caro tugged at Michael's sleeve; he looked back in time to see the two strange men disappearing along another path, one that led to the main road.

Caro opened her mouth—he held up a hand. Waited. Only when he was sure Ferdinand should be far enough away so that he couldn't hear their voices did he lower his hand and meet Caro's wide gaze.

"What on earth was all that about?"

"Indeed." Taking her arm, he guided her back to the path.

"I wondered at first if they could possibly be the men who attacked Miss Trice—although why Ferdinand would be talking to them I can't imagine—but they were too thin, don't you think?"

He nodded. They'd been about the same distance from the men who'd attacked Miss Trice; the pair in the clearing had been too short as well. He said so; Caro agreed.

They walked briskly for a while, then she said, "Why would Ferdinand, if he wanted to hire some men, meet them in . . . well, such secrecy? And even more, why *here*? We're miles from Leadbetter Hall."

The very questions he'd been pondering. "I have no idea."

The picnic site came into view. They heard voices—the younger guests had returned from their excursion, and their elders had revived. He paused, then stepped sideways off the path into the relative privacy afforded by a large bush.

Tugged after him, Caro looked at him in surprise.

He met her gaze. "I think we can safely conclude that Ferdinand is up to something—possibly something the duke and duchess, at least, might not be aware of or approve of."

She nodded. "But what?"

"Until we know more, we'll have to keep our eyes open, and be on guard." He bent his head and kissed her—one last, very last kiss.

He'd intended it to remind her, to stir her memories back

to life for just an instant; unfortunately, her response had the same effect on him, and left him aching.

Biting back a curse, he lifted his head, met her eyes. "Remember—when it comes to Ferdinand, be on guard."

She studied his eyes, his face, then smiled reassuringly and patted his shoulder. "Yes, of course."

With that, she turned, stepped back onto the path, and led the way into the clearing. His gaze locking on her swaying hips, he mentally swore, then followed, strolling as nonchalantly as he could in her wake.

CHAPTER
9

Michael debated whether or not to alert Geoffrey to their suspicions regarding Ferdinand. He spent a restless night, not, admittedly, primarily due to that concern. Then, during breakfast, a note from Geoffrey arrived asking him to dine with the family that evening.

The invitation was clearly a sign from the gods. He rode to Bramshaw House as the sun sank behind the trees and the day eased into a balmy evening. Aside from all else, when he and Caro had reentered the clearing, Ferdinand had been questioning Edward. He wanted to learn what Leponte's interest had been; he was sure Caro would have interrogated Edward.

Reaching Bramshaw House, he rode straight to the stable. Leaving Atlas there, he strode up to the house and found Geoffrey in his study.

Upstairs, Caro sat before her dressing table and idly poked at her hair. She was gowned and coiffed for dinner, not that this evening called for any great degree of sartorial accomplishment—it would be just the family. Her gown of pale gold silk was an old favorite; she'd donned it because it soothed her. Calmed and reassured her.

For the last twenty-four hours, she'd been . . . distracted.

Michael had surprised her. First by actively *wanting* to kiss her again and again. Then by wanting rather more. Even further, she was starting to suspect he might want more still, might possibly come to truly *desire* that.

Desire was a type of hunger, wasn't it? The notion that it could be what she sensed in him, welling and growing while they exchanged heated kisses, was too stunning and eye-opening a possibility to ignore.

Could it be so? Did he truly, absolutely and honestly, want her—*desire* her—in that way?

Part of her scoffed, contemptuously deriding the idea as pure fantasy; the more vulnerable part of her desperately wanted it to be true. Being in a position to actively consider that question was a novel development all its own.

One thing was clear. After their interlude by the pond, she had a decision to face: To go forward or stop, to say yes or no. If he did want more, should she, would she, agree?

That decision should have been easy enough for a twenty-eight-year-old unremarried relict of a political marriage to a much older man. Unfortunately, in her case, there were complications, definite complications, yet for the first time in her life she wasn't convinced she should reject the opportunity Michael *might* lay before her out of hand.

That uncertainty was unprecedented; it was what had kept her distracted all day.

Gentlemen had been offering to indulge in affairs with her for the past ten years—virtually since her marriage—yet this was the first time she'd felt even remotely tempted. All those others . . . she'd never been convinced their desire for her was any more real than Camden's had been, that they weren't instead driven by some more worldly motive, like boredom or simply the thrill of the chase, or even by political considerations. Not one of them had so much as truly kissed her, not as Michael had.

Thinking back . . . at no point had Michael asked her permission. If she'd understood him correctly, if she didn't specifically say "no," he was going to take her silence as "yes." That approach had worked, for both of them. Despite her reservations, he hadn't done anything, led her to do anything, she regretted. Quite the opposite. What they had done was driving her to contemplate doing a great deal more.

How far would he go before he lost interest? She had no idea, yet if he truly wanted her, desired her . . . didn't she owe it to herself to find out?

The sound of the gong reverberated through the house, summoning them to the drawing room. With a last glance at the at-present-relatively-neat corona of her hair, she rose and headed for the door. She'd resume her cogitations later; clearly it would be wise to have a firm idea of how she was going to deal with Michael before he next managed to get her alone.

Michael heard the gong and abandoned his well-meant but ill-fated attempt to alert Geoffrey to the potential threat emanating from Ferdinand Leponte. His fault, not Geoffrey's; he hadn't possessed sufficient hard facts to prod Geoffrey's less-well-honed instincts into action.

Although he'd been the local Member for a decade, Geoffrey had never been touched by the darker side of politics. When Michael had described Leponte's rabid interest in Camden Sutcliffe's personal life, Geoffrey had raised his brows. "How odd." He'd sipped his sherry, then added, "Perhaps George should show him around Sutcliffe Hall."

After that, he hadn't bothered mentioning Leponte's meeting with the two strangers in the forest. Geoffrey would probably suggest they were runners for Southampton bookmakers. Which could be true; he just didn't think it likely. Leponte was intent on something, but it wasn't which nag won the Derby.

Bowing to fate, he'd turned their conversation to a discussion of local affairs, none of which were in any way alarming.

"There's the gong." Geoffrey got to his feet.

Rising, Michael set down his glass and joined him; together they strolled down the corridor into the front hall and turned into the drawing room.

Caro, slender in old gold, was before them, as were Edward and Elizabeth. Standing in the middle of the room, Caro was facing the chaise on which Elizabeth sat; hearing their footsteps, she turned.

Her gaze first found Geoffrey, then moved on to rest on him.

She blinked, then looked back at Geoffrey. Other than that blink, no sign of surprise showed on her face or in her bearing.

Geoffrey gave her away. "Ah—my apologies, Caro—slipped my mind. I invited Michael to dinner this evening."

She smiled, confident and assured. "How delightful." Gliding forward, she gave him her hand. She glanced at Geoffrey. "Mrs. Judson . . . ?"

"Oh, I remembered to tell her."

Geoffrey ambled across to speak with Edward. Caro narrowed her eyes on his back; her smile took on a subtle edge.

He lifted her hand to his lips, briefly kissed. Had the satisfaction of seeing her gaze and her attention whip back to him. "I take it you don't disapprove?"

Caro looked him in the eye. "Of course not."

She would have liked more time to consider her position before they met again; however, that plainly was not to be. She would cope—coping was her specialty.

They didn't dally long in the drawing room. A discussion of the preparations for the church fete filled the minutes; they were still arguing the merits of Muriel's suggestion of an archery contest when they took their places at the dining table.

The meal passed off well. As always when Caro was in residence, Mrs. Judson outdid herself. Caro sympathized with the woman; during the rest of the year, she had only Geoffrey to cater for, and his tastes were plain beyond belief.

Tonight, the food was exceptional, the conversation relaxed and pleasant. Michael chatted easily with all of them; for her, and Geoffrey, too, it was easy to treat him as something very close to a family member.

As inviting Michael had been Geoffrey's idea, she wasn't sure what to expect when, all three men denying any wish for port, they all rose and returned to the drawing room together. Geoffrey suggested some music; Elizabeth dutifully went to the pianoforte.

Caro played, too, yet hung back, knowing Geoffrey liked to hear Elizabeth play and that Edward would, too, so he could stand beside her and turn the sheets . . . but that left her with Michael. Left her to ensure that he was entertained. . . .

She glanced at him and found him watching her. With an understanding smile, he offered his arm. "Come—stroll with me. I wanted to ask what Leponte tried to prise out of Edward."

The comment served to emphasize how distracted she'd been; she'd forgotten all about Ferdinand's odd behavior.

Sliding her hand onto Michael's arm, letting him steer her toward the far end of the long room, she assembled her facts. Looking down, she spoke softly, below the lilting air Elizabeth had started to play. "He wanted to know all sorts of odd things, but Edward said the crux of it was that Ferdinand wanted to know if Camden had left any personal papers— diaries, letters, personal notes—that sort of thing."

"Did he?"

"Of course." She glanced at him. "Can you imagine any ambassador of Camden's caliber not keeping detailed notes?"

"Indeed—so why did Leponte need to ask?"

"Edward's theory is that that was merely a gambit to elicit some reply alluding to where such papers might be."

"I take it the gambit failed?"

"Naturally." Halting before the French doors to the terrace, currently open to let in the evening breeze, she drew her hand from his arm and faced him. "Edward's entirely trustworthy—he gave Ferdinand no joy at all."

Michael frowned. "What else did Leponte ask? Specifically."

She raised her brows, recalled Edward's sober words. "He asked if it was possible to gain access to Camden's papers." She met Michael's gaze. "To further his studies into Camden's career, of course."

His lips thinned. "Of course."

She studied his steady blue eyes. "You don't believe him, do you?"

"No. And neither do you."

She wrinkled her nose. Turning, she gazed out, unseeing.

"Ferdinand knew Camden for years—only now has he shown any interest."

After a moment, he asked, "Where are Camden's papers?"

"In the London house."

"It's closed up?"

She nodded and met his eyes. "But they're not lying around in his study or anywhere easy to find, so . . ."

His eyes narrowed, then he glanced back up the room.

Half turning, she followed his gaze. Geoffrey's eyes were closed—he looked to be asleep; at the pianoforte, Elizabeth and Edward had eyes only for each other.

Michael's fingers closed about her elbow; before she could react, he'd steered her outside.

"You're not, by any chance, considering giving Leponte access to those papers?"

She blinked at him. "No—of course not. Well . . ." She looked ahead, let him link their arms and stroll with her down the long terrace. "At least not until I know exactly what he's looking for and, even more importantly, why."

Michael glanced at her face, saw the determination behind her words, and was satisfied. She clearly didn't trust Leponte. "You would have a better idea than most—what could he be after?"

"I never read Camden's diaries—I don't believe anyone has. As for the rest, who knows?" She shrugged, looking down as they descended the steps to the lawn; distracted by his question, she didn't seem to notice . . .

Then again, would Caro truly not notice?

It was an intriguing question, but not one he felt any need to press her over; if she was willing to go along with his direction, he wasn't foolish enough to erect hurdles in her path.

"I'm sure whatever it is, it can't be anything diplomatically serious." She glanced at him through the deepening dusk as they headed down the lawn. "The Ministry called Edward in for a debriefing as soon as we arrived back in England, and that was on top of the discussions both Edward and I had with Gillingham, Camden's successor. We spent our last weeks in Lisbon making sure he knew everything there was to know. If anything had cropped up since, I'm sure he, or the Foreign Office, would have contacted Edward."

He nodded. "It's hard to see what it might be, given Camden's been buried for two years."

"Indeed."

The word was somewhat vague. He looked at her, and realized she'd guessed where he was taking her.

She was looking at the summerhouse, at the dark expanse of lake beyond it rippling and lapping, ruffled by the rising breeze. Clouds were racing, overrunning each other as they streaked and tumbled across the evening sky, breaking up the lingering light. They would have a storm before dawn; it was still some distance away, yet the sense of its rising, of the air quivering at its approach, a primal warning of elemental instability rushing their way, was pervasive.

Heightening anticipation, tightening nerves.

Making senses stretch.

The summerhouse rose before them, blocking out the lake. "Do you think Camden's papers are safe where they are?"

"Yes." She looked down as they reached the summerhouse steps. "They're safe."

She reached down to lift her skirts. He released her elbow and started up the steps.

Immediately realized she hadn't; she'd remained on the lawn.

He swiveled on the step and looked down at her—at her pale face, her shadowed eyes; she was looking up at him, hesitating.

He caught her gaze, held it, then extended his hand. "Come with me, Caro."

Through the dusk, her eyes remained locked on his; for an instant, she didn't move—then she made up her mind. Transferring her hold on her skirt to one hand, she placed her fingers in his.

Let him close his hand about them and lead her up into the soft dimness of the summerhouse.

It took only seconds for their eyes to adjust; the last glimmer of light in the sky was reflected off the lake into the section of the summerhouse built out over the water. They moved into that gray half-light. She twitched her fingers and he let them go, content to prowl in her wake as she glided to one of the arched openings where a wide padded bench filled the gap, a tempting place to sit and look out over the lake.

He had no eyes for the lake, only her.

He halted a few feet away; Caro drew in a deep breath and faced him. She was aware of the onrushing storm, of the dance of charged air over her bare arms, of the breeze plucking at tendrils of her hair. Through the twilight, she studied his face—briefly wondered why, with him, it was all so different. Why, when they were alone, here, by the pond—she suspected anywhere—it was as if they'd stepped onto a different plane, one where things were possible, acceptable, even right, that weren't so in the normal world.

Regardless, they were here.

She stepped forward. Closing the distance between them, lifting her hands to slide them over his shoulders to his nape, she cupped his head, drew it down, stretched up and kissed him.

Felt his lips curve beneath hers.

Then they firmed, took control, parted hers. His tongue filled her mouth, his arms closed around her, and she had never been more certain that she was where she wanted, even needed, to be.

Their mouths merged, both eager to take, and then give. To participate fully in what they already knew they could share. Heat bloomed—in them, between them; the exchange quickly grew more demanding, more ravenous, more fiery.

His hunger was there, real, unfeigned, increasingly potent, increasingly undisguised. How strong was it? How lasting? Those were her burning questions—there was only one way to learn the answers.

She met him, taunted in response to his teasing, challenged and dueled. Then she stepped closer, fought to suppress her reactive shiver as their bodies met. Nearly fainted with relief—a delicious giddy faintness—at his reaction. Instantaneous, hot, greedy—almost violent.

Powerful.

His arms tightened, locking her to him, then his hand moved on her back, urging her closer still, then sliding, gliding lower, over the indentation of her waist, lower, over her hips to the swell of her bottom. To trace lightly, then cup, edging her closer, drawing her into his body so she could feel—

For one finite moment, all her senses stilled; for one instant, her mind refused to accept the reality, flatly refused to believe . . .

He shifted against her, deliberately, evocatively, seductively thrusting. The solid ridge of his erection rode against her belly, the soft silk of her old gown the flimsiest of barriers, in no way muting the effect.

Exultation rushed through her, welled, gushed; her mind seized, then whirled on a joyous tide.

He molded her to him; delighted, she wallowed, greedily grasping every sensation, holding each to her, balm to her old scars, and more, a tantalizing promise of what might be.

His desire for her was real, indisputably so; she'd actively evoked it. So could they . . . would he . . . ?

Was it possible?

Her breasts were swollen, hot, tingling; as deliberate as he, she shifted against him, sinuously pressing the aching peaks against his chest, easing and inviting, enticing.

Michael read her message with incalculable relief; never before had he been so driven by such a simple and powerful need. She was his and he had to have her. Soon. Perhaps even tonight . . .

He blocked off the thought, knew he couldn't—wouldn't if he was wise—rush her. This time he was playing a long game, one where his goal was forever. And that goal was too valuable, too precious, too fundamentally important to him—to who he was and who he would be, too much a central part of his future to in any way risk.

But she'd offered him an opportunity to make his case; he wasn't about to decline.

He found it surprisingly difficult to free enough of his mind to take stock, to assess the possibilities. The vision of the padded bench beside them flashed through his mind; he acted on it, eased her back enough to straddle the bench, then drew her down to the deep cushions with him.

Her hands framing his face, she clung to the kiss. Leaning back until his shoulders propped against the arch's side, he drew her with him, settling her within one arm. She went readily, leaning into him, her forearms on his chest, caught in the kiss.

He reached for her hips, eased her around within the V of his thighs, trapped her lips again, more greedily took her mouth, fed from it as he raised his hands, stroked down her back, and found the laces of her gown.

They were easily loosened. That accomplished, he slid his hands around, pushing her arms up, over his shoulders so he could close both hands about her breasts. She shuddered; he kneaded and she moaned. He drank in the sound, set himself the task of eliciting more.

But too soon she was quivering with need, her hands greedily, hungrily grasping—at his hair, his shoulders, sliding beneath his coat to spread and flex evocatively on his chest.

There were tiny buttons down the front of her bodice; fingers expertly flicking, he undid them, eased aside the fine fabric and reached within—cupped her breast through the thin silk of her chemise.

Her breath hitched, then her fingers firmed about his nape and she kissed him with almost desperate ardor.

His desire, already rampant, escalated; he met the demands of her greedy lips, then settled to pander to her ravenous senses. And his.

Within minutes they were both heated, both wanting and needing yet more. Unquestioning, he reached for the ribbon bows securing her chemise, with deft tugs unraveled them. Boldly drew the thin barrier down and set his palm to her breast, skin to naked skin.

The sensual shock shook them both. Their responses, instantaneous, seemed mutual, like strands of the same desire twining and tightening, growing stronger, gaining power through the simple fact that they both wanted this, needed this, somehow quite desperately needed the other, all the other could bring, could give.

He didn't doubt she was with him when he pushed the halves of her bodice aside and laid her breasts bare. Reverently cupped the firm, swollen mounds in his hands; thumbs cruising, brushing her nipples, already tightly furled, he drew his head back, broke from the kiss, and looked down.

In the faint light her skin shone like pearl; its exquisitely fine texture felt like silk. Fine silk heated by the provocative flush of desire. He looked his fill, examined, caressed, and she shuddered.

Caro briefly closed her eyes, fleetingly marveled at the intense sensations slicing through her, that he so easily evoked.

She'd been this far before, but this time she felt immeasurably more alive. Last time . . . she thrust the old memories away, buried them. Ignored their taunting. This time everything felt so very different.

Opening her eyes, she fixed them on Michael's face, drank in the lean, severe lines, handsome but austere. His attention was wholly focused on her, on her breasts . . . they weren't large, were, indeed, rather underweight, yet the concentration, the intensity in his expression, was impossible to mistake. He found them satisfying, worthy. . . .

As if he'd read her mind, his gaze flicked up to her face, briefly searched, then his lips curved . . . the tenor of that smile sent heat rushing through her.

He shifted. Eyes locking on hers, he released one breast, slid that arm around her waist, then eased her back over it.

And bent his head.

She closed her eyes, sucked in a breath as his lips touched her, as they cruised, firm and taunting, over the aching swell of her breast, then followed a tortuous path to its peak.

He teased, and she felt her body react as it never had before. Nerves unfurled, came alive, greedily reaching for sensation—for the sensations he created as he tormented her flesh, until it ached and pulsed. Spread over his shoulders, her fingers tightened involuntarily. She felt his breath warm on her nipple, then he lapped.

Licked, laved, and she gasped.

"Say my name."

She did. He drew her nipple into his mouth and suckled. Strongly. She nearly shrieked.

He released her with a soft chuckle. "There's no one near enough to hear."

Just as well; he bent his head to her other breast and repeated the torture until she begged. Only then did he take what she so willingly offered, and give her all she wanted.

All she'd never had before.

He was gentle yet forceful, experienced and knowing. But although he clearly took pleasure in pleasuring her, that at no time disguised his ultimate goal.

She wasn't the least surprised when his hand slid down from her now burning breast to splay over her stomach. To knead evocatively, then press lower, gently stroking her curls through her gown before reaching further, until his long fingers provocatively probed the indentation at the apex of her thighs.

What did surprise her was her response, the flood of heat that pooled low in her body, the tightening of muscles of which she'd never before been aware, the sudden hot throbbing in the soft flesh between her thighs.

He raised his head; his touch firmed, grew more demanding. She heard the taut tension that held him when he let out a short breath. His lips touched her throat, traced upward, circled her ear, brushed her temple. "Caro?"

He wanted her; she didn't doubt it, yet . . . "I don't . . . I'm not sure . . ."

The moment had come far sooner than she'd expected; she wasn't sure what she should do.

Michael sighed, but didn't retrieve his hand from the heated hollow between her thighs. He continued to caress her while verifying the information his senses had intuitively gauged. Confirmed that she did indeed want him, that she might, if he asked . . .

"I want you." He didn't need to embellish that; the truth

rang in the gravelly words. He was hard and aching, one step away from pain. With one fingertip, he circled the soft fullness of her flesh through her gown. "I want to come inside you, sweet Caro. There's no reason on earth we shouldn't indulge."

Caro heard; the words fell, dark and deeply seductive, into her mind. She knew they were true, at least as he meant them. But he didn't know . . . and if she agreed, and then . . . what if, despite all, it went wrong again? If she was wrong again?

She could feel her pulse pounding under her skin, could, for the first time in her life, imagine it was desire, hot and sweet, that she felt, that filled her and urged her to agree, to simply nod—and let him have his way. Let him show her . . .

But if it went wrong, how would she feel? How could she face him?

She couldn't.

With his hand stroking her, caressing her, blatant promise in every touch, with desire thrumming compulsively in her veins, it required immense effort to draw back. To gather enough will to resist, to say no.

He seemed to sense her decision, spoke quickly, urgently, almost desperately, "We can be married whenever you wish, but for God's sake, sweetheart, let me come inside you."

His words crashed over her in an icy wave, drowning all desire. Panic, full blown, reared from the coldness and gripped her.

She jerked back out of his hold. Horrified, she stared at him. "What did you say?"

The words were weak; her world was whirling, but no longer pleasantly.

Michael blinked, stared at her stunned face—mentally replayed his words. Inwardly grimaced. He frowned lightly at her. "For pity's sake, Caro, you know where we've been heading. I want to make love with you."

Very thoroughly. Multiple times. He hadn't realized just how powerful that need had grown, but it now had him in its grip and wasn't about to let go. Not until . . . Her sudden vacillation wasn't helping.

Her eyes had been fixed on his face, searching . . . she stiffened even more. "No, you don't—you want to *marry* me!"

The accusation hit him like a slap, one that left him disoriented. He stared at her, then felt his face set. "I want—and intend—to do both." He narrowed his eyes at her. "One once, the other frequently."

She narrowed her eyes back. "Not with me."

Her chin set; she reached for her chemise and yanked it up. "I don't intend to marry again."

He watched the gorgeous mounds of her breasts disappear behind the flimsy barrier; it might as well have been steel. He bit back an oath, forced himself to think . . . he thrust a hand through his hair. "But what . . . this is ridiculous! You can't expect me to believe you thought *I* would seduce *you*—my closest neighbor's sister—the past *Member's* sister—and not be thinking of marriage."

She was retying the straps of her chemise, her movements jerky and tense. He knew she was upset, but it was difficult to tell exactly in what way. She glanced up; her gaze clashed with his. "Try another tack." Her tone was flat and uncompromising. "I'm rather more than seven."

Looking down, she wriggled her gown back up and into place. "I'm a widow—I thought you wanted to seduce me, not marry me!"

Accusation still rang in her tone, still lit her silver eyes. His disorientation wasn't improving. "But . . . what's *wrong* with us getting married? For heaven's sake! You know I need a wife, and why, and here you are, the perfect candidate."

She recoiled as if he'd struck her, then her mask slammed into place and she looked down. *"Except* I don't want to marry again—I will not do so."

Abruptly, she stood, swung around, and presented him with her back. "You undid my laces—please do them up again."

Her voice shook. Narrow-eyed, he regarded her slender back, her hands locked on her hips, was conscious of a building impulse to simply seize her and be damned . . . but she suddenly seemed so fragile.

He swung his leg back over the bench and surged to his

feet, stepped directly behind her, caught her lacings and yanked them tight. Exasperation and an even more powerful frustration dug their spurs deep. "Just answer me this." He kept his eyes on the laces as he tightened, then tied them. "If my mentioning marriage is such a shock to you, what did you imagine what's been developing between us would lead to? How did you think this would play out?"

Head up, spine rigid, she looked straight ahead. "I told you. I'm a widow. Widows don't need to get married to . . ."

In lieu of words, she gestured.

"Indulge?"

Jaw setting, Caro nodded. "Indeed. *That's* what I thought *this* was about." He was almost finished with her laces; she wanted nothing more than to flee, to retreat with dignity intact before any of the emotions roiling within her could rupture her control. Her head was spinning so badly she felt sick. A deathly chill was slowly claiming her.

"But you're the Merry Widow. You don't have affairs."

The barb struck home in a way he couldn't have foreseen. She sucked in a breath, lifted her chin. Forced her voice steady. "I'm merely extremely finicky about whom I choose to have affairs with." His hands stilled; she tensed to leave. "But as that's not your real goal—"

"Wait."

She had to; the damned man had hooked his fingers in her laces. She let out a frustrated hiss.

"Having you is a very real goal of mine." He spoke slowly, his tone uninflected.

She couldn't see his face but sensed he was thinking, swiftly readjusting his strategy . . . she moistened her lips. "What do you mean?"

A full minute ticked by, long enough for her to grow aware of her own heartbeat, of the increasingly oppressive atmosphere building before the storm. Yet the elemental threat beyond the summerhouse wasn't sufficient to distract her from the turbulence within, from the potent presence standing in the dimness behind her. His fingers hadn't moved; he was still holding her laces.

Then she sensed him shift nearer; he bent his head so his

words fell by her ear, his breath brushing the side of her face. "If you could choose, how would you wish this—what's been growing between us—to develop?"

A subtle shiver tingled down her spine. *If she could choose* . . . she dragged in a breath past the vise gripping her lungs. Determinedly stepped forward—forcing him to let go. He did, reluctantly.

"I'm a widow." Halting two paces away, she pressed her hands tightly together, then faced him. Fixing her eyes on his, she lifted her chin. "It's perfectly feasible—a straightforward matter—for us to have an affair."

He looked at her for a long moment, then said, "Just so I have this perfectly straight . . . you, the Merry Widow, are agreeing to be seduced." He paused, then asked, "Is that correct?"

She held his gaze, wished she didn't need to answer, finally, briefly, nodded. "Yes."

He stood silent, still, studying her; she could read nothing from his face, in the dimness couldn't see his eyes. Then he stirred almost imperceptibly; she sensed an inner sigh.

When he spoke, his voice was stripped of all lightness, all seduction, all pretense. "I don't want an affair, Caro—I want to marry you."

She couldn't hide her reaction, the instinctive, deeply ingrained panic, her desperate recoil from the very words—from the threat in those words. Her lungs had clamped tight; head rising, muscles tensing, she faced him.

Even through the dimness, Michael saw her fear, saw the panic that dulled her silver eyes. He fought the urge to grab her, to haul her into his arms and soothe her, reassure her . . . what was this?

"I don't want to get married—I won't ever marry again. Not you. Not any man." The words quavered with emotion, charged, resolute. She dragged in a breath. "Now if you'll excuse me, I must get back to the house."

She swung away.

"Caro—"

"*No!*" Blindly, she held up a hand; her head rose higher. "Please . . . just forget it. Forget all this. It won't work."

With a shake of her head, she picked up her skirts and walked quickly across the summerhouse, down the steps, then hurried—almost ran—away across the lawn.

Michael stood in the shadows of the summerhouse with the storm closing in, and wondered what the devil had gone wrong.

Later that night, with the wind shrieking about the eaves and lashing the trees in the wood, he stood at his library window, a glass of brandy in his hand, watching the treetops flex, and thinking. Of Caro.

He didn't understand, couldn't even guess what was behind her aversion—her complete and unequivocal rejection—of another marriage. The sight of her face when he'd reiterated his wish to marry her replayed again and again in his mind.

Regardless of that reaction, his intention had deflected not at all. He would marry her. The thought of not having her as his wife had become simply unacceptable—he didn't completely understand that either, but knew absolutely that it was so. In some odd way, the events of the evening had only hardened his resolve.

He sipped his brandy, looked out, unseeing, and plotted his way forward; he'd never been one to back away from a challenge, even from a challenge he'd never in his wildest dreams imagined he would face.

As matters stood, his task was not to seduce Caro in the customary sense—it appeared he'd already largely succeeded in that, or could succeed whenever he wished. Instead, his true aim—his Holy Grail—was to seduce her into marriage.

His lips twisted wryly; he drained his glass. When he'd headed south from Somersham intent on securing his ideal bride, he'd never imagined he'd face such a battle—that the lady who was his ideal consort would not happily accept his proposal.

So much for blind arrogance.

Turning from the window, he crossed to an armchair. Sinking down, setting his empty glass on the side table, he steepled his fingers; propping his chin on his thumbs, he stared across the room.

Caro was stubborn, resolute.

He was stubborner, and prepared to be relentless.

The only way to undermine her resistance, so strong and entrenched as it clearly was, was to attack its source. Whatever that was.

He needed to find out, and the only way to learn was via Caro.

The best approach seemed obvious. Straightforward, even simple.

First he would get her into his bed, then he'd learn what he needed and do whatever it took to keep her there.

CHAPTER
10

*T*he following afternoon, Caro sat in the window seat of the back parlor and embroidered, while across the room Edward and Elizabeth played chess.

She was not good company; she'd spent all morning trying to distract herself with plans for the fete, now only three days away, but she remained upset and angry.

Angry with herself, angry with Michael.

She should have foreseen his direction. She'd deliberately displayed her highly developed social skills in order to demonstrate Elizabeth's relative lack thereof, so he'd turned his eye from Elizabeth—and fixed it on her!

Damn presumptuous male! Why couldn't he have simply wanted to . . . to . . . to have an *affair* and all that entailed? Wasn't she—?

She cut off the thought; she had good reason to know she wasn't the sort of female who inspired men to lust—not real, basic, raw, cannot-do-without-absolutely-must-have lust, only the sort encouraged by other motives, other wants. Like needing an experienced hostess, or an exceptionally well-trained diplomatic bride!

She seemed destined always to be chosen, never wanted. Never truly desired.

And for that—because for the first time in her life Michael had had her believing otherwise—she didn't think she'd ever forgive him.

Jabbing her needle into the canvas, she fought to calm her nerves. Apprehension snaked through her; she was very much aware that unless and until he gave up all thought of marrying her she was in danger—more danger than Elizabeth had ever been in.

She'd saved Elizabeth from a loveless political union, but there was no one to save her. If Michael made a formal offer, for the same reasons that would have applied in Elizabeth's case, it would be even more difficult for her to refuse. As a widow, theoretically she was in charge of her own life, yet she'd lived too long among her peers not to acknowledge that practically speaking, that wasn't so. If she accepted him, everyone would smile and congratulate her; if she sought to refuse him . . .

Contemplating the likely outcome did nothing to calm her nerves.

She was sorting through her silks when she heard footsteps approaching along the corridor. Bootsteps—not Geoffrey's ambling stride but a definite, determined one . . . her senses leapt. She looked up—just as Michael, attired for riding, appeared in the doorway.

He saw her, briefly glanced at Elizabeth and Edward, who'd looked up in surprise. Without breaking his stride, he directed a nod their way and continued across the room. To her.

She hurriedly gathered her embroidery; he barely gave her time to set it aside before he grasped her hand and pulled her to her feet.

He met her gaze. "We need to talk."

One glance into his eyes, at his set and determined expression, told her arguing was pointless. The way he turned and headed for the door, her hand gripped uncompromisingly tightly in his, underscored that conclusion.

He barely glanced at Edward and Elizabeth. "Do excuse us—we have matters to discuss."

They were out of the room and he was pacing along the corridor before she'd done more than blink. He was striding too fast; she yanked back on his hand. He flicked her a glance and slowed—a fraction—but his determined progress didn't stop. Reaching the garden door, he whisked her through. And continued on down the path.

"Where are we going?" She glanced back at the house.

"Where we won't be disturbed."

She looked at him. "And where's that?"

He didn't reply, but then they reached the end of the path and he set off across the lawn, and she had her answer. The summerhouse.

She pulled back on his hand. "If Elizabeth and Edward look out of the window, they'll see us."

"Will they be able to see us once we're inside?"

"No, but—"

"Then why are you arguing?" He glanced at her; his gaze was hard. "We have unfinished business and that's the obvious place to conclude it. If, however, you'd rather we pursued our 'discussion' in the middle of the lawn . . . ?"

She narrowed her eyes at him. Looked ahead at the summerhouse, rapidly nearing. Muttered sotto voce, "Damn presumptuous male!"

"What was that?"

"Never mind!" She waved toward the summerhouse. "In there, then, if you're so set on it."

Lifting her skirts, she climbed the steps beside him. If he was annoyed, as he seemed to be, then she was even more so. She'd never been one to brangle, but in this case she'd make an exception.

Her heels tapped imperiously as she and Michael crossed the wooden floor, heading to where they'd stood last night.

He stopped two yards from the bench, whirled her to face him, released her hand, raised his and framed her face—and kissed her.

Witless.

It was an assault plain and simple, but one her greedy senses leapt to meet; she grabbed hold of his coat to steady herself, to anchor herself in the giddy melee, the whirlpool of desire—hungry, ravenous, and hot—that he unleashed and sent raging. Through them both.

She drank it in, gasping as her senses exulted. As a hunger of her own rose in response.

He deepened the kiss and she was with him, mouths melding, tongues tangling, almost desperate in their need to touch, to take—to be with the other like this, on this otherworldly plane.

Michael knew he had her, that this at least she couldn't deny. Spreading the fingers of one hand, he speared them deeper into the fine, frizzy wonder of her hair, holding her head steady while he ravaged her mouth; his other hand he sent sliding about her waist, then he drew her to him, steady inch by inch, until she was locked against him.

The contact, breasts to chest, hips to thighs, eased one facet of his driving need, only to escalate another. Determinedly, he reined it in, promising himself that it wouldn't be for long.

It took effort to draw back, eventually to break the kiss, raise his head, and say, "That unfinished business . . . ?"

Her lashes fluttered; her lids rose. It took a moment—a moment he savored—before understanding swam into her eyes. She refocused on his, studied his face. "What did you want to discuss?"

He held her gaze. He had to get it right, had to walk a tightrope and not overbalance. "You said if you could choose, you'd choose an affair." He paused, then continued, his tone hardening, "If that's all you're offering, I'll take it."

Her eyes narrowed fractionally; she was practiced at hiding her emotions—he couldn't see past the beaten silver of her eyes. "You mean you'll forget all about marrying me, and we can just . . ."

"Be lovers. If that's what you wish"—he shrugged lightly—"so be it."

Again, he sensed rather than saw her suspicions. "You need to marry, but you accept I won't be your bride? You won't press me—won't make an offer, or talk to Geoffrey or anyone else?"

He shook his head. "No offer, no maneuvering. However"—he caught the flash of cynical disbelief in her eyes, had already decided how to counter it—"just so we understand each other completely, beyond misconstruction, if you change your mind at any time, I remain perfectly willing to marry you."

She frowned; holding her gaze, he went on, "My proposal stands—it stays on the table between us, but between us alone. If at any time you decide you wish to accept it, all you need do is say so. The decision's yours, totally in your hands, yours alone to make."

Caro understood what he was saying, understood not only the meaning of the words but the decision behind them. She felt mentally rocked; again the ground had shifted beneath her feet. This was something she hadn't, never would have, expected. She could barely take it in. Yet . . .

"Why?" She had to ask, had to know.

He held her gaze steadily, unwaveringly; his expression, hard, determined, if anything grew harder. "If setting aside my wish to marry you is the only way I'll get you into my bed, then I'll do it—*even that.*"

She knew truth when she heard it; his words held its ring. He knew what he was saying, and meant every word.

Her heart stilled, then swelled, soared . . . the impossible seemed possible again.

Captured by the prospect, by the sudden blossoming of hope, she paused. He raised an impatient brow. "Well?" She refocused and he baldly asked, "Will you have an affair with me?"

Trapped in the blue of his eyes, she again felt as if her world had tilted. Opportunity beckoned; fate tempted her not only with her most closely held dreams but also with her most deeply felt fears—and the chance to vanquish them. Fears that had held her in their cold, dead grip for the past eleven years, fears she'd never before believed she might challenge . . . not until the last few days.

Not until he'd come into her life and made her feel alive. Made her feel desired.

She felt giddy; a faint buzzing filled her ears. Over it, she heard herself say, quite distinctly, "Yes."

Two heartbeats passed, then she stepped toward him. He reached for her; hands slid—his about her waist, hers over his shoulders. He bent his head; she stretched up—

"Caro!"

Edward. They froze.

"Caro?" He was on the lawn, heading their way.

Michael exhaled through clenched teeth. "Campbell better have a damn good reason for calling you."

"He will have."

They stepped apart, turned to cross to the entrance; they were still within the summerhouse's shadows when Michael, close behind her, leaned down and whispered, "One thing." His hands closed about her waist, slowing her—reminding her he could draw her back if he wished. "We're now having an affair, so when I say 'Come with me,' you'll do just that, without argument. Agreed?"

If she wanted to go forward and learn what truly was possible between them, she had no real choice. She nodded. "Agreed."

His hands fell from her; he was at her heels as she hurried to the top of the steps.

"Caro?" Edward reached the steps as they appeared at the top. "Oh—there you are."

"What's happened?" Lifting her skirts, she went quickly down.

Edward glanced at Michael, following her, grimaced and looked back at her. "George Sutcliffe's here with Muriel Hedderwick. They're asking for you—it seems there was a burglary at Sutcliffe Hall last night."

They hurried to the drawing room where George, Camden's younger brother, sat waiting in an armchair.

Where Camden had been handsome to the grave, George, considerably his junior, about sixty now, had never laid claim to that adjective. He was not as clever as Camden, either. As the brothers had grown older, they'd grown less and less alike; there remained a superficial physical resemblance, but otherwise two more different men would be hard to imagine. George was now a dour, reclusive, rather cheerless widower; his only interests seemed to lie in his acres, and in his two sons and their sons.

Camden had died without heirs, so Sutcliffe Hall had passed to George. His elder son, David, and his wife and young family lived there, too; it was a large, classically

impressive but rather cold house. Although no longer residing there, Muriel, George's daughter, still considered the
Hall her real home; it was no surprise that she was present.

George looked up as Caro entered. He nodded. "Caro."
He started to struggle up; she smiled, welcoming and reassuring, and waved him back.

"George." Pausing by his chair, she pressed his hand
warmly, then nodded to Muriel, perched on the chaise.
"Muriel."

While George and Muriel exchanged greetings with
Michael, Caro joined Muriel on the chaise. Edward retreated
to stand by the wall. As Michael lifted a straight-backed
chair to join the circle, Caro fixed her gaze on George.
"Edward mentioned a burglary—what's happened?"

"Sometime last night, under cover of the storm, someone
broke into the sitting room at the end of the west wing."

During Camden's lifetime, the rooms in the west wing
had been his, left untouched while he was absent, always
ready for the few scattered weeks when he returned to his
home. Suppressing a frown, Caro listened while George
recounted how his grandsons had discovered a forced window, and described the signs that suggested whoever had
entered had searched the rooms thoroughly. However, as far
as they could tell, only a few knickknacks, none valuable,
had been taken.

Muriel broke in. "They must have been after something of
Camden's, something he'd left there."

George snorted. "More likely passing vagabonds—came
in looking for shelter and picked the place over while they
were about it. No serious harm done, but I did wonder if it
might have been those two who attacked Miss Trice." He
looked at Geoffrey. "Thought I'd put you on your guard."

Caro glanced at Michael.

Muriel all but snorted. "I think it *most* likely was something of Camden's they were after—that's why I insisted we
see you." She appealed to Caro. "What of his things left at
the Hall would be of interest to others?"

Looking into Muriel's dark, slightly protruberant eyes,
Caro wondered if she'd heard of Ferdinand's interest. "No,"

she said, her tone leaving no scope for argument. "There's nothing of Camden's, nothing valuable, left at the Hall."

She glanced at Edward, wordlessly warning him not to support or elaborate. Camden had never viewed the Hall, buried in rural Hampshire, as any real base of his. She and Edward knew her statement was absolutely true, but it was a truth few others were likely to know or guess. Muriel clearly hadn't; it would hardly be surprising if Ferdinand believed Camden's personal papers remained in his rooms at the Hall, his ancestral home.

Muriel frowned, unhappy with her answer, yet with little choice but to grudgingly accept it.

Caro had Edward ring for tea. Over their cups, George, Michael, and Geoffrey discussed crops, weather, and yields; she determinedly steered Muriel's thoughts to the fete, inquiring as to the numerous stalls, refreshments, and entertainments that were all coming together under Muriel's eagle eye.

Tea consumed, Muriel and George took their leave. Geoffrey retreated to his study; Caro, with Michael and Edward in train, made for the parlor.

Elizabeth had had her own tea tray brought in; she set down her cup and the novel she'd been reading as Caro entered. "I heard Muriel's voice." She grimaced. "I assumed if you needed me, you'd send for me."

Caro waved. "Of course." She sat on the chaise, fixed her gaze on Michael as he lounged in the armchair opposite; Edward perched on the arm of the other chair. "Those two weaselly men we saw Ferdinand speaking with in the forest. Do you think . . . ?"

Edward frowned. "What two men?"

Michael explained. Edward shot a concerned glance at Caro. "You think Ferdinand hired them to burgle Sutcliffe Hall?"

"I think," Michael broke in decisively, "that we're getting ahead of ourselves. While I agree that Ferdinand, with his sudden interest in Camden's papers, having a clandestine meeting with two men whom neither Caro nor I recognized but who certainly looked like thieves, and Sutcliffe Hall being burgled two nights later, is suggestive, it's hardly proof. Indeed, it *could* have been as George suggested—vagabonds seeking shelter from the storm."

He looked at Caro. "The end of the Hall's west wing is the most isolated part of the house, isn't it?"

She nodded. "Camden liked it for that reason—the others in the house didn't disturb him."

"Exactly. And the forest encroaches on that side, so if any vagabonds were looking for a refuge, it's the most likely place they'd enter."

Caro pulled a face. "You're saying it could just be coincidence."

He nodded. "I'm hardly a Leponte supporter, but there's insufficient evidence to charge the break-in to his account."

"But we can keep a closer eye on him." Edward's tone had hardened.

Michael met his gaze. "Indeed. Regardless of our lack of proof in this instance, I definitely think that would be wise."

Michael and Edward spent the next half hour discussing possibilities; they settled on alerting the Bramshaw House staff to watch for any intruders, citing the burglary at Sutcliffe Hall as the cause of their concern.

"Leadbetter Hall is too far away to mount a meaningful watch directly on Leponte." Michael grimaced. "And with the fete and the ball in the offing, there are too many easily constructed reasons for him to be out and about around Bramshaw anyway. Short of alerting half the county, there's not much more we can do."

Edward nodded. "The ball will be his best chance to search here, don't you think?"

"Yes—we'll have to make sure he's watched at all times."

Caro listened, agreed when appealed to, but otherwise held her tongue; she had enough to do organizing her ball without worrying about Ferdinand. Besides, it was clear she could leave that to Michael and Edward.

The sun was sinking behind the trees when Michael rose. She rose, too, watched while he took his leave of Elizabeth

and Edward; when he turned to her, she gave him her hand
and an easy smile. "Good-bye."

Discussion of the ball had reminded her just how much
there was yet to do, to organize, supervise, and manage.
Regardless of their decision to embark on an affair, she did
not need further distraction just now.

He held her hand, held her gaze, then raised her fingers
and brushed a kiss across her knuckles. "I'll call on you
tomorrow afternoon."

She turned with him to the door; he still held her fingers.
"Tomorrow will be very busy." She lowered her voice so
only he could hear. "There's a great deal we have to do with
both the preparations for the ball and our contribution to the
fete."

Pausing at the door, he looked down at her. "Nevertheless,
I'll be here midafternoon." The words were a promise,
underscored by the weight of his gaze. He again raised her
fingers; his eyes on hers, he kissed them, then released her.
"Look for me then."

With a nod and that same intent look, he left.

She stood in the doorway listening to his retreating footsteps, and wondered . . . in agreeing to an affair, just what
had she agreed to?

The question resonated in her mind the following afternoon
when she stood on the terrace, hands on her hips, and glared
at Michael.

She opened her mouth—

He pointed a finger at her nose. "*Without* argument.
Remember?"

She let out her breath in an exasperated hiss through teeth
unbecomingly clenched. "I—"

"You have precisely five minutes to change into your riding habit. I'll meet you on the front steps with the horses."

With that, he turned, went down the terrace steps, and
strode away toward the stables—leaving her with her mouth
open . . . and a sneaking suspicion she had no alternative but
to fall in with his plans.

She'd never been so dictated to in her life!

Swinging around, muttering dire imprecations against males, all males, presumptuous or otherwise, she whipped off her apron, swung through the kitchens to check with Cook and Mrs. Judson, then hurried upstairs. Ten minutes later, after remembering and delivering the instructions she'd been on her way to give when the sight of Michael striding purposefully up to the house had distracted her, she hurried into the front hall.

Looking down, tugging on her riding gloves, she ran straight into a wall of solid male muscle her senses had no difficulty recognizing.

"I'm coming, I'm coming!" she protested, bouncing off.

He steadied her, then locked one hand about one of hers. "Just as well."

His growl made her blink, but she couldn't see his face—he'd already turned and was striding for the door, towing her behind him. She had to hurry to keep up, frantically grabbing up her habit's skirt so she could clatter down the steps in his wake.

"This is ridiculous!" she grumbled as he towed her relentlessly to Calista's side.

"I couldn't agree more."

He halted by the mare's side, swung around to lift her up. He closed his hands about her waist, then paused.

She looked up, met his eyes. As always, she was screamingly aware of her giddy senses' preoccupation with him and his nearness, but she seemed to be growing used to the effect.

"Have you had an affair before?"

The question had her blinking her eyes wide. "No! Of course not . . ." The words were out before she'd thought.

But he merely nodded, somewhat grimly. "I thought not."

With that, he lifted her to her saddle, held her stirrup while she slid her boot in.

Settling her skirts, she frowned at him as he went to his horse and mounted. "What's that got to say to anything?"

Picking up his reins, he met her gaze. "You're not exactly making it easy."

She narrowed her eyes. "I told you." She brought Calista up beside him and they set out along the drive. "There's the ball, the fete—I'm busy."

"You're not—you're skittish, and looking for excuses to avoid taking the plunge."

She looked ahead; she made no attempt to meet his eyes, yet she felt his gaze on her face.

"You're the epitome of efficiency, Caro—you can't expect me to believe you can't take two hours out of the afternoon of the day before what for you is a relatively minor ball."

He was right, at least about that last. She frowned, more inwardly than outwardly. Was he right about the rest, too? She knew what she feared; had it really cut so deep, did the fear hold her so securely that she would unthinkingly, instinctively as he was suggesting, avoid any situation that might challenge it?

She glanced at him. He was watching her but, as their eyes met, she realized he wasn't seeking to pressure her. He was, most definitely, seeking to understand her; as yet, he couldn't.

Her heart gave a little twist, a small leap; she looked ahead. Unsure how she felt about being understood, or his wish to do so. After a moment of steady cantering, she cleared her throat. Drew breath and lifted her chin. "I might, indeed, appear to erect hurdles, but I assure you I don't mean to." She glanced at him. "I'm every bit as determined on our present course as you are."

His lips lifted; his smile was all male. "In that case, don't worry." He held her gaze. "I'll ignore your hurdles."

She humphed and looked ahead, not at all sure she approved of such a tack, yet . . . as they cantered through the golden afternoon, she drew a certain measure of comfort from it. Regardless of what silly vacillations her fears might drive her to, he wasn't going to allow her to avoid or resist him—to draw back. In battling her fears, it seemed she'd found an ally.

It wasn't until they were almost at the clearing that she realized they'd retraced their route to the Rufus Stone. When they cantered into the wide field carpeted in the green and gold of fresh grass and turning leaves, she wondered why he'd chosen this place, wondered what he was planning.

They halted; he dismounted, tethered the horses, then came to lift her down. He lowered her slowly; even when she was steady on her feet, he didn't let her go.

She looked up; their gazes locked. She felt the fascination between them draw tight, as he drew her closer and bent his head felt their mutual hunger awake.

With his lips, Michael brushed her temple, then bent lower to trace the curve of her ear and nuzzle the sweet hollow beneath. He inhaled, let her scent sink slowly through him, felt himself react. "I should probably admit . . ."

He let the words trail away as he drew her fully against him.

Her hands sliding up, over his shoulders, she blinked at him. "What?"

His lips curved. He lowered his head. "I would have ignored your hurdles anyway."

He took her mouth, felt her give it, and herself—felt her sink against him. For long moments, he simply savored her, and her implicit surrender. Yet the isolation of the clearing was not why they were here. Nevertheless, capturing her senses, focusing them, and her, on all that would be between them, on the ultimate intimacy that would soon exist before he broached his immediate objective, wasn't a bad idea.

Eventually, he drew back; when he lifted his head, she opened her eyes, searched his. "Why did you choose here?"

He might be able to addle her senses, but her wits were clearly more resilient. Releasing her, he took her hand, drew her to walk with him toward the stone. "When we came here last time . . ." He waited until she lifted her gaze to his, until he could capture her eyes. "As we rode into the clearing, I was baiting you." He saw that she remembered, was remembering. "I wanted a reaction, but the reaction I got was not one I can interpret, even now."

Looking ahead, she halted; he halted, too, but didn't release her hand. He shifted to face her. "We were discussing the life of an ambassador's wife, namely your own, and the duties you or any such lady had to perform."

Her features set. Without looking at him, she tugged her

hand; he tightened his grip. "You warned me of every ambassador's need for a suitable helpmate—I mentioned that the same held true for government ministers." Relentlessly he continued, "I then pointed out that Camden had been a master ambassador."

Her fingers twitched in his, but she refused to look at him; her expression was stony, her chin ominously set. "I brought you here to ask you what about that upset you. And why."

For a long moment, she remained utterly still, statuelike but for the pulse he could see thudding at the base of her throat. She was upset again, but in a different way . . . or the same way compounded by something more.

Finally, she drew in a deep breath, fleetingly glanced at him, but didn't meet his eyes. "I . . ." Again she breathed deeply, lifted her head and fixed her gaze on the trees. "Camden married me because he saw in me the perfect hostess—the ultimate ambassadorial helpmate."

Her voice was flat, without inflection; denied her eyes, any chance of reading her feelings, he was left guessing, trying to follow her direction. "Camden was a career diplomat, a very experienced and canny one by the time he married you." He paused, then added, "He was right."

"I know."

The words were so tight with emotion they quavered. She wouldn't look at him; he pressed her hand. "Caro . . ." When she didn't respond, he quietly said, "I can't see if you won't show me."

"I don't *want* you to see!" She tried to fling her hands in the air—found her fingers locked in his and tugged. "Oh, for goodness sake! Let me go. I can hardly run away from you, can I?"

The fact she recognized that made him ease his grip. Wrapping her arms about her, she paced, looking down, circling the stone. Agitation shimmered about her, yet her steps were definite; her expression, what he glimpsed of it, suggested she was wrestling, but with what he was still at a loss to guess.

Eventually she spoke, but didn't slow her pacing. "Why do you need to know?"

"Because I don't want to hurt you again." He hadn't even needed to think to reply.

His words made her pause; she glanced fleetingly at him, then resumed her pacing—from one side of the stone to the other, leaving the chest-high monument between them.

After another fraught pause, she spoke, her words low but clear, "I was young—very young. Only seventeen. Camden was fifty-eight. Think about that." She paced on. "Think about how a fifty-eight-year-old man, a very worldly, experienced, still handsome and devastatingly charming but ruthless fifty-eight-year-old man convinces a seventeen-year-old girl, one who hadn't even had a Season, to marry him. It was so easy for him to make me believe in something that simply wasn't there."

It hit him. Not like a blow but with the keen edge of a knife. He suddenly found himself bleeding from a place he hadn't even known could be cut. "Oh, Caro."

"No!" She rounded on him, silver eyes ablaze. "Don't you dare feel sorry for me! I just didn't know—" Abruptly, she waved her hands and turned away. Dragged in a huge breath and straightened, lifted her head. "Anyway, it's all in the past."

He wanted to tell her that past hurts properly buried didn't slice at one in the here and now. But he couldn't find the words, any she would accept.

"I'm not usually so sensitive about it, but this business with you and Elizabeth . . ." Her voice faded; she took in another breath, still looking away, into the trees. "So now you know. Are you happy?"

"No." He stirred, stepped around the stone and closed the gap between them. "But at least I understand."

She glanced over her shoulder as he slid his hands around her waist. Frowned at him. "I can't see why you need to."

He drew her around, closed his arms, and bent his head. "I know."

But you will.

He heard the words in his mind as he set his lips to hers. Not hungrily, but temptingly, coaxingly. She followed, not at first with her usual tempestuous yearning, but yet she went with him. It was a slower, more considered, more deliberate progression into the flames; step by step he led, and she followed.

Until they were burning. Until the heat of their mouths, the pressure of body against body, was no longer enough, not for either of them.

Caught in the moment, wrapped in its promise, needing the heat of it to drive away the past's chill, Caro resented even the moment he took to step back, shrug out of his coat, flick it out on the ground in the shade beneath a huge oak. When he reached for her and drew her down, she went eagerly, wanting, needing the contact, the wordless assurance that came with his kisses, with each increasingly bold caress.

As usual, he didn't ask permission to open her bodice, strip away her chemise, and lay her breasts bare—he simply did. Then he feasted, pressing delight upon sensual delight upon her, until she was gasping, skin taut and tight, fevered and burning.

He didn't ask, but simply reached for her skirt, tugged the front up between them and slid his hand beneath. His searching fingers found her knee, circled it, then traced upward, lingeringly caressing the inner faces of her thighs until the muscles flickered, until she shifted, pressed closer, wordlessly demanding . . .

She knew what she wanted, but when he touched her curls she nearly expired. Not just with delight, but anticipation. He boldly nudged her thighs apart, stroked through her curls, traced her soft flesh in a languid exploration that left her heated, slick, and throbbing. Then his touch firmed.

He released the breast he'd been tauntingly suckling; lifting his head, from under heavy lids he held her gaze as he slid one finger deep inside her.

Awareness gripped her, excruciatingly acute. She lost her breath, lost touch with her wits; every sense she possessed locked on that assured penetration, on the steady invasion as he pushed deeper, then reached deeper still.

Before she could catch her breath, he stroked, firmly, deliberately. Then he bent his head and covered her lips, kissed her as if she were a houri he owned.

She kissed him back as if she were, avid, greedy—demanding, commanding, even deliberately taunting. He responded in kind. Their mouths melded, tongues tangling as between her thighs he worked his hand, stroked, and drove her mindless.

Gripping his shoulders, she held him to the kiss, suddenly desperate on so many counts. Desperate for him to keep kissing her so he wouldn't see, wouldn't have a chance to see—so she wouldn't have a chance to give herself away by revealing how novel, how indescribably exciting yet glitteringly, fascinatingly new the sensations he was pressing on her were.

Desperate that he wouldn't stop.

Desperate to reach some sensual pinnacle, to shatter the tension growing and coiling and building within her.

She felt like screaming.

Even through the kiss, she sensed him swear, then between her thighs, his hand shifted.

She tried to pull back to protest; he refused to let her, followed her, holding her trapped in the kiss—then a second finger pressed in alongside the first, suddenly, startlingly, escalating the pressure. The tension racked up another notch; she could feel her body tightening against his.

He held her down, then his hand shifted again; his thumb touched her, stroked, searched, then settled—pressed in time with the stroking of his fingers.

She fractured like crystal in bright sunlight, shards of white-hot pleasure streaking through her, sharp, slicing, abruptly releasing the tension, letting it flow into a golden pool. The pool glowed, throbbed; its heat sank into her, pulsed beneath her skin, in her fingertips, in her heart.

The wonder held her, cradled her, ripped from the world for the very first time, afloat on the ecstasy of her senses.

Slowly, she returned—to the physical world, to comprehension. To the knowledge of what physical delight was, to some inkling of what she'd missed all these years—to a deeper knowledge of what she'd been waiting for, and what he'd brought her.

He'd raised his head; he'd been watching her and still was.

She smiled, slowly, lazily stretched, sensually sated for the first time in her life. Glorying in it.

Her smile said it all; Michael drank it in—decided it was even better than the smile she'd gifted him with when he'd told her he was no longer considering Elizabeth as his bride.

This was a smile worthy of the efforts he fully intended to make—mentally renewed his vow to make—to see it wreathe her face every morning, and every night. It was a smile she deserved as much as he did.

He drew his fingers from her; she'd been tight, very tight, but Camden had been dead for two years and had been getting on in years before that. But as he pushed her skirts down, he caught the frown in her eyes, the sudden dulling of the silvery glory. He raised a brow in mute query.

Her frown grew definite. "What about you?" She turned toward him; her hand found him, rigid as granite and equally hard. Her light caress would have brought him to his knees if he'd been upright.

He caught her hand, had to search to find breath enough to say, "Not this time."

"Why not?"

There was a hint of something beyond the obvious in her disappointment—a disappointment clear enough to lend an edge to his already intent glance. "Because I have plans."

He did, indeed, and he wasn't about to share them with her. Given her acknowledged propensity to erect hurdles, the less she knew, the better.

Her frown grew suspicious. "What?"

Flopping onto his back, he slid an arm around her and urged her over him. "You don't need to know." He drew her head down, caught her full lower lip between his teeth and gently tugged, then whispered, "But you're welcome to try to find out."

She chuckled; again he recalled she didn't laugh often, resolved, even as her lips pressed to his and she gave herself up to her quest to persuade him, to make her laugh more. To push away the clouds that beneath all the glamour seemed to have dulled her life for too long.

Then she shifted more definitely over him, put her heart

and soul into their kiss, and he forgot everything else and gave himself up to simply kissing her back.

Despite her efforts, Caro learned nothing of Michael's plans. When they returned to Bramshaw House, her neglected duties claimed her; not until her head hit her pillow late that night did she get a chance to think of what had transpired in the clearing. Of what he had wanted, what he had learned, what he had made her feel.

Just the thought of that last made her flesh throb in remembered delight; her body still glowed faintly with the aftermath of pleasure. True, Camden had touched her in similar ways; the veils she'd drawn over those few nights when he'd come to her bed obscured the details, yet she'd never sensed in Camden what she sensed in Michael—and had never reacted, never felt with Camden any of the excitement let alone the glory she felt in Michael's arms.

Despite the secret worry that still nagged—that something would yet go wrong, that at the end, when it came to the point, what she longed for simply wouldn't happen—she felt a countering eagerness, an anticipation, a compulsion to go forward, to explore and experience as much as she could. As much as he would show her.

Whatever his plans were, she would follow him regardless.

Regardless of all else, there was one vital point she simply had to know.

CHAPTER

11

Michael rose early the next morning. He tried to immerse himself in catching up with the London news, reading the news sheets and letters from various correspondents, but time and again he caught himself sitting in his armchair, booted ankle propped on one knee, his gaze fixed before him—thinking of Caro.

She'd spoken of hurdles she didn't mean to place before him, and then revealed one gigantic, triple-bar water jump that, unintended or not, he was going to have to find some way to clear.

Camden had married her for her talents, her undeniable skills. From what he knew of Camden, that came as no surprise; if any man had known which innate abilities were required to produce a topnotch hostess, and been able to recognize them in a raw young lady of seventeen, Camden had been that man. He'd already buried two highly talented wives.

That, however, wasn't the problem. Caro hadn't understood, had thought he'd been marrying her for other reasons, presumably the usual romantic reasons young ladies dreamed of, and Camden—

Michael gritted his teeth, but had no difficulty imagining the Camden he'd known and heard so much about deploying his charm and glittering, multifaceted personality to dazzle a young lady he'd wanted for his own. Oh, yes, he would have done it, knowingly led her up the garden path, let her think what she would—anything to gain what he'd wanted.

He'd wanted Caro, and got her.

But to her, it had all been under false pretenses.

That was what had wounded her, scarred her; the spot was still tender, even after all these years.

Just how tender, he'd seen for himself; he wouldn't willingly prod that point anew. He didn't, however, regret doing so. If he hadn't . . . at least he now knew what he faced.

Given that she was fully cognizant of his own urgent and very real need for just such a wife as Camden had wanted, just the sort of talented female she herself was, getting her to agree to marry him was going to be an uphill slog.

And that's where the gigantic, triple-bar water jump stood—not in the way of getting her into his bed, but between him and his ultimate goal.

He pondered that, then decided it lay too far ahead—who knew what might happen between then and now? Perhaps another, clearer route to marriage would open up, and he wouldn't need to front that gigantic, triple-bar water jump after all.

His plans were sound; one step at a time—secure one goal before moving on to take the next.

Leaving the subject, setting it aside, he tried to concentrate on his aunt Harriet's latest letter. He read one more paragraph before his mind wandered . . . to Caro.

Stifling a curse, he folded the letter and tossed it on the pile on his desk. Five minutes later, he was on Atlas's back, cantering toward Bramshaw.

Wisdom insisted that the day of a ball—and despite what he'd said, Caro's Midsummer Revels, attended by so many diplomatic personages, would be no minor event—was not the time to call on any lady. If he had any sense, he would have done as he'd planned and played least in sight. Yet here he was . . .

He decided that, aside from all else, it would be unfair to leave Edward to watch over Caro on his own. Geoffrey would doubtless have taken refuge in his study and would not be seen until dinner, so someone should be there who had some chance of reining Caro in, should that prove necessary.

He found her on the terrace, directing the placement of tables and chairs on the lawns below. Absorbed with waving two footmen carrying a table further to the right, she didn't realize he was there until he slid his hands around her waist and lightly squeezed.

"Oh—hello." She glanced distractedly up and back at him, slightly breathless.

He grinned down at her, let his hands drift down, lightly caressing her hips. The small army on the lawn below couldn't see.

She frowned—sternly warning. "Have you come to help?"

He sighed, resigned, and nodded. "What do you want me to do?"

Fatal words, as he quickly discovered; she had a list of errands as long as his arm. The first she shot his way involved moving furniture in and out of the reception rooms; some pieces had to be temporarily lodged in various other places. While the footmen struggled with sideboards and larger pieces, he, along with Edward and Elizabeth, was detailed to see to the lamps, mirrors, and other awkward but delicate and valuable items. Some needed to be removed, others repositioned. The next hour flew.

Once she was satisfied with the dispositions within doors, Caro returned outside. A marquee had to be erected to one side of the lawn; Michael exchanged a glance with Edward and they quickly volunteered. Better that than lug urns and heavy pots about the terrace and along the walks.

Elizabeth said she'd help. The canvas of the marquee lay folded at the edge of the lawn along with the clutter of its poles, guy ropes, and the stakes to anchor them. Between the three of them—Caro was off overseeing something else—they got the canvas laid out, then came their less-than-successful attempts to get the poles in position and hoist the canvas aloft. The marquee was hexagonal, not square—as they quickly learned, a much more difficult proposition.

Eventually, Michael got one corner aloft. Holding the

pole steady, he nodded at Edward. "See if you can get the central pole up."

Edward, by now in his shirtsleeves, eyed the mass of canvas, nodded once, grimly, and dived beneath. He had to fight his way through the folds.

Within seconds, he was lost. A series of poorly suppressed curses floated out from beneath the heaving canvas. Elizabeth, barely able to contain her laughter, called, "Wait—I'll help."

She, too, dove under the canvas.

Michael watched, indulgent and amused, leaning against the pole he was propping up.

"What *is* taking so long with this?" Caro bustled around the wall of canvas he was supporting. She took note of his hand wrapped about the pole, arm braced, then turned her attention to the still-heaving canvas and the muffled, indistinct but suggestive sounds coming from beneath it.

Hands rising to her hips, she glared. Muttered beneath her breath, "We don't have time for this nonsense."

Reaching out, he caught her around the waist; before she could protest, he tugged her to him. She landed against him, hands to his chest; the pole wobbled but he managed to keep it upright.

She caught her breath, looked up at him; he looked deep into her eyes, all but saw her wits marshaling a blistering reproof even while her senses danced a giddy jig. She blinked, fumbling to get her tongue to deliver the protest her brain had formed.

He smiled, watched her gaze fix on his lips. "Let them have their moment—it's not going to upset your schedule." He was about to add, "Don't you remember what it was like to be that young?" meaning that young and in the throes of first love; he remembered just in time that Caro almost certainly didn't remember, because almost certainly she'd never known. . . .

Bending his head, he kissed her, at first gently, until their lips melded, then with increasing passion. Theirs was not a young love, but a more mature engagement; the kiss reflected that, rapidly deepening.

The wall of canvas screened them from the myriad others hurrying about the lawns and gardens. Edward and Elizabeth were still struggling beneath the marquee.

Michael lifted his head the instant before Elizabeth emerged, shaking her skirts and valiantly stifling giggles. He released Caro as soon as he was sure she was steady on her feet.

Elizabeth saw his arm sliding from around Caro's waist; her eyes widened, sudden understanding writ large in her face.

Caro saw it; in an uncharacteristic fluster, she flapped her hands at Elizabeth—Edward was still under the marquee. "Do hurry up! We have to get this done."

Elizabeth grinned. "Edward's got the central pole in place, ready to hoist."

"Good." Stepping out quickly, back toward the house, Caro nodded. "Carry on!"

With that injunction, she bustled away—in a much greater fluster than when she'd bustled up. Michael watched her go, a smile in his eyes, then turned to Elizabeth. Ignoring the speculation in her face, he waved her to a pole. "If you can get the next corner in, we should be able to get the roof up."

They managed, albeit with much muted cursing and laughter. With the marquee properly erected and secured, they presented themselves to Caro, who fixed them with one of her more stern looks.

"Mrs. Judson needs help sorting all the cutlery and glassware for dinner, and for the supper to be laid out in the marquee." She fixed Elizabeth and Edward with a severe glance. "The two of you can go and help her."

Unabashed, the pair smiled and headed for the dining room. Caro turned her strait glance on him. "You can come with me."

He grinned. "With pleasure."

She humphed and marched past, nose high. He fell into step, half a pace behind her. The swish of her hips was distracting. A quick glance around showed no one else in the corridor; boldly, he reached out and ran a hand over those distracting curves.

He sensed her nerves leap, heard her breath catch. Her stride faltered, but then she walked on.

He didn't take his hand away.

She slowed as they approached an open doorway. Glanced over her shoulder, struggled to frown direfully. "Stop that."

He opened his eyes wide. "Why?"

"Because . . ."

He stroked again and her gaze unfocused. She moistened her lips, then halted at the open doorway and dragged in a breath. "Because you'll need both hands to carry these."

She waved into the room. He looked, and stifled a groan. "These" were huge urns and vases filled with flowers. Two maids were putting the finishing touches to the arrangements.

Caro smiled at him. Her eyes glinted. "Those two go in the ballroom, and the others are to be stationed about the house—Dora will tell you where each goes. When you've finished, I'm sure I can find something else to keep your hands busy."

Deliberately, he smiled at her. "If you can't, I'm sure I'll be able to suggest something."

She humphed as she turned away; he watched her walk down the corridor, distracting hips swishing, then he smiled and turned to the urns.

Carrying them hither and yon gave him plenty of time to think and plan. As she'd warned, there were arrangements to be placed all over the house, including on the first floor in and near the rooms prepared for the guests staying overnight. Most would arrive in the late afternoon, which explained the frenetic activity; everything before the green baize door had to be perfect before any guests climbed the front steps.

Carting flower arrangements all over reacquainted him with the house; he was familiar with it, but had never had reason to study the layout in detail. He learned which rooms were guest rooms, which were currently used by the family and Edward, and which would remain unused. There were a few rooms in the last category; after Dora released him, he disappeared upstairs.

Twenty minutes later he descended, and went looking for Caro. He found her on the terrace, a plate of sandwiches in one hand. The rest of the hungry household were scattered on the lawns, the terrace steps, on the chairs and tables, all munching and drinking from mugs.

Caro, too, was munching. Stopping beside her, he helped himself to a sandwich from her plate.

"There you are." She glanced at him. "I thought you must have left."

He met her gaze. "Not without giving you a chance to sate my appetite."

She caught the double entendre but, calmly looking forward, waved to the platters of sandwiches and jugs of lemonade placed along the balustrade. "Do help yourself."

He grinned and did so; returning to her side with a plate piled high, he murmured, "I'll remind you you said that."

Puzzled, she frowned at him.

He grinned at her. "Later."

Michael remained for another hour, being, Caro had to admit, helpful. He didn't do anything else to distract her. After his comment on the terrace, he didn't have to; that exchange replayed in her mind for the rest of the afternoon.

The man was a past master at ambiguity—a true politician, beyond doubt. *Later.* Had he meant he'd explain what he'd meant later, or that he'd remind her she'd told him to help himself later?

The latter possibility, linked with the phrase "giving you a chance to sate my appetite," constantly intruded on her thoughts—thoughts that should have been focused on the less personal challenges of the evening ahead. As she paused to tweak the delicate filigree headdress she'd chosen into place, she was conscious of not just anticipation, but expectation tightening her nerves, something very close to titillation teasing her senses.

Casting a last glance over her gown of shimmering ecru silk, noting with approval how it clung to her curves, how it brought out the gold and brown glints in her hair, she settled her large topaz pendant just above her décolletage, made sure her rings were straight, then, finally satisfied she looked her best, headed for the door.

She reached the main stairs to discover Catten waiting in the front hall. As she descended, he tugged his waistcoat into place and lifted his head. "Shall I sound the gong, ma'am?"

Stepping off the stairs, she inclined her head. "Indeed. Let our Midsummer Revels commence."

She glided into the drawing room, her words still ringing, her lips lifting.

Michael stood before the fireplace, Geoffrey beside him. Michael's gaze fixed on her the instant she appeared. She paused on the threshold, then glided on; they both turned to her as she joined them.

"Well, m'dear, you look fetching—very elegant." Looking her up and down, with brotherly affection Geoffrey patted her shoulder.

Caro heard him, but barely saw him. She smiled vaguely in response to the compliment, but her eyes were all for Michael.

There was something about seeing a gentleman in strict formal attire; true, she'd seen him in formal settings in the past, but . . . now he was looking at her, appreciating her, visually drinking her in, and watching her do the same, appreciatively taking in the width of his shoulders, the breadth of his chest, his height, the length of his long legs. In severe black, contrasting strongly with the pristine white of cravat and shirt, he seemed to tower over her even more than usual, making her feel especially delicate, feminine, and vulnerable.

Geoffrey cleared his throat, mumbled some comment, and left them; their gazes locked, neither glanced his way.

Slowly, she smiled. "Are you going to tell me I look fetching and elegant?"

His lips lifted, but his blue eyes remained intent, deadly serious. "No. To me you look . . . *superb*."

He invested the word with a meaning far beyond the visual. And she suddenly felt *superb*, as glowing, captivating, and desirable as his inflection painted her. She drew breath; an extra, unusual, novel confidence welled and filled her. "Thank you." She inclined her head, half turned toward the door. "I must greet the guests."

He offered his arm. "You can introduce me to those I've not yet met."

She hesitated, looked up and met his gaze. Recalled her determination not ever again to act as hostess for any man. She heard voices on the stairs; any minute the guests would appear. And if they saw her standing there with him . . . ?

If they saw him standing by her side at the door . . . ?

Either way, he would be seen to have taken a position with respect to her, one no other man had succeeded in attaining.

Which was true; he did, indeed, hold that position. He meant something to her, more than a mere acquaintance, more, even, than a friend.

Inclining her head, she slid her hand onto his sleeve and let him lead her to stand by the door. He'd said he wouldn't attempt to maneuver her into marriage, and she trusted him in that. Indeed, the dinner guests were primarily foreigners with no real influence within the ton.

As for the idea that people would see him as her lover . . . she viewed that prospect not just with equanimity, but with a subtle thrill very close to happiness.

Ferdinand, however, was one of the first to appear. He took one look at Michael and very nearly scowled. Luckily, with more guests arriving, he had to move on; he was quickly swallowed up into the general conversation as those who were staying at Bramshaw House overnight as well as those selected others who'd been invited for dinner before the ball rolled in.

From that moment on, she had barely an instant to call her own, and certainly not one second to think of anything personal. She discovered it was useful having Michael by her side; he was far more at home in this milieu than Geoffrey and could be relied on to recognize potentially difficult situations and handle them with suitable tact.

They made a very good team; she was conscious of that, knew he was, too, yet instead of making her uneasy, each shared, appreciative glance filled her with a sense of achievement, of satisfaction.

Of rightness.

She didn't have time to dwell on it; the dinner—ensuring all went as it should while keeping the conversation sparkling—claimed all her attention. It passed off well, without a hitch, and then the party was repairing to the ballroom. She'd timed it nicely; the dinner guests just had time to admire the floral theme and take note of the garlanded terrace with the lawns and walks beyond lit by lanterns, and the marquee with chairs and tables set ready for supper, before the first stir beyond the ballroom doors.

All was as it should be as the ball guests strolled in.

Michael returned to stand by Caro's side as, with Geoffrey, she greeted the incoming guests. She flicked him a glance, but made no direct comment, simply guided the newcomers his way, ensuring he had a chance to exchange a few words with everyone attending. As this group was primarily locals, none read anything into the arrangement. Geoffrey was the past Member, Caro his sister, and Michael the present Member; to them, all seemed as it should be.

As the tide slowed to a trickle, Michael touched Caro's arm; with his eyes, he indicated the Russian delegation, presently in the restraining company of Gerhardt Kosminsky. He pressed her arm, then left her, strolling through the crowd, stopping here and there to exchange compliments and comments, to eventually come up with the Russians and relieve Kosminsky. He and Kosminsky had agreed that one or other should keep the Russians in view, at least until the general bonhomie of the ball took hold.

Nodding to the senior Russian, Orlov, Michael resigned himself to playing his part; aside from all else, his selfless service would put him in Caro's good graces. Given his plans for later that evening, that wouldn't hurt.

Meanwhile, her Midsummer Revels had attracted enough senior diplomats to keep her supplied with dance partners throughout the evening. He was tall enough to see over most heads; while chatting with the Russians, then later with the Prussians, the Austrians, and the Swedes, he kept the delicate diadem she'd set in her hair in view. She was constantly on the move.

He saw Ferdinand propping a wall, watching her; he mentally wished him luck—in this setting, the hostessly bit between her teeth, Caro would be impossible to distract, totally ruthless in refusing to be detained. By anyone. He knew his limits. Later, he saw Ferdinand again, this time sulking, and deduced the handsome Portuguese had learned his.

There was a time and place for everything. The one weak link in his strategy lay in ensuring that when the supper waltz commenced, he was the gentleman in possession of Caro's hand. During a break in the music, he paused beside the dais on which the musicians were seated; a quick word and a few guineas strengthened his position. When the opening bars of the supper waltz sounded, he'd just returned to Caro's side, just reclaimed her hand, and had sotto voce informed her while bowing over it that the Russians and Prussians had thus far failed to come to blows.

She was smiling, relieved and entertained as the music swelled. He trapped her gaze. "My dance, I believe?" How could she refuse him?

With a laugh, she acquiesced and let him lead her to the floor. As she came into his arms and let him whirl her into the revolving circle, he realized she had no inkling that he was steering her in more ways than one.

He looked into her face, smiled into her eyes, found himself trapped in her silver gaze. Initially, she smiled back, as assured as he, yet gradually, as they twirled, their smiles faded, melted away, along with all consciousness of the noisy crowd around them.

Just that shared look, and he knew what she was thinking. That despite knowing each other for so long, inhabiting much the same circles, this was the first time they had ever shared a waltz.

She blinked; he saw her mind reach back . . .

"It was a country dance, last time."

She refocused. Nodded. "In Lady Arbuthnot's ballroom."

He couldn't remember. All he knew was that here, now, the moment was much different. It wasn't simply the waltz, the fact that they were both expert in the dance, that their bodies flowed effortlessly through the turns. There was something more, something deeper that left them more attuned, more alert, more aware, more acutely sensitive to the other.

Despite their training, to the exclusion of all else.

Caro felt the fascination, knew he did, too, and could only marvel. Nothing in her life had ever had the power to shut her ears, mentally shut her eyes, focus her senses to this degree. She was a captive, but a willing one. Her nerves tingled, her skin seemed alive, sensitive to his nearness, to the aura of strength that wrapped about her, not trapping her but holding her, promising sensual delights she craved.

Her senses led, her mind followed.

She was relaxed, yet excited, nerves taut yet assured.

Only when they slowed and she realized the music was ending did awareness of the present return. To them both. She saw it in his eyes; the reluctance she glimpsed in them mirrored her own.

The shield about them dissolved and chatter washed over them, for one instant a babel of incomprehensible tongues. Then over all the rest came Catten's stentorian tones directing everyone to the supper waiting in the marquee, to the chairs and tables, and the benches and well-lit walks, to the beauty of the midsummer night.

To a person, the throng turned to the three double French doors opened wide to the terrace. Delighted, exclaiming, guests poured out of the ballroom, stepping out into the balmy evening.

She and Michael had halted on the opposite side of the ballroom, not far from the main doors. She hung back, watching, making sure everyone was heading in the right direction. Once she was satisfied no guest had failed to understand the summons, she looked up, her hand firm on Michael's arm.

He smiled down at her. His hand covered hers. "Come with me."

She blinked; it took a moment to comprehend his meaning. *"Now?"* She stared at him. "I can't—" She looked toward the last stragglers disappearing onto the terrace.

Blinked again, then looked up at him. "We can't . . ." She

searched his eyes, aware her pulse had started to canter. She moistened her lips. "Can we?"

His smile deepened, his blue eyes held hers. "You'll never know unless you come with me."

Her hand locked in his, he led her up the main stairs. They saw no one, and no one saw them. Guests, household members, and staff were all outside on the lawns, or rushing back and forth between the kitchens and the marquee.

There was no one to hear them walk down the first-floor corridor to the small sitting room at its end. He opened the door and handed her through; she entered expecting to see chairs, chaise, and sideboard draped with holland covers. The room had been closed for years; it overlooked the side avenue and the orchard beyond.

Instead . . . the room had been cleaned, dusted, and swept and the covers all removed. The vase of lilacs standing on the small table before the open window suggested the when and how.

She'd forgotten the daybed. Wide, comfortable, it was now piled with cushions. Stopping beside it, she turned. And found him beside her, waiting to take her in his arms.

With confident ease, he gathered her to him and kissed her, parted her lips, sank into her mouth and claimed its softness. She met him, sank into his embrace, eagerly accepted every caress, returned them, and demanded more.

His head slanted over hers; her fingers speared through his hair and tightened on his skull as his tongue thrust deep in a definitely provocative rhythm. A rhythm that tightened her nerves, that sent heat pouring through her. And him. She wondered how much deeper, how much closer the simple intimacy of a kiss could get, how much more revealing.

The revelations were intoxicating—the hunger, the need, the simple human wanting, both his and hers. There seemed, between them at least, no disguise, no veil of propriety either sought to use to conceal the primitive nature of their desire.

Mutual desire. It had been her goal for a decade and more; in his arms, she knew it, felt it, recognized and acknowledged it. She gasped as he released her lips, then pressed her close as he trailed hot kisses from her temple to the hollow beneath her ear while his fingers undid her laces.

"Ah . . ." She couldn't think all that clearly, but she did remember she had a ballroomful of guests downstairs.

"Bear with me," he murmured. "In light of all the sharp eyes downstairs, returning with a crushed gown wouldn't be wise."

No, indeed. But . . .

His hands had earlier traced her curves, through the fine silk of her gown pressed flames and heat into her skin. The dewed flush she was starting to associate with his bolder caresses had already sprung up and raced across her more sensitive regions.

As her gown loosened, her mind belatedly caught up with his; she blinked, struggling to get her wits to work as he stepped back and drew her arms down, with his large palms slid the narrow straps of her gown over her shoulders, down over her arms—then he caught her wrists and raised them, draped her arms over his shoulders, and reached—not for her, but for her gown, for the folds that had collapsed at her waist.

She dragged in a breath, but the look on his face as he pushed the ecru silk over her hips, as the gown *shush*ed down to puddle about her feet, stifled her protest—one she realized was instinctive, another of her unintentional hurdles. The desire that lit his eyes as they traveled her body, revealed yet still tantalizingly concealed by her tissue-fine chemise, had her tensing, racking the delicious vise that held her one notch tighter.

The chemise's top was gathered above her breasts; the hem fell at midthigh, flirting with her ruched silk garters. Her body, its curves and hollows, the fine thatch of hair at the apex of her thighs, were only imperfectly screened by the diaphanous fabric.

His gaze, heated and bold, looked, traced, openly cataloged; he smiled when his roving eyes reached her garters, then he lifted his gaze, slowly, until his eyes met hers.

Desire burned in the blue—she couldn't doubt it; the same driving emotion etched the slow curve of his lips.

"I don't suppose you'd consider putting me out of my misery and removing that."

His eyes indicated her chemise, then returned to her face. Brazenly, she caught his gaze, arched one brow in query.

"I'm afraid if I touch it," his voice deepened as his gaze dropped to her breasts, "I'll tear it."

For an instant, reality—prudence and propriety—intruded; resolutely, she pushed them aside. She'd realized he'd imagined her more experienced than she was; in agreeing to an affair, in taking the road she'd wanted to take and fixing on the goal she was determined to reach, she'd accepted she'd have to play to his direction.

What she hadn't expected was that it would be so easy.

So easy to, while watching him watch her, raise her hand and tug the tiny ribbon bow nestled between her breasts undone. It slithered between her fingers, then the ends fell free.

There was only a handspan separating them; she could feel the tension holding him, feel it increase as, raising both hands, she slipped her fingers inside the chemise's neckline and eased it wide. Until it was wide enough to fall. To her hips. With a wriggle, she freed it and it joined her gown.

Heat reached for her—a heartbeat later he did, too, but she stopped him with a hand on his chest. "Wait."

He froze.

For an instant, she felt giddy—dizzy with the sense of power that suffused her—that she could, with just a word, with one small hand, hold him immobile, muscles, sinews, and masculine strength locked and quivering, simply waiting on her.

On her desire.

The realization sent a rush of heat through her. Swiftly, she bent, swiped up her gown and chemise and laid them over a nearby chair. She reached for her garters—

"No. Leave them."

The absolute command in his voice stayed her more than

the words. She was straightening, turning to him, when his hands touched her bare skin.

They spread, touched, slid; he drew her to him, flush against him, then locked her in his arms. Bent his head and kissed her, ripped her wits away and sent them spinning.

Then his hold on her eased, and his hands roved her body.

Emotions ignited, rippled through her, preceptions, revelations, and more. She'd thought him hungry before; now he was ravenous. Yet his control held firm; his touch was driven, urgent, greedy, and needful, yet masterful, almost reverent in taking all she wordlessly offered.

And offer she did; her own hunger, her own desire rose to meet his. She surprised herself, pressing herself to him, eager and enticing, flagrantly inviting; she hadn't known, not in her wildest dreams had imagined she had it in her to behave like this, wanton, abandoned, just a little wild.

She wanted more—wanted to feel his skin against hers. He was hot, so hot, and so hard. That need swelled until it became a physical ache. Driven, she drew her hands from where she'd clasped them about his nape, pressed them to his shoulders and tried to push back.

He broke from the kiss.

"Now you," she gasped, grasping the lapels of his coat.

"The coat, but nothing else." He suited action to the words, shrugging off his evening coat and flinging it to join her gown. "You have guests, remember?"

She blinked. "But I'm the one naked."

His lips curved; one large hand caressed her bottom, then he gripped and drew her back to him, molding her to him, bending his head to murmur against her lips, "Not naked. You're still wearing your stockings."

"But—"

He kissed her—lingeringly. "Not tonight, sweet Caro."

She was confused. "But—"

"Think of tonight as the second course in our sensual banquet."

A sensual banquet . . . the thought appealed. Her hands found his shoulders, felt the heavy, shifting muscles beneath the layers of waistcoat and shirt. Felt his hands spread over her bare back, stroking, caressing, then exploring. Roving anew.

His lips returned to tempt hers. His hands shifted.

"You're my hostess, remember? I told you I expected you to sate my appetite—you told me to help myself."

His thumbs were cruising her breasts, teasing her nipples to painful crests; his body was hard against hers.

"So just be quiet, lie back, and enjoy it while I do."

She had no choice—whatever his chosen road was tonight, it was outside her experience, yet she was eager to follow, to see where it led. There was no doubt in her mind, and none to color her responses; she met him freely, erected no more hurdles, nor felt compelled to create any restrictions.

Michael read her agreement in the way she allowed him to lower her to the daybed, in the way she relaxed, naked though she was, on the cushions alongside him and let him sculpt her body as he wished.

She flowed with him, with his caresses; he received her eager participation not just with inward triumph, but with a feeling very like thankfulness. He had himself, his raging lust and escalating desire, well in hand, yet if she pushed . . . he was increasingly certain he wouldn't be strong enough to resist her if she sought to tempt him.

Safety, therefore, lay in reducing her to helplessness; he set about doing so, conscious of a devotion to the exercise that exceeded any such situation in the past. She captured his senses, held them enthralled in some way no other woman ever had. When, one hand splayed over her waist, he eased back from their kiss and bent his head to her breasts, he couldn't remember a time when his whole being had been so focused, so acutely aware of taste, of texture, of tactile sensation.

When he'd reduced her to gasping moans, to arching wantonly beneath him, he replaced his lips and mouth with his fingers, and bent lower to trail kisses down to her navel. He dallied there, until her gasps came short and sharp, then nudged her thighs wide, shifted lower and settled between.

Felt the shock that gripped her. Set his lips to her soft flesh and felt the convulsive start that rocked her, that made her lungs seize, her fingers clench in his hair. Inwardly smiling, he settled to feast, to, as he'd warned her, sate his appetite—with her.

With her scent, with the apple-tart sweetness of her swollen flesh.

Caro shut her eyes tight, but that only made the sensations more intense. She couldn't believe—hadn't imagined ... her mental protests, her very wits melted away as he pressed heat and yet more heat on her, into her, impressed intimacy upon her through yet more shockingly intimate and flagrant acts.

Yet every touch was deliberate, expertly gauged, designed and executed with one primary goal—to give her pleasure. Mind-numbing, glorious, soul-drenching pleasure. His aim became clearer with every passing minute; delight welled, swelled—until she simply let herself flow with the tide.

Let herself whirl, then rise, spinning higher and higher as he delicately sucked, lapped, probed, as he orchestrated a dizzying splendor of sensation and sent it raging through her.

Heat built until within her a furnace roared. Her nerves were tight, and only grew tighter. Her lungs were starved, her breasts swollen and aching, her body a restless knot of need. And still he pushed her on. Gave her more and more ...

Until she shattered.

The bliss was deeper, longer, more intense than before. The pulsing of joy in its wake lengthened and stretched, the moment infinitely more truly intimate, infinitely more a sharing.

When she finally opened her eyes, he still lay propped between her widespread thighs, watching her face. He smiled knowingly; bending his head, he placed a kiss on her damp curls, then started kissing his way up her taut belly.

With weak hands, she reached for him, caught his shoulders and tried to tug. "Now you."

He glanced up at her face, met her eyes, tried to smile but it turned into a grimace. "Not tonight, sweet Caro."

She stared at him. "*Not?* But—"

"We've been absent long enough." He eased away from

her, swung his legs to the floor, then stood and looked down at her.

Still stunned, limbs weak, her wits in disarray, she blinked up at him.

He grinned, reached down, took her hands, and drew her to her feet. "You need to get dressed, then we need to appear again before your guests."

He might well be right, yet . . . she had to own to nagging disappointment. Accepting her chemise from him, she struggled into it, trying to think. He helped her into her gown, then expertly relaced it.

She put a hand to her hair.

"Wait."

He turned her to face him, resettled her diadem, touched the fine mass of her hair here and there, then stepped back and looked her over. Stopped at her breasts. Lifted her topaz pendant and settled it in place.

She met his eyes as they rose to hers. Searched them. Simply asked, "Are you sure?"

He didn't ask about what. Instead, his lips lifted; bending his head, he touched them fleetingly to hers. "Oh, yes." He straightened and his eyes met hers. "When I finally have you naked beneath me, I want at least two hours to play."

CHAPTER

12

*M*ichael elected to return to the ballroom via the secondary stairs at the end of the wing. Still pleasantly aglow and a trifle distracted, Caro allowed him to guide her. They were on the landing halfway down when the sound of a door closing brought them both to silent attention.

Below, in the corridor connecting the library and Geoffrey's study to the front hall, Ferdinand came into view. He walked confidently along; at one point, he looked around, but he failed to glance up.

Silent and still, they waited until he disappeared; they heard his footsteps fading across the hall tiles.

They exchanged a glance, then continued down. The door from which Ferdinand must have emerged led into the library. As they stepped off the stairs, it opened again; Edward stepped out. He closed the door, then started along, and saw them.

He smiled grimly. "Did you see?"

Caro nodded.

"I take it he searched?" Michael asked.

"Carefully and thoroughly for the past half hour. I watched him from outside."

Caro frowned. "I know there's nothing there, but did he take anything? Or look at anything in particular that might give us some clue?"

"No, but he went over the books very quickly. If I had to guess, I'd say he was looking for folios—the sort that look like books but are really folders of notes or letters."

Michael grimaced. "Camden's papers."

Caro humphed. "Well, at least he now knows there's nothing here."

"Or at Sutcliffe Hall." Michael took her elbow and steered her toward the ballroom, from whence sounds of guests regathering were emanating.

Edward followed. When they reached the ballroom, Michael released Caro; she headed for the terrace, no doubt intent on checking that her supper by moonlight had gone as she'd planned. He let her go. Pausing on the threshold, he scanned the heads, eventually locating Ferdinand's.

Beside him, Edward quietly said, "I wonder where Leponte will think of looking next."

"Indeed." Michael glanced at Edward. "We'll need to think more on that."

Edward nodded. "He's already checked the study, but I'll continue to keep an eye on him, just in case."

Inclining his head, Michael moved away. When he had a chance, he was going to have to try to put himself in Ferdinand's shoes, but the Russian attaché was, possibly unwittingly, standing next to the Prussian ambassador's wife—duty called.

Two hours, he'd said. As far as Caro could see, that meant she'd be waiting until the day after the fete, at the earliest, to learn the answer to her desperately urgent question.

She felt like having the gig harnessed, driving around to Eyeworth Manor, grabbing Michael by the cravat and hauling him off . . .

Where? That was the problem. Indeed, the more she thought of it, she couldn't imagine how he'd solve that particular difficulty at any time . . . unfortunately, today, she couldn't put her mind to devising a solution—she had a fete to help stage and a small horde of guests to herd to it.

The weather had held; the day had dawned fine, free of

any but the lightest clouds. The lilting breeze was just strong enough to rustle leaves and set ribbons dancing.

Breakfast was held late due to the previous night's festivities; as soon as it was over and the guests, refreshed, reassembled, she, aided by Edward, Elizabeth, and Geoffrey, shepherded them up the shady drive and across the village street.

For decades, the fete had been held in the meadow behind the church; a good-sized clearing, it was bound at the back and to the right by the forest, with a secondary clearing to the left, perfect for leaving horses and gigs under Muriel's stableman's watchful eye. Stalls set in a large circle displayed jams, cakes, and homemade wines amid a host of other local produce. There were wood carvings and paintings, horseshoes and ornamental brasses; the latter proved popular among the foreign visitors, as did Miss Trice's watercolors.

The offerings of the Ladies' Association—doilies, crocheted scarves, beribboned handkerchief sachets, embroidered tray cloths, antimacassars, and more—covered two long trestle tables. Caro stopped to chat with Mrs. Henry and Miss Ellerton, who were currently overseeing the wares.

While she talked she kept an eye on her guests, but they all seemed quite taken with this, for them uncommon, slice of English life. Lady Kleber and the general in particular seemed in their element; they'd stopped to talk with the woodcarver.

She was turning away when another large group came through from the stabling area. Michael steered the Swedish and Finnish contingents she'd billeted at the Manor into the main clearing, pausing to point out various stalls. She watched him smile and charm the Verolstadt girls, but when they went off, parasols gaily bobbing in their parents' wake, he remained where he was.

Then he turned his head, looked straight at her, and smiled.

A warm glow filled her; he'd known she was there. Not only that, but his smile—the smile he seemed to save just for her—was quite different. Somehow more real. He started toward her; she went forward to meet him. He took her hand, deftly raised it to his lips, kissed it.

His eyes on hers reminded her, stirred memories inappropriate to indulge in while in public. She felt a blush tinge her cheeks, tried to frown. "Don't."

His smile deepened. "Why not?" He wound her arm in his and turned her toward the homemade wines. "You look delicious when you blush."

Delicious. Of course he would use that word.

She retaliated by ensuring he bought two bottles of Mrs. Crabthorpe's elderberry wine, then guided him around the stalls, loading him with produce, even making him purchase two doilies from Miss Ellerton, who blushed even more rosily than she had.

His eyes laughed at her; indeed, he bore her managing in such good vein she started to become suspicious. Then they came upon Mrs. Entwhistle, who exclaimed at his load and insisted on relieving him of it; all the packages disppeared into her capacious bag while she waved aside his protests. "It's no difficulty at all, sir. Hardacre's here—he'll see me home."

"Ah, good." Michael's expression eased. "Given our guests won't be returning, I meant what I said earlier— please spend as long as you like here, all of you. I don't expect to be back until late. After all your hard work, you deserve some fun."

Mrs. Entwhistle beamed. "Thank you, sir. I'll tell the others. This *is* one of those occasions where we can catch up with our cousins and nieces and nephews—having the time to chat without thinking of ought else is a boon. I know Carter'll be happy to spend time with his mum."

"If I see him, I'll tell him, but do spread the word."

They parted; Caro felt her instincts pricking, but she couldn't fathom over what. Then Muriel saw them and swooped.

"Excellent! Just in time to perform the official opening." Muriel ran her eye critically over Michael, as if expecting to find something to correct.

When she frowned, defeated, Caro hid a smile; for this

setting, for his role, Michael was sartorially impeccable in a perfectly tailored riding jacket in brown-and-green tweed, his cravat snowy white, simply styled, his waistcoat an understated brown velvet, his breeches tight-fitting buckskins that disppeared into gleaming topboots. He looked the part he was there to play, the part he wished to project to this audience, that of a gentleman accustomed to moving in the highest circles, but who also was one of them, approachable, not above riding through their lanes, a man who appreciated their country pleasures as they did.

Had Muriel really thought he'd falter?

More, that if he had, that she, Caro, wouldn't have put him right?

Linking her arm more definitely in his, she nodded to a dray drawing up before the stalls. "Is that the platform?"

Muriel looked. "Yes, indeed! Come along."

Muriel strode ahead, calling to others to gather around. Seeing Reverend Trice, she imperiously directed him to the dray.

Michael caught Caro's eye; the glance they shared was one of complete understanding and politely suppressed amusement.

Reaching the dray, Caro slid her arm from Michael's and stood watching as he climbed up, assisted Reverend Trice up, then looked around, nodding and exchanging salutes with those he'd yet to chat with while they waited. Muriel came striding back; at her sharp command, numerous hands helped her up to the dray's tray.

Regaining her balance, Muriel smoothed down her skirts. She was a large woman, taller than Caro and rather heavier; in her dark green gown she looked imposing and severe. In a ringing voice, she called the crowd to order; briefly mentioning the long history of the fete and its purpose in raising funds for the physical betterment of the church, she graciously if somewhat superiorly thanked those who had assisted in staging today's event.

Muriel stepped back, inviting Reverend Trice to address the crowd. His tones imbued with the authority of his office, he accepted the support of the community and thanked all who had assisted and all who had come to share in the event in the name of the church and the Almighty.

Michael spoke last; it was instantly apparent he was the most gifted speaker of the three. His attitude was relaxed, his message succinct, his tone and inflections natural and assured as he applauded their community spirit, alluded to its strength, and how it owed its existence to each and every one of them. With just a few words, he bound them together, made each individual feel personally included. Then, drawing on local lore, thus subtly underscoring that he was one of them, he made them laugh, and then, speaking over the laughter, owned himself honored to declare the fete officially open.

The emphasis he placed on "officially" left everyone with a smile on their face; in true country fashion, no one had waited for any official sanction.

Caro had heard many such speeches, but not before from him. Yet she knew talent when she heard it; the Prime Minister's push to promote Michael into the Cabinet, where his eloquence would be of even more use to the government, now made complete sense.

Watching him shake hands with Reverend Trice and exchange a few words with Muriel, she sensed he was a politician who, although already successful, still had further to go. He had the talent to be a real power, but had yet to fully develop his strengths; to her experienced eyes, that was very clear.

He jumped down from the dray and rejoined her. Smiling, she took his arm. "You're very good at that, you know."

Michael looked into her eyes, read her sincerity, lightly shrugged. "It runs in the family."

Her smile deepened and she looked away; he seized the moment to tuck the compliment safely away in his mind. Such praise from her would have been gold in any case, yet now it meant much more.

The crowd had returned to the stalls and the various activities—the horseshoe throwing, the woodchopping and archery contests, among others. Despite her long absences, Caro was popular; as they strolled, people came up to greet her. And him. She was easy to spot in her summery gown of wide white and gold vertical stripes. She hadn't bothered with a hat; a gauzy gold scarf lay about her throat, protecting her fine skin from the sun.

Many members of the Ladies' Association stopped them, congratulating her on her idea of steering her ball guests to the fete, thus, as was quite evident about them, ensuring a special success for the day. Again he was struck by her facility for knowing what was happening in the lives of so many, even though she so rarely resided at Bramshaw; she picked up snippets from this one and that, and always seemed to remember to whom they applied when she next met that person.

He had more than one reason for clinging to her side; she commanded his attention on so many levels. Luckily, the fete was primarily Muriel's responsibility; when he asked, Caro confirmed that, as he'd supposed, once she'd delivered her guests as promised, her duty was discharged.

And she was free.

He bided his time, buying a selection of savories and two glasses of Mrs. Hennessy's pear wine to take the edge from their visceral hunger.

Normally, at such gatherings most participants would remain all day. The ball guests, who to a person had attended, had made their own arrangements for departure, instructing their coachmen to stop in the nearby clearing at prearranged times. There was no reason, therefore, that he and Caro could not remain until late afternoon.

He gave her no hint that he planned anything else. Arm in arm, they wended through the now considerable crowd, meeting others, in between amusing each other with observations and anecdotes that, unsurprisingly, were colored by their worldliness, by the background they shared.

Caro grew increasingly aware of that last, of just how much at ease in Michael's company she'd become. As they parted from Mrs. Carter, voluble in her thanks to Michael for having hired her son—which thanks he'd glibly yet sincerely turned aside with praise for Carter's service, thereby allaying any lingering doubts raised by Muriel's rejection of same, a fact Caro was perfectly certain he both knew and intended—she glanced at him. He caught her eye, lightly raised a brow. She merely smiled and looked away.

Impossible to tell him—explain to him—what a pleasure it was to be with someone who saw and understood as she did, to share even such minor yet significant matters with someone who thought and acted as she would. It was an emotional pleasure, not just an intellectual one, something that left her with a warm inner glow, a sense of shared achievement.

She'd grown used to his strength, to the sense of it surrounding her, to him being by her side, yet today she was conscious of the less obvious, less deliberate attentions he paid her. Without making any point of it, he seemed devoted to her pleasure, constantly seeking to smooth her way, to find things to amuse her, to please and entertain her.

If it had been Ferdinand, he'd have expected her to notice, and to reciprocate in kind; Michael hardly seemed aware he was doing it.

It occurred to her that he was taking care of her—that he considered her as being in his care, his to care for. Not as in a duty, but more as an instinctive act, an expression of the man he was.

She recognized the role; it was one she often assumed. Yet it was novel to find that role reversed, to discover herself the recipient of such unobtrusive, instinctive care.

They'd paused; she glanced at him. He was looking through the crowd, his expression impassive. She followed his gaze and saw Ferdinand talking to George Sutcliffe.

"I wonder," Michael murmured, "what Leponte is up to now."

"Whatever," she replied, "knowing George's taciturnity, *especially* with foreigners, I can't imagine Ferdinand will have much joy of him."

Michael raised his brows. "True." He glanced at her. "You're sure we shouldn't go and save him?"

She laughed. "Ferdinand or George? But regardless, I think we can leave them to their own devices." She had no wish to mar her day by having to deal with Ferdinand, to let him attempt to seduce her into revealing more about Camden's papers. He wouldn't succeed, and then he'd sulk; she'd known him for too long not to be certain of that.

Michael had pulled out his watch and was checking it.

"What's the time?" she asked.

"Nearly one o'clock." Returning the watch to his pocket, he looked over the crowd toward the forest. "They're starting the archery contest." He looked at her. "Shall we go and have a look?"

She smiled, took his arm. "Let's."

Many men had attempted to charm her, yet this—this simple day and his caring companionship—touched her in a way no other ever had.

The archery contest should have started by now; however, the participants, many eager to try their luck, had yet to agree on the precise structure of the contest. She and Michael were both appealed to, but were too experienced to get drawn in; laughing, they disclaimed all knowledge and, after a shared glance, beat a hasty retreat.

"Enough!" Taking her hand, Michael led her back into the crowd. They circled the central ring of stalls, passing three more, stopping to talk to the helpers who'd relieved those who had manned the same stalls earlier.

The crowd was dense, the sun high. Waving a hand before her face, regretting her lack of a fan, Caro tugged on Michael's arm. "Let's step to the side for a moment—catch our breath."

Instantly, he led her free of the bustle. A tall birch with a smooth trunk stood just within the clearing; reaching it, she turned and leaned against it, half closing her eyes, lifting her face to the sky. "It's really the perfect day for the fete, isn't it?"

Michael stood between her and the crowd; he let his gaze

dwell on her face, on the light flush the sun's warmth and their peripatetic exertions had brought to her fair skin. When he didn't immediately respond, she lowered her gaze and looked at him. Slowly, he smiled. "That's precisely what I was thinking."

Smile deepening, he reached for her hand. "Indeed." He drew her from the tree, almost into his arms as he leaned close to murmur, "As I was about to say—"

Whizz-thunk!

Startled, they looked up. Froze. Stared at the arrow quivering in the tree trunk precisely where Caro had been an instant before.

Michael closed his hand hard about hers. He looked down at her. Slowly, she brought her gaze back to his face. For one instant, her screens were down. Shock, bewilderment, and the first stirrings of fear were all there in her silver eyes. The fingers locked in his quivered.

He swore, drew her closer, into the protection of his body. One glance around showed that with all the noise and bustle, no one else had heard, much less seen, what had happened.

He glanced down at her. "Come on."

Keeping her close, he drew her back into the safety of the crowd, her hand still locked in his as they tried to disguise their shock. Caro put a hand on his arm, slowed him. He looked down. She was shaken, pale, but in control.

"It must have been an accident."

His jaw clenched so hard he thought it might crack. "We'll see."

He halted as the crowds parted and they got a clear view of the archery butts, now properly set up and with the contest in full swing. Laughing, Ferdinand laid down a bow. He appeared to be in high good humor, exchanging comments with two locals.

Caro grabbed his arm. "Don't make a fuss."

He looked down at her, grimaced. "I wasn't intending to." His protective instincts might have leapt at the sight of Ferdinand, bow in hand, but his wits were still functioning; he knew the two men running the contest—neither was so witless as to allow anyone to point an arrow toward the crowd.

And, as he'd assumed but had wanted to confirm, the butts all the contestants were aiming at had been positioned along the edge of the forest. There was absolutely no chance that even a stray arrow could have struck where he and Caro had been, all but in the opposite direction.

In addition to that, the arrow they'd left sunk in the tree trunk had been fletched with dark-striped feathers. All those for the contest carried plain white ones. He scanned the quivers standing filled and ready; not one arrow sported even a single stripe.

"Come on." He urged Caro back into the crowd.

She drew a tight breath and stayed close. After a few steps, she said, "So you agree. It must have been an accident."

From her tone, she was trying to convince herself.

"No." She glanced up; he caught her eye. "It was no accident—but I agree there's no point in making a fuss. Whoever fired that arrow wasn't in the crowd. He was in the forest, and he be long gone by now."

Caro's chest felt tight, her heart thudding in her throat as they pushed on through the crowd. But more people had arrived; they had to stop and talk as before. Both she and Michael slipped on their polished masks—no one seemed to guess that behind those masks, they were shocked and upset. However, the more they talked, the more they were forced to respond in a normal fashion to those about them, to discuss the gentle vicissitudes of country life, the further the incident, and the sudden fright it had caused, receded.

Eventually, she realized it really *had* to have been an accident—perhaps some boys larking about in the forest edge, as boys were wont to do, with no idea they'd shot at anyone. It was *inconceivable*—there was simply no reason—that anyone would want to harm her.

Certainly not Ferdinand. Even Michael seemed to have accepted that.

Only when they reached the far side of the clearing and

Michael continued on did she realize she hadn't, indeed, any idea what he was thinking.

"Where are we going?" Her hand still locked in his, he was heading for the clearing where the carriages and horses had been left.

He glanced at her. "You'll see."

Muriel's stableman was on watch; Michael saluted him and continued on, leading her to where a long line of horses were tethered. He marched along, then stopped. "Here we are."

Released, Caro blinked at a faintly familiar bay rump. Then Michael backed his big gelding out of the line.

Her instincts jerked to life. "What—"

"As I was about to say before being rudely interrupted by that arrow"—he lifted his head and met her gaze as his hand locked once more about hers—"*come with me*."

Her eyes widened with very real shock. "What? *Now?*"

"Now." Reins wrapped about his hand, he reached for her—and hoisted her up to sit in his saddle.

"What . . . but—" She had to grab the pommel, desperately fight for balance.

Before she could manage anything else, he slipped a boot into the stirrup and swung up behind her. Wrapping an arm about her waist, he lifted her, settled her against him, locked her there.

She looked up, fleetingly glimpsed the main clearing and the distant crowd as he wheeled the huge horse away. "We can't just leave!"

Michael touched his heels to Atlas's flanks; the big bay surged. "We have."

He'd planned, schemed, to make this afternoon their time—the only time when his house lay truly empty, no staff about. Everyone was at the fete and would remain there for hours, happy to while away the day.

While he and Caro seized their moment.

As they emerged onto the lane just outside the village and he turned Atlas away from Bramshaw, he was aware of the thud of the horses' big hooves—and the echo driving through his veins.

How much of the emotion that hardened his muscles, that fired his determination to cling resolutely to his plan and his goal—to grasp the hours he'd promised himself they would share—derived from the incident of the arrow he couldn't say, couldn't at the moment even reasonably guess. Some part of it certainly derived from a primitive conviction that he should claim her without delay, make her his and thus secure the right to protect her, yet while the incident might have acted as a spur, deepening his need to bring their wooing to a swift and satisfactory conclusion, the arrow hadn't given rise to that need.

She had.

She twisted before him, making him wince; she tried to glance back at his face, then back toward the fete. "What if someone misses me? Edward might—"

"He knows you're with me."

Leaning forward, she focused on his face. "Geoffrey?"

"As usual hasn't a clue, but he saw us." Looking ahead, he negotiated the turn into the lane that led to the Manor. He glanced at her as Atlas lengthened his stride. Raised his brows. "If he does wonder, he'll imagine you're with me."

Which she was.

Caro faced forward. Her heart was thudding again, but with an even more unsettling cadence. He was carrying her off like some knight in a minstrel's tale, tossing the maiden he desired over his saddle and making off for his isolated keep.

There to have his way with her.

It was a distracting thought.

She blinked back to the present—to the reality before her—when they clattered into the Manor's stableyard. Michael reined in the big horse, dismounted, then lifted her down. Quickly, he unsaddled the great beast. . . .

Two hours. That's what he'd said.

She tried to imagine it. Failed completely.

"Come on." Seizing her hand, he towed her out of the yard and on through the orchard.

She really should protest—shouldn't she? She cleared her throat.

Over his shoulder, he flicked her a glance. "Save your breath."

She frowned at the back of his head. "Why?"

He kept towing her along. "Because you're shortly going to need every last bit of it."

She frowned harder, tried to peer around and see his face. His jaw was set; the planes she could see resembled chiseled granite. She pulled back, dug in her heels. "Why? And anyway, you can't simply drag me off like this, like some"— with her free hand, she gestured wildly—"prehistoric caveman."

He halted, turned, met her gaze, then yanked, sending her tumbling into his chest—into his arms.

They locked around her; looking down, he met her wide eyes. "I can. I have."

He kissed her; what he'd left unsaid echoed through her brain. *And now I'm going to ravish you.*

The kiss stated that clearly; it was a storming that left her senses reeling and her wits disengaged.

That cindered every possible protest she might have made.

Her lips parted beneath his, gave before the devastating onslaught. He took her mouth, filled it and her with a heat that was already molten; hot as lava, he sent it flowing down her veins. His hands firmed on her back, holding her so she was acutely aware of his strength, and her relative weakness, then he molded her to him, making no secret of his desire, or his intent.

She clung to him, kissed him back, suddenly wanting as much as he, aware to her curling toes that this—*this*—was what she needed. This was the right answer—the answer she'd always longed for—to her question. He wanted her, desired her beyond doubt. If only . . .

As if he sensed her need, her real, impossible-to-state wish, he broke from the kiss, bent, and swept her into his arms.

He strode the last steps to the back door, juggled her and opened it, then strode through. His heels rang on the tiles as he made for the front hall, then he swung around and climbed the main stairs two at a time.

Clinging to his shoulders, she waited to be set down, but he didn't so much as pause. Glancing at his face, she found it set, his expression resolute and uncompromising. He paused before the door at the end of the corridor; with a quick twist of his wrist, he sent it swinging, and carried her through.

He heeled the door closed; the sharp snap as it shut echoed through the room.

It was a large, airy chamber; that was all she managed to gather as he swiftly carried her across it. To the large bed.

Again, she waited to be set down—again, he surprised her. Effortlessly, he raised her, and tossed her onto the coverlet.

She gasped—gasped again as he joined her, as his weight landing beside her made her bounce—and roll toward him. He helped her along, one large hand wrapping about her hip and pulling her flush against him. With his other hand he framed her face, held her still as his head came down and he covered her lips with his.

Fire. It poured from him into her, and ignited her starving senses. His lips moved on hers; he pressed her into the bed, and his tongue filled her mouth. No languor this time, just a burning, driving need that had her reaching for him, pulling him down to her, sinking her fingers into his shoulders, then spreading them, grasping his clothes, wanting—needing— to feel his body under her hungry hands.

He knew, understood. He drew back enough to shrug off his jacket; still trapped in the kiss, eyes closed, she searched and found the buttons of his waistcoat, frantically undid them. Then she pushed the halves wide and slid her hands over the fine linen of his shirt—over the hard ridged muscles beneath, up over the heavy planes of his chest.

Her touch—the heat of it, the flagrant greedy hunger of her fingers—distracted Michael. Eyes closed, sunk in savoring the wonders of her mouth, he paused . . .

She froze. Stopped. Suddenly hesitant.

He tore his mouth from hers. Groaned, "For God's sake, don't stop." Then he plunged back into the rich honeyed pleasures of her mouth—and felt her hands attack him again.

Felt her need of him in a flagrantly animalistic way.

Then she found the hem of his shirt where it had come loose from his breeches, and slipped her hands—first one, then the other—beneath.

Touched him. Spread her greedy little fingers wide and tactilely devoured him. He could barely believe the heat, the intensity of the desire she sent raging through him with each evocative touch.

Each evocative claiming.

For it was that. He wasn't sure she knew it, but he did. In the distant corner of his brain that still functioned, he knew, even as he groaned and urged her on, that he was surrendering—giving himself to her—that he would give whatever she needed to sate her.

Her hunger ran deep—deeper than he'd realized. He sensed it, sensed her response, her powerful yearning, through their kiss. They both held to the kiss avidly, their anchor, their most assured means of communication in a world suddenly full of heated longing that had reduced, drawn in to the limits of their tightly focused senses.

Riding the urgency of her unfurling desire, he mentally groaned and held his own back, let her take the first bite, at least enough to slake the edge from her appetite.

He managed to shrug out of his waistcoat; hands between them, he undid his cravat, then flung it away. Blindly groped, caught enough of his shirt to wrestle it up, then broke from the kiss to drag it off over his head.

She surged up, pressing him back to the bed; he dropped the shirt over the side, gasping, eyes closing the better to savor the feverish urgency of her touch, the way she spread her hands over his bare chest, fingers flexing, searching—as if he were hers and she was intent on possessing him.

He had no argument with her direction.

Opening his eyes, he studied her face, saw delight and something close to wonder in her expression. The sight made him ache. Then she lifted her gaze and her eyes met his. Molten silver, burning bright, then she veiled them, lowered her gaze to his lips.

He urged her more fully atop him; she obliged, then without further encouragement bent her head and set her lips to his.

He was waiting for her, waiting to draw her back deep into the kiss, to anchor her there, caught in the swirling, building heat of interlocking desires, while he set his fingers to her laces.

She drew back briefly to unwind her scarf, then sent it to join his shirt on the floor. His hand firming in the mass of her soft hair, he drew her back down, tongue thrusting boldly, finding and enticing hers, capturing her senses, holding her attention deep in the kiss as he skillfully eased her gown from her.

When he finally drew it free and it, too, hit the floor, he could no longer hold back his own need to touch her, to spread his hands over the lithe curves, to trace the sleek lines of her body with his palms. To fill his senses with her. To learn as she was intent on learning him, to possess as she was intent on possessing him.

She murmured through the kiss; he felt her breath hitch as he closed his hands over her breasts and kneaded. She responded by slanting her mouth over his and pressing deeper, flagrantly inviting. He met her, caught her nipples and squeezed, until her attention splintered and she gasped. Releasing her breasts, still holding her to their kiss, he boldly slid his hands down, proprietorially tracing her sides, her hips, to reach beneath the hem of her chemise and caress the globes of her bottom. He reveled in the dewed flush that sprang to his touch, at the urgency that rose and coursed through her.

She shifted upon him provocatively, quite deliberately teasing his aching erection. Not taunting, but with her sleek thighs exploring its contours, shifting hips and legs to sinuously stroke him.

He nearly broke, but caught his reins in time to remind himself they had hours. Even more than the two he'd promised himself. There was time to play, to savor. And there would be only one first time.

Spearing one hand into the glory of her hair, he anchored her head and kissed her. As ravenously as he—and she—wished, as blatantly, wantonly, primitively evocative as they both desired.

No rush.

He took his time savoring her mouth anew, feeding from her, stoking their passion as, with slow deliberation, he explored her body. Found each hollow and stroked, traced, searched for each point where her nerves fluttered, where any touch, however light, made her breath catch. High on the backs of her thighs—she was excruciatingly sensitive there. The undersides of her breasts, too. Inch by inch, he eased her chemise up, until finally he broke from the kiss and drew the fine garment over her head.

The instant it was free he let it fall where it would, caught her and rolled, pressing her back to the bed, leaning over her, hand splaying over her midriff, holding her down as he sank deeply into her mouth, then drew back.

And looked at the treasure he'd uncovered. Discovered.

At the feminine beauty of lithe limbs and svelte curves encased in ivory silk already delicately flushed with desire.

Wits barely engaged, breathless, Caro watched his face as he examined her body. Saw the austere planes tighten as with his hand he almost reverently sculpted her flesh. Her nerves tightened with an anticipation more delicious than she'd imagined. She felt on the brink of shivering, yet she wasn't cold.

It was a glorious midsummer afternoon; the window was open—a balmy breeze wafted in to caress them. To add its gentle warmth to the heat already pulsing so hotly within her. And him.

He was burning. For her.

She raised a hand, gently traced the harsh, almost graven lines of his face. His gaze deflected for one moment to her eyes, then he turned his head and pressed a kiss to her palm. Desire glowed in his eyes, turning the soft blue more solid, more intense. It was passion that etched his face, that hardened its lines as he returned his attention to her body.

To drawing fire beneath her skin, with each increasingly

intimate caress pulling her deeper into the vortex of her own hungry desire, tempting her need—a need only he had ever evoked. She watched his face, watched his concentration as he loved her, clung to that evidence of his commitment to their goal. The tension investing his large body, which had tightened his muscles to bands of steel, which she could feel through her fingers locked on his shoulder, likewise reassured. Then he bent and took one already ruched nipple into his mouth, and suckled. Deeply.

She moaned; sliding one hand to his head, clenching her fingers in his hair, she wordlessly lifted against him. Felt his rumble of approval as he shifted his attention to the other breast she so wantonly offered him, simultaneously soothing the first with clever fingers.

The path of his orchestrated worship was familar; she gave herself up to it, valiantly trying to mute her cries until he murmured, his tone gravelly and low, "Scream all you like. There's no one to hear . . . except me."

The last two words made it clear it pleased him to hear the sounds he drew from her. Just as well; she found it increasingly difficult to mute them, to spare enough wit and strength to do so.

All her attention, all her senses, were caught in the flames, in the pulsing conflagration he was so assiduously building within her.

But when he pressed her thighs wide and touched her, traced the slick folds already swollen and wet, sudden uncertainty gripped her. Opening her eyes, she reached for him, with one palm boldly found, and cupped him.

He froze, sucked in a sudden breath as if her touch were painful; she knew enough—had gathered enough—to know it wasn't pain that closed his eyes, that locked his features.

Then he opened his eyes, looked at her.

She met his gaze, hazed and burning. Caressed him, through his breeches let her fingers trace, then close about his length. Eyes locked with his, she licked her lips, forced herself to find breath enough to say, "I want you. This time . . ."

He shuddered; his lids started to fall, but then he forced them up. Impaled her with a burning blue gaze. "Yes. Definitely. This time . . ."

She sensed rather than heard his inward curse, saw the fight he waged to try to regain his control—then his fingers wrapped hard about her wrist and he drew her hand from him. "Wait."

He sat up and swung his legs off the bed. Coming up on one elbow, ready to protest if need be, she watched—relief and a surge of giddy anticipation flooded her when she heard the dull thud of one boot hitting the floor. The second followed; he glanced back at her as he worked the buttons of his waistband free, then he stood, stripped his breeches down, stepped out of them as he turned, kneeled, then fell back on the bed beside her.

Her heart leapt, swelled, ached. He was beautiful, fully aroused, elementally male. Her mouth was dry. She couldn't drag her eyes from him, from the evidence that his desire for her hadn't, yet, waned. She reached for him, traced lightly, trailing her fingers up the burning, baby-fine skin, then she closed her hand about his length, felt the weight of him fill her palm.

He groaned, the sound heartfelt. "Damn! You're going to be the death of me."

He caught her hand, lifted it from him, and rolled, coming over her, pressing her into the bed, nudging her thighs wide and settling between. Ground out as he shifted, "We'll take it slowly next time."

Caro's lungs seized; her heart leapt to her throat. The time had finally come; her question hovered, about to be answered. Unequivocally.

Her senses locked, focusing on the soft flesh between her thighs, feeling it throb as he reached down between them, with his fingers stroked, then probed, then parted her folds.

The broad head of his erection touched her, pressed against her, then eased in a fraction.

She nearly cried out; hips lifting in wordless entreaty, she closed her eyes, bit her lip, willing him to enter her. Every particle of her being strained, held poised on an emotional edge higher than any she'd previously climbed, acutely aware of the drop below her, of the ocean of disappointment that waited to swallow her if he didn't . . .

Spreading her hands over his back, she held him to her, pressed her hips nearer, urged him on.

Beneath her hands, the long planes of his back flexed. With one slow, powerful thrust, he joined them.

Eyes closed, savoring every inch of her scalding sheath as it stretched, took him in, and enclosed him, Michael noticed the tightness, then the constriction as he thrust through it; caught in her sensual web, he might not have understood if it hadn't been for the pained gasp she tried unsuccessfully to smother, and the telltale tensing that gripped her, held her.

Stunned, dazed, opening his eyes he looked down at her, into her eyes, molten silver looking back at him. Understood in that moment all she'd hidden, all she'd never told, him or anyone else.

Finally understood the truth of her past, the true reality of her marriage.

She was waiting, breathless . . . tense, nervous . . . he suddenly understood what she was waiting for.

Slowly, deliberately, he withdrew a fraction, then reseated himself fully within her.

Saw her eyes flare—with wonder, with a joy so profound he felt his own heart turn over. But this was no time for words or explanations. Bending his head, he covered her lips with his, and spun them both into the fire.

Into the intimate dance they both craved.

He didn't spare her, didn't try to be gentle, realized that that, assuredly, was not what she wanted, more, was very definitely not what she needed. He sank into her body, drove deep, then withdrew until he was almost free of her clinging heat and her fingernails had sunk into his skin, desperately holding him to her, before thrusting into her again, slowly, inexorably, so she could feel every inch of his throbbing erection as he buried himself inside her once more.

She pulled back from the kiss. Her sobbing gasp, echoing with relief, with pure happiness, urged him on.

He took her mouth again, pulled her ruthlessly back to him, back into the kiss, let his weight pin her, then sent one hand sliding down, around over her hip to cup her bottom, gripping, anchoring her at just the right angle beneath him, then he settled to ride her, to let his body plunder hers as he and she both wished. Let the driving rhythm take over, binding their heated bodies in an orgy of elemental lust, driven by desire, by the passion that swirled about them, unleashed and almost tangible.

She met him, matched him; not at any moment did he doubt that she wanted this. Every bit as much as he did.

It might be her first time, yet she was no wilting virgin; quite the opposite. She was a quick study; as their tongues tangled and their bodies strove, within minutes she'd learned how to meet his thrusts, how to most effectively ride them, how to clasp him within her body and drive him wild . . . he dimly realized that for her, this was a long-sought-after release—a freeing of all she'd held within her, trapped inside, denied outlet for so long.

A catharsis of passion, of desire, of the simple need for the intimacy of human mating.

He gave her all she needed, took all he wanted in return, conscious she surrendered it—all he wished to take—gladly.

It was certainly not his first time—he'd had more women than he could truly remember, all of them experienced ladies if not outright courtesans—yet as he sank into her body, into her mouth, plundered and gloried in her open welcome, there was something new, something different in the act.

Perhaps it was the simplicity—they knew each other so well, so completely in so many other ways, understood each other so instinctively that knowing each other in this way, skin to skin, hands searching, gripping, mouth to greedy mouth, tongues tangling, gasping, loins to heated loins, plunging, driving . . . all seemed so natural.

Meant to be. Without any veils or masks to disguise it.

Power, fueled by their joint passion, welled up, spilled through them both and took them.

Captured them, swept them into a sea of whirling, greedy need that suddenly, abruptly, coalesed.

Their skin was alive, nerves tense and tight; their bodies fused, driven by primal urgency. She pulled back from the kiss, gasped, eyes closed as she struggled to breathe.

He pushed her faster, harder; she strained upward, and with a cry touched the sun. Clutched, held tight to him as she shattered, then melted, pulsing around him.

Her release called on his own; he followed her quickly, drove deeper, harder, emptying himself into her, with a long groan finally collapsing atop her, sated to his toes.

CHAPTER
13

Caro lay beneath Michael and exulted. His hard body, his heavy muscles and even heavier bones, pressed her into the bed; she didn't think she'd ever felt so comfortable, so . . . simply happy.

So connected, physically and otherwise, to any other person in her life.

Tremors of excitement still racked her; aftershocks of glory still slid through her veins, leaving an indescribable sense of joy in their wake.

This, then, was intimacy. Something far more profound than she'd imagined it to be. Also a great deal more . . . *primitive* was the word that leapt to mind.

She smiled; she wasn't about to complain.

For long minutes, they simply lay entwined, trapped in each other's arms, both aware the other was awake, yet both needing to catch their breath, mental as well as physical. Slowly, the realization that he had guessed her secret, knew and understood it, intruded.

Staring up at the ceiling, she searched for words, for the right thing to say, in the end simply said what she felt. His head lay across her shoulder. Gently, almost tentatively, for such tender touching was still new to her, she riffled her fingers through his hair. "Thank you."

He dragged in a breath, his chest crushing her breasts,

then shifted his head and kissed her shoulder. "For what? Having the best time of my life?"

So he was a politician even in bed. She smiled, wryly cynical. "You don't have to pretend. I know I'm not particularly . . ." Words failed her; she gestured vaguely.

He lifted his shoulders, caught her waving hand, then pushed back enough so he could meet her eyes. He looked into them, then drew her hand to his lips. Turned it and placed a scorching kiss in her palm—caught her gaze as he did, then gently bit the mound at the base of her thumb.

She jerked. Realized he was still hard and solid within her . . . no . . . was *again* hard and solid within her. Puzzled, not quite sure, she refocused on his eyes.

His smile wasn't humorous, more forbearing. "I don't know what Camden's problem was, but as you can *feel,* I patently don't suffer from it."

The more she thought about it, the more obvious that last became.

As if to further demonstrate, he moved a little, rocking rather than thrusting. Nerves that a minute ago had seemed dead with exhaustion sizzled back to life.

He shifted over her again, settling on his forearms, one on either side of her. "Remember"—he kept the gently rocking motion going—"what I said earlier about taking two hours?"

Somewhat stunned, her mouth drying anew as, to her considerable astonishment, her body responded—ardently, eagerly—to his, to the promise in that gently repetitive motion and the rock-hard reality riding within her, she licked her lips, focused on his eyes. "Yes?"

His lips twisted; he lowered them to hers. "I thought I should warn you—I plan on taking three."

He did. For three bliss-filled hours he held her captive in his bed, until they'd reduced the originally neat covers to a froth of silk and linen, a sensual battlefield.

On resuming their play, he spent the next half hour ensuring she understood that once was very definitely not enough—not enough to sate him, or her. While outside, the pulsing heat of afternoon forced even insects to drowsing silence, inside his bedchamber, intimately entwined with him on his bed, heat of a different sort drew gasps, moans, and passionate cries from her.

Until she tumbled headlong into glorious oblivion and he swiftly joined her.

He had no interest in any passive submission; when he stirred her a third time, the engagement extended into a journey of intimate exploration and discovery—for them both. He not only blatantly encouraged her to be as wanton as she felt, in her wildest dreams desired, but teased, even taunted her to go further, to forget any restriction she might have imagined might apply and respond to him as primitively as he did to her.

Not once did he seek to conceal his desire for her, not once did he fail to impress on her his hunger, the power of his lust, his driving need to slake it by joining his body with hers.

When at the last she convulsed in his arms, held tight against him as he knelt on the bed, her thighs spread wide over his, him sunk to the hilt within her, she had finally learned what mating was—a sharing of passions, a mutual giving and taking, a melding that went far beyond the physical, touching deeper things.

It was a lesson she had waited more than a decade to learn.

As she slumped in his arms, Michael let his reins slide and surged within her, racing toward the shattering release that with every rippling contraction of her sheath about his painfully engorged length beckoned. Her body, still thrumming, drew him on, pulled him over that glorious edge and into sweet oblivion.

He didn't let himself sink too deep beneath the golden waves; couldn't. Yet still he lingered, glorying in the feel of her body in his arms, in the hot wetness that so tightly enclasped him. Drawing the scent of her deep into his lungs, he let his hands soothingly roam her sweet flesh. She was flushed, dewed after their exertions, yet her skin remained a wonder, the finest, most delicate silk. He nuzzled the tender hollow between her neck and shoulder, drew his face alongside hers, feeling the springy frizz of her hair against his cheek.

Matters between them had shifted, not so much changed as grown deeper, developed in ways he hadn't foreseen. Yet the changes had only made his ultimate goal all the more desirable, all the more precious.

Once his head had stopped whirling, he lifted her from him and laid her on the pillows. Eyes closed, exhausted, she slumped like one dead; wryly triumphant, he flicked the silk coverlet over her and slowly, reluctantly, left the bed.

Caro was dimly aware that this time he hadn't joined her amid the rumpled sheets, that his large, hot male body wasn't spooned around hers. Distant creaks, tiny rustles reassured her he was still in the room, yet many minutes passed before she could summon sufficient strength to lift her lids and see what he was about.

The sun was still strong, still beaming above the treetops, yet not by much; it had to be past four o'clock. Michael stood before the windows looking out at the trees. He'd donned his breeches, but remained bare-chested; as she watched, he raised his hand and sipped from the glass he carried.

His jaw was set. There was something in his stance, in the set of his shoulders, that told her something was wrong.

A sinking feeling assailed her. She closed her eyes . . . felt his hands on her, fingers sinking into her hips as he made love to her; opening her eyes, she resolutely pushed her fear aside.

If she'd learned anything about life, it was to face difficulties directly. Nothing good ever came from beating about any bush. She sat up. Her head spun once, but then steadied. She grabbed the coverlet as it started to slither down.

He heard the rustle, glanced around.

She caught his gaze. "What is it?"

He hesitated. The sinking feeling started to swell again, but then he moved, came closer, and she read enough from his face to know seeing her naked in his bed wasn't any part of the problem he was wrestling with.

He halted at the foot of the bed, sipped again from the

glass. She could now see it contained brandy. Lowering it, he fixed her with a steady, almost considering stare. Almost pensively said, "Someone's trying to kill you."

Michael had wondered how she'd react; his guess proved accurate—she started to smile reassuringly. Her lips curved, her eyes started to light—then the transformation paused. Faded as she read his face, and realized he was serious.

Eventually, she frowned. "Why do you think that?"

Inwardly, he gave thanks his marital lust had settled on an intelligent woman. "Consider these facts. One—that day when your horse, Henry, was spooked and you nearly came to grief in your gig, Hardacre found evidence that Henry had been hit with pellets, most likely from a slingshot."

Her jaw fell. "What?"

"Indeed. There seemed little point in worrying you at the time—Hardacre and I both reasoned it was some nonlocal lads larking about. Highly unlikely it would happen to you again." He nodded. "And it didn't. Something else did, or almost did."

She blinked, thinking back.

He watched, then told her, "Those men who attacked Miss Trice."

She focused on his face. "You think they were after *me*?"

"Think back. *You* were the first to leave the drawing room. If it hadn't been for me arguing, detaining you in the hall until Miss Trice had gone out, and then taking you up in my curricle, *you* would have been the first lone female walking down the village street. And there wouldn't, in normal circumstances, have been anyone close behind to aid you."

Realization sank in, chilling her; Caro shivered and pulled the coverlet closer. "But if they were intending to attack me—and I still can't see why"—she looked at him—"how could they have known I was about to leave, and that I'd be walking alone?"

"You'd walked there alone—reasonable to imagine you'd walk home alone, too, as, indeed, you'd intended. And the doors to the back garden were open—easy enough for anyone to have crept close and kept watch." He held her gaze steadily. "You made your farewells to Muriel, then headed for the front hall—the signs were clear."

She grimaced.

He went on, "And now we have an arrow striking a tree in precisely the spot where you'd been resting a mere instant before."

She studied his face, knew all his facts were true. "I still can't credit it. There's no point, no possible reason."

"Be that as it may, I believe there's no alternative but to conclude that someone, for what reasons we have no clue, is set on, if not killing you, then at the very least, causing you serious harm."

She wanted to laugh, to push the idea aside, to flippantly dismiss it. But his tone, and even more what she saw in his face, made that impossible.

When she said nothing, he nodded, as if acknowledging her acceptance, and drained his glass. He looked at her. "We need to do something about it."

She noted the royal "we." Some part of her felt she should be bothered by it, yet she wasn't. She wasn't convinced, either, yet knowing he would be by her side in dealing with whatever was going on reassured rather than unsettled her. Yet . . . her mind rapidly took stock, then she looked up and met his eye. "The first thing we need to do is get back to the fete."

They dressed; somewhat to her surprise, assuming their outward guise of tonnish lady and gentleman did not diminish the newfound sense of closeness, not just physical but more profound, that had infected not just her, but him, too. She experienced it as a heightened awareness of his body and his thoughts, his reactions; she sensed it in his gaze as it rested on her, in the light touch of his hand on her arm as they left his bedchamber, in the more definite, possessive engulfing of her hand by his as they threaded through the orchard.

Presumably three hours of naked play rendered reverting to any socially acceptable distance impossible. Not that she cared. Their new closeness was far more appealing, far more intriguing, and there was no one around to be shocked.

At her insistence, he harnessed his gig and drove her back to the fete in more conventional style. Leaving the gig in the secondary clearing, they rejoined the crowds still ambling about the stalls, now largely engaged in last-minute purchases and protracted farewells.

No one, it seemed, had missed them. Or if any had, none sought to remark on their mutual absence. Caro deemed that just as well; she had enough to do to appear normal, to keep a silly, far-too-revealing smile from her face. She kept banishing it, yet if she relaxed her vigilance, it crept back; on top of that, while she could walk well enough, she felt oddly exhausted, as if every muscle in her body had unraveled.

For the first time in her life, swooning delicately away— or at least pretending to—held considerable appeal. Instead, she applied her formidable skills to putting on a good show, chatting here and there as if she and Michael had, indeed, been present the entire afternoon.

Michael remained by her side, her hand anchored on his sleeve; although he was attentive to all those with whom they spoke, she was conscious that he was, if anything, being even more protective, alert to all around them as if on guard.

He confirmed that last when they moved away from the woodcarver's stall, murmuring, "The Portuguese have left."

She raised her brows. "The others?"

"No Prussians or Russians visible, but the Verolstadts are just leaving." With a nod, he indicated the small group gaily gathering to one side. Together, they strolled across to make their farewells.

The Swedish ambassador and his family had been delighted with their day; they were effusive in their thanks and good wishes, promising to meet in town later in the year.

They parted; Michael again scanned the clearing. "No more foreigners, nor any of the diplomatic crowd."

It had to be close to five o'clock, the accepted end of the day. Caro sighed happily, delighted that all had gone so well—on multiple counts. "I should go and help pack up the Ladies' Association stall." She glanced at Michael. "You can come and help."

He raised his brows at her, but followed her without complaint.

Muriel appeared as they reached the stall. She frowned at them. "There you are—I've been looking for you for some time."

Caro opened her eyes wide.

Michael shrugged. "We've been circulating—farewelling the foreign delegations and so on."

Muriel somewhat grudgingly conceded, "They all came, as far as I could tell."

"Indeed, and they enjoyed themselves hugely." Caro was too happy to take umbrage; she was perfectly prepared to spread the joy. "They all sent their compliments." She smiled at the other ladies folding unsold wares into baskets.

"And what's more," Mrs. Humphreys said, "they weren't above buying things. Those two young Swedish misses were buying up presents for their friends back home. Just think! Our embroideries on Swedish dressers."

A general discussion of the benefits of Caro's novel idea ensued; she helped stack tray covers and doilies, agreeing that if she was in residence at Bramshaw when next year's fete rolled around, she would consider hosting some similar dual event.

Standing a little behind Caro, Michael kept an eye on the clearing in general while scanning the thinning crowd. Eventually he spotted Edward and beckoned him over.

Stepping away from the ladies, he lowered his voice. "Earlier, someone shot an arrow at Caro."

His appreciation of the younger man's talents deepened when Edward only blinked, then returned, equally sotto voce, "Not an accident from the contest . . . ?" Reading the truth in his face, Edward sobered. "No—of course not." He blinked again. "Could it have been Ferdinand?"

"Not personally. I doubt he'd have the skill and regardless, he'd be more likely to hire someone to do the job. The arrow came from the direction of the butts, but had to have been fired from within the forest."

Edward nodded, his gaze on Caro. "This is starting to look very strange."

"Indeed. And there's more. I'll come around tomorrow morning and we can discuss the whole, and decide what we need to do."

Edward met his gaze. "Does she know?"

"Yes. But we'll need to keep a close watch over her." Michael looked at Caro. "Starting from now, and your journey home."

He couldn't drive Caro home; it would have looked too odd, what with Geoffrey, Edward, and Elizabeth all there, along with a host of Bramshaw staff—and the entrance to the drive was only across the village street. He did, however, keep a surreptitious watch from atop his gig, before, satisfied she was halfway down the drive, surrounded by numerous others, and no problem had occurred, he headed home.

On the one hand, he was thoroughly satisfied; on the other, anything but.

Next morning, he rode to Bramshaw House as soon as he'd breakfasted. Edward, seeing him striding up the lawn, left Elizabeth to practice the piano alone and came to meet him; together they went into the parlor.

"Caro's slept in," Edward informed him. A slight frown played across his face. "She must have been worn out by the fete—perhaps the heat."

Michael suppressed his smirk and sat. "Probably. Regardless, that gives us time to revisit the facts before she joins us."

Edward sat on the chaise and leaned forward, all attention. Michael settled in the armchair and recited the facts known to him, much as he had with Caro the previous day.

When, gowned for the summer day in a fluttery gown of pale apple-green muslin, Caro drifted downstairs after breakfasting—very late—in her room, she wasn't at all surprised to hear Michael's deep voice rumbling from the parlor.

Smiling, still serenely, dreamily content, she headed that

way, noting that Elizabeth was flexing her fingers in the drawing room.

Pausing on the parlor's threshold, she saw Michael and Edward, both frowning at their thoughts; they saw her, and stood. She glided in, smiling easily at Edward, then rather more privately at Michael.

His eyes met hers; she felt the heat in his gaze. Calmly, she sat on the chaise, waited until they'd resat. "What are you discussing?"

Michael replied, "The relative likelihood of Fedinand's being after something for himself, or having been sent after something for someone else."

She met his gaze. "I have to own to great difficulty in believing that what Ferdinand's after could have anything to do with him personally. He knew Camden, that's true, but diplomatically Ferdinand's a nonentity." She looked at Edward. "Don't you agree?"

Edward nodded. "I would assume with his background he'll eventually step up to some post, but at present . . ." He looked at Michael. "I can only see him as a lackey."

"Very well," Michael said. "If he's a lackey, who is he acting for?"

Caro exchanged a glance with Edward, then pulled a face. "I really couldn't see him acting for anyone but his family, not in such a way—trying to seduce me, asking after Camden's papers, arranging to have the Hall burgled, searching here." She met Michael's gaze. "No matter what else Ferdinand is, he is a member of an old aristocratic family, and Portuguese family honor is in some ways more stiff-rumped than English. He wouldn't risk the honor of his house in such a way."

"Not unless it was the honor of his house that he was seeking to protect." Michael nodded. "That's what I thought. So what do you know of Ferdinand's family?"

"The count and countess—his uncle and aunt—are the only ones I've met in Lisbon." Edward looked at Caro. "The duke and duchess are representatives of some description in Norway, I think."

She nodded. "I've met a few minor members who hold

lesser posts, but the count and countess are the two currently in favor at court. They're close to the king . . ." She paused, then added, "Thinking back, they've been steadily advancing their position over the last decade, certainly since I first went to Lisbon. They were only minor functionaries then."

"So it could be something that would damage their standing?" Michael asked.

Edward nodded. "That seems most likely."

Caro, however, remained sunk in thought. When she continued to stare blankly at the floor, Michael prompted, "Caro?"

She looked up, blinked. "I was just thinking . . . the count and countess's standing *might* be at risk, but I would have heard something from someone. . . ." She met Michael's gaze. "Even from the count or countess themselves."

"Not if it was something horrendously damaging," Edward pointed out.

"True. However, it's just occurred to me that the count and countess are *not* the head of the family—and that position means a lot."

"The duke and duchess?" Michael asked.

She nodded. "Ferdinand certainly gave me that impression, and the countess, too. I'd never met the duke and duchess before, not until this last Season in town, and that only briefly, *but*"—she looked at Edward, then at Michael— "I *should* have met them, sometime, at some function in Lisbon. But I didn't, I'm quite sure of that."

Edward blinked owlishly. "I can't even recall them being mentioned."

"Nor can I," Caro said. "Yet if they're the head of a house, and that house is close to the throne . . . well, something's wrong. Could it be they've been quietly banished?"

A pregnant silence fell as they all considered the prospect, all wordlessly accepted it as a possibility.

Michael glanced at Caro, then Edward. "Which begs the question, if so, for what—and could that 'what' be in some way connected with Ferdinand's obsession with Camden's papers?"

"The latter isn't hard to imagine," Edward said.

"Indeed not," Caro agreed. "Camden was in touch with virtually everyone. However, Camden would have placed anything pertaining to any sensitive subject in the official files, and they're with either the Foreign Office or the new ambassador."

"But Ferdinand wouldn't know that," Michael said.

"Possibly not. So that, potentially, explains his searching."

Edward frowned. "It doesn't, however, throw any light on why he might be trying to harm you."

She blinked. "You didn't seriously think . . . ?" Her gaze swept to Michael, then returned to Edward. "Even if these recent incidents are attempts to harm me, I can't see how they could have any diplomatic connection. Especially not with Ferdinand's family secret—that, whatever it is, most likely predates my time as Camden's wife."

Michael's steady, rather stern regard didn't waver. After a moment, he said, quietly but firmly, "That's because you don't know, never knew, or can't remember—for whatever reason are not aware of knowing—whatever it is these people think you know."

After an instant, Edward nodded decisively. "Yes—that could be it. In lieu of retrieving whatever it is from Camden's papers, someone—presumably the duke if our theorizing is correct—has decided you might know his secret, and must therefore be silenced." He paused as if turning his words over in his mind, then nodded again. "That makes sense."

"Not to me," she declared, equally decisively.

"Caro—" Michael said.

"No!" She held up a hand. "Just hear me out." She paused, listening to the distant music. "And we'll have to be quick because Elizabeth's almost at the end of that study, and she'll be along as soon as she's finished." She looked at Michael. "So don't argue."

He set his lips.

"You've decided these three incidents have been attempts to harm *me*—but have they? Couldn't they just as easily have been accidents? Only the first and third actually involved me—it's pure conjecture that the second was targeted at me. The men attacked Miss Trice, not me. If they'd been sent to kidnap me, why did they seize her?"

Michael bit his tongue; furnished with a sketchy description, in the deceptive twilight making such a mistake would be easy. He exchanged a long glance with Edward.

"As for the third incident," Caro rattled on, "an arrow shot from the forest too close to the edge of a crowd. Doing such a thing and successfully hitting a particular person—the archer would need to be a better marksman than Robin Hood. It was pure luck I happened to be there at that moment, that's all. The arrow had nothing to do with me specifically."

He and Edward kept silent. This was one argument Caro wasn't going to let them win; there was no point pursuing it even though they were convinced they were right. They'd simply watch her anyway.

"And even you and Hardacre thought the first incident with the pellets was just boys being stupid." Caro spread her hands. "So we have two likely accidents, and one attack. And while I grant the attack on Miss Trice wasn't an accident, there's no evidence it was me those men were after. Indeed, there's no reason to think that anyone wishes me, specifically me, ill."

She concluded on a definite note. She glanced at them, first one, then the other. They met her gaze and said nothing.

Caro frowned. She opened her lips—then had to swallow her "Well, what do you think?" as Elizabeth entered.

Michael rose; he and Elizabeth shook hands.

Bright-eyed, Elizabeth looked around. "Have you been discussing the fete—or business?"

"Both," Caro replied, and rose, too. She didn't want Michael and Edward worrying Elizabeth with speculations. "But we've exhausted both topics, and now Edward is free. I'm going for a stroll in the gardens."

Michael reached across and appropriated her hand. "An excellent idea. After all those hours amid the crowds, you're no doubt longing for silence and solitude." He drew her hand through his arm. "Come, I'll walk with you."

He turned to the door. She narrowed her eyes at him; he'd

taken the words out of her mouth and turned them to his own advantage.

"Very well," she assented as he guided her through the doorway. "But"—she lowered her voice—"I'm not going anywhere near the summerhouse."

The way he smiled in response, his expression shadowed in the dimmer corridor, did nothing for her equanimity.

But as they strolled across the lawns, then along the walks lushly bordered by beds burgeoning with the summer's verdant growth, the peace of their surroundings closed in, cocooning them from the world, and her serenity returned, bringing with it a degree of ease, of acceptance.

She glanced at him; he was looking about them. "I really can't believe anyone is seeking to harm me."

He looked down at her. "I know." He studied her eyes, then said, "However, Edward and I do."

She grimaced and looked ahead.

After a moment, he lowered his arm, took her hand in his, and said, his voice even, but low, "We both care for you, Caro—consider . . . if we were ultimately proved right, but hadn't taken any precautions, hadn't done what we could have and you were hurt, or killed . . ."

She frowned; they walked on.

"We'll keep watch over you—you won't even be aware of it."

Much he knew; she'd know every instant, would feel his gaze on her . . . would that be bad?

She inwardly frowned, thankful when he said no more but gave her time to wrestle with what for her was a novel situation. No one before had "watched over her" for the reasons he'd given. Camden had been protective, but only because she'd been one of his most treasured possessions, and she used the word "possessions" advisedly; that was what she'd been to him.

Edward was attached to her; they shared a common bond through their years with Camden and their respect for him and his memory. Edward and she were friends as well as associates; she wasn't surprised he was concerned for her safety.

But Michael . . . his quiet tone veiled yet, she suspected quite deliberately, didn't conceal a wealth of deeper emotions, and a need—a reason—to watch over her, to guard and protect her, which stemmed from a different source. It was a form of possessiveness, true, but one that arose not from an appreciation for and a need of her skills, her talents, but from an appreciation for and need of her, herself, the woman she was.

"Yes. All right." Her agreement was on her lips before she'd thought further, already distracted by a wish—a strong urge and desire—to learn more about his need of her, to understand the true nature of what drove him to protect her. Halting, she faced him. Looked into his eyes. "Will you spend the day with me?"

He blinked, briefly searched her eyes as if to confirm the invitation, then reached for her. "Gladly." He bent his head. "There isn't anywhere I'd rather be."

They were in a secluded walk, fully screened by thick bushes. She stepped into his arms, twined hers about his neck, and met his lips. Parting hers, she ardently welcomed him in, artfully teased.

Tempted, flagrantly taunted.

She knew what she wanted; so did he.

Within minutes, the reality was apparent; desire hummed through their veins, thrummed beneath their skins. Their mouths greedily, hungrily melded, sharing heat, fire, stoking their conflagration, reveling in it.

She pressed closer, arched against him; he shuddered and drew her closer still, molded her to him.

He broke from the kiss, laid a tracery of fiery kisses from temple to ear, ducked beneath to continue the line down the arched length of her throat. "The summerhouse is too risky." His words were a trifle rushed, fractionally breathless. Infinitely persuasive. "Come back to the Manor with me. The staff might be shocked, but they'll be discreet. They won't talk . . . not about us."

From his point of view, the matter was irrelevant; he intended to marry her, soon. More important and urgent was their mutual need for privacy.

Caro lifted weighted lids and looked at him. Moistened her lips, cleared her throat. "There's somewhere I know where we can go."

He forced his mind to think, but couldn't imagine where. . . .

She saw; the smile that curved her lips was essentially, fundamentally feminine. "Trust me." Her eyes lit, almost mischievous. Drawing back from his embrace, she took his hand. "Come with me."

It took him an instant to recognize the sultry invitation, his own seductive phrase given back to him, its potency multiplied a thousand times by the look in her eyes, by the spritelike way she turned and led him further along the path.

At no point did it occur to him to refuse.

She was a wood nymph leading him, a mere mortal, astray. He told her so and she laughed, the silvery sound drifting on the breeze—reminding him anew of his pledge to draw that magical sound from her more often.

Hand in hand, they descended through the gardens, eventually leaving the tended areas through a narrow gate in a hedge. Beyond lay a medley of meadow and wood, largely undisturbed by man. The path led underneath trees, then across open clearings where grasses encroached, reducing it at times to little more than a track.

Caro's feet seemed to follow it instinctively; she neither looked for landmarks nor searched for the path but strolled on, glancing at the birds flitting through the trees, occasionally lifting her face to the sun.

In the middle of one clearing, he halted, drew her back to him. Into his arms. The house was some distance behind them; he bent his head and kissed her, long, deep, letting his real yearning have full sway—a yearning he was learning, day by day, possessed a greater depth and breadth than he'd imagined it ever could.

Finally raising his head, he watched her face, watched her lids flutter, then rise, revealing the silvery sheen of her eyes. He smiled. "Where are you taking me?" Lifting her hand, he brushed a kiss across her fingertips. "Where is your bower of unearthly bliss?"

She laughed, a joyous sound, but shook her head at him. "You won't know of it—it's a special place." They started walking again; after a moment, she murmured, her voice soft, low, as magical as her laugh, "It is a bower of sorts." She glanced up, fleetingly met his eyes. "A place apart from the world." Smiling, she looked ahead.

He didn't press for more; she clearly wanted to surprise him, show him . . . anticipation flared, steadily built as she led him deeper into the wooded reaches of her family's property. She had spent her childhood here; she knew its grounds as well as he knew his own. He couldn't, however, guess where she was making for; he wasn't lost, but . . . "I've never been this way before."

She glanced at him, smiled, then looked ahead. "Few people have. It's a family secret."

After twenty minutes of strolling, they crested a small rise; beyond, a grassy meadow rolled down to the banks of the stream, here swiftly rushing. The swoosh of the water's gushing progress reached them; fine spray rose and swirled between the banks.

Caro halted; smiling, she waved ahead. "That's where we're going." She glanced at him. "Where I'm taking you."

On either side of the meadow, the woods marched down to the stream's edge, framing a tiny cottage that stood on an island set in the middle of the widening stream. A narrow plank bridge arched over the rushing waters; the cottage was old, built of stone, but was clearly in excellent condition.

"Come on." She tugged, and he obliging walked on at her side; his gaze remained riveted on the cottage.

"Whose is it?"

"It used to be my mother's." She caught his gaze as he glanced at her. "She was a painter, remember. She loved the light out here, and the sound of the stream rushing into the weir."

"Weir?"

She pointed to the right; as they descended through the meadow, a huge body of water came into sight.

He got his bearings. "Geoffrey's weir."

Caro nodded.

He'd known of the weir's existence, but had never had reason to come this way. The stream bubbled and boiled as it swept into the weir; even though it was summer and the flow far less than in winter, the island in the middle of the streambed forced the incoming water to split and rush past on either side.

Halting a yard from the bridge, he looked around. The stream banks were high, the water level at present much lower than that possible, yet even if the stream did overflow, as it would during a significant thaw, the island was higher than where they stood; much of the meadow flat would flood before the cottage's foundations got wet.

The bridge was as narrow as it had appeared from a distance, just wide enough for one person. It arched over its span to the island; a single handrail was fixed along one side.

But it was the cottage itself that commanded his attention; it looked to be one large room with numerous windows. The door, shutters, and window frames were brightly painted; flowers nodded and bobbed about a small paved area before the front door.

The cottage was not only in excellent repair, it was in use—not deserted.

"It was originally built as a folly," Caro said. Slipping her fingers from his, she stepped onto the bridge. "Rather more substantial than most, as it's such a long way from the house and so isolated. Mama loved it here—well"—starting across the bridge, she waved at the weir—"you can imagine the play of light off and over the weir at sunrise, at sunset, during storms."

"She came here at sunrise?" Michael followed her onto the bridge, wary at first, but it proved to be solid.

Caro glanced back. "Oh, yes." She looked ahead. "This was her hideaway—her own special place." Stepping onto the island, she spread her arms, lifted her head, whirled and faced him. "And now it's mine."

He grinned, caught her to him as he stepped off the bridge and backed her up the short path. "You weed the beds?"

She grinned back. "Not me. Mrs. Judson. She was Mama's maid when Mama first came here—she used to

keep the cottage and the garden perfect for Mama to use."
She glanced around, then turned out of his arms and reached
for the doorknob. "After Mama died, the others were all
grown and gone except for Geoffrey. He had no use for it, so
I claimed it for my own."

Setting the door wide, Caro walked through, then paused
and looked back. Michael filled the doorway, his large,
strong frame haloed by the sun. With his clothes thrown into
shadow, he appeared timeless, paganly, elementally male. A
shiver of awareness, of delicious anticipation, slithered
down her nerves. Lifting her chin, she locked her eyes on
his. "Other than Judson, who spends Friday afternoons here,
no one comes here but me."

It wasn't Friday.

His lips curved; for one long moment, he studied her,
then, his gaze unwavering, he stepped over the threshold,
reached behind him, and closed the door.

CHAPTER

14

She was waiting for him when he halted before her, waiting, when his hands rose and slid about her waist, to twine her arms about his neck, to step close, stretch up against him, and press her lips to his.

To tempt, taunt, and entice.

To move sinuously against him, soft curves and supple limbs caressing his muscled body in a siren's call as old as time.

Her invitation was explicit; it was clear in her mind—she wanted it clear in his.

His arms tightened about her, his tongue surged over hers as he accepted, as he relentlessly drew her to him, clamped his hands about her hips, and moved suggestively against her.

She sighed through the kiss, sank, openly seductive, against him, flagrantly invited him to take all he wished, to show her more of his hunger, and hers.

Sunshine shone through the wide windows, bathing the cottage's interior and them in a soft golden light. As they stood, bodies twining, mouths melding, knowing this was but a prelude—that they had no need to rush, that they had all day to orchestrate as they wished—memories of playing here while her mother painted slid into her mind, another time of discovery, of wonder found in the myriad flowers in the garden, in the variety of leaves, the strange and varied effects made by paint and brushes . . . it seemed all of a piece.

Today she was intent on exploring a fresh landscape, here, in the place of her childhood.

She arched against him, felt his hands slide up her sides, thumbs brushing her already sensitized breasts. It was his turn to tease, to artfully, skillfully tighten her nerves with caresses that promised, that made her flesh yearn, but which never assuaged.

Relief would come later. Possibly much later. As his hands continued to slide, to stroke her limbs, her curves through the fine muslin of her gown, as if he were learning her anew, she sensed . . . not a backtracking but a retracing of previous steps, so that he and she could dally at places along the road they'd hurried somewhat precipitously down the day before.

She made no demur, any temptation to impatience overridden by curiosity, by her determination to know all of what he felt for her, all of what he might reveal to her of his desire—for her, for what they, together, could conjure between them.

That much yesterday had taught her, that the power they both craved was created of them both, an amalgam of desires and needs and passions that necessarily required the input of two. Together, they could create the most wondrous whirlpool of sensations, the deepest, most satisfying of emotional connections.

They both wanted that, a shared goal, a mutual desire. As they stood locked together, the warmth of the sun like a benediction sinking into them, and gradually, step by slow step, allowed the kiss to deepen, she knew that beyond thought, beyond doubt.

Their lips parted; they paused to catch their breath. She felt his hands slide around her, felt his fingers tug at her laces. Eyes closed, she savored the moment, drank in every last sensation—the feel of his body, hard and aroused against hers, the steely muscles that surrounded her, that flexed in his arms as he loosened her gown, as he prepared to

strip it from her, the aura of strength that, more real than all
else, engulfed her, sank into her bones and reassured, the
sense of safety she found in his arms.

What if . . . ?

The thought teased. What if they'd come here years ago,
when she'd been sixteen—what would have happened if
he'd taken her in his arms then, and kissed her with the slow
burning hunger with which he kissed her now?

Impossible questions with no answer; they weren't who
they had been all those years ago. She was who she now was,
twenty-eight, confident and assured for so long that those
attributes were part of her character, acknowledged and
known to her, coloring her relative innocence, allowing her
to explore her newfound sensuality, her newfound appreciation of sexual interaction, of sexual intimacy, without guilt
or regret. And he . . . he was the man in her arms. No youth,
no young gentleman about town, but a man in his prime. In
all his strength, his desire mature, multilayered, and strong,
powerful and potent as, her laces all undone and her gown
loosened, he drew her back to him, into his embrace, into his
arms.

He kissed her; she willingly sank into the caress, into the
welling tide. The temptation to simply let go and flow with
it, let it and him take her as he would, burgeoned, yet . . .
she'd led him here today; she had her own agenda. Yesterday, of necessity, she'd had to follow his lead. Today . . . it
ought to be her turn.

When his hands rose to her shoulders, she readily
shrugged out of her gown. Let him break from the kiss to
help her from it; released from his arms, she stepped out of
the gown's folds, took the garment from his hands, shook it
out, and, turning, walked the few steps to a chair.

The cottage, outwardly small, contained only a single
large room. A dresser stood by the wall near the door, alongside a washbasin and ewer on an iron stand. Other chests and
benches and a long artist's desk were placed around the
walls; the fireplace and hearth took up half the wall opposite
the door. The center of the room had always been left clear,
reserved for her mother's easel, but that was now folded

away and propped in one corner, leaving only the beautiful daybed, two straight-backed chairs, and two small side tables deliberately placed, posed about the tiled space.

Thanks to Mrs. Judson, devoted to her mother and now to her, everything was dust-free, spick-and-span, always kept ready for her use, as was her room in the main house.

Laying her gown neatly over the back of one chair, she turned, met Michael's eyes across the room. Deliberately, she let her gaze wander down, over the long length of him. Returning her gaze to his eyes, she arched a brow. "Take off your coat."

Michael felt his lips ease, not in a smile; his features were already too set to permit that. He shrugged out of his coat, ready to play whatever game she wished—as far as he was able.

Her silver eyes gleamed at his obedience; she sauntered, hips swaying, closer; he let his eyes roam over the curves seductively shifting beneath her chemise. She paused before him until his eyes returned to hers, then lifted the coat from his hand. "The waistcoat, too."

He obliged. Handing the garment over, he asked, "Am I allowed to inquire just what your pleasure is?"

Brows rising, she draped coat and waistcoat over her gown; facing him, she smiled. "You may inquire, but I'm afraid I can't tell you." Her smile deepened as she returned to him. "Yet."

She reached up, boldly cupped a palm about his nape, and drew his lips to hers for a long, slow kiss, one intended to ignite every fire they'd laid and left waiting. He reached for her, hands sliding over skin screened only by diaphanous silk.

Hand splayed on his chest, she pushed back, broke the kiss. Met his eyes directly. "You still have on far too many clothes." She frowned disapprovingly. "Why is it men wear so much more than women? It hardly makes for evenhand-edness in this sphere."

He fought for a sufficiently languid tone. "True, but there's hay to be made there, after all."

As he'd intended, the allusion intrigued her. "From that? How?"

Looking innocent wasn't easy. "If I could make a suggestion?"

She smiled, as intent as he. "Suggest away." Her sultry tone indicated she'd seen straight through his ploy, but was interested nonetheless. That message was echoed in the shimmery silver of her eyes as he looked into them, as he paused to assure himself his control was strong enough to, even with her, attempt such sexual games. A sense of anticipation gripped viselike about his chest, an eagerness he couldn't recall feeling since adolescence infused him. Wound him one notch tighter.

"Once we're both naked, there won't be any reason to get dressed before we leave—I seriously doubt either of us will feel inclined to waste the energy. True?"

He arched a brow at her; puzzled, she nodded.

"So if we're going to harvest some of that hay . . ." He reached for her again, fingers flexing about her waist before he slowly turned her, then stepped close, his chest to her back, his thighs to her bottom. Sliding his hands around her waist, he locked her to him; bending his head, he nuzzled the hollow behind one ear. "Then we'd better do it now . . . don't you think?"

Lids falling, Caro leaned back into him, once again glorying in being wrapped in his strength. His breath wafted the fine curls about her ear; she fought to suppress a delicious shiver. Head back, resting against his shoulder, well aware they were embarking on some sensual game, she murmured, "I think . . . we should take advantage of every opportunity as it offers . . . don't you think?"

His deep chuckle dripped promise. "Absolutely." His lips traced the side of her throat, then he murmured, "Should we adopt that as our policy?"

His hands slid slowly upward until they cupped, then closed about her breasts; it was seriously difficult to draw breath enough to reply, "That seems an . . . appropriate notion."

Her hands, loosely clasped about the backs of his, had followed them upward; eyes closing, she savored the flexing muscles as he slowly, subtly kneaded, then she sighed.

"So . . ." Her words were a breathless whisper. "What should I do next?"

His answer came in a dark, deep murmur. "For the moment, all you need to do is feel."

An all-too-easy assignment; her senses were already mesmerized, caught by the skillful play of his fingers. They possessed, then teased, found her nipples and squeezed . . . until she gasped.

Releasing her breasts, his hands roamed, tracing the curves and indentations of waist and hips, the sleek upper faces of her thighs, the rounded globes of her bottom.

"Wait."

She blinked, felt him steady her on her feet. Then he stepped away, to the side; turning her head, she watched him pick up the second chair, and carry it back to where she swayed.

He set it down beside them, in the same movement regathered her into his arms, as before with her back to his chest, her bottom riding against his loins. Splayed, his hands were suddenly everywhere, hot and hard, sending heat pulsing through her. Bending his head, he pressed a kiss to her throat, over the point where her pulse galloped, then slowly traced his lips up the long taut curve; in the end, she turned enough to meet his hungry lips with hers, equally avid, equally greedy.

For long moments, the kiss and all it encompassed held them, then he lifted his head, waited for her lids to rise, looked into her eyes. "Your sandals—take them off."

So that was the purpose of the chair. She looked at it, shifted her weight, and raised one foot shod in a pretty Grecian sandal to the seat. The winding ties of the sandal wrapped around her ankle and reached halfway up her calf; she had to bend over to unpick the knot.

The movement pressed her scantily clad bottom more firmly against him—an inadvertent, yet hardly unintended invitation—one he was waiting to take advantage of. Her lips lifted as his large hand curved about her bottom, as his fingers stroked, evocatively caressed; she realized how hot her skin already was, how flushed, how tight with anticipation her flickering nerves had become.

Rightly so, it seemed; as she wrestled the leather laces undone, his fingers reached further, found her softness, boldly delved. Her lungs locked; bent over her raised leg, she felt increasingly giddy as he probed, as he made free with all, courtesy of the position, she offered.

She had to battle to draw in a huge breath, then straighten, one sandal free, dangling from her fingers. His fingers remained pressing into her softness, his hand intimately wedged between her thighs. She dropped the sandal, didn't wait for instructions but dragged in another breath, raised her other foot to the chair, and started—as fast as she could—to untie her other sandal.

He shifted behind her. His fingers reached deeper, probing more evocatively; with his other hand, he lifted the back of her chemise, exposing her bottom and back—then he bent and laid a long line of hot, open-mouthed kisses down her spine.

Lower and lower. She realized she'd stopped breathing—couldn't do more than take a shallow, far too shallow breath. His lips reached the base of her spine; he paused. His fingers still delved, caressing her heated slickness yet not as deeply while his other hand drifted from her, then she felt him move, press closer. His hand returned, wrapping about her hip, anchoring her—as the broad head of his erection, hot and hard, replaced his fingers between her thighs, shallowly penetrating her slick sheath.

She gasped, wanted more, much more of him, but wasn't sure which way to move.

He arched over her once more, again tracing her spine with his lips, keeping her bent over, open to his play.

And play it was; he pressed into her no more than an inch, if that, tantalizing her senses, making them writhe as he moved in and out. She closed her eyes, heard the soft exhalations that issued from her lips, savoring the sensations, the building urgency—the sheer need rising through her.

On the sensitive skin of her back, she felt his lips curve . . . realized she'd completely forgotten about her sandal. Summoning wit enough to complete the task was an effort. Opening her eyes, she pulled at the knotted lacings, eventually tugged them free.

His chuckle as she paused, not sure whether she wished to move, sent anticipation slithering through her.

His anchoring hand left her; he withdrew from her and straightened, allowing her to do the same.

The instant she dropped her sandal, he murmured, "Take off your chemise."

His fingertips grazed her hips, telling her she was to remain as she was, facing away from him. Excruciatingly aware of him just behind her, still clothed in shirt, cravat, breeches, and boots.

She slanted a glance back; she couldn't see his face, yet the sight of his broad shoulder, his muscled arm, confirmation of his strength so close, poised to possess her, sent a shiver of needy greed rushing through her.

The easiest way . . . facing forward, she reached for the hem of her chemise, and slowly, taking the time to gracefully untangle her arms and free her frizzy hair, drew it off over her head.

He plucked it from her fingers, tossed it she didn't know where. "Now . . ."

The word, breathed into the sensitive hollow behind her ear, held a wealth of dark, illicit promise.

She inwardly smiled, delighting in his devotion to her wishes, to her education, her fascination.

"Turn around."

She did, with alacrity. Her gaze went straight to his erection, jutting strong and proud from the open placket of his breeches. She exhaled in relief, in appreciation, reached— would have touched, stroked, but he caught her hands, one in each of his.

"Not this time."

Using his grip on her hands, he backed her a trifle so he could sit on the chair and settle, thighs wide. Changing his grip on her hands, interlocking their fingers, he drew her closer.

"This time, you get to pleasure me."

She looked into his eyes.

They beckoned. "Take me inside you."

Half command, half plea. It was impossible, she discovered, to smile, not with desire and passion riding her so hard; instead, she moved without hesitation, stepping over his thighs to straddle him, clinging to his hands as she sank slowly down, as she felt his hardness beneath her, adjusted, then, finding his eyes with hers, locking her gaze with his, she sank slowly down.

The pleasure—of him stretching her, filling her, of being able to feel every inch of his rigid invasion—was indescribable. He, and the blatant act of joining, filled her mind, drowned her senses.

Michael watched; he didn't try to take her lips even when she sank fully down, closed her eyes, and let out a shuddering sigh. He wanted her to know, for her senses to be free to feel all there was to be experienced.

As she wished. As, he accepted, she needed.

She was too mature to go gradually, to dally with simple sex, uncomplicated gratification. She was confident, too assured of her own self to be satisfied with any limited view; her nature insisted she see it all, learn all the activity had to offer. Given his ultimate aim, he was perfectly happy to accommodate that need—and slake it.

Happy to demonstrate every variation she might enjoy, the better to convince her to spend the rest of her life enjoying them with him.

Not once, not as he encouraged her to move upon him, to set her own pace, to ride him, to use her body to please and pleasure him, did he forget that ultimate aim. Once she'd mastered the basics, he left her to experiment; releasing her hands, he set his to her body, to learn more of her, to pander to her greedy senses, step by step to more deeply possess both them and her.

He recognized the moment when, heated and nearly frantic, she realized the implication of her nakedness, his clothed state. Even under her heavy lids, her eyes widened, molten silver burning with need. She gasped, slowed as full realization struck—that in the middle of the cottage in the midday sun, she was naked, straddling him, servicing him with abandon—a houri and her master. Slave and owner.

She stared into his eyes; he read her thoughts—she read his. He waited, unperturbed . . . then she closed her eyes and shuddered, tightened strongly about him.

Releasing her hands, he gripped her hips and took charge; spreading his fingers, he took her weight and urged her on. She gasped, adjusting to his more forceful penetration, then grabbed his shoulders, leaned close.

He nudged her head up and took her mouth, filled it as he filled her, deeply and thoroughly. Within minutes, she was aflame, her body writhing in his hold, straining to take him deeper, clutching, clinging, framing his face as she kissed him back.

And then they were flying.

Locked together, higher than the sky.

He hadn't expected her to take him with her, hadn't realized he was so deeply caught, but as her sheath contracted powerfully about him, he was already pressing deep, thrusting high within her.

To touch the sun a moment after she did.

To die and be reborn in that starburst of primitive pleasure.

To be one with her, sunk in her body, wrapped in her arms, as they floated back to earth.

As completions went, it would be hard to better.

Of course, he fully intended to try.

When Caro finally stirred, it was to remark, in her most prosaic tone, "I should have brought a picnic."

He couldn't help but laugh.

She struggled to lift her head from his shoulder. Planting her forearms on his chest, she managed it, and looked into his face. "Aren't you hungry?"

He grinned. "Ravenous." He caught a stray frizzy curl and tucked it back, met her gaze. "But I'm perfectly content to make do with you."

The comment pleased her, but also seemed to puzzle her. She studied his eyes. "You really do . . . like being with me."

He felt his heart contract. She wasn't fishing for compliments; she was trying to understand. "Caro . . ." With his fingertips, he traced her cheek. "I love being with you."

Hearing the words, he realized how true—simply true—they were. He would rather be with her than anywhere in the world, now or anytime.

She tilted her head. He realized he couldn't read her eyes not because she was hiding her feelings, but more because, or so it seemed, she was not yet sure what her feelings were. As in order to attain his desired goal, he needed to get her to change her mind, her mental assessing seemed a good sign.

Fingers firming about her jaw, he drew her face to his.

She hesitated just before his lips covered hers, murmured, "I like being like this with you, too."

He smiled, and kissed her, pleased and reassured by the hint of surprise he heard in her tone, by the implied suggestion she was of her own volition rethinking. He drew her into an easy, unpassionate, soothing exchange. It lengthened, took hold; he let it spin out, and on. He'd already lifted her from him, guessing what her next tack would be. Kissing her back, languid and slow, waiting while their bodies recovered and their senses awoke anew, he waited to see if he'd guessed right.

Caro eventually stirred and drew back, her spine once more straight, her muscles no longer lax. Gripping his shoulders, she pushed back, looked down at the solid evidence he was willing and able to further indulge her.

Her lips curved as her imagination ranged ahead, considering, wondering . . . for an instant she wondered if she shouldn't retreat to more restrained behavior. She considered, then pushed the thought from her mind, rejected it. There was too much she'd yet to learn, to experience, to know; so much of her life had already passed, she couldn't afford not to be bold.

Pressing down on his shoulders, she stood, pleased when her muscles, faintly aching but apparently still able, complied. Moving from him, she caught his gaze, arched an intentionally haughty brow. "My turn, I believe."

The ends of his lips lifted. "As you wish."

She studied him for an instant, then commanded, "Your boots—take them off."

She glimpsed his deepening smile as he bent and did as she'd asked. As soon as his second boot hit the floor, his stockings with it, she caught his hand—and his eyes.

He allowed her to tug him to his feet.

She drew him to the daybed. Released him, faced him. "I want you naked."

His gaze locked with hers; he raised his hands to his cravat.

"No." She caught his hands, drew them back to his sides before releasing them. "Let me."

No question—a command, one he obeyed without equivocation.

Stepping closer, she undid his cravat, slowly drew the folds from about his neck. Then she unbuttoned his shirt, his cuffs, helped him draw the linen folds over his head, allowing him to free his hands and toss the shirt aside. She paused, captivated by the expanse of hair-dusted muscle stretched over heavy bone. She'd seen his naked chest yesterday, but hadn't had time to appreciate the view, not like this with him displayed before her, hers to enjoy as she pleased.

Lips curving, she lifted her eyes to his and reached for his waistband, with both hands pushed his gaping breeches down. Followed them down with her hands, going down on one knee to release the closures below his knees and let the garment puddle about his feet. Hands spread, palms to his thighs, she slowly rose, running her hands upward as she did, cruising up over his hip bones, over the sides of his waist, up over the acres of his chest, ultimately stretching up to frame his face and draw his mouth to hers.

She filled it, surprising him, seizing the lead, then she retreated; lowering her heels to the floor, she placed a hot kiss in the hollow between his collarbones. She took a moment to look, to glory, then spread her hands over his chest. Stroked across the width, then ran her palms down, over his ridged abdomen. Muscles shifted beneath her fingers; eyes wide, briefly meeting his, she gripped his waist and moved closer, touched her lips to the flat disc of his nipple, lowered her lids and kissed, then licked. Lightly, teasingly . . . eyes closed the better to savor the feel of him, the tangy salty taste of him, she let her hands and her mouth roam, filling her senses.

With him. With the solid reality of his body, a sculpted masculine form she felt an overpowering need to explore. Fingers flexing, stroking, tracing, she followed her touch with her lips, sinking down once more to her knees as she followed the arrow of crinkly dark hair down the center of his body, past the hollow of his navel, down to where his erection stood rigidly awaiting her pleasure. Her attention.

She half expected him to stop her when she took him between her hands. Senses riveted, she barely noticed the light touch of his fingers on her hair, then his fingers speared through the frizzy tresses.

Absorbed with examining the baby-fine skin, the thick, pulsing veins, the heavily flushed velvety head, she was conscious of the rising beat in her blood, and his, the urgency that slowly, caress by caress, rose up to engulf them.

Ultimately it would draw them down, into that vortex of need with which she was growing increasingly familiar. Before then, however . . .

Michael hadn't expected her to take him into her mouth—hadn't expected her to *know* . . .

His lungs seized; his fingers tightened on her skull.

She sucked, and suddenly he couldn't see.

Every sense he posssessed, every last particle of awareness, rushed to that part of him she was so intent on exploring. Tasting. Possessing. She licked, curled her tongue and lightly rasped; he groaned and closed his eyes. He felt lightheaded, yet exhilarated. He'd been thoroughly engorged before; now he was aching.

The urge to thrust into the hot, welcoming cavern of her mouth was nearly overpowering; only the conviction that he didn't need to give her any further pointers, especially in that direction, held him back.

Gave him the strength to endure as she caressed his aching balls, toyed with his scrotum.

Then her hands slid around, caressed his buttocks, then gripped, fingers sinking in as she pressed closer, took him deeper.

For one finite instant, he felt as if he was clinging to the edge of the world by his fingernails. Then he dragged in a huge breath, gripped her head with both hands. "Enough." He could barely recognize his own voice.

He eased her back; she acquiesced and released him, rocked back on her heels and fluidly rose. Met his eyes, a witchy smile curving her lips.

The silvery light in her eyes promised hours of sensual torture.

Before he could fortify himself with another breath, she prodded his chest with all ten fingertips. "Lie down."

She meant on the daybed. He sat, looked up at her. She pushed at his shoulders. "On your back."

Stifling another groan, he did, swinging his legs up to lie prone. She knelt beside him, then straddled his hips. The daybed was of classic design—a raised head, but no sides, somewhat wider than a chaise. For their present occupation it was perfect; it was bed enough for her to ride him, as he was certain she meant to.

She settled her weight on him, wriggled her derriere, then leaned forward, framed his face, and kissed him.

To within an inch of sanity; he hadn't known she had it in her—that any woman could so completely capture his senses, his will, his awareness. She tried, and succeeded, until his wits were long gone, and the only thought left in his mind was the shuddering need to join with her.

He could feel her heat across his waist—tantalizingly just out of reach. Thus far, knowing she wished it so, he'd left his hands passive at his sides. Lifting them, he slid his palms across her back, then ran them down, caressing the supple muscles bracketing her spine, to cup her hips. He lightly gripped, wordlessly urged.

In reply, she shifted her hips not at all, but instead moved her shoulders sinuously side to side, caressing his chest with her swollen breasts, teasing him with the tight buds of her nipples.

With a gasp, he broke the kiss. "For God's sake, put me out of my misery."

She looked down into his eyes, with one hand lightly traced his cheek, then her fingers firmed; she bent and plunged wildly into his mouth—and edged her hips lower.

His relief stuck in his chest—a hard knot—when the head of his erection touched her heated flesh.

He went to reach down, to position himself; before he could, she shifted, adjusted, and got the angle right.

In the instant he registered that, she braced her arms and lifted her shoulders, simultaneously sinking down, enclosing him.

In the slickest, most scorching embrace he'd ever known.

Caro closed her eyes, blissfully savoring every second of her descent, of his steady invasion, one she controlled.

God! What joy she'd been missing.

The thought was simply there, in her head; she tightened about him, then moved, and it vaporized. As she'd suspected, there was yet more to learn, to feel, to know; this position was different again—she felt even more in control—of both of them.

At first she did the obvious, rising up, then sinking slowly down, then she experimented. Rolling her hips, incorporating a little thrust here, a grinding movement there.

Feeling the power slowly rise, grow stronger, investing them both.

She cracked open her lids, looked down at him beneath her, at his body, hard and immensely more powerful, absorbing her rocking movements, taking them in, absorbing the pleasure.

For there was pleasure in his eyes, in the way he watched her from under heavy lids. His hands lay passive on her upper thighs, letting her have her way, letting her take him—give herself—as she would.

She was immeasurably grateful.

As if he could tell, he reached up, cupped her nape with one large hand and drew her down, lifting his shoulders so their lips could meet and he could draw her into his fire.

Trap her there. Enmesh her in a web of desire that flamed

hotter with every rasping stroke of his tongue over hers, filling her mouth and her senses with pure heat. With a shattering physical need to move faster and burn.

He surged higher, propping on one elbow, one hand spreading over her back, holding her close so his chest abraded her breasts. His other hand gripped her hip, holding her against him as slowly, countering her rocking rhythm, he thrust upward, into her.

Steadily. Surging powerfully. Harder. Higher. Ultimately faster.

Until she was spinning, until the world her senses knew came apart, shards of sensation flying through her, slicing sharp with white-hot glory, burning, melting, until in the heat of the conflagration she was consumed.

And knew only ecstasy.

Michael caught her, turned and rolled her beneath him. Spread her thighs wide, wrapped her legs about his waist, and drove into her.

She was more open to him than before, more vulnerable, more his.

He took, driving solidly into her pulsing heat.

The steady pounding rhythm roused her, as he'd hoped it would. Her eyes gleamed, then a look of amazement, unfeigned and undisguised, crossed her features. Then she joined him.

Clutched his head and drew his lips down to hers, dueled with him for supremacy there even while their bodies did the same. She had a strength in her like flexing steel; she used it, not to challenge so much as to drive him on. Convince him to go further, to mate with her harder, deeper, to join with her without reserve.

He did. The result was something beyond his experience as surely as it was beyond hers, a gasping, clutching, frantic and desperate climb to an ecstasy greater, deeper, and infinitely more profound than either could have guessed, than either, when their eyes met in that last fraught moment before the maelstrom took them and whirled them from this world, had expected, or even imagined.

The cataclysm rocked them both. Fused them, seared them. Branded them with an awareness each of the other from which neither could ever shake free.

Finally, it released them. Exhausted, they collapsed. Gradually their senses returned, their surroundings reimpinged on their consciousness. Dimly. Neither had the strength to do more than settle into the other's arms.

Still breathing deeply, his heart still thudding in his ears, Michael kissed Caro's hand, laid it on his chest, and let his eyes close.

Never, not ever before, had he lost himself so completely, given himself so thoroughly. As he sank into beckoning oblivion, all he knew was that he wanted, desperately needed, to do it again.

That he needed to ensure that he had the chance.

Needed to ensure that she remained by his side.

Always. Forever.

When he awoke, the sun had moved on and shadows dappled the interior of the cottage. The day was warm; their lack of clothes posed no problem, yet the air within the cottage had grown sultry. Caro lay asleep, curled on her side, facing away from him, her bottom snug against his side. Smiling, he savored the sensation, locked it in his memory, then, easing away, rolled from the daybed.

Padding barefoot across tiles warmed by the sunshine, he quietly unlatched a window and set it wide. The sound of the stream gurgling and rushing drifted in; birdcalls added to the bucolic symphony.

He breathed in, then turned. A light breeze, warm and caressing, danced in, and followed him back to the daybed. He stood looking down at Caro, at the slender, shapely limbs relaxed in slumber, at the ripe swell of her hips, the lush curves of her breasts, at the delicate features lightly flushed with slumber. The breeze lifted strands of her fine hair, caressed and stirred them.

She slept on.

In the past two days, he'd spilled his seed inside her five times. He hadn't taken any precautions, hadn't tried to avoid it, and nor had she. Of course, the only interludes she until now had dreamed of had been with Camden, her husband. Instinct, distinctly primitive, urged him to leave the matter as was, leave that particular stone unturned. Yet . . .

Was it fair to simply let what might be—what was very likely to be—happen without her considered agreement? Without her consciously being aware of it and giving her consent?

Yet if he mentioned it . . . it would certainly break the spell, and he had no guarantee how she would react. He didn't even know how she felt about children.

A vivid image of Caro with his son in her arms, with two daughters clinging to her skirts, filled his mind.

For long moments, he was blind, held captured, entranced. Then he blinked back to reality . . . stunned, unsettled. Suddenly wary.

Never had any conjured vision made him feel his heart was standing still—and would until he had it, until he'd secured the thing he'd seen and now so desperately, beyond thought or doubt, wanted.

That thing he now sensed was critical for him, for his continued existence, for his future.

It took a moment or so more before he was breathing freely.

He looked again at Caro. His decision had been made—not, or so it seemed, by him. He wouldn't mention the risk of pregnancy.

He would, however, do whatever it took, give whatever was needed, to make his vision come true.

Caro woke to the feel of Michael's fingertips lightly tracing her bare skin. She lay still, eyes barely open, registering the sun still shining, the faint shadows playing across the tiles, the airy touch of a breeze drifting through a window he must have opened.

She was lying on her side, facing the fireplace. He was lying stretched out behind her, on his back, the fingers of his right hand idly stroking her hip. Smiling, she let her eyes close, the better to savor the warmth that still enveloped her and his light, repetitive caress.

A change in her breathing, or some tension in her body, must have given her away; a moment later, he shifted, coming up on one elbow, his body rearranging to spoon about hers.

Her smile deepened; he bent his head and nuzzled the spot where her shoulder and throat met, placed a hot, lingering, openmouthed kiss over the pulse point there.

Then he murmured, soft, low, infinitely dangerous, "I want you to keep your eyes closed, to just lie there, and let me make love to you."

Her breasts swelled, her nipples tightened even before he pushed his hand over her side, nudging her arm higher so he could close his hand and knead. Languidly, lazily. As if assessing her anew.

Heat spread beneath her skin, but this time in a gentle wave, not a rushing, tumultuous tide.

He caressed her—all of her—his touch assured yet never hurried, never driven. This, she concluded, was to be a slow engagement, each moment stretching, then sliding effortlessly into the next, each crest of sensation peaking, extending, before he let her fall back, catch her breath, and move on.

Through a landscape she saw only through touch, knew only via tactile sensation. Gentle, repetitive, tactile stimulation.

His hand moved over her bottom, fingers dipped, stroked, caressed. Until her need built, until she shifted her hips, gently moaned.

She started to turn, expecting him to roll her onto her back and part her thighs. Instead, her shoulder met his chest, her hip his groin.

"Other way," he murmured, pressing her back, his voice deep, murmurously sultry, stirring the thick molten heat inside her.

He edged her upper thigh higher, angled her hips over, then she felt him, hard, hot, rigid, press in.

Sink slowly in.

She shut her eyes tight, clung to the moment, exhaled softly as it ended, leaving him deeply inside her.

Then he moved. As slow and sultry as the sunshine, as

openly seductive as the breeze. His body moved against hers in a slow, surging evocative rhythm, a cadence he refused to vary even when she gasped, when her senses coiled tight, and she sank her fingers into his thigh.

He rode her gentle thrust after thrust until she could stand it no more, until a scream broke from her throat and she fractured, and the wonder poured in. It filled her up, and washed through her, leaving her blissfully free on some far distant shore.

And still he filled her, each controlled thrust definite and sure. She was dimly aware when he reached his own limit and release caught him, racked him, then the storm rolled on and he lay beside her on that golden shore.

CHAPTER
15

They walked home along the path, through the glory of the late afternoon. They exchanged glances, light touches aplenty, but few words; at that moment, a moment out of time, they needed none.

Caro couldn't think—couldn't form any opinion over what had transpired, couldn't make those glorious moments of sharing conform to any pattern she'd heard of or recognized. What had happened simply was; all she needed to do was accept it.

Beside her, Michael walked steadily, holding back branches so she could pass safely by, ready to grasp her arm and steady her if she slipped, but otherwise not holding her, leaving her free even while in his mind he acknowledged she was not, that he would never let her go. As they tramped through the woods and meadows, he tried to understand, conscious of a change, a realignment, a refinement of his feelings, a more acute defining of his direction.

They passed through the gate in the hedge, and walked up through the gardens. As they stepped onto the stretch of lawn leading to the terrace, they heard voices.

They glanced up and saw Muriel talking to Edward, who was looking faintly harassed.

Edward saw them; Muriel followed his gaze, then drew herself up and waited for them to climb the steps.

As they neared, both smiling easily, effortlessly adopting their social personas, Michael saw Muriel's eyes fix on Caro's face, faintly flushed, whether from their earlier exertions or their long walk in the sun that had shone throughout the day he couldn't say. What Muriel made of the sight he couldn't guess either; before she could comment, he held out his hand. "Good afternoon, Muriel. I must congratulate you again on the fete—it was a marvelous day and a wonderful turnout. You must be thoroughly gratified."

Muriel surrendered her hand, allowing him grasp her fingers. "Well, yes. I was indeed most happy with the way things turned out." Her tone was gracious, faintly condescending.

She exchanged nods with Caro, then continued, "I came to ask if there had been any difficulties at all with the diplomatic delegations. It was such an unusual idea to encourage them to attend—we need to gauge the success of the strategy in case we decide to try something similar again."

Muriel locked her gaze on Caro's face. "I have to say I find it hard to credit that the diplomatic crowd, especially the foreigners, found much to excite them at such an event. As Sutcliffes, we have a certain reputation to uphold—we don't want to be associated with any suggestion of foisting boring entertainments on those in diplomatic circles."

Beneath his polished veneer, Michael bridled; Edward, not so experienced in hiding his feelings, stiffened. Muriel's accusation, for that's what it amounted to, was outrageous.

Yet Caro simply laughed, lightly, apparently ingenuously— she put both him and Edward to shame. "You're worrying about nothing, Muriel, I assure you." She laid a hand briefly, reassuringly, on Muriel's arm. "The diplomatic crowd, especially the foreigners, were delighted one and all."

Muriel frowned. "They weren't just being polite?"

Caro shook her head. "It's the balls and glittering functions of which that crowd has a surfeit—simple pleasures, relaxing entertainments in the country—those are, for them, golden moments."

Smiling, she gestured down the terrace; still frowning, Muriel turned and walked beside her.

"From the diplomatic standpoint, and I'm sure Edward and Michael will bear me out in this"—with a wave, Caro included them as they fell in behind—"everything went perfectly, without the slightest hitch."

Muriel stared at the flagstones. After a moment, she asked, her tone flat, "So you don't have any suggestions on how we might improve things?"

Caro halted, her expression openly pensive, then she shook her head. "I can't think how one might improve on perfection." The words held a glimmer of steel. She caught Muriel's eye and smiled graciously. "Now, will you stay for tea?"

Muriel looked at her, then shook her head. "No, thank you—I want to call on Miss Trice. Such a terrible thing for those two men to have attacked her. I feel it's my duty to give her every support in overcoming her ordeal."

As they'd all met Miss Trice numerous times since the attack, and been reassured, not just by the lady herself but by her sunny good humor, that her "ordeal" had left no lasting mark, none of them could find anything to say.

With a telling sense of relief, they made their farewells.

"I'll see you out." Caro conducted Muriel through the open drawing room doors and on toward the front hall.

After exchanging a brief glance with Michael, Edward followed, hovering just behind, attaining that all-but-invisible state only the best political aides could achieve.

Michael remained on the terrace; within a few minutes, Caro and Edward rejoined him.

Edward was frowning at Caro. "It's true—she's jealous of you! You should have heard the questions she put to me before you two joined us."

Caro smiled reassuringly at Edward. "I know, but you mustn't take it to heart." When he continued to look mutinous, she went on, "Just consider—normally Muriel's the most . . . I suppose 'senior' is the right word—hostess or lady hereabouts. But when I come home, even for a few weeks, I—without exerting myself in the least—take her place. That has to be galling."

"Particularly," Michael put in, "for one of Muriel's disposition. She expects to be at the center of things."

Caro nodded. "She craves the notice, the position, but you have to admit she works hard for it."

Edward humphed.

"Anyway," Caro said, "Muriel might not have wanted tea, but I do." She glanced at Michael. "I'm ravenous."

He offered his arm. "Long walks through the countryside tend to have that effect."

Whether Edward believed them neither knew; they were both too experienced to look to find out.

They found Elizabeth in the parlor, and consumed vast quantities of scones and jam, then Michael, reluctantly, rose to take his leave. Caro met his eyes; he saw her consider inviting him to dine, then decide—to his mind correctly—against it. They'd spent all day so close; they both needed time alone—at least, he did; he suspected she did, too. Perspective was something they both knew the value of.

She walked with him to the parlor door, gave him her hand. "Thank you for a most . . . enjoyable day."

Holding her gaze, he raised her fingers to his lips, kissed. "It was truly my pleasure."

Pressing her fingers, he released her.

Caro noted the last glance Michael exchanged with Edward before he turned and left the room. A changing of the guard; it couldn't have been clearer. Michael had remained with her throughout the day; the evening was Edward's watch.

Inwardly smiling, she made no comment, accepting—allowing—their protection without argument. She was fond of them both, albeit in different ways; if watching over her made them happy, and they could manage it without bothering her, she could see no reason to complain.

The next morning, an hour after breakfast, Caro sat on the terrace and listened to Elizabeth practice a particularly difficult sonata. Edward had remained in the drawing room to turn the music sheets; she'd smiled and drifted out to sit in the cool air of the bright morning—and think.

About Michael. And herself.

Since they'd parted yesterday, she had, deliberately, not

thought about him, about them—wanting—needing—a certain distance from which to see more clearly, to be able to examine, study, and understand what was going on.

Despite all, yesterday had been a peaceful day. The hours spent with Michael had been soothing, untouched by any emotional upheavals. A time when they'd both simply existed and let what would be, be. The evening had passed in much the same vein, through a quiet dinner with Geoffrey, Edward, and Elizabeth, followed by their usual musical interlude in the drawing room and lastly a walk in the balmy evening, accompanied by Edward and Elizabeth, before retiring to her room and her couch.

Somewhat to her surprise, she'd slept very well. Long walks through the countryside—long hours wrapped in Michael's arms.

This morning, she'd risen, refreshed and eager for the day. After breakfast, she'd spent time with Mrs. Judson going over household matters; now, her slate clear, she was looking forward to turning her mind to what, running beneath all else in her life, was becoming an obsession.

Michael—yes, but not just him. She was either too old, too experienced, or had never been the sort to become infatuated, fascinated by another person, by his charms, by aspects of his personality. After spending so many years in diplomatic spheres, where such attributes were assumed, put on like costumes whenever necessary, she knew them for the flimsy things they were, knew their real worth.

Her fascination didn't center on Michael himself, but on what they, together, created between them.

That was where the power that both he and she were drawn to resided. It was something she could sense, at times so real she felt she could almost touch it; it arose from the link that was forming between them, that grew from the amalgam of their selves. . . .

Frowning, she rose, drew her fringed shawl about her shoulders, and stepped down onto the lawn.

It was so hard to *see* what was happening—impossible to reduce the emotions and sensations, and that simple overwhelming certainty that engulfed her when she was in his arms, to statement, to logical rational description from which an argument could be formed, a position defined, action planned. . . .

She stopped, tipped her head back, and looked up at the sky. "Heaven help me—I really have become far too much like Camden."

Shaking her head, she looked down and continued on, eyes fixed unseeing on the path before her feet. Trying to understand what was developing between her and Michael . . . using logic wasn't going to work. What she was dealing with operated beyond logic, of that she felt quite sure.

Emotion, then. That, indeed, seemed the more likely key. She needed, would feel more comfortable having, some sense of whither they—and their new and strange relationship—were heading, where it was leading them, both she and he. If she was to let emotion guide her . . .

She grimaced, and paced on.

No help there either; she didn't know—couldn't explain—what she felt. *Not* because she was unsure of what she felt, but because she had no words for it, no measure for it, no recognition of what the feelings burgeoning and growing stronger every time she and Michael met were, let alone meant.

She'd never felt like this before. Not about Camden, not about any man—and especially not *with* any other man. That was another aspect about which she was certain—whatever she felt, Michael felt it, too. It was a mutual development, affecting him as much, and in much the same way, as she.

And she suspected his reaction was the same as hers. They were both mature; they'd both seen the world, were comfortable in who and what they were, confident of their positions in society. Yet what was evolving between them was a fresh field, one on which neither had previously dallied, one with horizons neither had previously explored.

When faced with a new and different challenge, they both possessed temperaments that impelled them to walk confidently in and examine, study—assess what new opportunity life might be offering them. She was conscious of an eager interest, of something more compelling than mere fascination, a need more than an inclination to go forward and learn more. Understand more. And perhaps, ultimately . . .

She broke off her thoughts, blinked—and realized she stood facing the gate leading out of the garden. She muttered an oath and glanced back; she hadn't meant to walk this far, hadn't been conscious of doing so. She'd been thinking, and her feet had brought her here.

Her instinctive destination was clear, yet she knew Edward, once free of Elizabeth's sonata, would look for her to watch over her. But he knew of the cottage and that she often walked there; when he discovered she wasn't in the house, he'd guess. . . .

Facing forward, she looked at the path wending its way across the first meadow and into the first stretch of woodland. The path cut through a number of such wooded stands, but none were dark or dense; with the sun streaming down, it was difficult to imagine anyone skulking along the way, waiting to shoot or attack her.

And really, why would they? Looking along the path, she couldn't, no matter how hard she tried, drum up any fear. The pellets striking Henry and the arrow had been accidents; admittedly, the arrow striking the tree so close to her had been momentarily scarifying—she could still hear the dull *thwack* in her mind—and she could still remember the desperation, the cold clutch of fear that had gripped her when Henry had bolted, but Michael had rescued her—she'd come to no harm at all. As for the attack on Miss Trice, that had been nasty and shocking, but hadn't truly touched her at all; there was no reason to suppose she'd been the intended target.

She pushed the gate open and walked on. Her instincts had been right; she wanted to go to the cottage. Perhaps needed to be within those walls to revisit her feelings of yesterday and delve past the superficial to see what lay beneath. Besides, she was sure Michael would call soon—he'd know where she'd gone.

Eyes down, for once blind to the beauties of the countryside around her, she walked steadily on. And returned to her interrupted thoughts. To, perhaps, the most crucial point. Where, ultimately, was her liaison with Michael and the emotions that generated leading her? And was it, all aspects and feelings considered, a place she was prepared to go?

Michael left Atlas with Geoffrey's stableman and walked over the lawns to the house. He half expected to see Caro drift out onto the terrace to meet him. Instead, Elizabeth walked briskly out from the drawing room, looking about. She saw him and waved, then looked to his left.

Following her gaze, he saw Edward striding up from the summerhouse. The younger man waved and strode faster; premonition, faint but real, caressed Michael's nape.

Edward spoke as soon as he was within hearing distance. "Caro's gone off somewhere. She was on the terrace, but . . ."

He glanced at Elizabeth, who'd come down from the terrace to join them. "She's not in the house. Judson said she's probably gone down to the weir."

Edward looked at Michael. "There's a cottage—a retreat she often disappears to. She's most likely there."

"Or on her way there," Elizabeth said. "She couldn't have left that long ago, and it takes twenty minutes to walk there."

Michael nodded. "I know the place." He looked at Edward. "I'll catch up with her. If she's not there, I'll come back."

Edward grimaced. "If we find she's still here, I'll stay with her."

With a salute for Elizabeth, Michael strode back down the lawn, then took the path through the shrubbery, retracing the route he and Caro had taken the day before. He reached the gate; it wasn't latched. He'd latched it yesterday when they'd returned.

Going through, he strode quickly along the path. It didn't surprise him that Caro had a habit of walking alone through the countryside. Like him, she spent most of her life in ballrooms, drawing rooms, and elegant salons; the sense of peace he felt when he came home, the blessed contrast, the need to enjoy it while one could, was something he was sure she shared.

Nevertheless, he would much rather she wasn't rambling all alone. Not just at present, when he felt sure someone had designs on her life. Designs he didn't understand; designs he absolutely could not allow to succeed.

He didn't question from where the grim and steely purpose behind that "absolutely could not allow" came; at the moment, wherefores and whys didn't seem that pertinent. The need to protect her from all harm was deeply entrenched, as if etched on his soul, an immutable part of him.

It hadn't always been so; now it simply was.

Premonition stroked, chillingly cloying, again; he strode faster. Cresting a rise, he saw her, clearly visible in a pale muslin gown, her nimbus of fine hair glinting in the sunshine as she strolled across a meadow some way ahead. She was too far away to hail; she walked steadily on, looking down.

He'd expected to feel relief; instead, his instincts seemed to tighten—to urge him to hurry even more. He couldn't see any reason for it, yet he obeyed.

A little further on, he broke into a loping run.

Regardless of his insistence on watching over her, his rational mind did not expect another attack, not here on Geoffrey's land. Why, then, was his chest tightening—why was apprehension filling him?

He was running when he broke into the final clearing—and saw, across the meadow, Caro halfway across the narrow bridge. She was still steadily walking, looking down. Smiling, pushing aside his distracting premonition, he slowed. "Caro!"

She heard. Straightening, lifting her head, she turned, reached for the handrail as she grasped her clinging skirts and flicked them about. She smiled in glorious welcome. Grasped the rail as she released her skirts and raised her hand to wave—

The handrail broke. Fell away as she touched it.

She valiantly tried to regain her balance, but there was nothing to clutch, to cling to.

With a faint shriek, she toppled from the bridge, disappearing into the swirling mists boiling up from the racing waters funneling through the narrow gorge, hurling themselves into the deep waters of the weir.

His heart in his throat, Michael sprinted down the meadow. Reaching the bank, he frantically searched, simultaneously hauling off his boots. He was shrugging out of his coat when he saw her surface, a bobbing white welter of muslin skirts flashing into sight at the mouth of the weir. Her silk-fringed shawl dragged at her arms as she struggled to raise them, to stroke, to float.

The rushing current pulled her back down.

She was not a strong swimmer; the current, fueled by the torrents gushing past either side of the island, was sweeping her into the weir.

He dived in. A few swift strokes brought him to where she had been. He came up, trod water, trying to glimpse her, to more accurately gauge the current's direction. The undertow was ferocious.

She resurfaced, gasping, some yards farther on. He plunged back into the swirling waters, went with the tow, added his own powerful strokes to it—glimpsed a murky whiteness ahead and lunged for it.

His fingers tangled in her gown. Grabbing, grasping, he closed his fist about a handful—remembered just in time not to yank. Wet muslin would simply tear, rip away; desperate, he lunged again, touched a limb—latched his fingers around her upper arm and locked them.

Battling the powerful undertow, he fought not to get swept further into the convergence of the two arms of the stream. There, the water churned, its force powerful enough to pull him under, let alone her.

She was exhausted, gasping, fighting for breath. Steadily, he pulled her to him until her clutching fingers found his shoulders, until he could wrap one arm about her waist.

"Easy. Don't thrash!"

She responded to his voice, stopped flailing, but gripped him harder. "I can't swim well."

There was panic in her voice; she was battling to contain it.

"Stop trying—just hang on to me. I'll do the swimming."

Looking around, he realized the only safe way out was to move sideways into the quieter body of water between the two tumbling currents created by the arms of the stream. Once in the relative calm, he could tow her back to the island.

He juggled her, moving her to his left, then, still fighting the tow that wanted to swirl them on, he edged them inch by inch, foot by foot to the left. Gradually, the force pummeling them lessened until finally they were in calmer water.

Drawing her to him, brushing the wet hair from her face, he looked into her eyes, more blue than silver, darkened with fear. He kissed the tip of her nose. "Just hold on—I'm going to take us back to the island."

He did, exercising great care not to get swept back into the currents racing past on either side, then, as they neared the island, wary of rocks beneath the surface.

With an effort she lifted her head and gasped, "There's a small jetty to the left—that's the only place where it's easy to get up."

He glanced around and saw what she meant—a jetty less than a yard square stood out from the island, a few sturdy wooden rungs providing a means to climb up to it. Just as well; the sides of the island, now he could see them clearly, worn and cut by decades of floods, rose up, relatively sheer, no useful hand- or footholds, and with an unhelpful over-hang at the top.

A narrow paved path wound up from the jetty to the cot-tage. Readjusting his hold on her, he set course for the jetty.

She was exhausted and trembling by the time he got her onto it. They slumped side by side, gasping, simply waiting for some semblance of strength to return.

Lying back, shoulders propped against the bank, he stared unseeing at the sky. Her head lay cradled on his arm. After a few minutes, she turned his way, weakly raised a hand to touch his cheek. "Thank you."

He didn't reply—couldn't. He caught her fingers, trapped them in his, closed his eyes as reaction—realization— poured through him, so intense it was frightening, a fright that shook him to his soul.

Then her weight against him, the faint warmth reaching

through her drenched clothes, the gentle intermittent pressure of her breast against his side as she breathed, registered, and relief flooded him.

He realized he was squeezing her fingers; he eased his hold, raised them to his lips. He looked down; she looked up. Her eyes met his, a frown dulling the silver.

"You know," Caro murmured, trying valiantly not to shiver, "I think you're right. Someone is trying to kill me."

Eventually, they climbed up to the cottage. She refused to let Michael carry her, but was forced to lean heavily against him.

Once inside, they stripped; there was clean water to wash away the mud and linen towels with which to dry themselves. Michael wrung out their dripping clothes, then they hung them in the windows where the sun streamed in and the warm breeze could catch them.

She speared her fingers through her toweled hair, combed out the tangles as best she could. Then, draped in shawls her mother used to use in winter, she crawled into the V of Michael's thighs as he sat propped against the head of the daybed, and let him wrap her in his arms.

His arms tightened; he held her close, leaned his check against her damp hair. She crossed her arms over his and clung.

Simply held tight.

He didn't exactly rock her, yet she felt the same sense of caring, of being cherished and protected. They didn't speak; she wondered if he kept silent for the same reason she did—because her emotions were so stirred, roiling so close to her surface that she feared if she opened her lips, they'd come tumbling out, willy-nilly, without thought for what they might reveal, where they might lead. What they might commit her to.

Gradually, the slight shudders that still racked her—a combination of cold and fear—eased, driven out by the pervasive heat of his body, by the warmth that seeped slowly to her bones.

Yet it was he who stirred first, who sighed and eased his arms from under hers.

"Come." He placed a light kiss on her temple. "Let's get dressed and go back to the house." She shifted to face him; he caught her gaze, continued in the same even, determined voice, "There's lots we need to discuss, but first, you should take a hot bath."

She didn't argue. They dressed, pulling on their clothes, still slightly damp, then left the cottage. Crossing the bridge was no real problem; although it was narrow, she'd crossed it so often, she didn't truly need the rail.

Michael stopped just before he followed her off the bridge. Crouching, he examined what remained of the post that had supported the rail at that end. He'd caught a glimpse of it as he'd rushed down to the bank, before he'd dived in; what he saw now confirmed his earlier observation. The post had been sawn almost through; barely a sliver had been left intact. All three of the posts had been treated similarly; the upper portion of each had been virtually balancing on the lower section from which it had been all but severed.

No accident, but a callously deliberate act.

Rising, he drew a deep breath and stepped down to the bank.

Caro met his gaze. "I don't usually use the rail all that much, just for crossing. Did you, yesterday?"

He cast his mind back . . . recalled putting a hand on the post at the bridge's other end, not far from where Caro had grasped the rail today. "Yes." He refocused on her eyes, reached for her arm. "It was solid, then."

Had the perpetrator known that only Caro and Mrs. Judson used the bridge, and, it being Tuesday, that it was most likely Caro who would use it next?

Lips setting grimly, he steered her up the meadow. They walked back to the house as fast as she could manage. They entered via the garden hall; he parted from her in the corridor with a stern reminder of the advisability of a hot bath.

She cast him a sharp glance, with a glimmer of her usual manner tartly replied, "I'm hardly likely to want anyone to see me in my present state." Her wave directed his attention to her hair—now sun-dried, it seemed twice its normal volume and even more untameable than usual. "I'm going up the back stairs."

He caught her gaze. "I'll go home and change, then I'll meet you in the parlor."

She nodded and left; he watched her go, then headed for the parlor. As he'd hoped, the door was open; Elizabeth was on the window seat embroidering while Edward sat in a chair poring over some papers spread on a low table. Standing in the shadows of the corridor, out of Elizabeth's sight, Michael called to Edward.

Edward looked up; Michael beckoned. "If you can spare a moment?"

"Yes, of course." Edward shot to his feet and strode to the door, eyes widening as he took in Michael's state. He pulled the door closed behind him. "What the devil happened?"

In a few short sentences, Michael told him. Grim-faced, Edward swore he would ensure that after her bath, Caro came straight down to the parlor and stayed there, safe in his and Elizabeth's company until Michael returned.

Satisfied he'd done all he could for the moment, Michael left to ride home and change out of his bedraggled clothes.

He returned two hours later, resolute and determined.

While riding home, then bathing and changing his clothes, calming Mrs. Entwhistle and Carter, eating a quick luncheon, then riding back to Bramshaw House, he'd had plenty of time to think without the distraction of Caro's presence. Plenty of time not just to dwell on what might have been, but to draw some conclusions, firm enough for their purpose, and from that see ahead to how they should go on—what they needed to do to unmask whoever was behind what he now firmly believed were four attempts on Caro's life.

He walked into the parlor. Caro, recognizing his step, had already looked up, was already rising. Edward rose, too.

Elizabeth, still ensconced on the window seat, beamed a bright smile his way. Gathering her emboridery, she got to her feet. "I'll leave you to discuss your business."

Sunnily assured, she swept out. He held the door, then closed it behind her. Turning, he looked—just looked—at Caro.

She waved and sat again. "I don't want her to know and worry, and even less become involved, and she will if she knows, so I've told her you and I have some political business to discuss, and given the ambitions we all hold for Edward, that he should stay."

Edward shot him a long-suffering look and resumed his seat.

Michael took the armchair opposite Caro. He wanted to be able to see her face; she was often difficult to read, but given the subjects they had to discuss, he wanted to catch as much as she let show.

"I think," he said, glancing at Edward, "that we're all in possession of the relevant facts?"

Edward nodded. "I believe so."

Michael looked at Caro. "Do I take it you now accept that someone is intent on causing you harm?"

She met his gaze, hesitated, then nodded. "Yes."

"Very well. The question we clearly have to answer is: Who would want you dead?"

She spread her hands. "I don't have any enemies."

"I'll accept that you don't know of any enemies, but what about enemies who aren't motivated by personal connection."

She frowned. "You mean via Camden?"

He nodded. "We know of the Duke of Oporto, and the interest he apparently has in Camden's papers." Michael looked at Edward, then back at Caro. "Can we agree that it's possible there's some hidden reason in whatever's at stake there that the duke believes you know, that's sufficient to convince him he needs to do away with you?"

Edward considered for only a moment, then nodded decisively. "A possibility, definitely." He looked at Caro. "You must agree, Caro. You know as well as I do what's at stake at the Portuguese court. Murder has, indeed, been committed for less."

Caro grimaced; she glanced at Michael, then nodded.

"Very well. The duke is one suspect—or rather, his minions."

"Or, as it might be, Ferdinand's minions." His softly voiced correction drew a sigh, then a reluctant inclination of her head.

"True. So that's one potential nest of vipers."

His lips quirked, but only briefly. "Are there any other nests of that type?"

She met his gaze, then exchanged a long look with Edward.

It was Edward who finally answered, "I honestly don't know of any." His careful tone stated that that was the truth as far as he knew it, yet he was aware of the limits of his knowledge.

Michael watched Caro's face closely as she turned to meet his gaze. She noticed, searched his eyes, then smiled— lightly, genuinely; she'd realized what he feared. "Nor I." She hesitated, then added, "Truly."

The directness in her gaze assured him that was indeed the truth. With some relief, he let go of the worry that she would feel compelled to conceal something she considered diplomatically sensitive even though it might be a potential source of threat to her.

"Very well. So we have no direct personal enemies, and only one known from the diplomatic front. Which leaves us with Camden's personal life." Sitting back, he caught Caro's eye. "Camden's will—what did you inherit under it?"

She raised her brows. "The house in Half Moon Street, and a reasonable fortune in the Funds."

"Is there anything special about the house—could someone else covet it for some reason?"

Edward snorted. "The house is valuable enough, but it's what's *in* it that speaks to your question." He leaned forward, elbows propped on his knees. "Camden filled it with antiquities and antique furniture and ornaments. The collection ranks as impressive, even among other collectors."

Brows rising, jaw firming, Michael looked Caro. "In Camden's will, was the house and its contents left to you outright, or on your death does it revert to his estate or go to someone else?"

She met his gaze, then blinked, slowly. Glanced at Edward. "I really can't remember. Can you?"

Edward shook his head. "Other than that it went to you . . . I'm not sure I ever knew more."

"Do you have a copy of the will?"

Caro nodded. "It's in Half Moon Street."

"With Camden's papers?"

"Not in the same place, but yes, they, too, are in the house."

Michael briefly considered the alternatives, then evenly stated, "In that case, I believe we need to return to London. Immediately."

*I*n the end, the problem wasn't convincing Caro to go, but convincing Edward to stay.

"If you don't," Caro warned, "then Elizabeth will come, too—even if I don't take her, she'll invent some excuse to come up and stay at Angela's or Augusta's. She has open invitations in case she needs to shop, and she now has suffi-cient acquaintances in town to convince Geoffrey to let her go up, no matter what we might say when we leave. So!" She paused for breath; arms folded, she halted in her pacing and looked sternly down at Edward, still seated in the chair. "You, Edward dear, must remain here."

"I'm supposed to be your bloody secretary." Edward's jaw was set. He looked to Michael, something he had thus far managed not to do. "You must see my duty is to remain with her—it would be better if I come up to town and help you keep an eye on her."

He doggedly refused to look at Caro, refused to notice her narrowing eyes.

Michael sighed. "Unfortunately, I agree with Caro." He pretended not to see the startled look Caro threw him. "Given the potential danger, we really can't have Elizabeth involved. She's known as Caro's niece; it's obvious Caro is fond of her." He paused, held Edward's gaze. "As Caro's secretary, it's your job to aid her, and in this instance, strange though it may seem, you really can help best by keeping Elizabeth out of London."

Edward's determination wavered; Michael quietly added, "With the vital clue—whether it's in Camden's papers or in his will—in London, we cannot afford to give whoever's been pursuing Caro an avenue through which to coerce her—we don't need to give them any hostage to fortune."

The prospect of Elizabeth as a hostage tipped the scales. Michael had known it would; he understood Edward's dilemma, also his decision.

"Very well." Distinctly grim, Edward conceded. "I'll remain"—his lips twisted, briefly cynical—"and endeavor to keep Elizabeth distracted."

Caro began packing immediately. Michael remained for dinner to assist in excusing her whirlwind departure, sans Edward, to Geoffrey.

As expected, once apprised of Michael's intention to accompany Caro, having business to attend to in the capital himself, Geoffrey accepted the arrangement without quibble.

Michael took his leave as soon as the covers were drawn; he had to pack and ensure matters he'd expected to be at home to oversee were appropriately delegated. Caro, off upstairs to finish her own packing, saw him into the front hall. She gave him her hand. "Until tomorrow morning, then."

Her fingers felt so delicate in his; raising her hand, he placed a quick kiss on them, then released her. "At eight. Don't be late."

She smiled a very feminine smile and turned for the stairs.

He watched her climb them, then walked out and around to the stables.

Three hours later, he retraced his steps.

Quietly. It was close to midnight; the house was dark, silent under the fitful shadows thrown by the large oaks along the drive. Staying on the grass, he skirted the fore-court, circling to the west wing and the room at its end.

Caro's bedchamber. He'd learned its location on the day of her ball when she'd sent him traipsing through the house.

He'd finished packing an hour ago. He'd intended to go to bed and sleep; instead, here he was, slinking through the shadows like some lovelorn Romeo, and he wasn't even sure why. He was hardly a callow youth in the throes of his first romance, yet when it came to Caro, the feelings she evoked left him, if not in quite the same giddy and reckless state, then certainly compelled to actions and deeds his rational, experienced brain knew to be rash—and potentially far too revealing.

That that knowledge held no power to stop him was a revelation in itself. The risk of revealing too much, of leaving himself exposed and therefore vulnerable, barely registered against his need to know, not logically or rationally but physically via the immediate fact, that she was safe.

After hauling her out of the currents of the weir, after discovering the neatly sawn posts, he wasn't going to get any sleep unless she lay beside him under his hand.

Night, gently cool, engulfed the scene, settling, soothing; other than the rustle of some small creature foraging through the bushes, no sound disturbed the stillness. He'd left Atlas in the nearest paddock, left his saddle slung over the fence beneath a tree.

Rounding the west wing, he paused. Through the shadows, he studied the narrow balcony that the French doors of Caro's room gave onto. The balcony served only her room; built above the parlor's bay window, it could only be reached from this side.

He squinted at the wall to the left. His memory hadn't lied; a creeper grew there, thick and old. The west-facing wall caught the sun; over the years, the creeper had grown to the roof—past the balcony.

Quitting the dense shadows beneath the trees, he carefully crossed the path circling the house. Picking his way through the plants in the garden bed, he reached the creeper.

The base was over a foot thick, gnarled and solid. He looked up at the balcony, then sighed, wedged his boot into a suitable fork, and prayed the creeper was strong enough to take his weight.

Caro was on the brink of sleep when a muffled curse floated through her mind. It wasn't one she normally used . . . puzzled, her mind refocused, turning from the billows of slumber to wonder. . . .

A scrape reached her ears. Followed by another muffled curse.

She sat up and looked across the room to where she'd left the French doors to her balcony open to let in the elusive breeze. The lace curtains drifted, nothing looked amiss . . . then she heard a crack—a twig or branch—followed by a soft oath she couldn't make out.

Her heart leapt to her throat.

She slid from the bed. A heavy silver candlestick a foot tall stood on her dressing table; she reached for it, hefted it, taking comfort from its weight, then glided silently to the French doors, paused, then moved out onto the balcony beyond.

Whoever was climbing up the old wisteria was going to get a surprise.

A hand slapped onto the balustrade; she jumped. It was a male right hand, reaching, grabbing hold. It tensed, tendons shifting, muscles bunching as the man gripped, and pulled himself up—

Raising the candlestick, grimly determined, she stepped forward, intending to bring the heavy base down on the man's hand—

A gold signet ring winked in the weak light.

She blinked, peered, bent, and from a foot away looked more closely . . .

A vision flashed into her mind—of that hand, with that gold ring on the little finger, cupping her bare breast.

"Michael?" Lowering the candlestick, straightening, she stepped to the balustrade and peered over. Through the shifting shadows, she saw his head, the familiar set of his shoulders. "What on earth are you doing?"

He muttered something unintelligible, then more clearly said, "Stand back."

She took two steps back, watched as, both hands now locked on the balustrade, he hauled himself up, then swung a leg over the wide sill and sat astride.

Catching his breath, Michael looked at her, staring, not surprisingly bemused, at him, then he noticed the candlestick. "What were you intending to do with that?"

"Give whoever was sneaking up to my balcony a nasty surprise."

His lips twisted. "I didn't think of that." Swinging his other leg over, he stood, then leaned back against the balustrade as she stepped near and peered over.

"You didn't plan awfully well at all—wisteria isn't very strong."

Grimacing, he relieved her of the candelestick. "So I discovered. I'm afraid it took rather a beating."

"How am I supposed to explain that to Hendricks— Geoffrey's gardener?" Caro looked at him, found his gaze tracing down her body.

"You won't be here for him to ask." The words were vague; his gaze was still traveling down. It reached her feet; he hesitated, then slowly started upward again.

"And how would it have looked if you'd got caught? The local Member of Parliament climbing to a lady's window . . ." She stopped, intrigued. Waiting with feigned patience until his gaze returned to her eyes, she arched a brow.

His lips eased. "I'd imagined you as a demure cotton buttoned-to-the-throat type."

Raising both brows haughtily, she turned and walked back into her room. "I used to be. This"—she gestured to the delicate silk negligee gracing her curves—"was Camden's idea."

Following in her wake, Michael tore his gaze from the filmy confection that floated, flirted, a translucent sop to modesty, about her transparently naked form. "Camden?"

Even through the dimness, he could make out her peaked

nipples, the arousing curves of breast and hip and the long lines of her thighs. Her arms were bare, as was most of her back, the ivory silk shifting provocatively over the globes of her bottom as she led him into her bedchamber.

Camden must have been a glutton for self-punishment.

"He said it was in case the embassy caught on fire and I had to rush out *en déshabillé*." Halting, Caro faced him, met his eyes. "But I think it was more a case of what the servants would think. More a matter of protecting my standing than his." Her lips quirked self-deprecatingly. "After all," she murmured, fingers flicking the gown, "he never saw them."

Halting before her, he looked into her eyes. Then bent his head. "More fool him."

He kissed her, and she kissed him back, but then, one hand on his cheek, drew back to look into his eyes. "Why are you here?"

Closing his hands about her hips, he drew her nearer. "I couldn't sleep." The truth, if only part of it.

She searched his eyes; her lips curved teasingly. She let him settle her hips against him, then seductively shifted. "And you expect to *sleep* in my bed?"

"Yes." *From now until forever*. He shrugged. "Once we've indulged"—bending his head, he pressed a kiss beneath her ear, murmured even more softly—"once I've slaked my lust for you and sated my appetite"—lifting his head, he looked down at her—"I'll sleep perfectly well." *With you lying sated beside me*.

Brows high, she studied his eyes, then the curve of her lips deepened. "We'd better to get into bed then." Pushing back in his arms, her gaze dropped to his chest; her hands slid down from his shoulders. "You'll have to take off your clothes."

He caught her hands before she could embark on any fiendish—and doomed to be short-lived—game. The sight of her in her excuse for a negligee—and it seemed likely all her nightwear was of similar ilk, a point he didn't at that moment wish to dwell on—let alone the feel of her sinking, then sliding against him, had teased him from mere arousal to throbbing rigidity. He didn't need further encouragement. "I'll undress while you take off that creation—if I touch it, I'm bound to tear it. Once we're both naked, we can start from there."

Her laugh was sultry. "If you're sure you don't need any help?"

"Quite sure." He released her. She stepped back. Dragging in a breath, he moved to the end of her bed; leaning against it, he reached for his boots.

Hands rising to the shoulder clasps anchoring her nightgown, Caro murmured, "I'd always assumed these garments were designed so a man could remove them quickly."

"Those garments"—boots off, he straightened, hands rising to his cravat; his tones were distinctly strained—"were designed to drive men into a heightened state of lust in which, beyond the reach of sanity, they rip said garments off."

She laughed again, amazed that she could, that her heart felt so light even while her nerves were tightening. Two clicks and her negligee was free; the silk slithered down her body, pooling at her feet. "Well, you're in no danger now."

Shrugging out of his shirt, he glanced at her. "Much you know." His gaze felt like flame, caressing, burning. Emboldened, she bent and scooped the negligee up, tossed it on her dressing stool.

He looked away, flung his shirt aside, then, as if desperate, stripped off his breeches. Sending them spinning to join the rest of his clothes, he turned and reached for her.

She went into his arms, all laughter fading as their skins touched, and she felt his heat, felt his need—without thought gave herself up to it. To him.

Gave him her mouth and exulted when he took, sank into him, gloried in his ravenous, ravishing response. His hands roamed, not gentle but with undisguised yearning, with a heated hunger she shared.

That grew with every breath, with every gasp, every wickedly evocative caress.

Burying her hands in his hair, she clutched, arched against him, was only dimly aware when he lifted her and laid her on her sheets; she was caught in the flames, overwhelmed by their greedy heat, empty, aching, wanting.

His weight as he moved over her was a giddy relief, then he parted her thighs, pressed between, and entered her.

Thrust deep and joined with her.

Her gasp shivered through the night, a silver echo about them; eyes locked with hers, he thrust deeper still, then he bent his head, sealed her lips with his, and moved within her. Powerfully.

Unrestrained yet controlled, he whirled her into the dance her body and senses craved, that some part of her ached for. That her long-buried needs and wants, at last free, longed for. He wrapped her in dreams of hot skin slickly sliding, tongues sensuously tangling, muscled hardness and flushed softness supplely and intimately twining.

She arched beneath him, her body straining against his; he held her down and drove deeper, harder. Faster as she rose on the crest of that familiar wave, reaching higher, further, until it broke.

With a cry that he drank, she tumbled from the peak into his waiting arms.

Michael caught her, held her close, spread her thighs wider and sank deeper into her scalding heat, driving faster, harder, until her body claimed him and he followed her into sweet oblivion.

Later, he lifted from her; slumping beside her, relaxed, every muscle boneless with sated languor, he realized in the instant before sleep overcame him that his instincts had been right.

This was where he'd needed to spend the night—in Caro's bed, with her asleep beside him. One arm slung over her waist, he closed his eyes.

And slept.

He had to scramble the next morning to avoid the maids, both at Bramshaw House and the Manor. Returning to

Bramshaw as he'd promised at eight o'clock, he found Caro's traveling carriage waiting in the forecourt, the team between the shafts restless and ready to go.

Unfortunately for them all, while Caro herself was ready, the packing and stowing of her numerous boxes and valises had only just begun. Michael had had his groom drive him over in his curricle, his two cases strapped on behind; directing the two insignificant cases be placed alongside the mountain of Caro's luggage, he strolled to where she stood on the porch in conference with Catten and her not-so-young Portuguese maid.

Catten bowed in welcome; the maid bobbed, but the glance she threw him was severe.

Caro beamed, which was all he truly cared about.

"As you see"—she gestured to the footmen ferrying her luggage to the carriage—"we're ready—almost. This should take no more than half an hour."

He'd expected as much; he returned her smile. "No matter—I need to speak with Edward."

"He'll be supervising Elizabeth's piano practice, I expect."

With a nod, he turned away. "I'll find him."

He did, as predicted in the drawing room. A look summoned Edward from the piano; Elizabeth smiled, but continued to play. Edward joined him as he crossed the drawing room; at his intimation, they walked out onto the terrace.

He halted, but didn't immediately speak. Edward stopped beside him. "Last-minute instructions?"

Michael glanced at him. "No." He hesitated, then said, "More in the nature of forward planning." Before Edward could respond, he went on, "I want to ask you a question to which I would obviously like an answer, but if you feel you can't, for whatever reason, divulge the information, I will understand."

Edward was a skilled political aide; his "Oh?" was noncommittal.

Hands sunk in his pockets, Michael looked out over the lawn. "Caro's relationship with Camden—what was it?"

After Caro's explanation of her negligees, he had to know.

He'd chosen his words carefully; they revealed nothing specific, yet made clear that he knew what that relationship *hadn't* been.

Which, of course, raised the question of how he knew.

Silence stretched; he let it. He didn't expect Edward to reveal anything about Caro or Camden readily, yet he hoped Edward would allow for the fact that while Camden was dead, Caro wasn't.

Eventually, Edward cleared his throat. He, too, looked out over the lawn. "I'm very fond of Caro, as you know. . . ." After a moment, he continued, his tone that of one reporting, "It's common practice for all pertinent information about an ambassador's life, including his marriage, to be passed from each ambassadorial aide to his replacement. It's considered the sort of thing that might, in certain circumstances, be vital to know. When I took up my post in Lisbon, my predecessor informed me that it was common knowledge among the household that Caro and Camden never shared a bed."

He paused, then went on, "That situation was known to have been the case more or less since their marriage—at least from the time Caro took up residence in Lisbon." Again he paused, then more reluctantly went on, "The suspicion— and it was never voiced as more than that—was that their marriage might never have been consummated."

Michael felt Edward's quick glance, but kept his gaze on the lawn.

After a moment, Edward continued, "Be that as it may, Camden had a mistress throughout the years of his marriage to Caro—just one, a long-term relationship that had existed prior to their wedding. I was told Camden returned to the woman within a month or so of his marriage to Caro."

Despite his training, Edward hadn't been able to keep deep disapproval from coloring his words. Frowning as he digested them, Michael eventually asked, "Did Caro know?"

Edward snorted, but there was sadness in the sound. "I'm

sure of it. Something like that . . . she'd never have missed it. Not that she ever let on, not by word or deed."

A moment passed; Edward shifted, glanced at Michael, then looked away. "As far as I or any of my predecessors knew, Caro never took a lover."

Until now. Michael wasn't about to confirm or deny anything. He let the silence stretch, then looked at Edward. Met his gaze and nodded. "Thank you. That was, in part, what I needed to know."

It explained some things, but raised new questions, ones whose answers it seemed only Caro would know.

They turned back into the drawing room. "You will send for me," Edward said, "if there's any trouble in London?"

Michael considered Elizabeth, still engrossed in a concerto. "If you can better serve Caro there than here, I'll let you know."

Edward sighed. "You probably know this, but I'll warn you anyway. Keep a close eye on Caro. She's totally reliable in many respects, but she doesn't always recognize danger."

Michael met Edward's gaze, then nodded. Elizabeth sounded the last, triumphal chords; smoothly donning his politician's smile, he crossed to bid her farewell.

They rolled into London in the late afternoon. It was humid; warmth rising from the paved streets, the westering sun reflected from windows, its heat from high stone walls. In late July, the capital was half deserted, many spending the warmer weeks in their country house or farmhouse. The park, host to only a few riders and the occasional carriage, lay like an oasis of green in the surrounding desert of gray and brown stone, yet as the carriage turned into Mayfair, Michael was conscious of a quickening of his pulse—a recognition that they were reentering the political forum, the place where decisions were formulated, influenced, and made.

Politics, as he'd told Caro, ran in his blood.

Beside him, she shifted, straightening, glancing out of the window; with a flash of insight, he realized she, too, reacted to the capital—the seat of government—with a similiar focusing of her attention, a more keenly anticipatory air.

She turned to him. Met his gaze and smiled. "Where should I set you down?"

He held her gaze, then asked, "Where were you planning on staying?"

"At Angela's in Bedford Square."

"Is Angela in residence?"

Caro continued to smile. "No—but there'll be staff there."

"A skeleton staff?"

"Well, yes—it is the height of summer."

He looked forward, then said, "I think it would be infinitely wiser for us—both of us—to stay with my grandfather in Upper Grosvenor Street."

"But—" Caro glanced out as the carriage slowed. She glimpsed a street sign; the carriage was turning into Upper Grosvenor Street. The notion of having been an unwitting accomplice in her own kidnapping assailed her. She looked at Michael. "We cannot simply descend on your grandfather."

"Of course not." He sat forward. "I sent a messenger this morning."

The carriage slowed, then halted. He met her eyes. "I live here while in town, and Magnus rarely leaves—the house is fully staffed. Believe me when I say that both Magnus *and* his staff will be delighted to have us—both of us—stay."

She frowned. "It's stretching the proprieties for me to reside under your grandfather's roof while only you and he are in residence."

"I omitted to mention Evelyn, my grandfather's cousin. She lives with him and runs the house. She's seventy if she's a day, but then"—he met her gaze—"you're a widow—I'm sure the proprieties will remain unruffled." His voice gained in decisiveness. "Quite aside from all else, there's not a gossipmonger in town would dare suggest anything scandalous took place under Magnus Anstruther-Wetherby's roof."

That last was unarguable.

She narrowed her eyes at him. "You had this in mind all along."

He smiled and reached for the carriage door.

She wasn't convinced it was a good idea, but unable to think of any solid grounds on which to resist, she allowed him to hand her down, then conduct her up the steps.

A very large butler opened the door, his expression benevolent. "Good afternoon, sir. Welcome home."

"Thank you, Hammer." Michael handed her over the threshold. "This is Mrs. Sutcliffe. We'll be staying for the next week or so while we attend to a number of matters."

"Mrs. Sutcliffe." Hammer bowed low; his voice was as deep as he was large. "If there's anything you require, you have only to ring. It will be our pleasure to serve you."

Caro smiled charmingly; regardless of her reservations, she wouldn't allow them to show. "Thank you, Hammer." She waved at the carriage. "I'm afraid I've saddled you with rather a lot of luggage."

"It's of no moment, ma'am—we'll have it up in your room in no time." Hammer glanced at Michael. "Mrs. Logan thought the Green Room would be suitable."

Mentally locating that room in the huge house, Michael nodded. "An excellent choice. I'm sure Mrs. Sutcliffe will be comfortable there."

"Indeed." Caro caught his eye, tried to see past his mask to what was going on in his head—and failed. She turned to Hammer. "My maid's name is Fenella—she's fluent in English. If you could show her my room, I'll be up shortly to bathe and change for dinner."

Hammer bowed. Inclining her head gracefully, Caro turned to Michael and slid her hand onto his arm. "Now you had better present me to your grandfather."

Michael led her toward the library, his grandfather's sanctum. "You have met him, haven't you?"

"Years ago—I'm not sure he'd remember. It was at some Foreign Office function."

"He'll remember." Michael felt sure of that.

"Ah—Mrs. Sutcliffe!" Magnus boomed the instant Caro entered. "Do forgive me for not rising—demmed gout, y'know. It's a trial." Seated in a huge wing chair angled before the empty hearth, his swaddled foot propped on a stool, Magnus fixed her with a sharp, shrewd blue gaze as she walked across the room to greet him. "It's a pleasure to meet you again, m'dear."

He held out a hand; determinedly serene and unshakable, she placed her fingers in it and curtsied. "It's a pleasure to renew our acquaintance, sir."

Magnus glanced at Michael, his gaze, shaded by thick overhanging brows, penetrating. Meeting that searching glance, Michael merely smiled.

Clasping her hand, Magnus patted it lightly. "My grandson tells me we're to have the pleasure of your company for a week or so."

Releasing her, he sat back in his chair, his attention fixing on her.

She inclined her head. "If you're so disposed, of course."

A fleeting smile touched Magnus's lips. "My dear, I'm an ancient, and only too thrilled to have my declining years enlivened by the presence of wit and beauty."

She had to smile. "In that case"—sweeping her skirts about her, she sat on the chaise—"I'll be delighted to accept and enjoy your hospitality."

Magnus studied her, taking in her self-confidence, her calm, unruffled serenity, then he grinned. "Right then, now we've got the social niceties out of the way, what's this all about, heh?"

He glanced at Michael. Pointedly, Michael looked at her.

Understanding that he was leaving the decision to include Magnus entirely to her, she realized with faint astonishment that since they'd resolved to come to London, she hadn't had time to dwell on their reasons.

Refocusing on Magnus, considering his vast experience, she met his gaze. "Someone, it seems, is not well disposed toward my continuing existence."

Magnus's brows lowered; after a moment he barked, "Why?"

"That," she informed him, pulling off her gloves, "is what we've come to London to discover."

* * *

Between them, she and Michael explained; it was reassuring to find Magnus reacting much as they had. His experience of their world was profound; if he thought as they did, they were most likely correct.

Later that night, when Fenella had finally left her, Caro stood before the window in the elegant bedchamber decorated in shades of green, and looked out as the night wrapped London in its sultry arms. So different from the country, yet she was equally at home here, the constant if dim sounds of nighttime activity as familiar as the deep stillness of the countryside.

After speaking with Magnus, she'd retired to bathe and refresh herself, then they'd dined in semiformal state. Later, in the drawing room, with Magnus nodding in acquiescence, she and Michael had made plans to retrieve Camden's papers and her copy of Camden's will from Half Moon Street; she'd agreed that the mansion in Upper Grosvenor Street, under the constant eye of Magnus's considerable staff and with the old gentleman himself almost always present, would be a safer repository than the uninhabited Half Moon Street residence.

Their way forward on that matter was clear; she felt no qualms, no hesitations about their approach to unmasking and metaphorically spiking the guns of whoever now wished her harm.

On that score, she felt assured.

However, on the subject of what was developing between her and Michael, she was far less confident. She'd set out for the cottage intending to reach some conclusion; fate had intervened, setting in train a succession of events that subsequently had dominated her time.

Now, however, when at last she could return to consider that subject, it was only to realize she was no further along; Michael's continuing desire for her—all that she was discovering flowed from it, both from him and from her, such as his unexpected appearance by such a fanciful route in her bedchamber last night—was still so new to her, so enthralling, she couldn't yet see past it.

Couldn't see where it was leading her. Or him.

The house had fallen silent; she heard his muffled footfall an instant before the doorknob turned, and he entered.

She turned to watch him cross the room to her; she let her lips curve, but kept most of her smile within. She'd wondered if he would come—had donned another of her diaphanous nightgowns just in case.

He'd undressed; he appeared to be wearing nothing more than a long silk robe, loosely belted. As he walked unhurriedly to her, his gaze perused her form, absorbing the effect of the all-but-transparent gauze sheath rendered barely acceptable by three cleverly positioned appliqued roses—two buds, one full bloom.

Reaching her, he halted, lifted his gaze to her eyes. "You do realize, don't you, that such gowns on you deprive me of all ability to think?"

Her smile deepened, a sultry chuckle escaped her. He reached for her and she went into his arms, lifting her own to drape them about his neck. For a moment, he hesitated, his eyes on hers. The heat in his gaze assured her his comment was close to the literal truth. Then he lowered his head, his arms tightened—

Pressing a hand to his chest, she stayed him.

He stopped, met her gaze. Locking her eyes with his, she sent her hand skating down, found and tugged the tie at his hips free, slipped her hand between the edges of his robe, and found him.

Hard, hot, fully engorged, aroused with desire for her.

She still found it amazing, felt her lungs contract, her heart soar. Wanted to share her joy, her pleasure. Closing her hand, she squeezed, then stroked, watched his eyes blank, then close, his features ease of all expression, then tighten with surging desire.

With her other hand, she slid the silk gown from his shoulders, thrilled to the shush as it fell away. She pressed closer, placed a kiss at the center of his chest, then, one hand still wrapped around his rigid erection, used her other spread on his body to steady herself as she slid slowly down, her lips tracing down, until she was on her knees.

Boldly, she put out her tongue, with the tip delicately traced the broad head, then, urged on by the shudder that racked him, she parted her lips, and gently, smoothly, took him into her mouth.

His fingers slid through her hair, clenched as she lightly sucked, licked, then experimented. Fingers sinking into his buttocks, she held him tight as, tracking his response, his reactions—his tensing fingers, his increasingly ragged breaths—she learned how to minister to him.

Learned how to tighten his nerves as he had so often tightened hers—on, and on . . .

Abruptly, he hauled in a huge breath, closed his hands about her shoulders, and urged her up. "Enough."

The word was tortured; she obeyed, releasing him, leaning both hands on him, tracing them both upward as she allowed him to draw her upright.

His eyes, when they met hers, burned. "Take off the gown."

Holding his gaze, she lifted her hands to her shoulders, snapped open the clasps.

The instant the gauze hit the floor, he dragged her to him, kissed her ravenously—poured heat and fire down her veins until she was burning, too—then he lifted her.

She wrapped her arms about his neck, locked her legs about his hips, gasped, head falling back as she felt him nudge into her. Then he drew her down, slowly, steadily impaling her inch by inexorable inch, until he was fully seated within her, high and hard and oh so real.

Then he moved her upon him; she looked down, met his eyes, let him capture hers, draw her into the dance until she merged fully with him, one in thought, in deed, in desire. At some point, their lips found each other's again, and they left the world, stepped into another.

One where nothing mattered beyond this simple communion, this melding of bodies, of minds, of passions.

She gave herself up to it, knew he did the same.

Together, they soared and touched the sun, fused, melted, then, inevitably, returned to earth.

Later, wrapped in his arms, collapsed on her bed, she

murmured, "This is probably scandalous—it's your grandfather's house."

"His, not mine."

The words reached her as a rumble, vibrating through his chest on which she'd pillowed her cheek. "Is this why you wanted me to stay here?"

"One of the reasons." She felt his fingers toy with her hair, then they stroked and cupped her nape. "I have this trouble with insomnia I knew you could cure."

With a gurgle of laughter, weak but content, she settled her head.

Closing his eyes, Michael smiled and, equally content, surrendered to slumber.

CHAPTER

17

*C*aro slid her key into the lock on the front door of the town house in Half Moon Street. "Our old housekeeper, Mrs. Simms, comes in twice a week to air and dust so all will be ready should I wish to return."

Michael followed her into an airy hall tiled with black, white, and ochre mosaics, flecks of gold glinting in the veined marble. In returning to town, Caro hadn't elected to come here; apparently she hadn't considered it. Closing the front door, he glanced around as she paused in an archway he assumed led to the drawing room. The double doors were open; she cast a comprehensive glance within, then moved on to the next door, opened it, and looked in.

Noting the quality of the oak wainscoting, the side tables, and the huge mirror gracing the hall, he stolled up and looked over Caro's head, and felt his eyes widen. The room was the dining room; it contained a long mahogany table with the most wonderful glowing sheen, and a set of chairs even his less than expert knowledge labeled as antiques—French; he couldn't guess the period, yet their value was obvious.

He followed as Caro flitted from room to room; every item he saw was museum-quality, even the ornaments and fittings. Yet the house was neither cluttered nor cold and off-putting. It was as if it had been created with incredible love, care, and a superb eye for beauty, and then, for some reason, barely used.

As he climbed the sweeping staircase behind Caro, he realized Edward had been right; the house and its contents were highly valuable—something someone could conceivably kill for. He caught up with Caro at the top of the stairs. "The will first."

She glanced at him, then led the way down a corridor.

The room she turned into had clearly been Camden's study. While she went to the wall behind the desk, swung aside a painting—one that looked suspiciously like an old master—to reveal a large wall safe, and set about carefully unlocking it, he lounged in the doorway and looked around. Tried to imagine Camden here. With Caro.

Less overtly masculine than most studies were, the room testified to a sense of balance and taste; as in the other rooms, all the furniture was antique, the fabrics sumptuous. He examined, considered, conscious once again of not being able to get a clear picture of the relationship between Camden and Caro.

He'd seen them together on a number of occasions, diplomatic soirées, dinners, and the like. He'd never suspected that their marriage had been nothing more than a facade. He now knew it had been, yet here in the house Caro had told him Camden had created over the years of their marriage, essentially for her . . .

A folded parchment in her hand, she shut the safe, locked it, and swung the painting back into place; watching her cross the room, Michael inwardly shook his head. Camden may have created the house, but it was Caro's—it suited her to the ground, the perfect showcase for her and her manifold talents.

The instant the thought formed, he knew it was true, yet if Camden had cared enough to pour such a lot of himself—not just money but so much more—into creating this masterpiece for her, why had he left her untouched? Physically at least, unloved?

And given his attentions to a mistress instead?

Straightening, he took the thick sheaf Caro held out to him.

"It won't fit in my reticule."

He managed to tuck it into his inside coat pocket. "I'm not a legal expert—would it worry you if I got it examined by one, just to make sure there's no strange twist we can't see?"

She raised her brows, but nodded. "That might be wise. Now"—she pointed further down the corridor—"Camden's papers are along here."

To his surprise, she didn't lead him into another room, but instead stopped before a pair of double doors, a cupboard built into the corridor wall.

Caro set the doors wide, revealing shelves of linens and towels, all neatly stacked. The two halves of the cupboard were separate sets of shelves, like two bookcases abutting; reaching deep to the back of one shelf, she pressed the catch to release them—they swung open a little. "Stand back."

Michael did, watching, amazed as she swung first one set of shelves, then the other wide, revealing a storeroom lined with shelves on which boxes of files lay neatly stacked.

Stepping back, she gestured. "Camden's papers."

Michael considered them, then glanced at her. "Lucky we brought two footmen."

"Indeed." He hadn't understood when she'd requested them.

Turning, she led the way downstairs, through the back of the house, and down the garden path to open the back gate. Magnus's largest carriage stood waiting in the mews beyond.

Michael took charge. An hour later, with the Half Moon Street house once again closed and locked, they returned to Upper Grosvenor Street and proceeded to unload the accumulated records of Camden Sutcliffe's life.

Evelyn, a quiet but redoubtable lady whom Caro had met over dinner the previous evening, had suggested they store the papers in a small parlor on the first floor, not far from the main stairs in the central part of the mansion. "Safest," Evelyn had opined. "There's always some maid or footman traipsing about in sight of that door."

Magnus had grunted, but agreed. The boxes, therefore,

were carried upstairs and stacked neatly along one wall of the parlor, waiting for Caro to read through them. When the footmen finally retreated, their job done, she eyed the work before her and sighed.

Michael, shoulder propped against the doorframe, studied her. "Magnus would help at the drop of a hat."

She sighed again. "I know, but in deference to Camden, if anyone is to read his diaries and private correspondence, it should be me. At least until we know if there's anything of note in there."

Michael studied her face, then nodded and straightened. Downstairs, a gong clanged.

Caro smiled. "Saved—I'll start after lunch."

Tucking a wayward strand back into her coiffure, she took his arm, let him draw her out of the room and shut the door.

Over luncheon, they studied the will. All of them read it, even Evelyn, as crochety as Magnus could be irrascible yet also shrewd and experienced in her way. None of them felt confident they fully comprehended the convoluted legal language enough to pass judgment.

"Best get an expert opinion," Magnus said.

Caro graciously repeated her permission; Michael tucked the will back into his pocket.

Once the meal was ended, he accompanied her back to the parlor. They spent the next half hour rearranging the boxes into some semblance of order, then, the first box open at her feet, Caro sat in an armchair—and looked up at him. Raised a faintly amused brow.

He smiled. "No, I'm not going to stand here watching you read." He tapped his chest; the will crackled. "I'm going to get this examined. I'll ensure it's done with absolute discretion."

She smiled back. "Thank you."

Still, he hesitated. When she again a raised a brow, he asked, "Will you do something for me?"

She searched his face. "What?"

"Stay here—safe inside. Promise me you won't leave the house until I get back."

Her smile was gentle; she regarded him for a moment from steady silver eyes, then inclined her head. "I promise."

He held her gaze for an instant longer, then saluted her and left.

He didn't have far to go—just along Upper Grosvenor Street to where it fed into Grosvenor Square. He paced along the north side of the square, searching among the ladies, children, and nursemaids walking and playing in the central gardens, hoping to catch sight of familiar faces. In that he was disappointed. Reaching the imposing mansion in the center of the block, he went up the steps, praying the owners were in residence.

Fate smiled; they were.

It was Devil he asked to see.

Ensconced behind the desk in his study, his brother-in-law greeted him with raised brows and a devilish, faintly taunting smile. "Ho! I thought you were engrossed in the hunt for a wife. What brings you here?"

"A will." Michael tossed Camden's will onto Devil's desk and sank into one of the chairs facing it.

Sitting back in his chair, Devil considered the folded parchment, but made no move to take it. "Whose?"

"Camden Sutcliffe's."

At that, Devil looked up, met his gaze. After a moment of studying his face, he asked, "Why?"

Michael told him; as he'd expected, relating the attempts on Caro's life was all it took to focus his powerful brother-in-law's attention.

Devil picked up the will. "So the answer could lie in here."

"Either in there, or in Camden's papers. Caro's going through the papers—I wondered if you could get your people to go over that"—with a nod, he indicated the will—"with a fine-toothed comb."

He could have approached the firm of solicitors Magnus used, but those solicitors were as old as Magnus. Devil, on the other hand, Duke of St. Ives and head of the powerful

Cynster clan, and thus constantly embroiled in dealing with all types of legal affairs, employed the very best of the up-and-coming legal fraternity. If any solicitors could identify a potential threat to Caro buried in Camden's will, Devil's would.

Flicking through the document, Devil nodded. "I'll get them onto it immediately." He grimaced, then refolded the will. "Makes one wonder what became of the English language."

Laying the will aside, he reached for a fresh sheet of paper. "I'll add a note to the effect we want the answer with all speed."

"Thank you." Michael rose. "Is Honoria in?"

A faint smile lifted Devil's lips. "She is, and I'm sure your presence within her purlieu will by now have been reported." He looked up at Michael and grinned. "She's probably waiting to pounce the instant you leave this room."

Michael raised his brows. "I'm surprised she hasn't simply waltzed in." It wasn't like Honoria to stand on ceremony, and Devil had no secrets from her.

Devil's grin only deepened; he looked down and wrote. "I think she's trying to restrain herself from prying into your love life—the effort is probably killing her."

With a laugh, Michael turned to the door. "I'd better go and relieve her."

Devil raised a hand in farewell. "I'll send word the instant I have any news."

Michael left. Closing the study door, he headed back along the corridor to the front hall.

"I do hope"—his sister's crisp, unquestionably duchessy tones reached him the instant he set foot on the hall tiles—"that you intend to come up and call on me?"

Michael swung around, looked up the grand staircase to where Honoria stood on the landing. He grinned. "I was on my way up."

He took the stairs two at a time, then swung her into a hug, which she, smiling delightedly, returned.

"Now," she said, releasing him and stepping back to look

into his face. "Tell me your news. What are you doing back in town? Have you made an offer?"

He laughed. "I'll tell you, but not here."

She took his arm and led him to her private sitting room. Swinging around, she sat in an armchair, barely waited for him to do the same before demanding, "Now tell me. All of it."

He did; there was no point doing otherwise—any hint of evasion and she'd have pounced, and either wrung it out of him or out of Devil. The only information he omitted to mention, as he had with Devil, was the truth of Caro and Camden's marriage. He didn't specifically state that Caro Sutcliffe was the woman he'd set his heart on; he didn't have to—Honoria made the connection with ease.

The news of the attempts on Caro's life sobered her— Caro and she had once been close friends—but when he explained how they proposed to meet the challenge, she merely nodded. With three children whose welfare she supervised very closely, Honoria had too much on her plate these days to interfere. However . . .

"Bring her to afternoon tea." Honoria considered, then said, "It's too late today, but bring her tomorrow afternoon."

Michael knew he could count on Honoria to take his side, to tactfully and covertly steer Caro toward accepting his proposal. He couldn't wish for better support, but . . . it was a support that had better be informed. "I've asked her to marry me—she hasn't yet agreed."

Honoria's brows rose. She blinked, then smiled, entirely comprehending. "Then we'll have to see what we can do to help her make up her mind."

She stood. "Now come and do your penance—your nephews and niece are in the schoolroom."

With a smile, he rose, prefectly willing to pay her price.

Late July in London might be warm and muggy; it was, however, relatively free of unavoidable social engagements. Consequently, they gathered over the dinner table *en famille*—Caro, Magnus, Evelyn, and he; over the meal, they revisited the facts and refined their strategy.

"I've started on Camden's diaries." Caro grimaced. "He was incredibly detailed in his observations—it's perfectly possible he might have seen and noted something that some-one might now deem dangerous."

"Slow going?" Michael asked.

"Very. I've started from when he first took up his post as ambassador to Portugal—that seemed the most sensible place to start."

"What about his letters?"

"I'll go through them later, if I find nothing in the diaries."

Michael was aware that Magnus was restraining himself from demanding to help with the letters; he briefly described his visit to Devil Cynster, and Devil's agreement to get his solicitors to examine the will.

"There must be something else you can do." From under beetling brows, Magnus looked at Michael.

Faintly smiling, Michael glanced at Caro. "The Por-tuguese are firm suspects—it seems likely Leponte was behind the burglary at Sutcliffe Hall. We know he searched Bramshaw House. I think it would be wise to discover if he, or any of his family, have come up to town."

"And if they haven't," Magnus growled, "we need to set a watch."

"Indeed." Michael returned his gaze to Caro. "We need to pool our sources—what's the best way to learn who among the Portuguese delegation are in London?"

They tossed around names of aides and other officials in various capacities. Michael eventually assembled a short list. "I'll do the rounds tomorrow morning and see what they can tell me."

"It occurs to me"—leaning on one elbow, her chin propped in her hand, Caro studied him from across the table—"that between us, we have numerous contacts in diplomatic and political circles we could exploit—not offi-cially so much as socially. They might be able to help us, not just with news of who is in town, but with memories and also with current changes, any shifts in power in Portugal or else-where."

She glanced at Magnus. "We have no idea how far back the connection with Camden goes, nor do we know why it's suddenly assumed importance." She looked back at Michael. "Someone might know more, although how we're to approach the issue I can't yet see."

Magnus was nodding his shaggy head. "A sensible way forward, even if you can't yet see precisely how it might help. The first thing you need to do is let it be known you're back in town."

"Given it's midsummer, the circles are smaller and correspondingly more elite." Caro tapped the table. "It shouldn't be hard to wave the flag, put ourselves about—learn what we can regarding the Portuguese, and at the same time explore any other avenues that offer."

Michael studied her face, wondered if she'd realized why Magnus was so keen on them going about together among their social set. Yet it was she who'd suggested it. "Why don't we meet again over lunch tomorrow and see how far we've progressed, then we can make more definite plans to step back into the limelight."

Evelyn pushed back her chair; using her cane, she got to her feet. "I'll be out to both morning and afternoon teas tomorrow." She smiled. "We might be old, but we know what's what—and what's going on, what's more. I'll take note of which hostesses are entertaining in the next few days."

"Thank you." With a smile, Caro rose, too. Going around the table, she linked her arm in Evelyn's. "That would indeed help."

Together she and Evelyn left for the drawing room and the tea trolley; in an hour or so, they'd retire to their rooms.

Michael, who had also risen, sat again. He waited for Hammer to set out the decanters, then filled Magnus's glass and his. When Hammer had retreated and they were alone, he sat back, sipped, and looked speculatively at Magnus.

Perfectly aware, Magnus raised a shaggy brow. "Well?"

Michael savored his grandfather's excellent brandy, then asked, "What do you know about Camden Sutcliffe?"

*   *   *

An hour and a half later, having helped Magnus to his room, Michael returned to his own—to undress, don his robe, and join Caro in hers.

Pulling the gold pin from his cravat, he considered the picture Magnus had painted of Camden Sutcliffe. Magnus had, of course, known Camden, but not well; Magnus was over eighty, more than ten years older than Camden, and although throughout his long political career Magnus had frequently been involved in diplomatic events, none of those had involved Portugal during Camden's tenure.

Nevertheless, Magnus was a shrewd and acute observer; he'd painted Camden with a few deft strokes, leaving Michael with a clear vision of a gentleman born and bred, one who, like them, took his station for granted and saw no need to impress it on others. Camden, however, had been, as Magnus put it, *exquisitely* charming, a man who knew just the right degree of gloss to apply for whomever he was dealing with. A man who combined that lethal charm with a pleasant temperament and easy, well-bred manners in the service of his country—and of Camden Sutcliffe.

The picture Magnus had created was of a supremely self-centered man, but one who, simultaneously, had been a recognized patriot. A man who unstintingly put his country above all else, who held his service and loyalty to it inviolate, but who otherwise thought, first and last, of himself.

That vision fitted well with Caro's revelation that Camden had married her solely for her hostessly talents. It sat well with Edward's insights, too, and those Michael himself had gleaned over the years, not only from personal experience, but from Geoffrey, George Sutcliffe, and others who had known Camden well.

It did not, however, explain the house in Half Moon Street.

Michael shrugged on his robe, belted it. Inwardly shaking his head, putting aside the as yet inexplicable conundrum of Camden's relationship with Caro, he opened his door and set out to join her.

Camden's widow—his wife-to-be.

*   *   *

By lunchtime the next day, he'd learned that Ferdinand Leponte was in London. Returning to Upper Grosvenor Street, he joined the others about the luncheon table. Taking his seat, he glanced at Caro.

She caught his gaze. Her eyes opened wide. "You've learned something. What?"

He was surprised; he knew he wasn't that easy to read. But he nodded, and told them his news. "Neither the duke, duchess, count, or countess are with him—apparently they're still in Hampshire. Ferdinand, however, has left his yacht and the lure of the Solent in summer, and come up to London—he's staying in rooms attached to the embassy."

"When did he come up?" Magnus asked.

"Yesterday." Across the table, Michael exchanged a glance with Caro.

She nodded. "Easy enough to call at Bramshaw House, ask for me, and learn I'd left for town."

He reached for his glass. "I didn't learn anything more of interest. Did you turn up anything?"

Caro grimaced and shook her head. "It's all very colorful, but there's no hint of anything nefarious—any item that could now be dangerous to know."

They looked at Evelyn; she'd pulled a note from her pocket and was smoothing it out.

"I made a list of who's entertaining tonight." She passed it to Caro. "That should get you started."

Glancing up from perusing the list, Caro smiled gratefully. "Thank you—this is perfect." Across the table, she met Michael's eyes. "Your aunt Harriet is giving a soirée this evening."

Although nothing showed in his face, she was sure he was thinking of his last meeting with his aunt, and Caro's subsequent encounter with Harriet. Harriet thought he was pursuing Elizabeth.

Caro smiled. "Quite obviously we should attend."

A faint grimace crossed his face, but he inclined his head.

When they rose from the luncheon table and dispersed, Caro paused in the hall, tapping Evelyn's note in her hand, planning.

Returning from helping Magnus back to the library, Michael found her there. Paused to take in her slender figure, erect, head high, her absorbed yet focused expression, before strolling to join her. "Are you heading back to the diaries, then?"

She glanced at him, smiled. "No—if we're to plunge back into the whirl, I need new gloves and more stockings. I think I'll go to Bond Street." Fleetingly, she pulled a face. "I've had enough of Camden's writings for one day."

He could detect no sadness in her, yet would he? Would she let such a reaction show? He had no idea what manner of revelations Camden might have set down in his diaries.

"I'll come with you." The words, and his intention, were instinctive; he hadn't needed to—didn't need to—think.

She blinked at him. "You *want* to go to Bond Street?"

"No. But if that's where you're heading, then that's where I'll go."

For what seemed like a full minute, she looked into his eyes, then a faint smile curved her lips; she turned to the stairs. "We may as well go now, but I'll have to change."

He stifled a sigh. "I'll wait in the library."

He was reading a treatise on the recent history of Portugal when she opened the library door and looked in. He rose; Magnus glanced up from his own researches, on much the same topic, grunted, and waved them off.

Joining Caro in the corridor, he ran an appreciative eye over the creation she'd selected, a gown in spotted voile of a delicate ice-blue. The vision of ice on a hot summer's day flashed into his mind; his mouth watered. With a smile, she led the way back to the hall and the front door, transparently oblivious of the effect the sight of her swaying hips, clothed in such fantasy, was having on him.

When she paused by the door Hammer was holding open and, haloed by the sunshine outside, looked back at him, waiting, expectant, he hesitated—for one second toyed with the notion of inveigling her back upstairs . . . realized she wouldn't immediately understand, that despite all they'd thus far shared, she didn't yet truly comprehend the depth of his desire for her. She wouldn't necessarily react accordingly, not immediately.

Dragging in a breath, forcing his features to relax into an expression of indulgent ease, he reached for her arm. "The carriage should be waiting."

It was; he handed her up, then sat beside her as they rattled through the streets. Bond Street wasn't far; soon they were strolling arm in arm past the fashionable shops. Caro entered only two establishments—one for gloves, one for stockings. He waited on the pavement in both instances, giving mute thanks that she wasn't one of those females who had to look through every shop she passed.

The street was far less crowded than during the Season. It was pleasant enough to walk along, nodding to this lady and that. The bulk of society was absent, cavorting in the countryside; those of the haut ton presently in town were there because they needed to be—because they were involved in one or other arm of government, or were essential players in some similar sphere.

Caro drew eyes, both male and female. She had a style that was elegant and exclusive—exclusively hers. Today the attention she attracted often resulted in recognition; many of the ladies currently in Bond Street were the more senior hostesses who regarded her as one of their own.

Parting from Lady Holland, the hostess of note they'd encountered, he arched a brow as Caro reclaimed his arm. "Just gloves and stockings?"

She smiled. "It was an obvious opportunity. If we're to rejoin the pack, then these ladies are the first who need to know."

"Speaking of obvious opportunities, I forgot to mention"—glancing down, he caught her eyes as she looked up inquiringly—"Honoria asked that I bring you to tea today. I gathered it was to be private—I think, entertainingwise, she's lying low at present."

Caro's face lit. "I haven't seen her—not to talk to—in years. Not since your parents died. I only glimpsed her a few times this last Season in the ballrooms—we never had a chance to really talk." She met his eyes. "What's the time?"

He pulled out his watch, consulted it; she peeked. Slipping it back into his pocket, he looked around. "If we stroll to the corner, then return to the carriage, we can go straight there—our timing will be perfect."

"Excellent." Settling her hand on his arm, she stepped out. "Let's see who else we meet."

Two more hostesses, then, to their surprise, Muriel Hedderwick appeared in their path.

"Caro." She directed a nod Caro's way, then looked at Michael.

He reached for her hand and bowed over it. Muriel returned his polite greeting, then turned to Caro.

"Have you come up for a meeting?" Caro knew Muriel rarely came to town for anything else.

"Indeed," Muriel replied. "The Older Orphans' Temperance Society. The inaugural meeting was yesterday. Our aim, of course . . ." She launched into an impassioned description of the society's predictable aims.

Michael shifted; Caro pinched his arm. There was no point interrupting; Muriel would say what she would say. Any attempt to distract her would only prolong the exercise.

Muriel's eloquence finally ended. She fixed her gaze intently on Caro. "We're holding a steering committee meeting tonight. As you're now residing in England, I should think it's the sort of association to which you would wish to devote some of your time. I would most strongly urge you to attend—the meeting will be held at eight o'clock."

Caro smiled. "Thank you for the invitation—I'll make every effort to attend." From experience she knew this was a case in which a simple prevarication worked to everyone's advantage. If she demurred and said she was already committed elsewhere, Muriel would feel compelled to argue her case until Caro broke down and agreed to attend. She made a mental note to make her excuses when next they met.

She felt Michael's gaze, pressed his arm to keep him silent. Smiled at Muriel.

Who nodded, as haughty as ever. "We're meeting at Number Four, Alder Street, just past Aldgate."

Michael inwardly frowned; he glanced at Caro—she wouldn't know London all that well, not beyond the fashionable areas.

She confirmed that by smiling and inclining her head. "I'll hope to meet you and the rest of your committee there."

"Good." With another firm nod and a regal glance his way, Muriel made her good-byes.

He suppressed an impulse to tell her that if she was going to Aldgate, she should take a footman—a burly one—with her; Muriel would consider the comment unforgivably presumptuous.

He waited until she was out of earshot to murmur, "You're not attending any meeting near Aldgate."

"Of course not." Caro retook his arm; they strolled on. "I'm sure the steering committee is full of eager and interested members—they'll manage perfectly well without me. But Muriel's obsessed with her societies and associations— she doesn't seem to appreciate that others aren't as interested, at least not to the same extent as she." She smiled up at him. "But each to her own."

He met her gaze. "In that case, let's go to tea."

Much more frivolous than a temperance society meeting— also much more relaxing.

They sat not in the formal drawing room but in a beautiful sitting room that gave onto the back terrace of the mansion in Grosvenor Square, drank tea, consumed cakes and scones, and caught up with the past.

Within seconds of taking Honoria's hands and being pulled into a warm embrace, Caro felt as if the years had, if not fallen from them, then been bridged. Honoria was three years older than she; throughout childhood they'd been firm friends. But then Honoria and Michael's parents had been killed in a tragic accident; the event had parted Caro and Honoria, not only physically.

They had been—still were, Caro suspected—alike in many ways; if Honoria had been and still was the more assertive, she was the more assured, the more confident in herself.

She had remained in Hampshire, the much-loved youngest daughter of the happy household at Bramshaw House—until she'd been swept off her feet into her marriage with Camden. While Honoria had been very much alone, she, catapulted into the highest echelons of society, had been wrestling with hostessly demands that had initially been well beyond her years. She had coped; so had Honoria.

While Honoria glossed over the years she'd spent with distant relatives in the shires, virtually alone in the world but for Michael, Caro was quite sure those years had left their mark, as the accident itself must have done. Now, however, there was not the faintest vestige of cloud to be found in Honoria's eyes; her life was full, rich, and transparently satisfying.

She had married Devil Cynster.

Over the rim of her cup, Caro glanced at the lounging presence talking with Michael; they had taken chairs opposite the chaise where she and Honoria sat. It was the first time she had seen Devil beyond a glimpse.

Within the ton, the name Cynster was synonymous with a certain type of gentleman, with a certain type of wife. And while Honoria certainly fitted the mold of a Cynster wife, Devil Cynster, from all she could see and all she had heard, was the epitome of the Cynster male.

He was large, lean, harsh featured. There was very little softness about him; even his eyes, large, heavy lidded, a curious shade of pale green, seemed crystalline, his glance hard and sharp. Yet Caro noted that every time his eyes rested on Honoria, they softened; even the austere lines of his face, of his lean lips, seemed to ease.

Power was his—he'd been born to it, not just physically but in every imaginable way. And he used it; that Caro knew beyond doubt. Yet talking to Honoria, sensing the deep, almost startlingly vibrant connection carried in shared glances, in the light touch of a hand, she sensed—could almost feel—that another power ruled here. That just as Honoria seemed to have surrendered to it, so, too, had Devil.

And they were happy. Deeply, powerfully content.

Caro set down her cup, reached for another scone, and asked Honoria who else was in town; Honoria had confirmed that Michael had explained the real reason for their presence in the capital. "In order to learn whatever we can, we must make an effort to be seen."

Honoria raised her brows. "In that case, Therese Osbaldestone came up two days ago. A select gathering has been summoned to attend her tomorrow for morning tea." She grinned. "You should come with me."

Caro met Honoria's eyes. "You know perfectly well she'll pounce on me and lecture me. You're just trying to divert her attention."

Honoria opened her eyes wide, spread her hands. "Of course. What are friends for, after all?"

Caro laughed.

Devil and Michael rose; she and Honoria turned to view them inquiringly.

Devil grinned. "I'll return your late husband's will. While my people couldn't find anything significant in it, there are a number of matters I need to clarify with Michael, so if you'll excuse us, we'll retire to my study."

Caro found herself smiling and inclining her head—even while her mind retreaded his words and found no request for permission in them. But by then, the door was closing. Looking at Honoria, she raised a quizzical brow. "Tell me— were those 'matters' to be clarified to do with the will, or something else entirely?"

"Your guess is as good as mine. Devil and Michael share other interests; however, I, too, suspect those matters are most likely questions about Camden's will." Honoria shrugged. "No matter. I'll get it out of Devil later, and you can drag the information from Michael.

Rising, she waved Caro up. "Come—I want to show you the other half of my life."

Caro rose. The doors to the terrace were open; she could hear the shrill laughter of children playing on the lawns beyond. Linking her arm in Honoria's, she strolled with her outside. "How many?"

"Three."

The satisfaction and deep happiness that rang in Honoria's voice slipped under Caro's guard, and touched her. She glanced at Honoria, but she was looking ahead. Love and pride glowed in her face.

Caro followed her gaze to where three children romped on the lush lawn. Two brown-haired young boys held wooden swords; under the watchful gaze of two nursemaids, they were staging a fight. One of the nursemaids juggled a toddler, a dark-haired poppet, on her knee.

Honoria steered her down the steps. "Sebastian—sometimes known as Earith—is nearly five, Michael is three, and Louisa is one."

Caro smiled. "You have been busy."

"No, Devil's been busy—I've been occupied." Not even her laughter could disguise Honoria's joy.

The dark-haired poppet saw them and waved chubby arms. "Mama!"

The demand was imperious. They walked that way, then Honoria lifted her daughter into her arms. The child cooed—literally—wrapped her arms about her mother's neck, and snuggled her curly head onto Honoria's shoulder. Her wide, pale green eyes, impossibly long- and lushly-lashed, remained fixed—openly inquisitive—on Caro.

"Contrary to all appearances"—Honoria squinted down at her daughter—"this is the dangerous one. She's already got her father wrapped about her little finger, and when her brothers aren't busy fighting each other, they're her knights to command."

Caro grinned. "A very sensible young lady."

Honoria chuckled, gently jigging Louisa. "She'll do."

At that moment, a wail rent the air. *"Oowww!* You did that on purpose!"

All eyes deflected to the would-be swordsmen; they'd progressed further down the lawn. Michael was rolling on the grass holding his knee.

Sebastian stood over him, a scowl on his face. "I didn't hit you there—that would be a foul blow. It was your own silly sword—you stuck yourself with the hilt!"

"Didn't!"

The nursemaids hovered, unsure whether to intervene, given that their charges had not yet come to blows.

Honoria took one look at her eldest son's face—and untangled Louisa and thrust her into Caro's arms. "Here— hold her. Any minute now a deadly insult is going to be uttered—and then it'll have to be avenged!"

Left with no option, Caro hefted Louisa, a warm, resilient bundle, into her arms.

Honoria walked quickly down the lawn. "Hold hard, you two! Let's just see what's going on here."

"Prrrt."

Caro refocused on Louisa. Unlike her behavior with Honoria, the little girl sat up in Caro's arms and stared into her face.

"Prrrt," she said again, chubby fingers not very steadily pointing to Caro's eyes. Then the tiny fingers touched her cheeks. Louisa leaned close, peering at first one eye, then the other.

She clearly found them fascinating.

"You, my sweet, have very pretty eyes, too," Caro informed her. They were her father's eyes, yet not—a similar shade, yet softer, more beguiling . . . oddly familiar. Caro searched her memory, then realized. She smiled. "You have your grandmother's eyes."

Louisa blinked at her, then lifted her gaze to Caro's hair. A huge, delighted smile wreathed Louisa's face. "Prrrtttt!"

She reached for the corona of frizzy golden brown; Caro tensed to feel a tug—instead, the tiny hands touched gently, patting, then lacing lightly through. Louisa's face filled with wonder, big eyes wide as she stiffened her pudgy fingers and drew strands free, marveling. . . .

Caro knew she should stop her—her hair was wayward enough as it was—yet . . . she couldn't. She could only watch, her heart turning over, as the little girl explored, curious and enthralled.

The wonder of discovery lit the small, vivid face, glowed in her eyes.

Caro fought, tried so hard to keep the thought from forming, but it wouldn't be held down. Would she ever have a child like this—hold a child of her own like this—and witness again this simple joy, be touched by such open, innocent pleasure?

Children had never been part of the equation of her marriage. Although she was close to her nieces and nephews, she'd rarely seen them as babies, or even as young children—she couldn't recall carrying any of them, not even at Louisa's age.

She hadn't thought of children of her own—hadn't allowed herself to; there'd been no point. Yet the warm weight of Louisa in her arms opened a well of longing she hadn't until then realized she possessed.

"Thank you." Honoria returned. "War has been averted and peace restored." She reached for Louisa.

Caro gave her up, conscious of a reluctant tug—made all the stronger by Louisa, who made protesting noises and leaned back toward her until Honoria allowed her to place her little hands on Caro's face and plant a damp kiss on her cheek.

"Prrttt!" Louisa said as, satisfied, she turned back to Honoria.

Honoria smiled. "She thinks you're pretty."

"Ah." Caro nodded.

Bootsteps on stone had them looking toward the house; Devil and Michael had come out onto the terrace. The boys saw them; with whoops, they pelted past, swords waving, charging up to the terrace and male company.

Smiling indulgently, Honoria glanced back, checked that the nursemaids were gathering the scattered toys, then, Louisa in her arms, together with Caro started back up the gently sloping lawn.

As she paced alongside, Caro tried to rid herself of—or at least suppress—the thought that had taken up residence in her mind. Marrying just to have children was surely as bad as marrying just to gain a hostess. But she couldn't stop herself from glancing at Louisa, secure and settled in Honoria's arms.

The little girl's eyes were wide, her gaze open, yet intent, not serious, yet seeing . . . Caro remembered again why those eyes seemed familiar. Old eyes, knowing eyes, ageless and all-seeing.

Drawing in a breath, she looked up as they reached the steps to the terrace. She murmured to Honoria as they ascended, "You're right—*she's* the dangerous one."

Honoria only smiled. Her gaze fell on her eldest, standing by his father's side, relating some tale of male significance. Michael was talking with his namesake. She made a mental note to give orders that they could have extra dessert tonight—and Louisa, too, of course.

She couldn't have managed their recent scene better if she'd tried.

CHAPTER
18

What did Devil have to say about Camden's will?" Caro swiveled on the carriage seat so she could see Michael's face.

He glanced at her, smiled faintly. "The house was left to you outright, in your name, and doesn't revert to Camden's estate or anyone else on your death—it would go to your heirs."

She sat back. "My heirs . . . that's Geoffrey, Augusta, and Angela, who definitely aren't trying to kill me. So there's no reason buried in Camden's will for anyone to want me dead."

"Not directly, no. However, there were an unusual number of bequests to unrelated individuals. Devil asked if you'd mind if he had two of his cousins quietly look over the legatees."

She frowned. "Which cousins? And why?"

"Gabriel and Lucifer."

"Who?"

Michael had to stop and think. "Rupert and Alasdair Cynster."

Caro cast her eyes heavenward. "Such nicknames."

"Appropriate, or so I've been told."

"Indeed? And how are these two supposed to help us?"

"Gabriel is the Cynsters' investment expert—no one within the ton has better contacts in finance, business, and banking. Lucifer's interest is antiques, principally silver and jewelry, but his knowledge and expertise are wide."

After a moment, she inclined her head. "I can see that in this case such talents might be useful."

Michael considered her expression. "I didn't think you'd mind, so I agreed on your behalf. Given Gabriel's and Lucifer's backgrounds, discretion is assured." He caught her gaze. "Are you comfortable with that?"

Caro studied his eyes—and thought it more a question of whether such an investigation made him more comfortable. She'd accepted that someone—to her mind some nebulous person she'd never met—wanted her dead, presumably so she couldn't relate something they thought she knew; she couldn't see the house or any piece it contained as a likely reason for murder.

He, however, had without hesitation volunteered to brave the terrors of Bond Street. What had prompted his request that she didn't leave his grandfather's house without him wasn't hard to guess. Never before had anyone so concertedly focused on her safety; she couldn't help but be touched and grateful, even though to her mind pursuing the bequests would prove wide of the mark.

Smiling, she settled back against the seat. "If they wish to investigate discreetly, I can see no harm in that."

That evening, she walked into Harriet Jennet's salon on Michael's arm. They hadn't been invited, yet as a family member, Michael had permanent entree there; as a celebrated diplomatic hostess, Caro could claim the same.

She'd expected to detect at least mild surprise behind Harriet's eyes; instead, Harriet greeted her with her usual hostessly aplomb touched, if anything, by faintly amused understanding. Seeing Caro arrive on her nephew's arm had been precisely what she'd been expecting.

"Did you send word?" Caro pinched Michael's arm as, leaving Harriet, they moved into the salon in which the crème de la crème of political society mingled.

He glanced at her. "Not I."

She humphed. "Magnus, then. I was *so* looking forward to

seeing Harriet blink. I don't think anyone has managed that in years."

They spent a pleasant evening circulating among the political elite, a milieu in which they both blended with ease. Her appearance with Michael undoubtedly raised questions, but among that crowd, no one would leap to any conclusions; they were who they were because they knew better than to make unwarranted assumptions.

At twelve, they returned to Upper Grosvenor Street, content to have so easily established their presence in London among the political crowd. Diplomatic circles were more varied; climbing the stairs by Michael's side, Caro mulled over the most efficient way forward there.

Later, as was fast becoming habit, Michael joined her in her room, and in her bed. She found his continuing desire, his continuing hunger for her glorious and enthralling, yet amazing, too; she couldn't bring herself even to consider, let alone believe, that it would last.

So she enjoyed it while she could, took all he offered and returned it fullfold. The liaison remained a source of wonder; it had happened so fast—her initial, unexpected trust in giving herself to him, and all that had followed so easily, so naturally from that. She still hadn't come to grips with it, with what it meant, what she felt and why . . . it seemed as if she were another person, some other woman, when in his arms.

The following morning, Honoria took her up in her carriage and they went to call on Lady Osbaldestone at her daughter's house in Chelsea.

The house was old, its terrace overlooking the river. The assembled ladies of the haut ton—all matrons or widows—sat in the sunshine, sipped tea, and spoke of their world.

It was, she had to admit, another perfect venue in which to advertise her return to the capital. Over wafer-thin sandwiches and biscuits, she informed the many who asked that she was presently residing with the Anstruther-Wetherbys in Upper Grosvenor Street.

The only difficult moment occurred, predictably, when Therese Osbaldestone cornered her.

"Honoria tells me you're staying with that old fool, Magnus Anstruther-Wetherby." Therese fixed her with a interrogatory look. "Now why is that?"

No one else would dare ask such a question in such an outrageous way. Then again, no one else would refer to Magnus Anstruther-Wetherby as "that old fool." Caro gestured airily. "I was in Hampshire with my brother and had to come up to town—some matters to do with Camden's estate. Michael Anstruther-Wetherby is our neighbor—as he was coming to town on business, he accompanied me." Caro prayed her expression was as innocent as it needed to be. "As I haven't opened up the Half Moon Street house, and Angela is still in the country, Michael suggested I stay in Upper Grosvenor Street."

For a long moment, Therese Osbaldestone studied her, then both her brows rose. "Indeed? So there was nothing particular behind your appearing at Harriet's last evening on Michael's arm?"

Caro shrugged. "We were both interested in attending."

One of Therese's brows quirked higher. "I see."

Caro greatly feared she might.

However, after another pregnant pause, she merely said, "Camden's estate? I would have thought such matters had been resolved long ago."

"There was a question over the individual bequests." Caro wasn't keen to invite further discussion; her tone made that clear.

Therese seemed to accept it; mildly, she said, "I was glad to see you about this last Season, glad you're not about to hide yourself away. To my mind"—her black eyes trapped Caro's—"you have no excuse not to use your talents and experience where they will do most good."

Safety assuredly lay in silence; Caro kept mum.

Therese's lips twitched. "Now tell me, who of the diplomatic crowd was gallivanting in Hampshire?"

Caro told her, mentioning her Midsummer Revels and the fading contretemps between the Prussians and the Russians. In her time, Therese Osbaldestone had been a premier hostess in diplomatic circles; her husband had been variously a Minister, an ambassador, and an elder statesman. He'd died over a decade ago, but Therese remained closely linked with diplomatic and political circles, as influential there as she was in the ton at large.

She had a soft spot for Caro, and Caro had one for her. They had always understood each other, understood the challenges of diplomatic life as those outside it could not. "And the Portuguese were there, too—just part of the legation. The ambassador is at Brighton, I believe."

Therese nodded. "I know him only vaguely, but you must know that whole crew well." She snorted reminiscently. "The Portuguese were forever Camden's specialty, even before he took up his post there."

"Oh?" Caro pricked up her ears. Therese was a contemporary of Camden's.

"I don't suppose you would have been told, but Camden was hand in glove with a veritable rabble of courtiers there. I always suspected they made him ambassador to force him to acquire some restraint in that regard—before he could get himself involved in anything regrettable."

"Regrettable?" Caro gave her a look of unfeigned interest.

Therese shook her head. "I never knew any details—it was one of those things, an understanding running beneath a decision that one grasped without explanation or proof."

Caro nodded; she understood what Therese meant. But Therese's recollection was the first intimation they'd stumbled on that there could indeed be something in Camden's past, in his papers, that some Portuguese might kill to suppress.

A chill touched her; she shivered.

"The breeze is rising—come inside."

Therese led the way. Caro followed. There was no point questioning Therese further; if she knew anything more, she would have said.

After returning to Upper Grosvenor Street and taking luncheon with Magnus and Evelyn—Michael was still out doing the rounds of the political and diplomatic clubs—Caro retired to the upstairs parlor and settled to her task of plodding through Camden's diaries.

Therese's words had given her renewed purpose, making the likelihood of some entry buried in the accummulated papers being the reason behind the attempts on her life much more real. Her slow progress through the closely written diaries became increasingly frustrating.

Adding to that was a welling sense that the entire business of the attacks on her was merely a distraction, an irritating circumstance deflecting her from more important matters— such as what was happening between herself and Michael. Such as what she'd sensed and felt during her visit with Honoria, whether she should pursue the idea that had struck her with such force while holding Louisa.

All those things—ideas, concepts, and feelings—were new to her. She wanted to explore them, to think through them and understand, but solving the mystery of who was trying to kill her logically took priority.

Setting a diary on the pile beside her chair, she sighed; she looked at the row of boxes stacked along the wall. She'd finished two.

She needed help. Dare she summon Edward to town? He would come immediately; she could trust him to read Camden's letters.

But Elizabeth would follow, of that she had no doubt, and that she would not allow.

Grimacing, she estimated how long it would take her to get through all the boxes. The answer was a depressing number of weeks. Again, she racked her brain for someone who could help, someone she could trust to go through Camden's personal writings. There didn't seem to be anyone . . .

"Yes, there *is!*" She sat up, enthused by the possibility that had popped into her mind. She examined it, developed it. Not the diaries—they contained highly personal comments and notes—but the letters . . . she could entrust those to him.

"Knowing him, he's probably in town. . . ."

She hesitated, then, chin firming, rose and tugged the bellpull.

* * *

"Good afternoon. Is Viscount Breckenridge in?"

The butler—she'd never met him before and didn't know his name—blinked at her. Hesitated. "Ma'am?"

Caro handed over the card she had ready in her hand and walked in; the butler gave ground. "Take that to him immediately—he'll see me."

Glancing around, she spied the drawing room through an open door. "I'll wait in the drawing room, but before you take my card up, please tell my footmen where they may store these boxes."

"Boxes?" The butler whirled to face the front door; he goggled at the two footmen standing on the threshold, sturdy boxes in their arms.

"The boxes are for Breckenridge—he'll understand once he's seen me." Caro waved the men in. "There are quite a few of them—if he has a study or a library, that might be the best place."

The butler blinked, then drew himself up, and conceded. "His lordship's study is this way."

He went to show the footmen; smiling, Caro strolled into the drawing room. She looked around, then, pulling off her gloves, settled in a wing chair and waited for Timothy to join her.

Five minutes later, the door opened and Timothy Danvers, Viscount Breckenridge, strode in. "*Caro?* What's happened?"

He paused, taking in her wide-eyed perusal of his thoroughly disarranged locks and the flamboyant silk dressing robe he'd transparently shrugged over hastily donned breeches.

Caro fought to keep her lips straight as she raised her gaze to his narrowing hazel eyes. "Oh, dear—I seem to have called at an inopportune moment."

His lips set, she was quite sure over a curse. Turning, he shut the door on his interested butler, then faced her. "What the devil are you doing here?"

She smiled, intending to calm him yet not quite able to keep the twinkle from her eye. He was thirty-one, three years older than she, and an extraordinarily handsome man, tall, broad shouldered, powerful but lean, with a face like a Greek god and grace to match; she'd heard him described as excessively dangerous to any female under the age of seventy. He wasn't, however, dangerous to her. "I have a favor to ask, if you will."

He frowned. "What favor?" He stalked forward, then abruptly halted and held up a hand. "First, tell me you arrived cloaked and heavily veiled, and had the sense to use an unmarked carriage."

Again, she had to battle to keep a straight face. "No cloak or veil, but I did bring two footmen. They were necessary to carry in the boxes."

"What boxes?"

"Camden's letters." She sat back, watching him study her. Then he shook his head as if shaking off a distraction.

"Your carriage?"

"It's not mine—it's Magnus Anstruther-Wetherby's—but it is unmarked."

"*Where* is it?"

She raised her brows, surprised. "Waiting in the street, of course."

Timothy stared at her as if she'd grown two heads, then he cursed and strode to the bellpull. When his butler appeared, he rapped out, "Send Mrs. Sutcliffe's carriage to await her in the mews."

The instant the butler had departed, Timothy looked at her straitly. "It's a damn good thing you never attempted to play Camden false."

Haughtily she raised her brows; she was tempted to ask him how he knew she hadn't.

He dropped into the other armchair and fixed her with a steady gaze. "Now cut line. Why have you brought Camden's letters here?"

She told him; his face grew grimmer with every succeeding sentence.

"There must be someone I can wring information from . . ."

She didn't like the look in his eyes, the set of his jaw. "No—you can't." The unequivocal statement brought his gaze to her face; she caught it, held it. "I, or Michael, or one of the Anstruther-Wetherbys or Therese Osbaldestone might, but not you. You have no business in and no connection with diplomatic circles. If you stalked in there, everyone would be instantly suspicious."

She gave him a moment to digest that, then said, "I came to ask for your help, but I need from you something only you can give." She waited a heartbeat, then went on, "Camden's papers. The answer has to be in there somewhere, but I can't—won't—trust anyone else with them. You more than anyone else know why."

Again, she paused, then, holding his gaze, continued, "I'll read the diaries—they're full of references only I, or maybe Edward or one of Camden's previous aides, would understand. His letters are different—more specific, more formal, more clear. *You* are the only other person I would trust to read them. If you want to help, then read."

He was very definitely a man of action, yet he was also, she knew, highly educated and intelligent. After a moment, he sighed, less than happy, but resigned. "We're looking for reference to some politically illicit affair with the Portuguese—is that correct?"

"Yes. And from what Therese Osbaldestone said, it's likely to be early in his tenure as ambassador, or possibly just before."

He nodded. "I'll start straightaway." His gaze drifted upward.

She grimaced. "I'm sorry—I didn't think. I've interrupted—"

"No. That's not important. You and this are." He grimaced. "And I could do without you thinking about what you interrupted." His lips thinned; he fixed her with a severe glance. "I have one condition."

She raised her brows. "What?"

"That under no circumstances will you call here again. If you want to see me, send word—I'll come to you."

She pulled a face. "Nonsense!" She rose, started to tug on her gloves. "I'm the Merry Widow, remember? The entire ton knows I don't seduce that easily."

She looked down at him. For a moment, he remained lounging in the armchair, looking at her, then he came to his feet.

Rapidly, in a movement so redolent with male power it—to her considerable surprise—had her breath tangling in her throat.

He ended standing very close, looking down into her eyes. His lips curved in a flagrantly predatory line. "The entire ton knows," he purred, his voice seductively low, "that I don't give up that easily."

She remained, gaze locked with his, for a heartbeat, then she patted his arm. "I daresay. That, however, has nothing to do with me."

Turning to the door, she heard him curse beneath his breath. She smiled. "You may now see me to my carriage."

He muttered something unintelligible, but followed and opened the door for her. When she turned toward the front door, he caught her arm and swung her in the opposite direction. "If you insist on visiting one of the ton's foremost rakes, you need to learn the correct procedure. Your carriage waits in the mews so no one will see you depart, or know when you do."

She raised her brows, once more battling her smile. "I see."

He led her along a corridor, then through the morning room onto a terrace and from there down the garden path to a gate set in the high stone wall at the rear of his property. Opening it, he glanced out, then drew her out and handed her straight into her carriage, waiting with its door aligned with the gate.

He was about to step back and shut the carriage door when she leaned forward and said, "Incidentally, I do like the peacocks."

He blinked, then glanced down at his robe. Swore softly. He looked up at her, eyes blazing. "Next time," he bit out, "send word!"

The carriage door shut with an ominous click, the gate with a definite thud. Sinking back on the cushions, she gave way to her laughter as the carriage rocked and rumbled away.

* * *

She and Michael had a soirée to attend that evening—a small affair at the Corsican consulate at which the Italian and Spanish legations would be present.

"Do you think the Spaniards might know something?" she asked as the carriage rattled over the cobbles. "Could it be some incident during the wars?"

Michael shrugged. "Impossible to say. All we can do is keep our ears open. If someone is so desperate to bury irretrievably whatever this secret is, then there must be some reason they've been prodded into action now, so long after the event."

She nodded. "True. We might hear a clue from an unexpected source."

His hand wrapped about hers on the seat between them, Michael felt his attention literally divided—as if he were a swordsman simultaneously defending on two fronts. The Portuguese seemed the most likely villains, yet . . . "Devil caught up with me today. He's spoken to Gabriel and Lucifer. Gabriel agreed that the long list of bequests warrants further scrutiny—he's already looking into the individuals, seeing if there's any reason to imagine they might harbor deeper designs on Camden's property, now yours. Lucifer apparently took one look at the list of bequests themselves and declared he needs to examine the contents of the Half Moon Street house."

He glanced at Caro. "Devil at first suspected Lucifer simply wanted to get a look at the collection, but Lucifer explained that forgery—at least of items such as those bequeathed—was a thriving business. He thought Camden might inadvertently have got caught up in that—unknowingly been used to pass forgeries off as authentic."

She frowned. "I didn't take much notice of Camden's collecting—he'd been doing it for decades before I met him. It was simply something that was always going on. That said, I know he dealt with the same people constantly, that those associations went back many years. He only dealt with people he trusted." She met his eyes. "He'd learned to be very careful."

"Be that as it may, do you have any objection to Lucifer's looking around the house?"

She shook her head. "No. Indeed, I think it might be wise. The more things we can reassure ourselves are not in question . . ."

He squeezed her hand. "Precisely."

Recalling their other lines of inquiry, Caro said, "Incidentally, I remembered an old, very trusted friend of Camden's—I called on him today and asked him to read Camden's letters. He agreed."

The carriage rocked to a halt before the steps of the Corsican consulate; a waiting footman opened the door. Michael nodded, indicating he'd heard her, stepped down, then handed her down.

Their hostess was waiting just beyond the open door; they both smiled and climbed the steps to be welcomed with a great deal of delight and Corsican camaraderie. The crowd was small and select; while superficially the customary formalities held sway, beneath, a more informal atmosphere reigned. Everyone knew everyone else, what they did, what their current aims were; the usual games were still played, but openly.

Caro was the only one there who did not have a defined role. While the stage was familiar, she felt rather strange not having any clear part to play. The lack made her more aware of others' roles, especially Michael's. Although the evening was a diplomatic affair, there were numerous civil servants present, those with whom the consular staff interacted in promoting their country's interest. Every such gentleman made a point of stopping by Michael's side, making sure he knew who he was, his present position, and his role in foreign affairs.

In no other sphere, not even the haut ton, was the grapevine more efficient.

Her presence by his side was remarked by all, but none knew what to make of it. They presented themselves as old family friends, and were accepted as such, at least on the face of it. Yet as the evening wore on, she found herself aiding him much as she had at Muriel's supper—it was so much a habit, so easy for her to do, it seemed churlish not to assist. Especially when he was so busily assisting her on so many other fronts.

When a member of the Spanish legation bowed before them, she instinctively knew Michael couldn't place him. Smiling, she gave Señor Fernandes her hand; while he was bowing and complimenting her on her appearance, she glibly dropped his name, position, and a little of his past into the conversation. Without a blink, Michael took things from there.

Later, when the conversation had parted them, she glanced over, alerted by some sixth sense, and saw the wife of a senior Foreign Office mandarin cutting Michael out from the knot of diplomats with whom he'd been speaking.

That was dangerous—the possible future Foreign Minister speaking too privately with the wife of one who would be jockeying for position beneath him. A fast way of creating rancor among the ranks. From her one brief glance, she realized Michael was aware of the unwisdom, yet was having trouble extricating himself from the lady's clutches.

She smiled at the Corsican deputy consul. "Do excuse me. I must have a word with Mr. Anstruther-Wetherby."

The deputy consul glanced at Michael and needed no further explanation. He returned her smile and bowed. "Mr. Anstruther-Wetherby is a lucky man."

Caro smiled easily. Leaving the deputy consul, she glided around to come up on Michael's free side.

"There you are!" She slid her hand onto his arm as she rounded him, apparently only then noticing his companion. "Lady Casey." She smiled. "It's been some time since I've had the pleasure."

She held out her hand; Lady Casey met her gaze, clearly wished her elsewhere, but had to take her hand, press fingers, and smile in return.

"My dear Mrs. Sutcliffe." Lady Casey twitched her shawl higher. "I had thought you'd retired from the fray."

"I may no longer be an ambassador's wife, but you know what they say. . . . Why," she artlessly continued, "I've already been lectured once today that I absolutely must not hide myself away. I was given to understand that it's my duty to continue to participate in diplomatic activities."

Lady Casey looked as if she'd like to argue the point, however, ex–ambassador's wife or no, Caro outranked her by several rather telling degrees. Deciding retreat was the better part of valor, Lady Casey inclined her head. "If you'll excuse me, I must join my husband."

They parted amicably.

The instant Lady Casey was out of earshot, Michael exhaled. "Thank you—she was trying to bully me into accepting a dinner invitation."

"Quite out of order," Caro declared. "Now, have you spoken privately with Monsieur Hartinges?"

Michael glanced at her. "Monsieur Hartinges being?"

"One of the French ambassador's senior aides. He's clever, he'll go far, and he's well disposed."

"Ah." He closed his hand over Caro's, anchoring it on his sleeve—anchoring her by his side. "Obviously he's someone I should know."

"Indeed. He's standing by the windows, and he's been watching you all evening, waiting for his moment."

He grinned. "Lead on."

She did; he spent the next twenty minutes talking to the Frenchman, one inclined to let bygones be bygones and deal more effectively in trade—one of the most important issues that would face the next Foreign Minister.

Parting most cordially from Monsieur Hartinges, they circulated again, this time with a view to leaving.

"I should speak with Jamieson before we leave—he's just come in." Michael nodded to a lanky, faintly harassed-looking gentleman bowing over their hostess's hand, clearly making obsequious apologies for his tardiness.

"Odd that he's so late," Caro murmured.

"Indeed." He steered her to intercept Jamieson, an under-secretary at the Foreign Office. Jamieson saw them as he parted from the consul's wife, and came their way.

He bowed to Caro, whom he knew of old, and nodded deferentially to Michael. "Sir."

Michael held out his hand; relaxing a trifle, Jamieson shook it. "Anything amiss?"

Jamieson grimaced. "Strangest thing. There's been a break-in at the office—that's why I'm late. Two of our storerooms holding nothing but old archives were searched." He looked at Caro. "The strange thing is they're the Lisbon files."

Caro frowned. "Why is that particularly strange?"

Jamieson glanced at Michael, then back at her. "Because we just received word that our place in Lisbon was burgled two weeks ago. The packet was delayed by storms, but, well, there it is. First them, now us. Nothing like it ever happened in Camden's day." Jamieson focused on Caro. "Have you any notion who might be behind it?"

Caro kept her eyes wide and shook her head. "What were they after? Was anything taken, either here or there?"

"No." Jamieson glanced at Michael. "Every sheet in our files is numbered, and none are missing. It's clear the files were searched, but beyond that . . ." He shrugged. "There isn't anything remotely useful, diplomatically speaking, in there. The Lisbon station's in my sector, but the files searched date from before my time. However, Roberts, my predecessor, was precise in the extreme—I can't imagine anything would have slipped past him."

"What period," Caro asked, "did the files that were searched cover?"

"They span the years before and after Camden took up his position there. We're inclined to think someone's looking for information on some activity Camden put a stop to." Jamieson grimaced. "I'm glad I bumped into you—I would have called in the next few days to ask if you knew anything. If you do think of any possibility that might account for this, do let me know."

Caro nodded. "Of course."

They parted from Jamieson, and shortly afterward left the consulate.

"You know," Michael said as, later, having joined Caro in her room, he drew her into his arms, "I'm starting to wonder if someone's panicking over nothing. If there's nothing in the Foreign Office files . . ."

"That," Caro admitted, winding her arms about his neck, "is entirely possible."

Gripping her waist, anchoring her, he held back against her tug, and studied her face in the dimness. "I detect a 'but.' "

Her lips curved, not so much in humor as in resignation over his perspicacity. "Knowing Camden and his love of intrigue, and his deep connections with Portugal's elite, it's equally possible there's something quite explosive buried somewhere in his papers."

She studied his eyes, then continued, "Therese Osbaldestone reminded me how personally involved with the Portuguese Camden was, even before his appointment to Lisbon. Given that, it's perfectly possible there's nothing in the Foreign Office files—Camden might have considered the matter as something outside the office if the contact had come before he took up the position."

"You mean he buried all mention of it?"

"If nothing came of it that subsequently affected the office for which he was responsible, then yes," she nodded, "I can see that he might have."

"But mention might remain in his papers."

"Indeed." She sighed. "I had better put more effort into reading them, but at least now I know over which period I need to search."

At that moment, however, in the shadows of the night, standing within Michael's arms, Camden's papers were not uppermost in her mind. She tightened her arms, stretched up against his hold. "Kiss me."

Michael smiled, and did, taking full advantage of her invitation—making a mental note to later ask who the old friend she'd entrusted with Camden's letters was—but then her invitation deepened, broadened, sensual horizons expanding . . . capturing him, his thoughts, his body, his mind.

Ultimately his soul.

With no other woman had he shared such a connection;

with no other could he imagine doing so. With every passing night, every day, every soirée, every hour in their mutual world, they seemed to become more definitely, ever more clearly the compatible halves of a powerful whole.

The knowledge shook him, and thrilled him. Sent impatient exultation surging through him. No matter that she hadn't yet recanted her opposition and agreed to their wedding, he couldn't see—had no intention of countenancing—any other outcome. The path between now and then might be shrouded in impenetrable shadow, uncertain both in length and events, yet their eventual destination remained fixed and unwavering.

Later, sated and replete, he gathered her, boneless and drowsy, against him, settling them comfortably in the billows of her bed. He'd meant to ask her something . . . couldn't quite focus his mind. . . . "Who lectured you on your duty?" He hoped it hadn't been Magnus.

"Therese Osbaldestone." Caro sleepily rubbed her cheek against his arm. "She's pleased I'm not hiding myself away."

He made a mental note to keep an eye on Lady Osbaldestone. He didn't need her queering his pitch, pressuring Caro in any way whatever.

If he'd harbored any reservations that he needed her—specifically her—by his side, the past two evenings would have put the matter beyond doubt. Yet that was his professional life; while such considerations provided a major impetus—an increasingly powerful motive for him to marry her with all speed—the very same arguments were those she would most distrust . . . and he couldn't fault her in that.

Marriage—the more he thought of it, considered it in its totality, the more he appreciated that it had to be based on more than professional interests, on far more than a sense of duty. Not only would Caro not bow to duty again, he didn't want her to come to him that way. Not for that reason.

Above all, not for that reason.

As he lay in the warmth of the rumpled bed and let sleep draw near, heard Caro's soft breaths, felt them ruffle the hairs on his chest, felt her soft warmth, her feminine curves, pressed to him, a promise clearer, more potent than any words, he was aware of impatience, yet equally conscious of the wisdom of waiting.

Of letting her make up her mind on her own, no pressure, no persuasions. . . .

A thought rippled through his mind as sleep drew him under. Perhaps there was something he could do.

Subtly influencing people was a politician's stock-in-trade. He was an excellent politician; the following morning, leaving Caro ensconced in the upstairs parlor leafing through Camden's diaries, he reminded himself of that as he paced down Upper Grosvenor Street and into Grosvenor Square.

Not pressure, not persuasion, but there were other avenues, other means. Aside from all else, actions spoke loudest, were always more convincing.

Honoria was at home; she joined him in the sitting room. The children barreled in in her wake; after dutifully admiring Sebastian's and young Michael's new bat and ball, and spending a few minutes tickling Louisa, he glanced at Honoria. She saw and efficiently shooed her brood out through the terrace doors to play on the lawn where their nursemaids were waiting.

"There!" Standing on the threshold, she looked at him. "What is it?"

He joined her, allowing her to keep a distant eye on her sons' antics while they talked. "I want to marry Caro, *but* . . ." Staring out at the lawns, he continued, "Her marriage to Camden was based on his need of her talents—what he correctly perceived as her potential hostessly skills. Those, of course, are precisely the same skills *I* need in a wife, but such a need is the very last thing that would persuade Caro to a second marriage."

Honoria grimaced. "I can see her point. Camden was a great deal older than she."

"Indeed. Worse, it was very much an arranged marriage, primarily for Camden's benefit. Caro, however, was not initially aware of that."

Honoria's grimace turned pained. "Oh, dear." She glanced

briefly at him. "So if you approach her offering the position of your wife . . ."

He nodded, a touch grim. "If that was all I offered, I would stand no chance of winning her." He drew breath, exhaled, stated his decision. "To win Caro, I need to offer more—a lot more."

He looked at Honoria, met her eyes. "Which is why I'm here. I wanted to ask why, when initially you were so set against it, you changed your mind and accepted Devil's proposal. What tipped the scales?"

Honoria studied his face, his eyes; she understood exactly what he was asking. Her mind flitted back seven years, to that long-ago summer. Remembered . . . recalled. Facing the lawn, she searched for words to explain what had compelled her to accept Devil's offer, to seize the chance, accept the challenge—pick up the gauntlet fate had so unexpectedly flung in her path.

How could she explain the allure, the compelling temptation, of love? Of a heart offered, however reluctantly, however much against the grain. That that very reluctance could in certain circumstances make the gift even more precious, because it could never be seen as something lightly yielded.

She drew breath, thought how to phrase her answer. Eventually said, "I changed my mind because he offered me the one thing I most truly needed, the thing that would make my life into what—or even more than—I had dreamed it could be. Because he was prepared to give me that, and through that, all that was most important to me."

Her gaze focused on her children. Should she mention that Caro wanted children, yearned for them in much the same way she had? A hidden, very private yearning that only another who had felt the same might guess. She'd guessed, and had seized the opportunity to let Louisa confirm it, prodding that yearning to life.

But if she told Michael . . . he was male—would he understand how to effectively use the knowledge? He might think the promise of children, of itself, was enough, and not see it as the outcome, the consequence of that even more precious gift.

Quite aside from her sisterly desire to see him happy and settled, married to a lady of the type he deserved, she also felt a compulsion to do all she could to see Caro happy, too. To have her childhood friend experience the same happiness she had found.

The last thing she wished was for Caro's unsatisfactory first marriage to dim her chances of attaining that happiness.

She glanced at Michael, realized that despite his impassive expression he was wrestling with her words, trying to interpret them. "I can't explain better than that. For each woman, the outward expression of what is most important will differ, yet giving her that one critical thing that enables all else, being willing to do so, is the key."

He met her gaze. Smiled a touch wryly. "Thank you."

She sighed. "I hope that helps."

Michael took her hand, squeezed lightly. "It does—it will."

Casting a last glance at his nephews and niece, cavorting, shrieking, on the lawn, he released Honoria's hand, nodded in farewell. "I'll leave you to your dream."

She snorted, but by the time he reached the door, she'd already gone out on the terrace.

He stopped to speak to Devil, who had nothing further to report, then set out for the clubs. As he walked, he turned Honoria's words over in his mind.

When she'd spoken, she'd been looking at her children. Given their background, the tragic loss of the rest of their family, he had no difficulty understanding that for Honoria, home, family, and therefore children, mattered a great deal—that those things were as important to her as they were to him.

Had she meant that those things were just as important to Caro?

If she did, where did that get him?

What, indeed, was Caro's deepest need?

CHAPTER
19

*H*e returned to Upper Grosvenor Street just before three o'clock, still no further along, either with his inquiries or his cogitations on Caro's needs. Putting both aside, he took the stairs two at a time; opening the parlor door, he beheld Caro, seated in an armchair and deep in one of Camden's diaries.

She looked up. Her fine hair formed a nimbus about her head; the sun striking through the window gilded each strand, a quiveringly alive filigree halo for her heart-shaped face with its delicate features and tip-tilted silvery eyes.

Those eyes lit at the sight of him. "Thank God!" Shutting the diary and setting it atop the pile, she held out her hands. "I sincerely hope you're here to rescue me."

Smiling, he walked in, took her hands, and pulled her up—and into his arms. Closing them about her, he bent his head; she lifted her lips.

They kissed. Long and slowly, deeply, yet both aware that they had to hold passion at bay, had to keep the flames suppressed.

Their lips parted only to meet again, to taste, take, give.

Eventually, he raised his head.

She sighed. Opened her eyes. "I suppose we must go."

Her transparent reluctance delighted him. Yet. . . . "Unfortunately, we must." Releasing her, he stepped back. "Lucifer will be waiting."

They'd agreed to show Lucifer around the Half Moon

Street house that afternoon at three. When they arrived, he was lounging, tall, dark, and rakishly handsome, against the front railings.

Grinning, he straightened and stepped forward to hand Caro down from the hackney, then bowed gracefully. "Your servant, Mrs. Sutcliffe. It's a pleasure to make your acquaintance."

She smiled. "Thank you—but please call me Caro."

Lucifer nodded to Michael, then waved up the steps. "I confess I'm agog to view the collection."

Opening the door, Caro led them into the front hall. "I hadn't realized Camden was such a well-known collector."

"He wasn't, but once I started asking around, he was definitely known, mostly for his eccentricity in collecting as he had." Lucifer studied a sideboard and the vase that stood upon it. "Most people collect one type of thing. Sutcliffe collected all sorts of things, but for one house—this house." He gestured at the round table in the hall, at the mirror on the wall. "Everything was chosen specifically to fill a particular place and function in this house. Everything is unique—the collection itself is unique."

"I see." Leading the way into the drawing room, she crossed to the windows and dragged back the heavy drapes, letting light spill across the gorgeous furniture, fracture and refract through crystal, gleam across gilt and beaten silver. "I hadn't thought of it as strange." She turned. "So what do you need to see?"

"Most of the major rooms, I suspect. But tell me, do you know who he dealt with? I have some names, but wondered which other dealers he used."

"Wainwright, Cantor, Jofleur, and Hastings. No others."

Lucifer looked up. "You're certain of that?"

"Yes. Camden refused to deal with anyone else—he once told me he wasn't interested in getting bilked, and that's why he insisted on dealing only with men he trusted."

Lucifer nodded. "He was right about those four, which means we can forget any likelihood of forgery. If any of them discovered they'd sold him a fake, they would have offered him his money back. If he dealt solely with them, that's one scam we don't need to imagine was involved here."

"One scam." Michael raised his brows. "There's another possibility?"

"One that's looking more likely every minute." Lucifer glanced around. "Wait until I've seen more, then I'll explain."

Caro dutifully guided him about the ground floor, answering his questions, confirming that Camden had kept excellent records of all his purchases. In the dining room, waiting while Lucifer studied the contents of a glass-fronted cabinet, she noticed a candlestick normally in the center of the sideboard now stood to the left. She centered it again; thinking back to when she'd glanced in when she and Michael had come to fetch Camden's papers, she was sure the candlestick had been in its accustomed place.

Mrs. Simms must have called; the housekeeper must have been distracted not to have replaced the candlestick precisely. Nothing was missing, nothing else had been moved. Making a mental note to send a message to let Mrs. Simms know she was back in town, she turned as Lucifer straightened. "Come—I'll show you upstairs."

Michael followed in their wake, listening with half an ear, otherwise looking about him. Not as Lucifer was doing, examining individual objects, not as he himself had done the last time he was here, but looking to learn what the house could tell him of Caro, what hints it might give him of what she needed, what she might covet that she didn't already have. What was missing in this apparently wonderful house?

Children leapt to mind, but, as he looked and considered and compared, it wasn't simply little people with grubby fingers thundering pell-mell down the corridors, sliding with whoops down the elegantly carved banister, that were missing.

This house was empty. Truly empty. Camden had created it for Caro—that Michael no longer doubted—yet it lay cold, without a heart, without the life, that indefinable pulse of family, that should have enlivened it and filled it with joy. It was presently an exquisitely beautiful shell, nothing more.

The one thing needed to bring the house to life was the one gift Camden had not given Caro. Either he'd neglected to do so, or it hadn't been in him to give.

What was it that brought a house to life, that didn't just create a family residence, but transformed it into a home?

Michael was standing in the upstairs corridor when Caro and Lucifer came out of the study.

Lucifer waved to the stairs. "Let's go down." He looked a touch grim.

In the hall, he faced them. "There's a danger here that could account for the attacks on Caro. The collection as a whole is no temptation, but individual pieces are. Sutcliffe had an eye for the highest quality—many pieces here are beyond superb. More than enough to tempt a rabid collector, one of those who, having once seen, absolutely must have."

Lucifer looked at Caro. "Given Sutcliffe's reason for assembling such a collection, I doubt he could have been induced to sell any piece once he acquired it. Is that right?"

Caro nodded. "He was approached on numerous occasions over different pieces, but as you say, once he had the perfect piece for a certain spot, he wasn't interested in selling it. For him, there wasn't any point."

"Indeed. And that's *my* point." Lucifer glanced at Michael. "There are those among the rabid collectors who will, in pursuit of a particular piece, ignore all rules and laws. They grow obsessed, and simply must have that piece regardless of what they have to do to get it."

Michael frowned. "Why not simply buy the piece from Caro?"

Lucifer looked at her. "Would you sell?"

She met his gaze. After a long moment, said, "No. This was Camden's creation—I couldn't pull bits out of it."

Lucifer looked at Michael. "That's why; they'd *assume* she wouldn't sell, that she would be as obsessed with the item as they were."

"Why not break in and steal it?" Michael gestured about them. "The locks may be sound, but a determined thief—"

"Would achieve little in terms of what rabid collectors

want. They want the provenance, too, and that they can only legitimately claim via a sale."

Caro stared at him. "They're trying to kill me to force a sale?"

"Whoever inherits if you die—would they feel as you do about this place? Or, if they were quietly and honorably approached, would they, after a suitable period had elapsed, feel they might as well sell at least bits of the contents?"

She blinked, then looked at Michael.

He didn't need to read her eyes. "Geoffrey, Augusta, and Angela would sell. Not immediately, but after a time."

She nodded. "Yes. They would."

"When I asked around, I was surprised how many people were aware of this place, of individual pieces in it." Lucifer once again glanced around. "There's definitely enough motive here for murder."

Instead of narrowing, their net seemed to be widening, the reasons to murder Caro piling up rather than diminishing. After joining them in Upper Grosvenor Street for tea, Lucifer went off to further investigate, first the list of those who'd received bequests, and then more widely through his contacts in the antiquarian underworld for any whisper of one he termed a "rabid collector" with designs on any of the more obvious pieces in the Half Moon Street house.

Over dinner, they discussed the situation with Magnus and Evelyn; Magnus humphed, clearly chafing that he couldn't do more to assist, that in this case his contacts, these days all political, were of no help. It was Evelyn who suggested Magnus and she should call on old Lady Claypoole.

"Her husband was the ambassador to Portugal before Camden—Lord Claypoole is long gone, but Ernestine might recall something useful. She's in town at present, visiting her sister. No reason we can't call and see what she has to say."

They all agreed that was an excellent idea; leaving Magnus and Evelyn making plans, Michael and Caro left for their evening rounds—two small soirées, the first at the Belgian embassy, the other at Lady Castlereagh's.

Entering the Belgian embassy drawing room, Caro glimpsed a dark head through the shoulders. On Michael's arm, she leaned close. "Is that Ferdinand by the windows?"

Michael looked. His lips thinned. "Yes." He glanced at her. "Shall we ask him what he's doing in town?"

She smiled, with her lips but not her eyes. "Let's."

But by the time they wove their way through the crowd, chatting and greeting, and finally gained the windows, Ferdinand had gone. Lifting his head, Michael scanned the room. "He's no longer here."

"He caught sight of us and beat a hasty retreat." In such company, Caro was careful not to frown, but her gaze when she met Michael's was severe. "What does that say of his conscience, I wonder?"

Michael arched a brow. "Does he have one?"

Eloquently shrugging, Caro turned to greet Lady Winston, the Jamaican governor's wife, who came bustling up to talk with them.

She introduced Michael, remained by his side, then and later as they circled the room. That done, they traveled on to Lady Castlereagh's; again, they worked the room together. Caro wasn't sure if their unvoiced decision to act as a team owed more to her reaction to Michael's need—a need she more and more clearly perceived, a need it was all but instinctive for her to fill—or to his desire to keep her close, protected and within reach; his hand lay heavy over hers on his sleeve, communicating that desire without words.

The evening revealed nothing regarding any long-buried secret the Portuguese might be keen to bury even deeper, but she did become aware—more aware—of other things.

Later, when they'd returned to Upper Grosvenor Street, when Michael had joined her in her bed, when they'd shared and indulged, bathing in an ocean of mutual pleasure to finally lay slumped, limbs tangled, sated and relaxed in her bed, with their heartbeats slowing and sleep drifting ever nearer . . . she let herself think of all she'd seen, all she'd become conscious of, all she now knew.

Of Michael. Of his need for her, not just the physical need they'd so recently slaked, not his professional need, even though she was coming to realize that was far more acute than she'd supposed, but that other need that lingered in the way his arms closed around her, in the way, sometimes, his lips touched her hair. In the way his arm lay heavy over her waist even in sleep. In the way he tensed and came alert, ready to step forward and shield her from danger, physical or otherwise.

The need he revealed through his compulsion to protect her.

He'd said he wanted to marry her, that the offer remained so that all she had to do was agree and it would happen. She hadn't believed anything could make her change her mind, make her rethink her aversion to matrimony, especially to another politician, yet his elusive need had. It possessed a power against which even her hardened heart—the heart she'd deliberately hardened—wasn't immune. While she was no longer so young, so innocent and naive as to take anything at face value, by the same token the years had taught her the wisdom of not unthinkingly rejecting fate's gifts.

Such gifts weren't offered frequently. When they were . . .

Was she prepared to again face the risk of loving a politician? A man to whom charm was intrinsic, to whom the facility for glib persuasiveness was a necessary skill?

Yet it wasn't Michael's words that were persuading her. It was his actions, his reactions. And the emotions that drove them.

Sleep slunk into her mind and weighed heavily, pressing her down, wiping out her thoughts. Beckoning her dreams.

The last whisper of consciousness of which she was aware was the sensation of Michael's body, hot, naked, heavy with the languor of satiation, wrapped protectively about hers, a tacit statement—he wasn't Camden.

Sunk beside her in the bed, Michael felt sleep take her; for himself, he tried to hold it at bay—to wrestle with his prob-

lem, to try to see further, to identify what her heart most
desired, what were her most secret dreams.

A home, a family, a husband, the position of a political
and diplomatic hostess, a Minister's wife—a stage on which
her highly polished skills would be most highly regarded
and appreciated . . . all that he could give her, but what was
the key—what was the one thing that would persuade her to
marry him?

Sleep wouldn't be denied; ruthlessly, it caught him and
dragged him down, and left him still searching for his answer.

Over the next days, Caro devoted herself assiduously to
Camden's diaries. Other than attending the most select
soirées with Michael every evening, she remained indoors,
in the parlor, and read.

If the clue to what was behind the threat to her lay in
Camden's papers, then it clearly behooved her to apply herself to discovering it.

Magnus and Evelyn thoroughly enjoyed their excursion to
interrogate Lady Claypoole, although other than confirming
via vague recollection that there *had* been some political turmoil in Lisbon toward the close of her husband's tenure, her
ladyship proved of little help. However, the outing improved
both Evelyn's and Magnus's moods, so that much at least
was gained.

Michael continued playing the part of a soon-to-be-
Minister very likely to be appointed to the Foreign Office for
all it was worth, exploiting the readiness of others to impress
him to glean all he could on current Portuguese affairs. He
laid seige not only to the relevant British offices, but to the
Spanish, French, Corsicans, Sardinians, Belgians, and Ital-
ians, too. Everyone had their sources—someone had to
know something of use.

And then there was Ferdinand.

Michael didn't forget him, or the Portuguese embassy
staff. But he couldn't act directly there; with Devil's assistance, he organized others to infiltrate and see what they
could learn, but such operations necessarily took time.

Time he was increasingly worried they might not have.

Returning to Upper Grosvenor Street late one afternoon, still no further along and running out of useful avenues to explore, he climbed the stairs, paused in the parlor doorway to watch Caro read. When she glanced up and smiled, he joined her.

With a sigh, he sank into the armchair that was the mate of the one she occupied.

She raised a brow. "Nothing?"

He shook his head. "Patience, I know, is a virtue, *but . . .*"

She grinned; looking down, she returned to her reading.

He sat and watched her, oddly pleased that she did not feel the need to entertain him as any other lady would. It was a comfortable feeling, to be accepted with such ease, to simply be together without any of the customary social barriers between them.

The simple togetherness soothed his aggravation, stroked his impatient irritation away.

In the distance, the front doorbell pealed. Hammer's muffled steps crossed the tiles; a moment passed, then the front door closed. An instant later, they heard Hammer ascending the stairs, heading their way.

Hammer appeared in the open doorway. He bowed to them both, then advanced to offer his salver. "A note for you, ma'am. The boy expected no reply."

Caro took the folded sheet. "Thank you, Hammer."

With a bow, Hammer departed. Michael watched Caro's face as she opened the missive and read. Then she smiled, glanced at him as she laid the single sheet aside. "It's from Breckenridge."

Michael stared. "*Breckenridge?*" Had he heard aright? "Viscount Breckenridge—Brunswick's heir?"

"The same. I told you I asked an old and trusted friend of Camden's to read his letters. Timothy's just written to say he hasn't found anything yet." Her gaze on the note, her expression turned affectionate. "I daresay he was worried I'd call to ask in person, so he sent word instead."

Timothy? Call in person? Michael felt poleaxed. "Ah . . . you wouldn't, would you?" Caro looked at him, puzzled. He cleared his throat. "Call on Breckenridge in person." His voice faded as he took in her increasingly puzzled expression.

She blinked. "Well, I had to take him the letters. Or rather, have two footmen carry the letters into his house. Then I had to explain what I needed him to do, what he should look for."

For a suspended moment, he simply stared. "You entered Breckenridge's establishment alone." His voice sounded strange; he was struggling to take it in.

She frowned at him. Severely. "I've known Timothy for more than a decade—we danced at my wedding. Camden knew him for nearly thirty years."

He blinked. "Breckenridge is barely thirty."

"He's thirty-one," she tartly informed him.

"And one of the foremost rakes in the ton—if not *the* foremost!" Abruptly, he stood. Raking a hand through his hair, he looked down at Caro.

She fixed him with a narrow-eyed silver gaze and crisply advised, "Don't start."

He took in the increasingly mulish set of her lips, the militant light in her eyes—felt his own jaw set. "For God's sake! You can't simply . . . *call* to see a man like Breckenridge as if you're visiting for morning tea!"

"Of course I can—although now you mention it, he didn't offer tea."

"I can imagine," he growled.

Caro arched her brows. "I seriously doubt you can. You're starting to sound as bad as he, what with insisting I leave via the mews. Unnecessarily exercised for no cause at all."

Fixing him with a very direct look, she continued, "As I reminded him, let me remind you—*I* am the Merry Widow. My widowhood is established—no one in the ton imagines I will readily succumb to the blandishments of any rake."

Michael simply stood and stared down at her—pointedly.

She felt faint heat rise in her cheeks. Lightly shrugged. "Only you know about that—and anyway, you're no rake."

His eyes narrowed along with his lips. "Caro . . ."

"No!" She held up a hand. "Hear me out. Timothy is an old and dear friend, one I trust implicitly, without reservation. I've known him for an age—he was an associate—well, more a connection—of Camden's, and while I know what he is, what his reputation paints him, I assure you that I am in absolutely no danger from him. Now!" She glanced at the pile of diaries. "While I'm very glad Timothy sent around a note because I don't have time to call to see how he's faring, I likewise have no time to waste in silly arguments."

Picking up a diary, she looked up at Michael. "So rather than scowling at me for no reason and to no avail, you can help, too. Here—read this."

She tossed the book at him.

He caught it. Frowned at her. "You want me to read it?"

She'd already reopened the volume she'd been perusing. Looking up at him, she raised her brows. "I'm sure you can read as well as Timothy. I gave him the letters, but the diaries are crammed and much harder going." Looking down again, she continued, her tone softer, "And while I trust Timothy with the letters, there are references in the diaries I would rather he didn't see."

Michael stared at her down-bent head, absentmindedly hefted the volume in his hand. He was too astute not to recognize blatant manipulation when it was so shamelessly practiced on him—she trusted him where she didn't trust Breckenridge—Timothy!—yet . . .

After a moment, he shifted back to the chair, slowly sat. Opened the diary, flicked through a few pages. "What am I looking for?"

She answered without looking up. "Any mention of the Portuguese court, or the names Leponte, Oporto, or Albufeira. Anything you find, show it to me—I'll know if it's what we're after."

Discovering that the lady he was determined to make his wife consorted, apparently without any degree of caution, with the ton's most dangerous rake, would, Michael told himself, rattle any man.

It certainly rattled him, to the point of making him actively consider hedging her about with guards, an action he was well aware would simply lead to another argument, another he wouldn't win.

He knew, better than anyone else could, that, as she'd intimated, Caro had never consorted in the physical sense with Breckenridge or any of his peers. In light of that knowledge, he might be overreacting, yet . . .

While Caro readied herself for dinner at Lady Osterley's, he sat in the library and pored over *Burke's Peerage*.

Timothy Martin Claude Danvers, Viscount Breckenridge. Only son of the Earl of Brunswick.

The usual background—Eton, Oxford—with the usual clubs listed. Quickly, Michael read further, cross-referencing between the Danverses, the Elliots—Breckenridge's mother's family—and the Sutcliffes. He could find no hint of the connection to which Caro had alluded.

Hearing her footsteps on the stairs, he shut the tome and returned it to the shelf. Mentally adding Breckenridge at the top of the list of things he intended to investigate tomorrow, he headed for the front hall.

Caro wasn't at all sure how she felt about Michael being jealous of her association with Timothy. From observation, she knew jealous males tended to dictate, to restrict, to try to hem women in; she was, to her mind sensibly, wary of jealous men. However . . .

She'd never had a man jealous over her before; while irritating in some respects, it was, she had to admit, rather intriguing. Subtly revealing. Interesting enough for her to endure Michael's silence all the way to the Osterleys'. He wasn't sulking; he was brooding, thinking—about her more than Timothy.

Yet when they reached the Osterleys' and he stepped down, then handed her down, she was conscious of his attention focusing dramatically. On her. As they went up the steps, greeted their hostess, then moved into the drawing room to join the other guests, regardless of his occupation, that's where his attention remained. Locked, squarely, on her.

Far from annoying her, she found being the cynosure of

his attention quite enjoyable. Having a man jealous over one wasn't all bad.

The Osterleys' drawing room was awash with blue political blood. Aside from all the usual suspects, the gathering included Magnus, who had come ahead of her and Michael, Michael's aunt Harriet Jennet, and Therese Osbaldestone. Devil and Honoria were there, too.

"Lord Osterley is distantly connected to the Cynsters," Honoria told her as they touched fingers, brushed cheeks.

There were few among the company Caro did not know; she and Michael spent a few minutes with Honoria and Devil, then both couples moved on, as all were expected to, to converse, reestablish and strengthen ties. This group formed the political elite, the ultimate power in the land. All sides of politics were represented; although government men might presently wield the whip, all accepted that that would at some election in the future change.

Renewing acquaintances, making new contacts—exchanging names, learning faces, noting to which clubs each gentleman belonged, his present position, and, although never stated aloud, his ultimate ambition—that was the unabashed purpose of the gathering. Such congresses of the powerful were held two or three times a year—there was rarely need for more; those who attended had long memories.

Gaining the far end of the drawing room, Caro glanced back, estimating, considering.

"What?" Michael asked, leaning close.

"I was just thinking it's a goodly crowd, but one selected with care." She met his eyes. "Not even all Ministers are present."

"Some"—taking her elbow, he guided her on—"have blotted their copybook. Others are, much as it pains me to admit, hidebound—they're not amenable to change, and change most definitely is in the air."

She nodded; over the past two years, freed of the necessity of concentrating on Portuguese affairs, she'd been monitoring political vicissitudes nearer to hand. Plebiscite reform was only one of a multitude of challenges staring the government in the face.

It would no longer be enough to govern by default; the times—the immediate future—called for action.

Diplomacy and politics were old bedfellows; her experience in one arena stood her in excellent stead in the other. She encountered no difficulty moving through the throng, charming and allowing herself to be charmed, interacting and absorbing all that her questions and comments drew forth.

Michael needed no help in this sphere, no prompting, no direct assistance; he was more at home here than she was. He could, however, use a foil, one who comprehended not only words but their nuances, who could artfully extend a topic or introduce a new one, seeking more, revealing more.

As they left Lord Colebatch and Mr. Harris from the War Office, Caro caught Michael's eye. The smile they exchanged was brief, and private. He leaned closer. "We make an exceptional team."

"Colebatch didn't want to tell you about his association with the new railway."

"He wouldn't have if you hadn't asked—how did you know?"

"He was uncomfortable the moment Harris mentioned the subject—there had to be a reason." She glanced up, met his eyes. "And there was."

He acknowledged her astuteness with an inclination of his head, and steered her on to fresh fields.

As usual with such gatherings, the time in the drawing room before the meal was extended, and even after they were all seated about the long board, the conversation remained scintillating and sharp. At such a dinner, food wasn't the main course. Information was.

Ideas, suggestions, observations—all had their place; in this company, all were treated with respect. Visually, the scene was glittering, gorgeous, subtly and pervasively elegant, outrageous only in its undeniable worth, the gold-plated cutlery, the Sevres dishes, the crystal flashing in poor imitation of the diamonds circling the ladies' throats.

They all noticed, yet were barely aware. To a person, their attention remained riveted on conversation—on why they were there.

Caro found it tiring, yet exhilarating. It had been more than two years since she'd attended such an event. To her surprise, her enthusiasm, her enjoyment of the rapierlike cut-and-thrust of comment and dialogue, of witty repartee, all swirling and dipping and connecting, hadn't died; if anything, her delight in participating and succeeding had grown.

Toward the end of the meal, when for a moment she sat back and sipped her wine, and caught her breath after an extended and quite hilarious exchange with George Canning, she caught Lady Osterley's eye. Seated at the far end of the table, her ladyship, one of the great hostesses, smiled, inclined her head, and lifted her glass in a silent toast of patent approval.

Caro smiled back, wondered, then allowed her gaze to travel the table. Realized, confirmed, that each recognized hostess—each recognized power—was spread among the guests so that each could command a section of the table, ensuring no group did the unthinkable and let conversation die.

She had been included in the roster of female powers.

Her heart tripped, gave a definite jump of joy, of very real satisfaction.

Five minutes later, Lady Osterley rose and led the ladies back to the drawing room, leaving the gentlemen to discuss parliamentary business over their port.

The ladies had other issues to address, ones equally relevant.

Entering the drawing room toward the rear of the female crowd, Caro found Therese Osbaldestone waiting to waylay her. Taking her arm, Therese nodded to the long windows left open to the balcony. "I need some air—come and walk with me."

Intrigued, Caro matched her steps to Therese's slower ones as they crossed the wide room. As always, Therese was supremely well dressed in a high-necked maroon silk gown.

Rings flashed on her gnarled fingers as she moved her cane; she used it sparingly.

Content with her own appearance, with her skillfully draped *eau de nil* silk and the carved green amber set in silver that adorned her throat and wrists, Caro followed Therese onto the narrow balcony. They had the space to themselves, as, she was certain, Therese had intended.

Hooking the ornate silver head of her cane over one arm, Therese gripped the balcony rails and studied her. Consideringly.

Caro met that black stare, one she knew disconcerted others—indeed, was intended to disconcert—with unruffled serenity.

Therese's lips curved; she looked out over the darkened gardens. "Most others would be apprehensive, but of course you're not. I wished to compliment you on your good sense."

Good sense in what? Before Caro would voice the question, Therese continued, "I think too often we forget to tell others when they take the right road. Then, when hurdles appear and they falter, we criticize, quite forgetting we hadn't taken the time to encourage when, perhaps, we should have. You may consider my comments in that light, if you please—while I have no wish to manage your life, in your case"—glancing at her, Therese caught her eye—"I suspect a few encouraging words will not go amiss."

Caro waited.

"You may not recall, but I was *not* one of those who applauded your marriage to Camden." Therese faced the gardens once more. "To me, it seemed very much a case of socially sanctioned cradle-snatching. But then, as time went on, I changed my mind. *Not* because I thought Camden an appropriate husband for you, but because I realized he was most definitely a highly suitable *mentor* for you."

Caro let her gaze drift out over the gardens, black in the night. She felt Therese's gaze on her face, but didn't meet it.

"If I'm not mistaken," Therese continued, her voice low, her tone dry, "the concept of tutor and pupil most closely describes your relationship with Camden. Consequently, I wished to enthusiastically applaud your return to the fray." Her voice strengthened. "You have a great deal of skill, of honed talent and experience—and believe me, this country needs them. There are turbulent times ahead—we'll need men of integrity, commitment, and courage to weather them, and those men will need the support of . . ."

Therese paused. When Caro glanced at her and met her eyes, she smiled faintly. "Ladies like us."

Caro let her eyes flare with surprise; being classed with Therese Osbaldestone—*by* Therese Osbaldestone—was astounding. And an honor.

Of that, Therese herself was fully aware; she inclined her head, lips lifting self-deprecatingly. "Indeed, but you know that I mean what I say. Your 'right road,' dear Caro, lies in evenings such as these. There are only so many of us who can cope at this level, and you are one. It's important to us all, and yes, I speak for the others, too, that you continue within our circle. We all sincerely hope you will marry again, and be there to specifically support one of the upcoming men, but regardless, this—our circle—is where you most definitely belong."

Caro found it difficult to draw breath. Therese held her gaze; there could be no doubt of the sincerity with which she spoke, equally no doubt of the power she still wielded. "This, my dear, is your true life—the circle, the position that will most satisfy you, that will afford you the greatest fulfillment." Therese's lips quirked. "If I was given to the melodramatic, I would declare this your destiny."

Therese's black eyes were impossible to read; her expression, Caro knew, showed only what she wished it to. Yet the impression she received as Therese regarded her was one of fond kindness.

As if to confirm her reading, Therese smiled and patted her arm. Reclaiming her cane, she turned toward the drawing room. Caro paced beside her as they slowly strolled back into the light.

Just inside the windows, Therese paused. Caro followed her gaze—to Michael. He'd just walked into the drawing room in company with the Prime Minister and the current Foreign Minister, George Canning.

"Unless I much mistake the matter," Therese murmured, "your 'full tide,' as the Bard so aptly put it, is upon you. I wished to reassure you that you are on the right path, that when opportunity presents, you should not pass it up, but instead take heart, claim your courage, and seize the day."

With that, Therese inclined her head and regally moved away. Caro remained for a moment, committing her words to memory, laying them aside for later examination, then glided forward to join the nearest group. To return to her annointed role.

Michael saw Caro join a group of guests on the far side of the room. Absentmindedly, he tracked her, his attention otherwise on the conversation between the three gentlemen beside him—Liverpool, Canning, and Martinbury. He made no attempt to join in; he knew Liverpool and Canning wished to speak with him, but were waiting for Martinbury to leave them.

Caro moved on, joining the group of which Honoria was a part. He caught the glance his lover and his sister exchanged; pleased, he tucked it away—another example of how well Caro fitted in his life.

A movement in a group beyond the first drew his attention. Arrogantly assured, Devil detached himself from two grand dames, and went to join his own. Honoria was standing with her back to Devil, yet as he neared, she turned.

Across the large room, Michael watched his sister's face—saw her heart-stopping smile, saw her expression soften, almost glow. Glancing at Devil, he glimpsed, not the same but an answering response, the outward expression of a connection so deep, so powerful it was almost frightening.

Was frightening, given the man on whom it had laid its mark.

Honoria's words replayed in his ears. *The one thing . . . that gave me all that was truly important to me.*

He'd thought she'd meant on the physical plane, had searched for what was important to Caro on that basis. Yet perhaps Honoria had meant something else—something simpler, more ethereal, and much more powerful.

The one thing on which all else depended.

"Ah, Harriet! Well met, my dear."

Michael refocused to find Liverpool greeting his aunt Harriet. Martinbury nodded and stepped away. Canning bowed over Harriet's hand as Liverpool turned to Michael. "Opportune as ever, Harriet—I was about to have a word with Michael here."

The three—Liverpool, Harriet, and Canning—all turned to him and drew closer; for one fanciful instant, Michael felt as if they'd cornered him. Then Liverpool smiled, and he was no longer sure the impression was such a fantasy.

"Wanted to let you know, m'boy, that George here is moving on sooner rather than later." Liverpool nodded to Canning, who took up the tale.

"The extended negotiations with the Americans rather took it out of me, what?" Canning tugged down his waistcoat. "It's time for fresh blood, new energy. I've done my best, but it's time I handed the baton on."

Harriet was watching with an eagle eye, ready to step in if anything showed any signs of going awry.

Liverpool huffed out a breath and looked over the room. "So we'll have a vacant seat at the cabinet table, and at the F.O., in a matter of weeks. Wanted you to know."

His features impassive, Michael inclined his head. "Thank you, sir."

"And Caro Sutcliffe, heh?" Liverpool's gaze found Caro; his eyes lit with something close to delight. "*Quite* a find, m'boy—a supremely capable lady." His gaze returning to Michael's face, Liverpool was as close to jovial as he ever became. "Glad to see you took my hint to heart. Difficult thing these days, promoting an unmarried man. The party doesn't have the stomach for it just now. And you couldn't have chosen better. I'll look forward to receiving the wedding invitation in the next few weeks, what?"

Michael smiled, made the right noncommittal response; he suspected only Harriet picked up his sleight of words, the subtle evasion. Nevertheless, when with the usual comments and assurances the group broke up, Harriet merely smiled and went off on Canning's arm.

Relieved, Michael escaped, strolling to join another group, eventually circling around to come up with Caro.

Caro looked up and smiled when he joined her. With a word and a look, she drew him into the conversation she'd been having with Mr. Collins from the Home Office.

She was glad Michael had come to her; there were a number of people she thought he should speak with before the evening was over. With a smile, they parted from Mr. Collins. Her hand on Michael's arm, she deftly guided him on.

As was usual at such affairs, the night wore on, the conversation undimmed. They continued circulating; Caro caught more than one intrigued look, more than one interested glance. Gradually, she realized that the reality of the connection between her and Michael must show; Therese Osbaldestone was clearly not the only one to have seen past their facade.

Therese's words, ringing with undeniable wisdom, replayed in her mind . . . slowly sank deeper to wind about her heart. As she stood beside Michael and effortlessly played her role, some part of her studied the prospect, detached, impassively—almost unemotionally—assessing.

It was the life, the position, the purpose she wanted, indeed needed. At functions like these, the truth shone clearly; this was where she belonged.

She glanced at Michael, at his strong profile as he spoke with others. Wondered if he knew, if he'd seen that reality, too.

In a way, it was about power—feminine power; she'd had it once in her life, and had grown accustomed to wielding it, to gaining satisfaction from all it could achieve. That was what Camden had taught her, his greatest and most enduring legacy to her. To be involved in the political and diplomatic game was now essential to her continuing happiness, her fulfillment. Therese Osbaldestone had been right.

She glanced again at Michael, acknowledged that Therese had been right there, too. With Camden, she'd always been in his shadow—he'd been the great man, the celebrated ambassador. Michael was a different proposition—a completely different man. A relationship between them would be—and would be seen and accepted as being—a full partnership, a coming together of equals, each needed by the other.

Oh, yes, Therese had been right. Caro felt the inward surge of recognition, of the desire to step into the position that was there before her. The tug of the flood tide.

It could be so different, this time.

She looked at Michael; when he glanced at her, she merely smiled and tightened her hold on his arm. Felt, an instant later, his hand close more firmly over hers as they excused themselves and moved on.

They'd just joined the next group when they saw Liverpool beckon. Michael stepped back, tried to draw her with him, but she stood firm. "No." She spoke softly. "You go. It might be confidential."

He hesitated, then nodded and left her.

Two minutes later, while she was quietly following the group's discussion, she felt a touch on her arm, turned to see Harriet smiling.

"A quick word, Caro, then I really must go." Harriet glanced across the room at Michael. "It's been a long evening."

Murmuring agreement, Caro stepped aside, joining Harriet by the wall.

Harriet spoke quickly; happiness threaded through her words. "I just wanted you to know how thrilled I am—well, we all are, really, not only that you're back, but on Michael's arm." Harriet put a hand on Caro's wrist, a reassuring touch. "It's *such* a relief—I can't tell you how worried I was that he wouldn't bestir himself."

Harriet's assumption was obvious. One glance at her face reassured Caro that Harriet wasn't attempting to pressure her; Harriet's bright eyes and open expression made it abundantly clear she'd taken a wedding between Michael and Caro for granted, a decision already made if not announced.

Harriet rattled on, "My main concern, of course, was the time!"

Caro blinked; Harriet continued without prompting, "Now that Canning has all but officially vacated the F.O., then the appointment has to be made in September, and it's already August." She blew out a breath, her gaze going to Michael. "He always was one to leave things until the last minute, but really!"

Then she smiled, and looked at Caro. "At least from now on, it'll be *your* job to keep him up to the mark."

Giving silent thanks for her years of training, she managed a smile.

Harriet continued chatting; one part of Caro's mind monitored her words. Most of her mind was fixed on one fact: September was only weeks away.

CHAPTER

20

*I*f Michael had been quiet on the way to the Osterleys', Caro was silent, sunk in her thoughts, all the way home. Michael, too, seemed absorbed, presumably thinking of his pending appointment; the likelihood made her thoughts churn even more.

Arriving in Upper Grosvenor Street, they climbed the stairs. Magnus had left the Osterleys' an hour before them; upstairs, all was quiet. With a light touch on her hand, Michael parted from her at her door and continued on to his room to undress.

Caro entered her bedchamber; Fenella jumped up from the chair on which she'd been dozing and came to help her disrobe. For the first time since coming to Upper Grosvenor Street, Caro clung to the moments, let them spin out; Michael wouldn't come to her until he heard Fenella pass his room on her way to the servants' stair.

Carol had so much to think about; everything seemed to have rushed on her at once, yet she knew in reality that wasn't so. She'd been reassessing for days, even weeks— ever since Michael had so definitively left the decision about whether they should wed to her. Not resigning his goal, but acknowledging her right to choose her own life. He'd deliberately placed the reins of their relationship in her hand and closed her fingers about them.

What she hadn't until the last hour fully appreciated was

that, with complete understanding and certainly thus far unshakable resolve, he'd handed her the reins to his *career*, too.

Clad in a diaphanous nightgown covered by a silk robe barely opaque enough for decency, she went to stand before the uncurtained window, staring out over the rear garden while Fenella tidied.

Deliberately, she looked into the future—considered whether she should simply acquiesce and let the flood tide sweep her on. Imagined, weighed, recalled all Therese Osbaldestone had said, all she'd seen and comprehended that evening, before sighing and rejecting that course. Her resistance was too deep, the scars too deeply scored, to pursue that path—not again.

It had been so very wrong the last time.

Yet she was no longer set against marriage, not to Michael. If they had time—enough for her to be sure that what bound them was what she thought it was, that that indefinable something was as strong and, most importantly, as enduring as she thought it might be—then yes, she could see herself happily becoming his wife.

There was no other impediment—just her and the lessons fate had taught her.

Just her memories, and their ineradicable effect.

She could not, again, agree to a marriage by default. She could not allow herself to be swept into it with nothing more than hope as a guarantee. The first time she'd gaily jumped in and let the tide carry her away; it had landed her on a shore she had no wish to visit again.

Not that her life with Camden had been hard; she'd never lacked for material wealth. Yet she had been so alone. Her marriage had been an empty shell, just like the house in Half Moon Street. That was why she continually put off returning to it—because no matter how beautiful it was, how crammed with expensive objects, there was simply nothing there.

Nothing of importance. Nothing on which to build a life.

She barely noticed Fenella bobbing a curtsy; she dismissed the maid with an absentminded wave.

She didn't yet know if she could believe and go forward.

If the love—and yes, she thought it was love—that had grown between her and Michael would endure, would live and grow and be strong enough to be the cornerstone of her future, rather than dissipating like mist within a month, as with Camden.

And this time, the risk was far greater. The young girl's infatuation she'd felt for Camden, while it might have grown to more with time, was nothing, a mere cipher against what now, at twenty-eight, she felt for Michael. The comparison was laughable.

If she let the tide take her this time, and the vessel of their love foundered, the wreck would devastate her. Would scar her far more deeply than Camden's turning from her within days of their marriage had done.

The latch of her door clicked. Turning, through the shadows she watched Michael enter and shut the door. Watched him stroll easily, confidently, toward her.

There was only one thing to do.

She straightened her spine, lifted her head. Fixed her gaze on his eyes. "I need to talk to you."

Michael slowed. A single candle burned by the bed, too far away to illuminate her eyes, yet her stance warned him; she didn't expect him to like what she wished to say. Halting before her, he searched her face—could read nothing beyond implacable resolve. He arched a brow. "About what?"

"Us." Her gaze on his eyes, she drew a deep breath—hesitated. Then spoke, her tone ruthlessly even. "When we first became close, you told me that whether or not we married was entirely my decision. I accept you meant that sincerely. I knew you'd been urged to marry to enable your appointment to the ministry—I assumed that meant, as it usually would, an announcement of an engagement by October or so."

Drawing a tight breath, wrapping her arms about her, she looked down. "Tonight, I heard that Canning's resignation is imminent, making his replacement urgent." She looked up at him. "You now need to marry by mid-September at the latest."

He held her gaze for a finite moment, then replied, "I didn't know that until tonight, either."

To his relief, she inclined her head. "Yes, well . . . regardless, we now have a problem." Before he could ask what, she drew in a huge breath, turned to the window, and said, "I don't know if I can."

He didn't need to ask what she meant. An iron hand clutched his gut . . . yet it seemed she hadn't ruled out an engagement by October. . . . The cold tension dissolved; hope flared, but . . . he wasn't sure what was going on.

Shifting, he leaned against the window frame so he could better see her face limned by the faint moonlight flowing through the window. She was tense, yes, but not overwrought. A frown tangled her brows, her lips were compressed; she seemed to be wrestling with some insurmountable problem. The insight gave him pause. Evenly, unaggressively, he asked, "Why not?"

She glanced briefly at him, then looked forward. After a moment, she said, "I told you Camden"—she gestured—"swept me off my feet. Yet even then, I wasn't a complete ninny—I did have reservations. I wanted more time to be certain of my feelings and his, but he had to marry in less than two months and return to his post. I allowed myself to be persuaded—I *allowed* myself to be swept away.

"And now here I am, eleven years later, considering marrying another politician—and again due to the pressure of political events having to simply accept that all is as perfect, as right as it seems." She drew in another breath; this time, it shook. "I care for you—a lot. You know I do. But not even for you—not even for what might be—will I commit the same folly again."

He saw the problem; she confirmed it.

"I won't allow my decision to be made by default. This time, *I* have to make it—I have to be sure."

"What did Harriet say to you?"

She glanced at him. "Only that Canning was retiring—the timing." She frowned, following his thoughts. "She didn't pressure me—not her, or anyone else." Looking out at the garden, she sighed. "It's not people who've been persuading me this time—it's everything else. All the tangible and not-so-tangible things—the position, the role, the possibilities. I can see that everything fits . . . but it seemed to fit the last time, too."

He was feeling his way. Glancing at her face, he judged her calm enough to ask, "You're not imagining—not about to suggest—I look elsewhere for a wife?"

Her lips set. For a long moment, she didn't answer, then said, "I should."

"But you won't?"

She blew out a breath. Still not looking at him, she quietly stated, "I don't want you to marry anyone else."

Relief washed through him. So far, so good—

"But that's not the point!" Abruptly, she speared her hands through her hair, then whirled from the window. "You *have* to marry within a few weeks, so I *have to* make up my mind—and *I can't!* Not like this!"

He caught her hand before she could dash away across the room. The instant he touched her, he realized she was more tense than she appeared—her nerves far more taut. "What you mean is not yet."

Her eyes, limpid silver, locked with his. "What I mean is I can't promise that within a few weeks I'll happily agree to be your bride!" She held his gaze, no veil, no shield, nothing to screen the turmoil, close to anguish, in her mind. "I can't say yes"—she shook her head, almost whispered—"and I don't want to say no."

He suddenly saw it, the answer to his most urgent question. What was truly most important to her. The insight was momentarily blinding, then he blinked, refocused. On her. His eyes locked on hers; using his hold on her hand, he drew her closer. "You won't have to say no." Before she could argue, he continued, "You won't have to declare your decision until you're ready—until you've made it."

Steadily, he drew her nearer; reluctantly, frowning, she came. "But—"

"I told you at the outset—no pressures, no persuasions. Your decision, and yours alone." He finally saw the truth, saw it all; drawing breath, he looked into her eyes. "I want you to make that decision—between us, there's no hourglass with its sand running out." He raised her hand to his lips, kissed. "It's important this time—for you, for me, for us—that *you* make your decision."

He'd only just comprehended how vital, how essential that was—not just for her but for him as well. It might be his commitment she questioned, but unless she made her decision, actively and not by default, he would never be sure of her commitment either.

"I'll do anything—give anything—to allow you your choice." His voice deepened, each word intent. "I want to know you've knowingly accepted—that you've actively chosen to be my wife, to combine your life with mine."

She studied his eyes; confusion filled hers. "I don't understand."

His lips twisted, ironically self-deprecatory. "I don't care about the appointment."

Her eyes flared; she tried to jerk back as if he were joking.

He caught her waist, held her. "No—I know what I'm saying." He trapped her gaze, felt his jaw set. "I *mean* it."

"But . . ." Eyes wide, she searched his. "You're a politician . . . this is a *cabinet* post . . ."

"Yes, all right—I do care, *but* . . ." He hauled in a breath, briefly closed his eyes. He had to explain—and get it right; if he didn't, she wouldn't understand, wouldn't believe. Opening his eyes, he looked into hers. "I'm a politician—it's in my blood, so yes, success in that field is important to me. But being a politician is only a part of my life, and it's not the most important part. The other part of my life, the other half of it, is."

She frowned.

He went on, "The other part—the part that's most important . . . think of Devil. His life is spent running a dukedom, but the reason he does so—what gives his life purpose—is the other side of it. Honoria, his family, both immediate and wider. That's why he does what he does—that's where the purpose, the raison d'être of his life springs from."

Caro blinked, studied his eyes. "And you?" From the tension she sensed rising through him, he wasn't enjoying the discussion, but was grimly determined to see it to its end.

"The same holds true. I need . . . you, and a family, to

anchor me—to give me a base, a foundation—a sense of personal purpose. I want you as my wife—I want to have children with you, to make a home with you, found a family with you. That's what I need—and I know it." His jaw tensed, but he went on, "If passing up this chance at the Foreign Office is the price I have to pay to have you as my wife, I'll pay gladly. The post doesn't matter as much to me as you do."

She searched his eyes; no matter how hard she looked she could see nothing but brutal honesty. "I really mean that much to you?" Not just a surprise, but something beyond her wildest dreams.

He held her gaze, then quietly said, "My career is at the periphery of my life—*you* are at its center. Without you, all the rest is meaningless."

The admission hung between them, stark and clear.

She felt compelled to ask, "Your grandfather—your aunt?"

"Strangely enough, I think they'll understand. Magnus, at least."

She hesitated, but had to ask, "You really want me that much?"

He clenched his teeth. "I *need* you that much." The intensity of the words shook him as much as her.

"I . . ."—she searched his blue eyes—"don't know what to say."

He released her. "You don't have to say anything yet." Lifting his hands, he framed her face. Let his thumbs cruise the fine skin of her jaw, then brought his gaze to her eyes. "You just have to believe—and you will."

He tipped up her face, lowered his head. "However long it takes, I'll wait until you do."

The vow resonated between them, shivered through them. He kissed her.

Whether it was the touch of her hand on the back of his, or that they'd spoken so blatantly of their needs, or whether it was simply him owning to his—to that force that compelled, that beat in his blood, pounded through his veins, surged through his body—whichever or all, they ignited him. Cindered the last of his restraint, left him with undisguised hunger raging through him. A potent, driving, primitive desire to show her beyond doubt, beyond confusion, what she truly meant to him.

How elementally deep his need for her ran.

Caro felt the change in him. She was already adrift on an unchartered sea; his words had ripped her from the rock her past had chained her to, and whirled her into the surging waves of the unknown. Onto the flood tide.

The raging currents sucked her down. Dragged her into some dark inferno where he waited for her, ablaze with hunger, with greedy need.

Their tongues tangled, but he was the aggressor, openly, dominantly so. He shifted into her, steering, then pressing her against the wall beyond the window; his hands released her jaw, one reaching further to slide through her hair until his strong fingers wrapped about her nape, holding her steady so he could plunder. So he could feast on the softness of her mouth, so he could brand her with the heat that seemed to pour from him. Then his other hand found her breast, and the flames leapt.

She pushed her hands up, gripped his shoulders as her world, her senses, spun, as his hand closed possessively, as he kneaded and she ached, and want and need spilled like an elixir down her veins.

His or hers, she wasn't sure, couldn't tell.

Then his fingers found her nipple and she moaned. He plunged deep into her mouth, tightened his fingers—her lungs seized. She sank her fingertips into his shoulders, came up on her toes to meet him, to urge him on.

The resulting duel sent heat and fire raging through them both, hungry, ravenous, surging and building. Her skin burned; his was even hotter, stretched over tensed muscles, scalding, branding her wherever he touched. Her peignoir and negligee were no protection; pressing her to the wall, his hands roved, searched, flagrantly explored, possessed.

Abruptly his hard hands rose to her shoulders; he stripped off her peignoir—discarded, it drifted to the floor. Her gauzy negligee was designed to be an erotic temptation; when he bent his head and through the fine material licked and laved her nipple, then closed his mouth over it and suck-led fiercely until she cried out, she was no longer sure who was tempter, who the target.

He used the material, shifting it over her excruciatingly tight nipples, sliding it over her heated skin, veiling his caresses, sensually distracting, disconcerting. Then he pressed closer, one hard thigh parting hers, forcing hers wide enough so hard muscle rode against her mons. He pressed, rocked, aroused her until she was gasping through their kiss, clinging to his shoulders, reaching to twine her fingers in his hair.

To anchor her against the fire and the yearning, the achingly empty sensation growing inside her, the welling, burgeoning, all-consuming need.

One hand at her hip, anchoring her against the wall, he eased back, pressed a hand between their bodies, reached down. Found her curls through the distracting gauze and stroked, then reached further. Through the shifting gossamer silk he caressed her, traced her swollen folds, parted them, probed, pressed a finger, encased in gauze, into her, deeper, then deeper still, pulling the material tight over her mons.

He stroked, pressing in, easing back, each successive movement shifting the filmy material over the sensitive bud hidden between her folds. Over and over. Breaking from the kiss, he leaned into her, holding her against the wall while he pleasured her. His head was beside hers; she felt his gaze on her face. Could barely think through the haze of escalating sensations.

She cracked open her lids, found his eyes waiting to trap hers. She moistened her lips. Managed to find breath to say, "Take me to the bed."

"No." His voice was dark, deep. "Not yet."

There was something in his tone, something in his face that was harder, clearer, more defined. She studied it, understood more by instinct than reason, shuddered and closed her eyes.

Felt her senses close in, felt them start the now familiar giddy climb.

"Michael . . ." She pushed back on his shoulders; he moved not an inch.

Ruthlessly pushed her on.

"Here. Now. Let go."

She had to. He gave her no choice, stroking again and again deep inside her until the glory took her and she broke apart.

Sagging against the wall, she felt his hand leave her—expected him to step back, sweep her up in his arms, and carry her to the bed.

Instead, she felt him pull up her gauzy skirts, gathering the fabric above her hips; the night air, warm and redolent with the scent of night stock, caressed her flushed and heated skin.

He shifted, and his silk robe gaped open; wrapping his hands about her thighs, he lifted her.

Braced her against the wall, and pushed into her.

She gasped, raised her head as he pressed deeper, as her slick and still-throbbing flesh surrendered, stretched and took him in. She felt every inch of his penetration as he impaled her, thrust powerfully up and filled her.

Without instruction, she wrapped her legs about his waist, desperate to gain some solid hold in a world that was suddenly whirling.

Then he moved and the flames flared again. Within seconds he'd driven her deep into the conflagration.

She sobbed, wrapped her arms about his shoulders and clung, held tight as he sent her rocketing into that fiery sea, with each powerful thrust sent the twin currents of passion and desire raging ever more hotly through her.

Until she burned.

Until she felt sure even her fingertips were pulsing with flame.

Then he slowed. Continued moving heavily, powerfully surging within her, but not hard enough, not fast enough.

His head, until then alongside hers, lifted; he drew back enough to look into her eyes. With an effort she opened them, knowing he would wait. . . .

He caught her gaze. Moved once, twice, within her. Leaned closer. Their breaths mingled, their breathing ragged and harsh. His gaze dropped to her lips, then his lashes lifted and their eyes locked again.

"I will never, ever, turn from you." The words were guttural, low, resonant with the weight of a vow. "Not tonight, not tomorrow, not in fifty years." He continued to move within her, his thrusts punctuating his words. "Don't ask it of me. Don't expect it to happen, don't imagine it ever will. It won't. I won't."

His gaze fell; her lips throbbed.

He covered them.

And the firestorm took them. Melded them. Fused them.

Yet when, driven far beyond the world, she shattered, fractured by the pulsing glory, he didn't follow. He hung back, anchoring her, driving rhythmically into her—drawing her back.

When she finally drew in a shuddering breath and lifted her head, bracing her arms, straightening her spine, opening her eyes to look at him in disoriented puzzlement, Michael clamped a desperate hold on his raging passions, felt her contract about him, confirming he'd yet to seek his release.

Before she could speak, he withdrew from her, slowly lowered her. "First act." His voice was so gravelly he wondered if she would even make out the words. He waited while she unwound her legs, then swept her up into his arms. Carrying her to the bed, he caught her gaze. "Tonight, I want more."

Much more.

Her widening eyes suggested his meaning—primitive, basic, less than civilized—had reached her. He didn't feel anything like his smoothly sophisticated self as he tumbled her onto the bed. As he followed her and swiftly arranged her as he wished, bent over her knees before him.

His facade, his mask, had long gone as he pushed her nightgown up to her waist, as he ran his hands over the dewed globes of her bottom, then opened her and eased his throbbing staff into the hot haven between her thighs.

He heard her sob, catch her breath, felt her silent gasp as she instinctively tightened, then surrendered and let him in. He pushed further; her sheath stretched, easing in welcome, then clasped about him, a scalding lover's caress. Closing his hands about her hips, anchoring her before him, he adjusted her position as he worked deep and filled her.

Then he rode her.

As he had told her, demanding more, wanting more, needing more. And she gave without reservation. Her already sensitized nerves leapt to every explicit caress; her nightgown simply added another layer of sensual taunting.

Her hips rocked as he rhythmically thrust, angling to penetrate as deeply as he could—and she met him. Sensuously shifted, wanton in her passion, riding each movement, taking him in, pressing her bottom into his groin as he joined with her.

He heard her pants, heard the soft moans she struggled to suppress, then surrendered and let free. The sound of female abandonment added yet more impetus to the primal passion driving him. He could no longer think. Didn't need to. Instinct had claimed him, decisive, urgent, and commanding.

Reaching forward, he filled his hands with her breasts, ripe and sumptuous, the nipples hard pebbles he rubbed and taunted, then squeezed. She cried out, lifted, and felt his hand on her back holding her down, only then realized her inherent helplessness.

With a gasp understood, then gave herself over to it.

Let go as he'd asked, gave herself up to the turbulent tide, let it and him sweep her where they would. Let him take all he wished of her—give all he wished to her. Show her all.

He employed no restraint, no finesse, simply dropped all pretense and let her feel what she was to him, feel the primitive urges that whipped through him, that she and only she evoked.

Let her sense through him, through the power that drove him, all she meant to him, all she called forth in him. All that she controlled in him.

Whether she recognized that last or not, he didn't care. His need for her transcended any logic, any consideration of self-protection. There was no longer any existence for him but with her.

The driving, pumping rhythm had escalated beyond his

control or hers. Desire roared; passion lashed out and caught them in its fiery embrace.

And they burned.

When she fell from the peak, she took him with her—this time, he went willingly. Surrendering to the glory. Surrendering to her.

Surrendering to the power that bound them, now and forever.

He stirred her again in the deep watches of the night.

Caro woke as he shifted behind her. She lay on her side; he must have moved them onto the pillows and dragged the covers over them. The power of their extended joining pulsed, a faint echo in her bones. Hours must have passed, yet she still felt wrapped in the moment, in the passion, the raw hunger, the urgent desire.

Not just his, but hers.

Despite the many times they'd come together, enjoyed, indulged, and shared, she hadn't understood—hadn't truly comprehended from what source the power that commanded him, that compelled him and drove him, sprang. Yet this last time . . . even though she hadn't been able to see his face, she'd felt that power, so strong it had been palpable, surrounding them, holding them, welding them. Until there'd been just them—not him or her, but one entity.

She felt his hand on her thigh, felt him raise the back of her nightgown, drawing the material to her waist. He caressed her bottom; she reacted instantly, her skin dewing, heating. His hand slipped lower, pressed between her thighs, found her. Fondled, probed, then, pushing her upper thigh higher, he opened her, and slid in.

She'd wondered if he'd known she was awake; he certainly knew as he sank into her to the hilt and she arched, a soft gasp falling from her lips as, head back, eyes closed, she savored that incredible moment.

He held still, let her enjoy it fully.

Then, when she eased, very gently, rocked.

Into her, about her, with her.

He slid his hand, palm splayed, over her stomach, holding

her against him. She spread her hand over the back of his, murmured, caught her breath as he pushed deeper still.

The familiar heat rose within them, between them, poured through them. The tide rose and she went with it, whirling gently, senses aware, into its sensuous sea.

No urgency this time, just a long, slow, unhurried loving, one neither was eager to rush.

For her part, just the feel of him, hard, hot, unforgivingly rigid, drawing out of, then pressing back into, her body was bliss. As the minutes ticked by and the tempo remained severely restrained, she felt certain he knew.

But the slow pace allowed her mind to function, to drift, to snag on the question. "Why?" She was sure she wouldn't need to elaborate.

Propped on one elbow behind her, he leaned close, nuzzled the curve of her throat.

"Because of this." His voice was low, deep, a male promise in the dark of the night. "Because of all the women I could have, I want you—like this."

He slowed, let her feel again how much he wanted her, let their loins come together as he sank deep. "Like this. Lying naked beside me in my bed, mine whenever I wish." His voice deepened, darkened. "Mine to have, to fill with my seed. I want you to bear my children. I want you by my side when I grow old. Because at the end of all the explanations, it comes down to this—that you are the only wife I want, and for you, for that, I'll wait forever."

She felt her heart swell, was so glad he couldn't see her face, see her eyes as tears welled and silently fell.

Then he picked up their rhythm, the tempo escalated, and there were no more words, but a wordless communion. An age-old melding; he held her tight, his chest to her back as she crested the peak and fell through the stars. He followed immediately, with her—as he wished, as she wished—when they found their distant shore.

CHAPTER

21

Michael left the house the next morning feeling for the first time in weeks as if he were walking in mental sunshine rather than fog. As if a miasma had blown away and he could finally see clearly.

Caro was all that truly mattered to him. It wasn't just sensible but completely justifiable to devote himself wholly, single-mindedly, to her protection. To set aside all other concerns and concentrate solely on that, for she was the key to his future.

He'd left her still sleeping, sated and warm in her bed, safe in his grandfather's house. He headed for the clubs and scouted through his contacts; none had anything to report. After lunching at Brooks with Jamieson, who was still puzzled and uneasy over the break-in, not so much over it happening but because he couldn't see why, Michael headed for Grosvenor Square, confident there was no piece of accessible information he'd overlooked.

Devil had summoned him to a meeting at three o'clock; Gabriel had turned up something odd among the legatees that Lucifer agreed needed to be investigated. The meeting was opportune; Michael could report his findings, or lack thereof, and Devil would have news of Ferdinand and his doings.

Devil's butler, Webster, was waiting to admit him;

Michael surmised Honoria had not been informed a meeting was taking place. His brother-in-law had deeply entrenched prejudices against involving his wife in any potentially dangerous game. He now shared—fully—those same prejudices, and other similar reactions and emotions to which he'd never thought to fall prey. Thinking of Caro and all she made him feel, he wondered that he'd been so self-blind.

Devil and Lucifer were waiting in the study; Gabriel arrived as he sat in one of the four armchairs facing each other across the empty hearth. As Gabriel sank into the last, Michael glanced around at the faces; he'd grown close to all the Cynsters. Since Honoria's marriage they'd treated him as one of them; he'd come to regard them in the same light. Helping each other was an unwritten Cynster code; it didn't seem odd, even to him, that they'd put aside other things and devoted time and effort to aiding him.

Gabriel looked at him. "Let's hear your news first."

Michael grimaced; it didn't take long to summarize nothing.

"Leponte has been lying low," Devil said. "Sligo's certain he hired someone to watch the Foreign Office buildings, but he's been careful to work through intermediaries. However, for the night in question, we can't place Leponte anywhere. He might have remained within the emabassy all night— then again, he might not."

"If he's searching for something incriminating," Michael said, "presumably he won't want anyone else to read it. While at Sutcliffe House, he could have asked others to bring away anything they found, removing an entire archive. . . ."

Devil nodded. "He would have had to go through it. He probably did, but as he's not going about much anyway, his social absence that night can hardly be cited as evidence."

They all grimaced, rather grimly, then turned to Gabriel.

"Whether this means anything or not I don't know," he said, "but it's definitely deuced odd. I checked the list of bequests, all those involving items of value. There were nine such bequests, all of antiques, specific pieces that Camden had collected over the last decade.

"All the pieces were highly valuable. Eight went to men Camden had known for decades, most from his early years in diplomatic circles. Those eight fit the mold of old and valued friend. I ran the list past Lucifer—"

"All eight are known collectors," Lucifer said. "The pieces each received fit perfectly into their collections. From what I saw in Half Moon Street, those bequests didn't leave holes in Camden's collection. He'd clearly viewed the pieces as gifts from the first, so it's no surprise they were listed in his will."

"Subsequently," Gabriel resumed, "I quietly asked around and confirmed none of those eight are in any way pressed for cash."

"Nor do any of them have the reputation of those I term 'rabid collectors,'" Lucifer added.

"So eight bequests make eminent sense and raise no hares," Michael said. "What of the ninth?"

"That's where things become interesting." Gabriel met Michael's eyes. "On first reading, I didn't realize its significance. The ninth bequest is described as 'a Louis XIV desk set in marble and gold, jewel-encrusted.'"

"However," Lucifer took up the tale, "that particular piece is not simply a desk set created in the time of Louis XIV—it was *Louis XIV's* desk set. It's worth a not-so-small fortune."

"Who is the ninth legatee?" Devil asked.

Gabriel looked at him. "He's listed as T. M. C. Danvers."

"Breckenridge?" Michael stared. "Is he a collector, too?"

"No," Lucifer said, a touch grimly. "He isn't—not at all."

"But you know of him," Gabriel said. "I searched everywhere, but I couldn't find any connection between Camden Sutcliffe and Breckenridge, other than that, due to some reason, they knew each other."

"Caro said they'd known each other for thirty years—all Breckenridge's life." Michael frowned. "She's given Breckenridge Camden's letters to read, explained what we're looking for." He glanced at the others. "She trusts him completely."

Their frowns stated that they, as he, thought Caro had no business trusting a man of Breckenridge's ilk.

"Did she explain what the connection between Sutcliffe and Breckenridge was?" Devil asked.

"No, but it's not through political or diplomatic circles— I'd know if Breckenridge was a player there, and he isn't." Michael felt his face hardening. "I'll ask her." He looked at Gabriel. "If he's not a collector, could money be the motive?"

Gabriel grimaced. "I'd so like to say yes, but all the answers I got say otherwise. Breckenridge is Brunswick's heir, and Brunswick is as financially solid as the proverbial rock. When it comes to money, Breckenridge is his father's son; his investments are sound, even a touch conservative for my taste, and his income greatly exceeds his expenditures. Breckenridge certainly has a vice, but it's not the tables, it's women, and even there, he's careful. I couldn't find the slightest sign any harpy has her talons in him, let alone to the extent of bleeding him."

Devil murmured, "From all I've heard, Breckenridge is considered a dangerous man to cross. There seems no reason to think him a blackmailer, yet equally I can't see him as a blackmailer's victim."

"Forced to act as a pawn in bleeding Sutcliffe?" Lucifer asked.

Devil nodded. "Highly unlikely, I should think."

"So what we have is a nobleman with no explainable connection to Sutcliffe being left a disguised but sizeable fortune in his will." Michael paused, then added, "There has to be a reason."

"Indeed," Devil said. "And while we know the Portuguese are attempting to suppress something in Sutcliffe's past, and can surmise they might wish to permanently silence Caro, there's the possibility the attempts on her life stem from something quite different."

"Like Sutcliffe's treasures." Lucifer rose. "We need to learn what the connection between Sutcliffe and Breckenridge was with all speed."

"Caro knows what it is." Michael rose, as did the others; he glanced at them. "I'll go and ask."

Devil clapped him on the shoulder as they turned to the door. "If it's anything potentially damning, let us know."

Michael nodded.

Lucifer opened the door—just as Honoria swept up. She halted in the corridor, her hazel eyes noting each one.

"Good afternoon, gentlemen." Her tone was all grande dame. "And what have we here?"

Devil smiled. "There you are." Surreptitiously, he prodded Michael in the back.

Michael moved forward, through the door; Honoria stepped back, allowing him into the corridor.

Devil efficiently ushered Gabriel and Lucifer through the doorway—into freedom. "I was just on my way to tell you our news."

Michael glanced back as he, Gabriel, and Lucifer retreated down the corridor; the look on his sister's face was disbelieving in the extreme.

Her "Indeed?" was incredulous.

As they turned into the front hall, they heard Devil's answering purr, "Come in, and I'll tell you."

They could imagine Honoria's "*Humph!*" but an instant later, they heard the click of the study door closing.

Pausing on the front steps, they exchanged glances.

"I wonder how much he'll tell her," Lucifer mused.

Gabriel shook his head. "That's one question on which I wouldn't like to wager."

Michael agreed; with a grin, he saluted them, then strode down the steps and headed for Upper Grosvenor Street. Turning his thoughts to his mission, his grin faded.

"Breckenridge." Michael stood before Caro, his face impassive as he looked down at her.

She blinked up at him. She was seated in an armchair in the parlor, one of Camden's diaries in her hands. About them the house was peaceful, basking in the late afternoon sunshine.

He read her surprise in her eyes—she didn't try to hide it.

He'd walked in, nodded a greeting, shut the door, and baldly said, "Breckenridge."

Some of the tension eased from his shoulders. Glancing around, he moved to the armchair facing her.

The last time she'd seen his face, it had been dawn and his expression had been slack with sated passion. Calmly shutting the diary, she inquired, "What about Timothy?"

Her use of the name touched a nerve, but Michael suppressed his reaction. Grimly stated, "You said Breckenridge was an old and trusted friend of Camden's, that their association stretched back to when Breckenridge was a child." He met her gaze. "What was the basis of the connection?"

She raised her brows, waited. . . .

It was like a shield being reluctantly lowered; she could almost sense his deliberation, the subsequent conscious submission.

"We were checking the bequests in Camden's will." He explained the information Gabriel and Lucifer had gathered, Devil's report on Ferdinand's movements, and his own lack of success in learning what it was the Portuguese were after, or why.

She listened without comment, but when he outlined their reasoning that the attempts on her life might in some way stem from Camden's collection, she went to shake her head, then stopped.

He saw, waited, then raised a brow back.

She met his gaze, then inclined her head. "While I can't dismiss the notion that someone might be motivated by a piece in Camden's collection, I can and do assure you that I can be absolutely certain Breckenridge is not in any way involved—*either* in anything illicit to do with Camden's collection or with the attempts on my life."

He studied her face, searched her eyes, then somewhat bleakly asked, "You trust him that much?"

She held his gaze, then reached out, threaded her fingers through his and squeezed. "I know it's not easy for you to accept or understand, but yes, I *know* I can trust Breckenridge that much."

A long moment passed. She saw in his eyes his decision to

accept her reassurance. "What," he asked, "is or was the nature of the connection between Camden and Breckenridge?"

"It's 'is'—the connection continues. And while I know what it is, I'm afraid, much as I wish to"—she let her eyes show how much she wished, that it wasn't because she didn't or wouldn't trust him that she felt forced to say—"I can't tell you. As you've discovered, the connection is a secret, concealed from the world for a multitude of good reasons. It's not my secret to share."

She watched as he digested her answer . . . and decided he had to accept it. Had to respect the confidence she wouldn't break, even for him. Had to trust her to be right.

Refocusing on her eyes, he nodded. "All right—it's not Breckenridge, then."

Her heart swelled; she hadn't realized his simple acceptance would mean so much, yet it did.

She smiled.

He sat back in the chair, slowly smiled in return. "Where have we got to with the diaries?"

She couldn't simply change her mind and say yes, she would marry him. Not after last night and all she now understood of both herself and him.

They sat in the parlor a few feet apart and read more of the diaries; while part of her mind followed Camden's accounts of social gatherings, the rest followed a different tack.

Ever since she'd woken that morning, languorous and exhausted in the rumpled disaster of her bed, she'd been reassessing, reevaluating—hardly surprising given the tectonic shift in the landscape between them that the night had brought. That Michael had wrought. Quite deliberately.

She'd tried to tell herself he hadn't meant it. That he couldn't really not care.

One glance at the bruises circling her thighs, the lingering evidence of the intensity that had gripped him, had brought the power that drove him, that when they were together caught her and drove her, too, forcibly to mind.

She'd felt it, experienced it, recognized it; she knew it wasn't fabricated or false. Indeed, gripped by it, it was impossible to be false, to play false, not between them. She believed in it—that between them that power existed, simply was. Replaying his words, the fervor, the certainty with which he'd made his declarations, she'd come to believe in them, too.

He'd made no subsequent reference to his decision. It seemed to have become a part of him; he clearly felt no need to try to convince her further. He'd told her all he needed to. All he had to.

All she needed to know.

Glancing up, she watched as he turned a page and continued reading. For a long moment, she studied his face, him, drank in his strength, the reliability and steadfastness that was so much a part of him one hardly noticed, then looked down.

There was still something missing in their equation. She and he were in unknown territory; neither had been this way before. She didn't know what it was that had yet to manifest between them, yet her instincts, instincts she was too experienced to ignore, assured her there was something more. Something they yet lacked that they needed to have, to find, to secure if their relationship, the relationship they both wanted and needed, was to thrive.

That last was now her aim. By freeing her to make her own decision, he'd given her the opportunity to get everything right. More, he'd revealed how important it was to him that their relationship was strong and well founded.

So she wouldn't let herself get swept away—she would grasp the chance he'd created. She'd wait and keep searching until she found that vital piece; he'd given her the strength to stand against the tide.

They'd gone down to report to Magnus and were climbing the stairs to change for dinner when Hammer strode into the hall. Glancing up, he saw them.

"Mrs. Sutcliffe."

They halted on the landing. With stately tread, Hammer ascended, then, bowing, proffered his salver. "A lad delivered this to the back door. No reply required, I gather, for he disappeared without a word."

"Thank you, Hammer." Caro took the note; her name was printed on it. As Hammer retreated, she unfolded the single sheet.

She glanced at the contents, then held it up so Michael could read over her shoulder. She scanned the words more carefully, then exhaled. "Someone from the Portuguese embassy, do you think?"

Michael considered the careful clerkish script and the phrasing—diplomatic formal.

Should Mrs. Sutcliffe wish to learn the reason behind the recent strange events, she is invited to meet with the writer at her Half Moon Street house tonight at eight o'clock. Provided Mrs. Sutcliffe comes alone, or with only Mr. Anstruther-Wetherby as escort, the writer is willing to reveal all they know. If, however, more people are present, the writer cannot undertake the risk of coming forward and speaking.

The note concluded with the customary formal *Yours, et cetera*, but unsurprisingly was unsigned.

Caro lowered the sheet and looked at him.

He took the note, folded it, and tucked it into his pocket. "Yes, I agree—it sounds like a foreign aide." He met her eyes. "Sligo, Devil's majordomo, has been quietly putting the word about that we're looking for information."

"And here it is." She held his gaze. "We are going, aren't we? One foreign aide in my house—that's no great risk, surely?"

Expression impassive, Michael waved up the stairs. Caro turned and went; he grasped the moment to consider his response.

Instinct was pulling him one way, experience and Caro's commonsense assessment in another. Aside from all else, it was already after seven o'clock; if he alerted any of the

Cynsters, it was unlikely they could take up any position covertly before eight.

And if instead they were seen . . . no more than Caro did he believe their would-be informant would appear. Diplomatic games had rules like any other; a show of trust was essential.

They gained the top of the stairs. Caro halted and turned to him. He met her gaze, read her question, curtly nodded. "We'll go. Just you and me."

"Good." She looked down at her flimsy day gown. "I'll need to change."

Consulting his watch, he nodded. "I'll go and tell Magnus what's happened and what we're doing. I'll be in the library when you're ready."

At twenty minutes before eight o'clock, a hackney set them down before the Half Moon Street house. Climbing the steps, Michael glanced up and down the street. It was long enough, the area fashionable enough that even in summer at that hour there were carriages drawn up before houses and others rattling past.

There were gentlemen lounging against railings, chatting, others strolling, some alone. Any carriage, any stroller, could be their man; it was impossible to tell.

Caro opened the front door; Michael followed her into the hall, reminding himself to rein in his protectiveness. Whoever arrived to meet them most likely wouldn't be a threat, not unless this was some kind of trap.

Recognizing the possibility, he'd grasped the few minutes he'd spent with Magnus to refine a plan and put it into action. Sligo, Devil's sometime batman, now his major-domo, had ways, means, and experience beyond that of most servants; Michael hadn't hesitated to send for him. He would arrive close to eight and keep watch from outside; even if they saw him, no one would imagine the slight, unprepossessing man was of any consequence.

As for inside the house . . . Michael tightened his grip on the head of his cane; the blade concealed within was rapier sharp and well honed.

Caro opened the double doors into the drawing room.

He followed her inside, saw her crossing to the windows. "Leave the curtains closed." It was still full light outside. "Whoever it is won't want to risk being glimpsed."

Caro looked at him, then nodded. Going instead to the sideboard, she lit two three-armed candelabra. The flames flared, then settled, casting warm light across the room. Leaving one candelabra on the sideboard, she carried the other to the mantelpiece. "There—at least we'll be able to see."

It wasn't that dark, but the candlelight was comforting.

Michael glanced around, struck again by the sense that the house was a shell, prepared and waiting to be used as a home. He glanced at Caro—

A grinding groan—the scrape of wood against stone—reached them.

Caro's eyes flared. Then puzzlement filled her face. "That's from downstairs," she hissed.

His face leaching of expression, he turned and went back into the hall. Pushing through the swinging door at the end, he considered—fleetingly—ordering Caro to go back and wait in the drawing room. Recognized the futility; standing there arguing wouldn't help. Besides, she might well be safer with him.

The corridor beyond the door was narrow and dim; it was relatively short, ending in a ninety-degree turn to the right. Faint scuffling came from beyond the turn. Treading carefully, silently, he went on.

Caro's hand touched his back; reaching past him, she pointed to the right, then walked her fingers down . . . stairs lay immediately around the corner. He nodded. He considered drawing his swordstick, but the sound would carry in the enclosed space, and if the kitchen lay down the stairs . . . a naked rapier in close confines might be more dangerous than helpful.

Tightening his grip on the cane, he halted at the corner; the sounds below had resolved into definite footsteps.

Reaching back with one hand, he found Caro; stepping out onto the landing beyond the corner, he simultaneously held her back.

The man standing at the foot of the stairs looked up. What little light came through the fanlight above the back door didn't reach his face. All Michael could tell was that he was tall, lean, and broad-shouldered, with brown, slightly wavy hair. Not Ferdinand, but not anyone he knew either.

For one fraught instant, they stared at each other.

Then the stranger charged up the stairs; with an oath, Michael flung himself down them.

The man hadn't seen his cane; Michael brought it up across his body, intending to stop the man's murderous charge with it and push him back down the stairs. It certainly stopped the man's rush, but he caught hold of the cane. They wrestled, then both lost their balance and fell, tumbling down the stairs.

They landed in a wild tangle on the flagstones; both checked—each instantly knew the other wasn't incapacitated. Both sprang to their feet. Michael threw a punch, but it was blocked; he had to duck quickly to avoid a fist aimed at his jaw.

He grabbed the man; furious wrestling ensued, both trying to land a telling blow. Dimly, he heard Caro yelling something; avoiding another jab, he was too busy to pay attention.

Both he and his attacker thought of tripping each other at the same time; they lurched, but their death grips on each other kept them upright—

Icy water hit them. Struck them, drenched them.

Gasping, spluttering, they broke apart, furiously dashing water from their eyes.

"*Stop* it! Both of you! Don't you *dare* hit each other!"

Dumbstruck, they stared up at Caro.

The now empty ewer from Mrs. Simms's room in her hands, she glared down at them. "Allow me to introduce you. Michael Anstruther-Wetherby—Timothy, Viscount Breckenridge."

They glanced at each other, eyes narrow.

She hissed in frustration. "For goodness sake! Shake hands—*now!*"

Both looked at her, then at each other, then, reluctantly,

Michael held out his hand. Equally reluctantly, Timothy gripped it. Briefly.

Michael eyed him coldly. "What are you doing here?" He spoke softly, yet there was unmistakable menace in the words.

Timothy studied him, then glanced up at her. "I received a note. It said you were in danger and if I wanted to know more, to meet the writer here at eight o'clock."

It was plain Michael didn't believe him.

His usually infallible instincts starting to operate again, Timothy looked from her to Michael, then he narrowed his eyes at her. "What have you been up to? What's this all about?"

His tone should have set Michael's suspicions to rest; it rang with typical aggravated male concern. She elevated her nose. "I got a note, too. Very similar. We came to meet the writer." She peered across the kitchen at the clock Mrs. Simms kept wound. "It's ten minutes to eight, and we're down here arguing."

"And now we're wet." Bending his head, Timothy ran his hands through his hair, dislodging droplets.

Michael, brushing water off his shoulders, didn't take his eyes from him. "How did you get in?"

Timothy glanced at him. Even though Caro couldn't see it, she could imagine his smirk as he softly answered, "I have a key, of course."

"Stop it!" She glared at him; he tried to look innocent and as usual failed. Transferring her gaze to Michael's stony face, she explained, "There's a perfectly sensible, acceptable reason."

Michael bit his tongue. The most notorious rake in London had a key to his wife-to-be's house—and she was insisting there was an acceptable explanation. He managed not to snort. With an exaggerated wave, he gestured for Breckenridge to precede him up the stairs.

His expression faintly amused, Breckenridge did; he followed.

Caro had disappeared. As he and Breckenridge turned

into the corridor, she emerged ewerless from the house-keeper's room; shutting the door, she led them back to the front hall. "I hope our writer didn't knock while we were down there. I'm not sure if the bell's still working."

She glanced back at Timothy.

He shook his head. "I don't know, either. I haven't dropped by for some time."

Michael digested that as they crossed the hall and entered the drawing room. Caro led the way to the area before the hearth. As he followed, Breckenridge beside him, Michael was aware of the man glancing from Caro to him, and back again.

They halted at the edge of the exquisite rug before the hearth; both were still dripping from various extremities.

Breckenridge was studying Caro. "You haven't told him, have you?"

She raised her brows, fixed him with an irritated look. "Of course not. It's *your* secret. If anyone is to be told, you have to tell them."

It was Michael's turn to glance from one to the other; their interaction seemed more like his with Honoria than anything remotely loverlike.

Brows lifting, Breckenridge faced him, studied him levelly, then, his voice free of any drawl, said, "As there's presumably a reason Caro wants you told, and as it's difficult to explain my presence without knowing . . . Camden Sutcliffe was my sire."

Amusement gleamed in Breckenridge's eyes; he glanced at Caro. "Which makes Caro my . . . I'm not quite sure what. Stepmother?"

"Whatever," Caro firmly stated. "That explains your connection to Camden, with this house, and why he left you that desk set."

Breckenridge's brows rose. He glanced at Michael with a touch more respect. "Twigged to that, did you?"

Michael refused to be drawn. "There was no evidence of any connection . . ." He broke off as things fell into place.

Breckenridge smiled. "Indeed. It was not just kept quiet

but thoroughly buried by both parties. My mother, God rest her soul, was perfectly content with her husband, but in Camden she found what she always claimed was the love of her life. A short-lived love, but . . ." He shrugged. "My mother was forever a pragmatist. Camden was married. The liaison occurred during a brief visit to Lisbon. Mama returned to England and bore my father—by whom I mean Brunswick—his only son. Me."

Moving past Michael, Breckenridge went to the side-board, where a decanter stood. He looked at Michael, waved at the glasses; Michael shook his head. Breckenridge poured. "Aside from the obvious considerations, there was the fact that if I wasn't there, as Brunswick's heir, the title and estates would revert to the Crown, pleasing no one except the royal treasurer."

He paused to sip the brandy. "My father, however, is a stickler—if he knew, he might feel forced to disown me, sacrificing himself, the wider family, and me in the process. Not, I should add, that the decision was ever mine to make—it was made for me by my mother. She did, however, inform Camden of my birth. As he had no other children, he kept informed of my progress, although always from a distance.

"Until I was sixteen." Breckenridge looked down, sipped, then went on. "My mother accompanied me on a tour of Portugal. In Lisbon, we met privately with Camden Sutcliffe, the famous ambassador. Together, they told me that he was my father." A faint smile curved his lips. "Of course, I never thought of him as that—to me, Brunswick is and always will be my father. However, knowing Camden was my *sire* explained much that wasn't, until then, all that easy to understand. And although Camden knew my filial allegiance remained with Brunswick—to his credit, he never attempted to challenge that—he was always helpful and interested in my welfare. I never leaned toward diplomatic or political life—I intend to succeed Brunswick and continue to nurture all he and his forebears have worked for. In spite of that, Camden was . . . I suppose as devoted as it was in him to be."

Breckenridge's gaze had grown distant. "I visited Lisbon frequently until Camden's death. Getting to know him, learning about him, taught me a great deal." He drained his glass, then glanced at Michael. "About myself."

He was turning to set the glass on the sideboard when the clock above the mantelpiece stuck eight o'clock.

It was a large clock; its bongs reverberated through the room.

They glanced at each other.

Caro noticed the drawing room door swinging shut.

She straightened, eyes widening. Both men noticed and swung around.

Muriel Hedderwick stepped from the shadows; the half-closed door had until then concealed her.

Caro stared, literally not knowing what to think. Muriel walked slowly forward, a smile on her lips. Reaching the middle of the room, she halted and lifted her arm.

She was holding one of Camden's dueling pistols; she trained it, very steadily, on Caro.

"*At last.*" The words held a wealth of feeling, the hatred ringing through them so intense it held them silent.

Muriel's dark eyes glowed as with transparent satisfaction she viewed them. "Finally, I have the two people I hate most in the world at my mercy."

Michael shifted to face her, simultaneously moving closer to Caro. "Why do you hate me?"

"Not you!" Muriel's expression turned contemptuous. "*Them!*" With her chin, she indicated Caro and Breckenridge; the pistol didn't waver. "The two who took what was rightfully *mine!*"

Evangelical fanatacism rang in her voice. Michael glanced at Breckenridge, caught his equally mystified look.

Caro stepped forward. "Muriel—"

"*No!*" The roar exploded around the room. Muriel fixed Caro with a gaze glittering with rage. Breckenridge grasped the moment to edge further away; Michael guessed what he intended doing—didn't like the odds, but couldn't think of a better plan.

"Don't tell me I have it wrong—don't try to explain it all away!" Muriel's fury turned mocking.

"I've only met you in passing." Breckenridge drew her attention. "I barely know you. How could I have harmed you?"

Muriel bared her teeth at him. "You were his bright-eyed boy." She spat the words at him. "He cared about you—he talked to you. He *acknowledged* you!"

Breckenridge frowned. "Camden? What has he to say to this?"

"Nothing anymore—it's too late for *him* to make amends. But he was my father, too, and I *will* have my due."

Michael glanced at Caro, saw her shock, her consternation. "Muriel—"

"No!" Again Muriel's eyes glittered, this time with patent malice. "You think I'm inventing it? That your dear Camden didn't lie with his sister-in-law?" Her gaze darted to Breckenridge; her lips curled. "See—he knows it's true."

Caro glanced at Timothy; briefly he met her eyes. Lips tightening, he looked back at Muriel. "It makes sense of references in letters from George's wife to Camden."

Muriel nodded. "Indeed. Mama told Camden of my birth—she never loved George, it was Camden she adored. She gave George two sons, then Camden came home to bury his first wife. It was perfect timing, or so she thought, but Camden married Helen and returned to Lisbon—and I was born at Sutcliffe Hall." Muriel snarled at Timothy, "*Me*! *I'm* Camden's firstborn, but he never paid attention—not a jot. He never even spoke to me as his—he always treated me as *George's* daughter!"

Her eyes gleamed. "But I wasn't, was I? I was his."

"How did you learn about me?" Timothy asked. He sounded merely interested, unconcerned.

Caro looked at the pistol in Muriel's hand; it remained resolutely steady, pointed at her heart. It was one of a pair. She hoped Timothy and Michael realized; she knew Muriel—she was an excellent shot, and she planned carefully. She'd organized for all three of them to be there; she wouldn't have faced them with only one pistol, and she'd kept her other hand out of sight.

"You came to tender your condolences when Helen died. I saw you and Camden walking in the gardens. You didn't look that alike"—Muriel sneered—"except in profile. I saw the truth then. If Camden could lie with his sister-in-law, why not others? But I didn't care, not then—I was convinced that at last, now he'd lost Helen, and he was old, after all, at last Camden would open his arms to *me*. I didn't care if he called me his niece and not his daughter, but I'd trained for the position." Muriel lifted her chin. "I was excellently well prepared to act as his hostess at the embassy."

Slowly, her gaze swung to Caro; the murderous intent that contorted her features had both Michael and Timothy stiffening, battling the instinct to move protectively nearer.

"Instead"—the words were deep, seething with barely suppressed violence; Muriel's chest heaved—"*you* caught his eye. He ran after *you*—a girl younger than his own daughter and totally inexperienced! He wouldn't talk to me—*refused* to talk to me. He married you, and made you his hostess *in my place*!"

Rage poured from Muriel; she physically shook, yet the pistol remained uncompromisingly aimed. "For years— *years!*—all I've heard is how wonderful you are, not just from Camden, but from *everyone*! Even now, you drop by out of the blue and every lady in the Ladies' Association falls on your neck. All they talk of is *your* wonderful ideas, how capable *you* are—they forget about *me*, but *I'm* the one who does all the hard work. *I'm* the one who does everything right, but you always steal my *glory*!"

Her voice had risen to a shriek; Caro was so shaken she could barely take in the hatred spewing out in Muriel's words.

"Driving back from the meeting at Fordingham, I'd had enough. I realized I had to get rid of you. I'd confiscated Jimmy Biggs's slingshot and his bag of pellets the day before; they were lying at my feet in the gig as I followed you home. I didn't think of them until you turned off to the Manor—it was the perfect opportunity, obviously meant to be."

Muriel's gaze shifted to Michael. "But you saved her. I didn't think it mattered—there were other, probably better ways. I hired two sailors to kidnap and get rid of her, but you delayed her and they grabbed Miss Trice instead. After that, I didn't trust anyone else. I would have killed her at the fete—*again* you pulled her away just in time." Muriel snarled at him; stony faced, Michael held her gaze, aware that to his right, Breckenridge was edging farther away.

"And then I sawed through the railings above the weir. She should have drowned, but *yet again* you pulled her out!" Her eyes glittered. "You're a *nuisance*!"

She looked at Caro. "And why didn't you come to the meeting I arranged for you? Of course, you wouldn't have met the steering committee, but some others I'd hired, but you never came."

Strangely, Muriel appeared to be calming; her lips curved in a travesty of a smile. "But I forgive you for that. Because of it, I came here and looked around. I'd copied the key years ago, but never used it." Her dark eyes blazed; she drew herself up. "Once I saw this place, I realized it should be *mine*. *I* deserved it—*I* deserved his love—but he gave it to you. Now I want it."

Breckenridge took another half step away.

Muriel noticed. Realized what he was doing.

Everything slowed. Michael saw her blink. Saw her cold-blooded decision to shoot—he knew Muriel was an excellent shot.

Knew, absolutely, that in seconds Breckenridge would be dead. Breckenridge, whom Caro cared about, who through no fault of his own had become a target for Muriel's hate.

And his death wouldn't change anything; Muriel assuredly had the second pistol loaded and primed.

He wasn't aware of making the decision; he flung himself at Breckenridge. Took him down in a tackle as the pistol discharged.

Caro screamed.

They hit the floor. Michael registered Breckenridge's jerk—he'd been hit—but then his own head met the heavy iron claw-foot of an elegant chaise. Light exploded through his skull.

Pain followed, washing over him in a nauseating wave.

Grimly, he clung to consciousness; he hadn't planned this—hadn't intended to leave Caro to face Muriel and that second pistol alone. . . .

He felt Caro leaning over them; she'd flung herself on her knees beside him. Her fingers touched his face, burrowed beneath his cravat, feeling for his pulse. Then she was tugging his cravat loose.

Through a cold fog, he heard her cry, "Muriel, for God's sake, help me! He's bleeding."

For a moment, he wondered, but it was Breckenridge Caro meant. She shifted to work over him, trying to staunch a wound, where he couldn't tell. He tried to open his lids, but couldn't. Pain battered his senses; blank unconsciousness drew closer, beating down his will.

"Stop." Muriel's voice was colder than ice. "Right now, Caro—I mean it."

Caro paused, froze. Then quietly said, "There's no point killing Michael."

"No, that's right. I'll only kill Michael if you don't do as you're told."

A pause ensued, then Caro asked, "What do you want me to do?"

"I told you I want this house, so I've arranged for you to make a new will. It's waiting with a solicitor in his office at Number 31, Horseferry Road. Mr. Atkins—don't bother to ask him for help. He won't oblige. Once you've signed the will he's drawn up for you, he and his clerk will witness it, then give you a token to signify that all has been done as I wish.

"If you want Michael to live, you must bring that token back here to me before," Muriel paused, then said, "nine-thirty."

He wanted to make sure Caro realized that Muriel would never let him live, but the black tide was steadily dragging him under.

But Muriel had thought of that, too. "You don't need to worry I won't let Michael live if you do as I say—I only want what rightfully should be mine, and when all is said and done, once you're dead, he won't be any threat to me—

he'll bury you and Breckenridge and let me go, because if he doesn't he'll hurt and damage any number of others. Brunswick and his family, George and my brothers, their families—if Michael exposes me, the victims of Camden's legacy will only grow."

Memory flickered; they had a chance, a faint one, yet all he could do was with all his heart will Caro onto the right path. She touched his cheek; he sensed her rise. Then the black wave breached his guard, poured over and through him and dragged him down.

CHAPTER
22

Caro stood, her mind racing. She was used to emergencies but not of this sort. She swallowed, glanced at the clock—she had less than an hour to return with the token. "Very well." She didn't have time to argue, and from the light in Muriel's eyes, the expression on her face, there'd be no point. "Number 31, Horseferry Road. Mr. Atkins."

"That's right." Muriel waved to the door with the second pistol. She dropped the one she'd used; she'd been carrying its twin in her other hand, as Caro had suspected. "Off you go."

Casting one last glance at the men slumped at her feet, she said a silent prayer and went.

"Hurry back!" Muriel called after her, then laughed.

Suppressing a shiver, Caro flew out of the front door. Dragging it shut, she looked up and down the street. Where was a hackney when one needed one?

She clattered down the steps. Should she run for Piccadilly, where hackneys were plentiful, or head in the direction she wanted to go? She paused on the pavement, then turned north and started running for Grosvenor Square.

She'd passed three houses when an unmarked black carriage slowed alongside.

A small wiry man opened the door and leaned out. "Mrs.

Sutcliffe? Sligo, ma'am—I'm in the employ of His Grace of St. Ives."

Caro stopped, stared, then leapt for the carriage. "Thank God! Take me to your master immediately!"

"Indeed, ma'am. Jeffers—home as fast as you can."

On the way, Sligo explained that Michael had asked him to keep watch; Caro gave thanks and prayed all the harder. They rattled into Grosvenor Square minutes later—just as Devil and Honoria, dressed for the evening, were descending their front steps.

Caro all but fell from the carriage. Devil caught her. Steadied her.

She poured out her desperate tale.

Honoria knew Muriel; she paled. "Good God!"

Devil looked at Honoria. "Send word to Gabriel and Lucifer to meet us at the south end of Half Moon Street."

"Immediately." Honoria met Caro's gaze, squeezed her hand. "Take care." Turning, she hurried back up the steps.

Devil lifted Caro back into the carriage, called to the coachman, "Horseferry Road, Number Thirty-one. Fast as you can." He leapt in, acknowledged Sligo's nod. Sitting beside Caro, he took her hand. "Now tell me exactly what Muriel said about this will."

They returned to the south end of Half Moon Street less than thirty minutes later. The ride back and forth had been wild, the incident in the solicitor's office managed with ruthless dispatch.

At Devil's suggestion, she'd played the witless female; it hadn't been hard. Supported by Sligo, she'd entered the solicitor's office; Devil had hung back in the shadows outside the office window. A greasy individual with an equally greasy clerk, the solicitor had had her new will ready and waiting. She'd signed; the clerk and Sligo had witnessed it, then the solicitor, rubbing his hands in unctuous delight, had handed her the "token"—a jay's feather.

With it clutched in her hand, she'd turned to the window. Devil had entered in a swirl of dark drama and black evening cape, twitched the will from the stunned solicitor's fingers, and ripped it to shreds.

They'd been back in the carriage, she with the feather clutched in her hand, within a minute.

She peered out of the carriage window; the light was fast fading, the sky turning purple and deep blue. Still on Piccadilly, the carriage slowed before the corner. Devil opened the door and leaned out; two large shadows detached themselves from a nearby wall and approached.

In hushed tones, they conferred. All three were against her delivering Muriel's feather. "There has to be a better way," Gabriel insisted.

At Devil's request, she described the scene in the drawing room. Lucifer shook his head. "Too risky to just walk in. We need to make sure she's still in that room."

"I have the keys to the back door and back gate."

All three men looked at her, then exchanged a silent glance, then Devil was helping her from the carriage.

"Stay with Jeffers," he told Sligo. Pulling out his watch, he glanced at it. "Drive up to the house exactly fifteen minutes from now."

Sligo looked at his own watch and nodded.

Devil shut the carriage door, took her arm; with Gabriel and Lucifer following, they walked quickly down the narrow mews that lay behind the houses on Half Moon Street.

"This is it." She stopped before the garden gate and opened her reticule to get her keys.

Lucifer reached forward and lifted the latch—the gate opened.

They all looked at her; she stared at the gate. "The housekeeper might have left it unlocked." That was possible, but was it likely?

Gabriel and Lucifer led the way up the garden path; despite their size, all three Cynsters moved with silent grace. The garden was overgrown—Caro caught herself making a mental note to have a gardener in, to make the place habitable now that—

She broke off the thought, looked ahead. Gabriel ducked

out of sight. Lucifer crouched, then looked back and signaled. Devil drew her off the path into the shadows of a large rhododendron.

"What?" she whispered.

"There's someone there," Devil murmured back. "The others will take care of it."

On the words, she heard a faint thump, a muted scuffle, then the others returned propelling a man almost as tall as they were, a hand clamped over his mouth, his arms twisted behind him.

The man's eyes met hers—and flared.

Stepping out from the bush, she glared. "Ferdinand! What the devil are you doing here?"

He looked mulish; removing his hand, Gabriel checked Ferdinand's face, then did something that made him gasp.

Caro suppressed a wince, but this—Ferdinand surrounded by three murderous Cynsters—was the perfect opportunity to get a straight answer. "We don't have time to waste, Ferdinand. Tell me what you're after—now!"

He glanced at Lucifer, then through the dimness met Devil's gaze. Paled and looked down at her. "Letters—an exchange of letters between the duke and Sutcliffe from many years ago. The duke has been pardoned and wants to return home, but if those letters ever surface . . . he would be exiled again." He paused, then went on more fervently, "You know what it's like, Caro, at court. You know—"

She held up a hand. "Yes, I know. And yes, you can have the letters. We'll have to find them, if they exist. . . ." Her gaze had gone to the house, her mind to Michael and Timothy. "Call on me tomorrow and we'll sort it out. We don't have time for this now—something's happening in the house we must stop. Go now—I'll see you tomorrow."

Ferdinand would have clutched her hand and poured out his heartfelt thanks, but Lucifer gave him a not-too-gentle shove toward the gate.

They turned their attention to the house. The lock on the back door was well oiled; it turned without a sound. The door opened easily; Caro led them through the kitchen, up the stairs, and into the narrow corridor. Stopping before the door into the hall, she looked back and noticed that Ferdinand had followed, but was hanging back and, most important, keeping quiet.

"The drawing room is three rooms forward on the right—closest to the front door," she whispered.

They all nodded. Silently, she pushed open the door. Devil held it for her as she crept forward. He went with her; the others hung back. No sound reached them from the drawing room.

Just before the double doors, Devil closed his hands about her shoulders and halted her; he stepped silently past her, briefly looked, then rejoined her and motioned them all back beyond the service door. Once there, he softly said, "She's sitting in a chair facing the hearth. She has a pistol in her hand—there's another on the floor beside the chair. Michael still appears to be unconscious." He glanced at Caro. "Breckenridge has lost a lot of blood."

She nodded. Only distantly heard the three Cynsters conferring; dragging in a breath, she forced her ears to function—fought to ignore the hollowness in her stomach, the chill flowing through her veins.

"You're right," Gabriel grudgingly conceded. "If we barge in, she's too likely to fire and we can't guess what she'll aim for."

"We need a diversion," Devil murmured back.

They looked at each other; nothing sprang to mind. Any minute the carriage would roll up outside and Muriel would expect her to enter.

Ferdinand reached forward and tapped Gabriel on the shoulder. Gabriel glanced back, stepped back as Ferdinand joined them and whispered, "I have a suggestion. The lady with the pistol—it is Muriel Hedderwick, yes?" Caro nodded; Ferdinand went on, "Does she know these three?" Caro shook her head. Ferdinand grinned. "She knows me—she'll recognize me. I can walk in and play the 'crazy Portuguese,' yes? She will let me get close—she won't see me as a danger. I could take the pistol from her."

Caro understood immediately—not just what he was proposing, but why. If he did this and saved Michael and Timothy, she'd be in his debt—he could claim the letters as a reward.

The Cynsters were unconvinced, but ultimately looked to her. She nodded. Decisively. "Yes. Let him try. He might pull it off, and we can't."

Ferdinand looked at Devil. Who nodded. "Get the pistol she's holding—we'll be there as soon as you've got your hands on it."

With a nod in reply, Ferdinand moved past them. He paused before the door to resettle his coat, then he lifted his head, squared his shoulders, and pushed through, walking confidently, his boots ringing on the tile.

"Caro?" He called. "Where are you?"

Silently, they followed him into the front hall.

He reached the drawing room, looked in, then smiled hugely and walked in. "Ah—Mrs. Hedderwick. What a pleasant surprise. I see you, too, have come up from the country—"

The last word changed, steely purpose breaking through. They heard an outraged female gasp, then the sounds of a struggle.

Like angels of death, Gabriel and Lucifer swept in. Caro started after them. Devil caught her about the waist and held her back.

Furious, she struggled. "Damn it, St. Ives—let me go!"

"All in good time," came the imperturbable response.

A shot rang out, echoing through the house.

Devil released her. She dashed for the door; he still got there before her, momentarily blocked her path as he scanned the room, then he let her in, and followed as she flew across the room to her fallen men.

She glimpsed Muriel struggling like a fiend; all three men were battling to restrain her. The second pistol had been kicked to the side of the room; Devil detoured and picked it up. The one that had fired lay at Muriel's feet.

Caro fell to her knees beside Michael and Timothy. Frantically she checked Michael's pulse, felt it steady and strong, but he didn't respond to her touch or her voice.

Timothy's pulse, when she found it, was thready and weak. Blood had soaked his shirt and coat and lay pooled beneath him. In his upper chest, the wound looked to have stopped bleeding. She reached to lift the wadded cravat she'd pressed over it to check—Devil stopped her.

"Best leave it." He called to Lucifer to send Sligo for a doctor.

Glancing over, Caro saw Muriel being held down in the chair, Gabriel winding curtain cords around her to hold her there.

Across the room, Muriel's eyes locked with hers. For one long moment, Muriel stared, then she threw back her head and screeched.

All four men flinched. When she barely paused for breath, Gabriel swore, whipped a handkerchief from his pocket, balled it and shoved it into her mouth. Reduced to raging mumbles, eyes starting, Muriel flung herself against her bonds, but they held.

The tension gripping the room eased; the men stepped back. Shrugging his coat into place, Ferdinand walked over to Caro. He looked down at Michael and Timothy, then glanced at Devil. "They will live?"

Devil had checked Michael's head, lifted his lids; Caro had grasped the moment to shift Michael's shoulders so she could cradle his head in her lap. Glancing at Timothy, Devil nodded grimly. "Both should. Luckily, the ball missed the lung."

Ferdinand hesitated, then said, "It will be better if I am not here when your doctor arrives, I think."

From her position on the floor, Caro looked up at Ferdinand. "Probably. Call on me tomorrow—the Anstruther-Wetherby house in Upper Grosvenor Street." She smiled. "You were very brave, acting as you did."

Ferdinand's usual grin broke through. He shrugged. "A woman with a pistol—that is hardly a problem."

She held his gaze. "Except when the woman is a marksman."

He looked down at her; his grin faded. "It is a joke, yes?"

She shook her head. "Unfortunately not."

Ferdinand muttered a curse in Portuguese. He glanced back at Muriel, still wrestling futilely with Gabriel's knots. "Why did she do it?"

Across Michael and Timothy, Caro met Devil's eyes. Quietly said, "I suspect we'll never know—she's quite mad."

Ferdinand nodded and left. Devil remained on the floor beside Timothy and Michael; Gabriel sat on the chaise and kept a close eye on Muriel. Caro studied Michael's face, with her eyes traced the lines that had become so familiar, stroked his hair.

Then Lucifer returned with the doctor; she stirred and, giving thanks to the gods, gave herself up to caring for the two men she held closest to her heart.

The final scene in the drama was played out in Magnus's library. All the family involved gathered late that night to hear the full story, to understand, to be reassured, ultimately to help protect.

Michael sat in a deep armchair, his head, still distantly pounding, cushioned on a silk pillow. A bump the size of an egg on the back of his skull throbbed; he raised his glass and sipped—a cordial. Caro, sitting on the chair's arm no more than inches away, had insisted on the tonic. All the other men were drinking brandy, but with Caro so close and Honoria on the chaise nearby, her eyes fixed on him, he had no option but to drink the ghastly stuff.

Devil was present, along with Gabriel and Lucifer and their wives, Alathea and Phyllida. Magnus sat in his favorite chair listening intently as they recounted the facts, put together the pieces. Evelyn, too, hung on their words.

"I didn't really believe it until I remembered Muriel was a marksman." Caro glanced at Michael. "She excels at all those things at which girls normally don't—like driving, archery, and pistols."

"And," Michael grimly added, "slingshots."

She nodded. "That, too."

"So," Honoria said, "when you returned to Bramshaw, Muriel told you of the Ladies' Association meeting, insisted you attend, then when you did and the local ladies treated you, unsurprisingly, as a celebrity, she saw red?"

Caro met Michael's gaze. "I think it was more the straw

that broke the camel's back." She glanced at the others. "Muriel always saw herself as the rightful lady of Sutcliffe Hall. *She* was a true Sutcliffe, Camden's firstborn—the heir of his talents if you will, but then, in marrying me and making me his hostess, he chose me over her. Bad enough. She then worked hard to be the premier lady of the district—that position was all hers. Yet despite my long absences, all I had to do was appear and the other local ladies put me on her pedestal, displacing her. Camden wounded her, but then every time I returned home, salt was rubbed into the wound."

Michael squeezed her hand. "That wasn't your fault."

"No." She looked down, after a moment raised her head and went on, "But once she started trying to get rid of me, in her usual dogged fashion, she just kept at it. Then she saw the house, and also the chance to even her old if secret score with Timothy, and . . ."

"*However,*" Magnus said, looking up at her from under his shaggy brows, "her true target, the one she wished to punish, was Camden. But he's dead. You and Breckenridge were merely the two on whom she could vent her rancor." Sternly, he held Caro's gaze. "All this has been more about the loose ends of Camden Sutcliffe's life than about either you or Breckenridge."

Caro looked into his old eyes; after a moment, she inclined her head.

"Regardless," Devil said, "we're now left with the final tying of those loose ends." He looked at Gabriel and Lucifer, who had taken Muriel, still bound and gagged, to her London home. "How did Hedderwick take it?"

Gabriel grimaced. "He didn't argue, nor even seem all that surprised."

"He *was* surprised over what she'd done," Lucifer amended, "but not surprised she'd finally done something."

"He must have known how obsessed she was," Gabriel said. "He was quick to take our points. He's a quiet sort, but seems competent and decisive enough, and we left him in no doubt over what he needs to do to ensure our silence."

"So he's undertaken to keep her restrained?"

Gabriel nodded. "She's immensely strong, and given her

skills she'll always be dangerous. Hedderwick has an iso-lated cottage on the Cornish coast he intends taking her to; she'll be guarded night and day."

Devil glanced at Caro. "The doctor intends to remain with Breckenridge overnight, just to make sure, but he felt certain that with time he'd recover fully." He looked at Michael, raised a brow.

Michael nodded, winced, resettled his head carefully. "In the circumstances, we'll need to consult with Breckenridge, and also with George Sutcliffe, but allowing any of this to become public is pointless. Quite aside from tarnishing Camden Sutcliffe's memory—and despite his personal shortcomings, his public service was exemplary—any for-mal proceedings will cause considerable anguish and diffi-culties for the other Sutcliffes, and even more for the Danverses."

He glanced around the circle; no one argued. He nodded. "It's a sorry enough tale as it is—best we end it here."

They all agreed, drained their glasses, then, reassured that all was as well as could be, took their leave.

Michael woke in the night, in the small hours when the world lay blanketed and asleep. About him, the huge old house lay silent and still; he rested warm beneath soft cov-ers, Caro curled against his side.

He smiled, felt relief and quiet joy spread through him. Realized his head had stopped throbbing. Reaching up, he touched the bump, confirmed it still hurt if touched, but oth-erwise was bearable.

Beside him, Caro stirred. She seemed to realize he was awake; lifting her head, she peered into his face, then blinked her eyes wide. "How are you feeling?"

He'd barely made it to her room before collapsing; she'd helped him undress and crawl beneath the covers—he'd fallen asleep the instant his face touched the pillow. "Much better." He studied her face, put out a hand to stroke her hair, smiled. "Your tonic worked."

Her look said "I told you so," but she refrained from utter-ing the words. Instead, she searched his eyes, then, shifting further over, crossed her arms on his chest and settled to look into his face. "If you are properly awake and compos mentis, I wanted to ask you a question."

He hid a frown; she seemed terribly serious. "I'm awake. What question?"

She hesitated, then drew a deep breath—he felt her breasts press into his chest. "How soon can we marry?" It came out calmly enough; she continued, "I've made my decision. I know what I want—there's nothing more I need to wait for. That is," she held his gaze, arched a brow, "assuming you still want to marry me."

"You don't have to ask." He closed one hand over her waist—over her latest silk confection. He hadn't yet seen it; he would—soon. "But . . ." He tried to stop himself questioning fate, yet he had to know. "What convinced you—brought on your decision?"

"You. Me." She searched his eyes. "And seeing Muriel point a pistol at your head. That . . . opened my eyes—I suddenly saw things terribly clearly." She paused, her eyes on his, then went on, "You'd convinced me that I should marry you, that being your wife was the right position for me, but I sensed some element was missing, some last vital thing." Her lips twisted ironically. "I realized what was missing was me, or rather my decision itself. I had to, in Therese Osbaldestone's words, 'claim my courage and seize the day.' Until I did, until I knowingly accepted the risk and went forward, what's grown between us couldn't develop further."

She shifted, her legs tangling with his. "Muriel and her threats brought home to me all I was risking by *not* deciding—by not taking the risk. Life is for living, not hating, but it's not for wasting, either. You and I, we've both wasted years, but now we have a chance to go forward."

She met his gaze openly, without any veil or shield. "Together we can build a family, fill the Manor with children and joy. And the Half Moon Street house, too—I could imagine living there with you, being your hostess, your helpmate to a much greater degree than I ever was with Camden."

Her eyes were purest silver in the night. "Together, we've

a chance to create our future as we want it to be. Whether what we feel will see us through . . ." She tilted her head. "It's a risk, yes, but one worth taking." Her lips lifted lightly as she refocused on his eyes. "It's a risk I'm willing to take with you."

He smiled, felt every last vestige of concern fall from him. "Thank you." He closed his arms about her, held her close, felt her warmth sink to his bones. "We can be married as soon as you like—I've got a special license."

Before she could think too much about that last, he bent his head, nudged hers up, and kissed her—a kiss that rapidly spun out of control, his or hers.

Several heated minutes later, she pulled back, gasped, "What about your head?"

"It'll be fine," he groaned, "if you'll just"—throwing back the covers, he caught her knees, drew them up to his sides, adjusted beneath her, sighed and closed his eyes—"sit back."

Caro did, smiling blissfully, exhaling slowly as she took him in.

And all was well. Very well.

They dealt with the last loose end of Camden Sutcliffe's life the next morning. When they'd taken Timothy home the day before, Caro had retrieved Camden's letters. Ferdinand called at eleven o'clock, armed with a list of dates; it was a simple enough matter to find the relevant letters.

Caro read them, confirmed they were not only what Ferdinand wanted but also seriously inflammatory; they dealt with a proposed coup to be led by the duke many years ago, a few months before Camden had been appointed ambassador to Portugal. Satisfied there was nothing in the letters to concern the present British government, she handed them to Ferdinand. "Why didn't you just ask?"

He looked down at her, then smiled his winning smile. "Dear Caro, you are known too well for that. If I'd asked, you would have looked, and then you might have felt compelled to let someone in your Foreign Office know. . . ." He shrugged. "It *could* have ended badly."

Considering what she'd just read, she had to agree; for the duke, the stakes had been, and still were, high.

With smiles all around, Ferdinand shook hands and left.

She turned to Michael, raised a brow. "If you're up to it, I'd like to visit Timothy. Given your views on my visiting his house, I imagine you would prefer to accompany me?"

Michael met her gaze. "You imagine correctly."

They went, and found Breckenridge lying in bed, interestingly pale, very weak, but fully conscious—and not at all receptive to Caro's fussing, let alone her tonic. Michael saw the desperate plea in Breckenridge's eyes and took pity. Wincing as if from a headache, when Caro noticed he suggested that perhaps he needed to return home to rest.

She reacted as he'd expected with instant solicitude. Behind her back, Breckenridge rolled his eyes, but wisely remained mute.

Later in the afternoon, on his way to his club to meet with Jamieson, Michael looked in again on Breckenridge. This time, Timothy was propped up in bed; Michael lounged in the doorway.

Timothy eyed him, then faintly smiled. "I suppose I should thank you. I had no idea she was such an excellent shot."

"So I assumed. But you can avoid doing violence to your feelings—I saved you because of Caro. Strange to tell, she seems to value you."

Letting his head rest against his pillows, Timothy grinned. "Indeed. Do bear that in mind for the future." He considered Michael, then added, "Of course, you wouldn't have saved me if you'd known in doing so you'd incapacitate yourself in the process."

Michael didn't smile. "I would never knowingly leave Caro unprotected."

Timothy's eyes glinted from beneath his heavy lids. "Just so." His smile dawned.

Michael was sure they understood each other perfectly.

"So," Timothy lifted a glass and sipped Caro's cordial, grimaced, "why are you here?"

"To prey on your gratitude," Michael replied. "This might well be the only chance I get."

Brows rising, Timothy studied him, then waved him to a chair. "What do you want?"

Pushing away from the doorframe, Michael closed the door. Crossing to the chair, he turned it and sat astride; folding his arms along the back, he met Timothy's eyes. "I want to know what the relationship between Caro and Camden was."

Timothy's eyes widened. "Ah . . ." He blinked, refocused on Michael. Hesitated, then said, "I presume you know . . ."

"That their marriage was unconsummated? Yes. What I want to know is why."

Timothy smiled. "That, as it happens, is easy to explain— because the great Camden Sutcliffe, womanizer of the world, bit off more than he could chew."

Michael blinked. Timothy explained, "Camden was a connoisseur of women. From the moment he set eyes on her, he lusted after Caro—not as she then was so much as for the potential he correctly identified, for what he knew she could become. On *all* levels. That was what drove him to marry her. However, Camden was very much aware he was forty years her senior; when it came to the sexual side of things, he became so anxious that he wouldn't be able to satisfy her, or keep satisfying her, he couldn't perform at all."

Michael stared. "You're sure of that?"

Timothy nodded. "He told me himself, years after they were wed. He simply couldn't, not with her."

Michael digested that, eventually again met Timothy's eyes. "Did he love her?"

"I'm not sure Camden knew the meaning of the word 'love,' not as you use it—not as Caro would use it. He was devoted to her, but more in a sense of being obsessed with the aspects of her potential he could and did unlock. But love?" Timothy grimaced deprecatingly. "If Camden ever loved anyone other than himself, it would, I suppose, be me."

Michael raised his brows. "Because you're like him?"

Timothy inclined his head. "So he believed."

Michael suspected that was another mistake Camden had made.

"I don't think Caro ever knew his reason—I'd take an

oath Camden never told her. He was a confusing man—selfless and devoted to his country, but in all things personal, utterly self-centered." Timothy caught Michael's gaze. "If I'd believed it would have helped, I'd have told Caro myself, but . . ."

His face hardened, but he didn't look away. "The past can't be changed—believe me, I know. It can only be laid to rest. That's what Muriel wouldn't accept." His features eased, his lips curving. "Caro was always much wiser."

Michael studied his face, heard truth ring in his tone. Wisdom from the mouth of one of the ton's foremost rakes?

Timothy looked away, took another sip of his cordial. "One thing—before he leaves town with Muriel, can you tell Hedderwick about me?" He met Michael's eyes. "While I shudder at the thought that she's my half sister, I will want to keep track of her."

Michael agreed; Timothy might want to remain advised of Muriel's whereabouts purely for his own protection, but Michael was starting to suspect that Timothy was more likely to protect Muriel, and ensure her welfare, than anything else. For all he wasn't like Camden, he was in one respect his sire's son—a complex character.

Timothy grimaced. "I have two older sisters—half sisters. I've always in jest referred to them as my evil, ugly sisters." He winced. "Never again."

The words had barely passed his lips when a tap on the door heralded his man. "Lady Constance has arrived, m'lord. She's heard about your injury and is demanding to see you."

Timothy stared at him, then slumped back and groaned. Feelingly.

Michael laughed. Standing, he gripped Timothy's hand, assured him he'd let Hedderwick know of Timothy's interest, then beat a hasty retreat.

Timothy muttered darkly—something about deserting fallen comrades and leaving them to the enemy.

On the stairs, Michael passed Lady Constance Rafferty, a handsome matron grimly set on her task; they exchanged nods, but she didn't pause, regally sweeping into her brother's chamber.

Grinning, Michael left the house, abandoning Timothy to Lady Constance's tender mercies.

Later that night, when he'd joined Caro in her bedchamber and she stood within the circle of his arms, he smiled down at her and mentioned his visit to Timothy and Lady Constance's arrival. "He seemed stronger. I'm sure between you and his sisters, he'll make an amazing recovery."

Caro narrowed her eyes at him. "Was he taking my cordial?"

"I witnessed it with my own eyes."

"*Humph!* Just as well." She leaned into him, reached up and carefully speared her fingers through his hair, gently explored the back of his skull. "It still hurts," she said when he winced.

"Nothing like it did." He spread his hands and drew her to him, molded her to him. "And my head isn't spinning in the least."

Her eyes searched his; her smile was slow, filled with sultry promise. "Perhaps I should rectify that."

"Indeed. I'm quite sure that falls under the heading of wifely duties." He'd used the term deliberately; her lashes had been lowering, but now they rose and she met his eyes.

She read them, then drew breath, exhaled. "We haven't discussed the details."

"The details," he informed her, "remain up to you. Whatever you want, whatever you wish. Whenever you wish."

She studied his eyes, smiled. "I believe you mentioned a special license?"

She had remembered; he'd wondered. He nodded. "I have one."

Gently, within his arms, she swished her hips side to side, back and forth, the exquisitely sheer figured silk of her gown a tantalizing whisper shielding her svelte curves. Her eyes never left his. "Perhaps we should marry as soon as possible. . . ." Her gaze dropped to his lips; she licked hers, then met his gaze again. "Can you see any reason to wait?"

He could see every reason to rush ahead. "Three days." He tightened his hold on her, anchoring her distracting hips, almost groaning as he realized how aroused she'd succeeded in making him. "Soon!"

She laughed, that light airy, truly carefree sound he'd heard too infrequently to date. "It's the height of summer—hardly anyone's in town. And they'll never forgive us if we slip away and tie the knot without them."

Michael thought of Honoria, and groaned aloud. "Invitations, organization." More delay.

"Don't worry—I'll handle it." Caro smiled up at him. "Let's say the end of next week. . . ." Her smile faded; her eyes remained on his, open, yet . . . "Can we hold the wedding breakfast at the Manor?"

"Of course." He didn't ask why, left the choice to her.

Her silver gaze remained locked with his. "When I married Camden, we had the breakfast at Bramshaw House. But that's the past, one I've left behind. I want our wedding to be a fresh start—for me, it is. It's a new start, walking a different road, with you."

He looked into her silvery eyes, clear, decided, resolute. He'd been weighing whether to tell her what Timothy had revealed, to help her understand that the sexual failure of her first marriage had never been her fault, or whether to simply let the past die.

She'd just made the decision for him—she'd put the past behind her, shut the door and turned away. And now she was committed to walking into the future with her hand in his, and making the best they could of it together.

He smiled into her eyes. "I love you."

Her brows lightly rose; her eyes glowed softly. "I know. I love you, too—at least, I believe I do." She searched his eyes, then said, "It has to be that, don't you think—this feeling?"

He knew she wasn't referring to the warmth that was spreading through them, heating their skins, sliding through their veins, but the force that drove it—that power that most tangibly manifested when they were locked together, when they gave themselves each to the other, the power that at such times waxed so strong they could feel it, could almost touch it. The power that day by day bound them ever more closely.

"Yes," he said, and lowered his head, found her lips, accepted her invitation and sank into her mouth. And devoted himself to showing her that to him she was the most desirable woman in the world.

By giving himself up to that power.

They were wed in the church in Bramshaw village. The ton turned out in force; so, too, did London's diplomatic elite. It might have been a political and diplomatic nightmare, yet with Caro decreeing and Honoria enforcing, with able lieutenants among the many Cynster ladies and connections, no one dared create a fuss over anything, and the event passed without a single hitch.

From the packed church, running a gauntlet of flowers and a fine hail of rice, Caro and Michael made their way through the crowd that hadn't managed to squeeze inside, then climbed up to an open barouche for the drive back to the Manor.

There, a massive feast had been laid out; everyone was welcome—everyone came. The crowd was enormous, the good wishes unfeigned; the sun shone down in glorious benediction as, hand in hand, they did the rounds, greeting, thanking, talking.

The crowd didn't start thinning until late in the afternoon. Still wearing her ivory lace wedding gown heavily beaded with tiny seed pearls, Caro saw Timothy, a glass in his hand, sit down on the orchard wall, grinning as he watched the younger crew playing bat and ball along the back section of the drive. She leaned close to Michael, brushed his jaw with her lips, met his gaze. Smiled serenely. "I'm going to talk to Timothy."

Michael looked over her head, then nodded. "I'm going to get Magnus inside. I'll find you when I come out."

Drawing away, leaving his side yet aware some part of her never truly would, she followed the lawn bordering the drive, and came up beside Timothy.

He glanced up as she sank onto the stone beside him. Grinned, and raised his glass to her. "An exceptional event." He held her gaze, then took her hand and raised it to his lips.

"I'm pleased you're so happy." Gently squeezing her hand, he released it.

They sat in the sunshine and watched the game, then she remembered and murmured, "Hedderwick sent his felicitations. He's staying in Cornwall with Muriel. He's a quiet man, but a steady one—I think he truly loves her, but she never seemed to see it."

"Or wasn't content with it." Timothy shrugged. "That was Muriel's choice." Facing her, he smiled his rakish smile. "You, at least, have had the sense to plunge into life and live it."

Caro arched a brow. "And you?"

He laughed. "As you know full well, that's always been my creed." His gaze went past her; he stood as Michael joined them.

They exchanged easy nods.

"How's the shoulder?" Michael asked.

Caro listened as they swapped quips, inwardly smiled. They weren't at all alike, yet they seemed to have settled into an easy camaraderie based on mutual masculine respect.

Then Timothy glanced down at her; she rose and slipped her hand onto Michael's arm.

"I must leave," Timothy said. "I'm off north to spend the next weeks with Brunswick." He glanced at Michael, then leaned close and kissed Caro's cheek. "I wish you both the very best of happiness."

With an almost boyish smile, he stepped back, then turned and started up the drive.

Three paces on, he halted and looked back. Frowned at Caro. "When you come up to town, *don't call*—send word. You've damaged my reputation enough as it is."

She laughed; hand over her heart, she promised. Timothy humphed, saluted Michael, then strode away.

Michael frowned. "Just how did you damage his reputation?"

Caro looked into his eyes and smiled. "His, not mine." She patted his arm. "We should speak with Mrs. Pilkington."

Noting the subject for investigation later, Michael let her distract him.

They moved through the crowd, chatting, accepting wishes and farewells. There were children aplenty present, running hither and yon through the gardens and shrubbery, whooping through the orchard, playing games in the drive. Michael caught a wild throw; releasing Caro, he lobbed the ball back, stopping for a few moments to compliment the boys on their style.

Watching him smile at a towheaded lad and tousle the boy's hair, Caro felt her heart catch. She thought she might be pregnant, but . . . just the thought made her so emotional it was a battle to keep her face straight, to keep the blissfully happy tears from her eyes. Not yet; today, she'd enjoy today's joys. Once she was sure, she would share the news with Michael—a new joy for them both, one to share privately—one she'd once thought she never would know.

So she waited for him to return to her, a smile on her face, giddy exultation in her heart. When he did, they passed once more into the crowd, chatting here and there until Therese Osbaldestone summoned her with an imperious wave.

"I'll wait here," Michael said. Lifting her hand from his sleeve, he kissed her fingertips, and released her.

She looked at him. "Coward."

He grinned. "Indeed."

She laughed, and left him. Michael watched her go, saw the sharp glance Lady Osbaldestone threw him, pretended he hadn't.

Gerrard Debbington strolled up. "I wanted to ask if you and Caro would consent to sit for me sometime."

Michael looked his surprise. "I thought you only did landscapes?" Gerrard had built a spectacular reputation as a painter of English country scenes.

Gerrard grinned. Hands in his pockets, he looked across the thinning crowd at Caro, seated beside Lady Osbaldestone. "That's my forte; however, I've recently realized there's a special challenge in painting couples—one I hadn't previously appreciated. I stumbled across it when I did a family portrait for Patience and Vane. To me, it's like a different dimension—one that simply doesn't exist in landscapes."

He met Michael's gaze. "I'd like to paint you and Caro—together, you have that extra dimension. As a painter, if I can capture it, I'll be rich beyond measure."

Michael looked across at Caro, thought of a painting that would capture what had grown between them. He nodded. "I'll tell her." He glanced at Gerrard. "Maybe when next we're in town?"

Delighted, Gerrard agreed. They shook hands and parted.

Michael remained where he was, in the center of the forecourt. Others came up to make their farewells; a few minutes later, Caro rejoined him.

The sun was sinking; the next hour was one of good-byes. Only they and Magnus and Evelyn were remaining at the Manor; the London-bound crowd left in a steady stream, then the locals followed.

Devil and Honoria were the last to leave—they were driving back to London and their children, then retreating to Somersham for the next several weeks. Caro and Michael had, of course, been summoned to the family Summer Celebration and, of course, would go.

As the St. Iveses' carriage rumbled out through the gateposts, Caro heaved a patently happy, deeply contented sigh. Equally content to hear it, Michael looked down at her, at the glorious sun-shot frizz of her golden brown hair. She glanced up; her silver eyes met his.

Then she smiled and looked across at the grass verge. "It was just there that this all started—do you remember?"

She walked the few steps to the spot on the verge a few yards from the memorial stone. His hand about hers, Michael went with her.

Glancing up, she grinned. "You called me witless."

Staring at the grass, he squeezed her hand. "You frightened me. I knew, even then, that I couldn't afford to lose you."

Deliberately, he shifted his gaze to the stone. Waited . . . but all he heard was the birds settling in the trees, the soft whisper of the breeze. All he felt was Caro's warmth as she leaned against him.

No screaming horses. No cold and deadening fear.

The memory hadn't gone, but the effects had dimmed, been overlaid.

By something much more powerful.

He looked at Caro, caught her silver gaze, smiled. Lifting her hand, he kissed it, then turned away. Hand in hand, they walked to the house.

He glanced up at the windows, looked up to the attics below the roofline, and felt a sense of completion well. A sense of sureness, of anticipation—of simple happiness.

His lost family was his past; Caro was his present and his future.

He'd found his ideal bride—together, the future was theirs.

STEPHANIE LAURENS's CYNSTER NOVELS
continue with

The Truth About Love

Available now in hardcover
from William Morrow

The next wave of elegant gentlemen who've learned at
the feet of the masters continues with the tale of
Gerrard Debbington, brother-in-law and protégé of
Vane Cynster, and the passionate adventure through
which he discovers the unexpected truth
about matters of the heart.

Following is an excerpt from
The Truth About Love

Gerrard Debbington is faced with a stark choice—he wants to paint the renowned but highly private gardens of Lord Tregonning's estate, Hellebore Hall, in Cornwall, but to do so he must also paint a portrait of Lord Tregonning's daughter. Gerrard has no wish to paint any flighty flibbertigibbet, but with no alternative offering, and encouraged by Patience, he agrees. Jaded by tonnish society, tired of being the target of too many matchmaking mamas, Gerrard, joined by his friend the Honorable Barnaby Adair, kicks the dust of London from his elegant boot heels and journeys into Cornwall.

⬥⬥⬥

Gerrard tooled his curricle between a pair of worn stone gateposts bearing plaques proclaiming them the entrance to Hellebore Hall.

"It's certainly a long way from London." Relaxed on the seat beside him, Barnaby looked around, curious and mildly intrigued.

They'd set out from the capital four mornings before, and spelled Gerrard's matched grays over the distance, stopping at inns that caught their fancy each lunchtime and each evening.

The driveway, a continuation of the lane they'd

taken off the road to St. Just and St. Mawes, was lined with old, large-boled, thickly canopied trees. The fields on either side were screened by dense hedgerows. A sense of being enclosed in a living corridor, a shifting collage of browns and greens, was pervasive. Between the tops of the hedges and the overhanging branches, they caught tantalizing glimpses of the sea, sparkling silver under a cerulean sky. Ahead and to the right, the strip of sea was bounded by distant headlands, a medley of olive, purple and smoky gray in the early afternoon light.

Gerrard squinted against the glare. "By my reckoning, that stretch of water must be Carrick Roads. Falmouth ought to lie directly ahead."

Barnaby looked. "It's too far to make out the town, but there are certainly plenty of sails out there."

The land dipped; the lane followed, curving slowly south and west. They lost sight of Carrick Roads as the spur leading to St. Mawes intervened on their right, then the tree sentinels that had lined the lane abruptly ended. The curricle rattled on, into the sunshine.

They both caught their breath.

Before them lay one of the irregular inlets where an ancient valley had been drowned by the sea. To their right lay the St. Mawes arm of the Roseland peninsula, solid protection from any cold north wind; to their left, the rougher heathland of the southern arm rose, cutting off any buffets from the south. The horses trotted on and the view shifted, a new vista opening as they descended yet further.

The lane led them down through sloping fields, then steeply pitched and gabled roofs appeared ahead, between them and the blue-green waters of the inlet. Swinging in a wide, descending arc, the lane went past the house that majestically rose into view, then curved back to end in a wide sweep of gravel before the front door.

Rounding the final curve, Gerrard slowed his horses; neither he nor Barnaby uttered a word as they descended the last stretch. The house was . . . eccentric, fabulous—*wonderful*. There were turrets too numerous to count, multiple balconies laced with wrought iron, odd-shaped buttresses aplenty, windows of all descriptions, and segments of rooms forming fanciful angles in the gray stone walls.

"You didn't say anything about the house," Barnaby said as the horses neared the forecourt and they were forced to stop staring.

"I didn't *know* about the house," Gerrard replied. "I'd only heard about the gardens."

Arms of those gardens, the famous gardens of Hellebore Hall, reached out of the valley above which the house sat and embraced the fantastical creation, but the major part of the gardens lay hidden behind. Poised sentrylike at the upper end of the valley that ran down to the inlet's rocky shore, the house blocked all view of the valley itself and the gardens it contained.

Gerrard let out the breath he hadn't been aware

he'd been holding. "No wonder no one ever succeeded in slipping in to paint undetected."

Barnaby shot him an amused look, straightening as Gerrard tightened the reins, and they entered the shaded forecourt of Hellebore Hall.

Seated in the drawing room of Hellebore Hall, Jacqueline Tregonning caught the sound she'd been waiting for—the clop of hooves, the soft scrunch of gravel under a carriage's wheels.

None of the others scattered about the large room heard; they were too busy speculating on aspects of the nature of the visitors who'd just arrived.

Jacqueline preferred not to speculate, not when she could view with her own eyes, and make up her own mind.

Smoothly, quietly, she rose from the armchair beside the chaise on which sat her closest friend, Eleanor Fritham, and Eleanor's mother, Lady Fritham, of neighboring Tresdale Manor. Both were engaged in a spirited discussion with Mrs. Elcott, the vicar's wife, over the descriptions of the two gentlemen shortly expected that Mrs. Elcott's and Lady Fritham's correspondents in the capital had provided.

"Bound to be arrogant, the pair of them, my cousin said." Mrs. Elcott grimaced disparagingly. "I daresay they'll think themselves a cut above us."

"I don't see why they should," Eleanor returned. "Lady Humphries wrote that while both were from excellent families, very much the haut ton, they were perfectly personable and amenable to being entertained." Eleanor appealed to her mother. "Why would they turn their noses up at us? Aside from all else, we're all the society there is around here— they'll lead very quiet lives if they cut us."

"True," Lady Fritham agreed. "But if they're half as well bred as her ladyship makes out, they won't be high in the instep. Mark my words"—Lady Fritham nodded portentously, setting her multiple chins and the ribbons in her cap bobbing—"the mark of a true gentleman shows in the ease with which he comports himself in any company."

Unobtrusively slipping away, gliding silently up the long room to the window that gave the best view of the front portico, Jacqueline cynically noted the others present; aside from her father's sister, Millicent, who after her mother's death had come to live with them, none had any real reason to be there.

Not unless one deemed rampant curiosity sufficient reason.

Jordan Fritham, Eleanor's brother, stood chatting with Mrs. Myles and her daughters, Clara and Rosa, both as yet unwed. Millicent stood with them, Mitchel Cunningham by her side. The group was engrossed in discussing portraiture, and the singular success of Mitchel and her father in persuading society's foremost artistic lion to grace Hellebore Hall and favor her with his talents.

Calmly, Jacqueline approached the window. Regardless of her father's, Mitchel's, or the artistic lion's belief, *she* would be the one bestowing the favor. She hadn't yet decided whether she would sit for him, and wouldn't, not until she'd evaluated the man, his talents, and, most importantly, his integrity.

She knew why her father had been so insistent this man, and only he, could paint the portrait her father required. Millicent had been nothing short of brilliant in planting the right seeds in her father's mind, and nurturing them to fruition. As the one most intimately involved on all counts, Jacqueline was aware that the man himself would be pivotal; without him, his talents, and his vaunted integrity regarding his work, their plans would come to naught.

And there was no other way to turn.

Halting two paces from the window, she looked out at the occupants of the curricle that had just rocked to a stop before the portico; in the circumstances she felt no compunction in spying on Gerrard Debbington.

First, she had to identify which of the two men he was. The one who wasn't driving? That tawny-haired gentleman stepped lithely down, then paused to throw a laughing comment to the other man, who remained on the box seat, the reins held loosely in his long-fingered hands.

The grays between the curricle's shafts were prime horseflesh, and had been well-spelled; Jacqueline registered that in the briefest of glances. The man holding the reins was dark-haired, with strong, chiseled features; the tawny-haired one was prettier, the darker the more handsome.

In the second it took her to blink, she realized how odd it was for her to notice; male beauty rarely impinged on her mind. Then she looked again at the pair in the forecourt, and inwardly admitted that their physical attributes were hard to ignore.

The man on the box seat moved: a groom appeared and he descended from the carriage, handing over the reins.

And she had her answer; *he* was the painter. He was Gerrard Debbington.

A dozen little things confirmed it, from the strength apparent in those very long fingers as he surrendered the ribbons, to the austere perfection of his clothes, and the reined intensity that hung about him, every bit as real as his fashionable coat.

That intensity came as a shock. She'd steeled herself to deal with some fashionable fribble or vain popinjay, but this man was something quite different.

She watched as he answered his friend with a quiet word; the line of his thin lips didn't so much curve as ease—the veriest hint of a smile. Controlled power, intensity harnessed, ruthless determination—those were the impressions that sprang to her mind as he turned.

And looked straight at her.

Her breath caught, suspended, but she didn't move; she was standing too far from the pane for him to see her. Then she heard skirts rustling, footsteps pattering at the far end of the room; glancing sideways, she saw Eleanor, both Myles girls, and their mothers crowding around the far window that was angled to the forecourt. Jordan peered over their heads.

Unlike her, they'd crowded close to the glass.

Looking back at Gerrard Debbington, she saw him studying them, and inwardly smiled. If he sensed someone watching him, he'd think it was them.

Gerrard regarded the cluster of faces blatantly staring from the wide windows facing the forecourt. Raising a supercilious brow, he turned away; avoiding the gaze of the single woman standing back from the window closest to the portico, he looked at Barnaby. "It seems we're expected."

Barnaby could see the goggling crowd, too, but the angle of the nearer window hid the lone woman from him. He gestured to the door. "Shall we make our entrance?"

Gerrard nodded. "Ring the bell."

Strolling to an iron handle dangling by the door, Barnaby gave it a tug.

Turning his head, Gerrard looked once more at the woman. Her stillness confirmed she thought he couldn't see her. Light spilled into the room from windows behind her, diagonally across from where she stood; courtesy of that she was, indeed, primarily a silhouette, barely illuminated. She was intelligent enough, then, to have realized that.

But she'd forgotten, or hadn't known of, the effect of painted woodwork. Gerrard would take an oath the frame surrounding the window was at least eight inches wide and painted white. It threw back enough light, diffused and soft, true, but light nevertheless, to let him see her face.

Just her face.

He'd already glimpsed three youthful female faces, every bit as uninspiring as he'd expected, in the other group. Doubtless his subject was one of them; God knew how he'd manage.

This lady, however . . . he could paint her. He knew it in an instant; just a glance, that's all it took. Even though her features weren't that clear to him, there was a quality—one of stillness, of depth, of a complexity behind the pale oval of her face—that commanded his attention.

Just like his dream of the Garden of Night, the sight of her face reached for him, touched him, called to the artist that was his soul.

The front door opened and he turned away. Outwardly set himself to the task of greeting and being greeted. Cunningham was there, doing the honors; Gerrard shook his hand, his expression mild, his mind elsewhere.

A governess, or a companion. She was in the drawing room, the doors of which he could now see, so unless she beat a very rapid retreat, he would meet her. Then he'd have to find some way of ensuring she was included along with the gardens in the other subjects he was permitted to paint.

"This is Treadle." Cunningham introduced the butler, who bowed. "And Mrs. Carpenter, our housekeeper."

A stern-faced, competent-looking woman bobbed a curtsy. "Anything you need, sirs, please ask." Mrs. Carpenter straightened. "I've not yet assigned rooms, not being sure of your requirements. Perhaps, once you've looked around and decided which rooms would best suit, you could let Treadle and me know, and we'll have everything arranged in a blink."

Gerrard smiled. "Thank you. We will." The charm behind his smile worked its usual magic; Mrs. Carpenter's face eased, and Treadle unbent a fraction.

"This is Mr. Adair." Gerrard introduced Barnaby, who with his usual air of genial bomhomie, nodded to the two servants and Cunningham.

Gerrard looked at Cunningham.

Who seemed suddenly on edge. "Ah . . . if you'll come this way, I'll introduce you to the ladies, and inform Lord Tregonning that you're here."

Gerrard let his smile grow a fraction more intent. "Thank you."

Cunningham turned and preceded them to the double doors leading into what Gerrard had surmised must be the drawing room.

He was right. They stepped into a room long enough to boast three separate areas for comfortable conversation. At one end, no longer by the window but gathered about the chairs angled before a large fireplace, was the group of ladies and the young man who'd peered out at them, and one other, middle-aged lady he hadn't previously seen.

Directly ahead, on the chaise that faced the doors,

were two matrons, one of whom was eyeing Barnaby and him with incipient disapproval.

Although he didn't glance her way, Gerrard was instantly aware of the single lady, standing alone and regarding them levelly from the other end of the room.

Suppressing his impatience, he halted beside Cunningham, who'd paused a yard over the threshold. Barnaby halted just behind his shoulder. Gerrard looked at the bevy of young misses, waiting to see which one came forward—which of the three he was going to hate to have to paint. To his surprise, they all hung back.

The middle-aged lady, a welcoming expression on her face, started toward them.

As did the lone lady on his left.

The middle-aged lady was too old; she couldn't be his subject.

The younger lady drew nearer; he could no longer resist, but looked directly at her.

And saw her, her face, for the first time in good light.

He met her eyes, and realized his error.

Not a governess. Not a companion.

The lady his fingers were already itching to paint was Lord Tregonning's daughter.

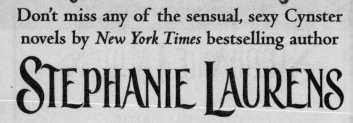

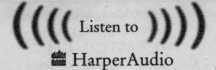